The age-old cla
rarely been brought
evocative tale set
Americ

The Wolf is often viewed as Man's oldest enemy, we hold him at arm's, sometimes rifle's length, seldom permitting him to live alongside us. This book conveys an even more disquieting truth.

The shadowy worlds of Tarka and White Fang come to life again in this story pitting Man against Man against Nature.

This compelling tale takes the reader on a journey through family conflict, betrayal and loyalty. It is a sensitive and realistic story which raises many questions.

The long-standing animosity between Man and Wolf is tackled in an often violent narrative where the author succeeds in portraying the wolves' desperate plight whilst highlighting the conflicts which arise in safeguarding him.

A ruthless patriarch – a son with a mission – an environmental dilemma: this is a tense thriller, revealing a number of inconvenient truths.

Published in Great Britain in 2009 by
GreenVineBooks, 28 Green Lane,
Blackwater, Camberley. GU17 9DH

The right of K E Slocombe to be identified
as the author of this work has been asserted in accordance
with the Copyright, Designs and Patents Act 1988.

Copyright © K E Slocombe 2009

All rights reserved. No part of this publication may be
reproduced, stored in a retrieval system, or transmitted, in any
form or by any means, without the prior permission in writing of
the publisher, nor be otherwise circulated in any form of binding
or cover other than that in which it is published and without a
similar condition including this condition being imposed on the
subsequent purchaser.

This book is a work of fiction. Names, characters,
places and incidents are either the product of the author's
imagination or are used fictionally. Any resemblance to other
actual persons, living or dead, is purely coincidental.

A CIP catalogue record for this book
is available from the British Library

ISBN 978-0-9562043-0-1

Printed and bound in Great Britain by
Printondemand-worldwide.com

Cover Design by Flying Fish
Design Consultants

BITTER ENEMIES

BY

KRIS SLOKUM

*To Veronica
Have A Howling Good Read!
Kris Slokum*

GreenVineBooks

This book is dedicated to animal conservationists: professional, amateur and volunteer, who work for the good of wildlife across the world.

Chapter One

'Don't lie down...!' It was Lys, my sister, yelling at me. 'Don't lie down...not in the snow!' she cried angrily.

I felt her kneel beside me. She began pummelling my shoulders. I opened my eyes briefly and watched snow tumbling, wave on wave, down the bank. My right side was lost under the white blanket, soon my whole body would be engulfed. I had to move! But as I tried to lift myself the bones of my left leg ground savagely together. The pain was unbearable. Mercifully I passed out.

When I regained consciousness I sensed a change. Above, the winter sun shone fiercely from the noonday sky intensely blue in the crisp air. The great trees stretched tall and still, their bowed limbs laden with snow. And the forest was totally silent. Not the silence of peace but of suffocation. And Lys had gone. Perhaps she'd never been there. I was suddenly frightened. I couldn't move, couldn't feel the intense cold. When I moved my head, fighting down the spasms of pain, I saw that the dense fur mitten had been torn from my left hand. The fingers, resting on the white crusted snow, were in jeopardy from frostbite.

I'd broken all the rules. Don't hunt alone, or in deep snow. Don't leave the hunting party, always leave a plan of your route, always...... But I'd done it all. Except for Gary and myself all the rest of the group had left for home yesterday. It was the last day of the hunt but we'd tracked a magnificent caribou stag through until sunset. I had wanted to bag him so I got up next day before dawn and was out of the cabin before Gary woke.

The snow was knee-high right to the end of the

heavily-wooded valley, there the caribou's track turned up a narrow incline through still denser conifers. Finally, I caught up with him. He was moving along a small bluff. As I fired he ran down the far side of the hill. Was he hit? Leaving a wounded animal is against all hunting lore, so I followed him and almost immediately snagged my foot on a rock. I plunged over the edge of the bluff into a small col setting off the avalanche which now threatened to entomb me.

I sighed and looking beyond the pale fingers of my hand, saw the gleam of the rifle barrel. The end of the butt, a rich mahogany, lay half-hidden under a conifer bough crushed by heavy clods of snow. Helpless, I gazed down at my arm, the whitened fingers and the rifle, just out of reach, and became aware of movement in the distance.

The col was really just a small depression, a few hundred yards across, within a larger valley. Dense groves of conifers edged down both sides, opening out where the ground fell away to reveal a distant hillside of more open woodland. The conifer forest here was ancient, the trees tall and haughty in their maturity but here the cliff fell away sharply and there were few trees in the nearer end of the valley. Probably one of Minnesota's innumerable glacial lakes nestled below.

Snow banked thickly below the trees but the lip of the col had only a shallow coating. A stream must run there in summer to feed the lake. It was on this shallow skim of snow that I sensed rather than saw the movement, a long mottled back, the muted tones of the hide, disappearing under branches half buried in snow.

The creature's movements were slow and halting. A wounded animal might walk like that, in pain, pausing with every laboured footstep, hungry for breath, its vision blurred. I had aimed for the caribou's crown right between its jutting antlers. How could it have survived? Fiercely, I struggled to focus against the blinding snow.

Whatever the creature was it had reached the first of the conifers. But instead of antlers a pair of broad pointed ears breasted the rim of the snow. I may have gasped, though my lips were dry and half-frozen. But something caused the animal to stop mid-stride, its grey paw held above the snow like a lurcher dog. Through eyelashes fringed with rime I now saw him clearly.

Instantly anger welled up inside me. Not fear, not loathing. But anger, sending such great waves of heat through my brain that it fairly boiled. The wolf's heavy brows seemed to furrow. Dark lines running down from his forehead twitched and the full orange eyes came to focus across the distance between us. From the width of his brows he was an adult, with a long sturdy body and strong muscles indicative of a male. He had come for the kill. And I was the victim, trapped, helpless.

All the words I'd heard since childhood, came tumbling into my mind: vicious heartless killer, treacherous and loathsome, the names we'd given the wolf were endless - and all deserved. They killed for the fun of it, savaging caribou and cattle alike. And they paid the price. Hunters hated them, farmers trapped them.

They'd been shot and killed by the hundreds, by the thousands, until we thought we'd driven them from our land. Yet still they returned: menacing livestock, taking an unwonted toll of deer and moose and caribou that were the hunter's rightful quarry. So I had to find the strength to kill this wolf, had to do justice one last time to the rifle my father had given me for my sixteenth birthday.

****

It was such a high-powered rifle, so much heavier than I thought it would be, but then I hadn't expected anything as magnificent, not in my wildest dreams. I held the weapon high so friends and family might admire it. The smooth polished butt glowed red in the firelight and the long dark line of the barrel seemed to go on for ever. Men shouted and laughed around me. They clapped me on my back, and grasped my arms till I felt dazed and bruised.

Men like Uncle Gary, with weather-beaten jowls and a hearty smile beside his pretty wife, Sandra. Jeff and Carl, their twin sons, older than me, full of mischief, a little jealous too, but enjoying the throng; a host of men from the hunting lodges, their faces ruddy in the firelight, shouting encouragement; and even Jasper was here, now in his seventies, his weathered face rugged and glistening, a lifetime of hunting and scorn for all his fellow creatures, except perhaps my father, behind him.

There must have been fifty people in the room when the roar went up. They were all so ludicrously excited you would have thought it was everyone's birthday not just my own. But of course it wasn't just a birthday, it was a coming of age. I lowered my arm to roars of approbation, grasped the weapon even tighter in both hands and turned back to face my father. To say that his features glowed with pride would do him a disservice. His eyes did sparkle in the firelight and there was a broad grin on his face, a face grown lined with trauma and loss.

Another son, my elder by twelve years had died when I was only six. But as I looked at my father he seemed to have grown older and come to look like the man in the painting behind him. Unwilling to acknowledge my own thoughts I looked instead at the heavy chimneybreast, the solid brick walls groaning with guns of all ages: great blunderbusses with flaring barrels, shotguns with such heavy stocks only a modern-day wrestler might handle them, modern rifles their gunsights almost as large as the flintlocks above.

I let my eyes settle finally on the painting. It portrayed a scene familiar to our numerous customers: another father and son, my great, great .... I never remember how many, grandfather, Louis François Delacroix, a French-Canadian trapper, with his own son by an Ojibwa woman. She had died at the boy's birth. Two further marriages had left him with only girls. The boy, named Francis, had been the only child to carry on the family name. The two men stood rigidly as they might in a photograph, except photography hadn't been invented in 1820.

The artist hadn't been very good, he gave them a stilted, uneasy look. Their surroundings had more animation: a stack of moose, deer and caribou trophies, mounted heads and antlers all jumbled together, and three great racks of wolf skins, said to be the sum of five complete packs, stood beside the young Francis Delacroix. Louis was a great mountain of a man, broad of shoulder and with a steely look to his eye.

Standing as my father did before the portrait the likeness was quite striking, he had almost the same build, the shock of iron grey hair and the thin uneven lines on the forehead: so similar you would have thought they were same man. There was far less of a resemblance to the young Francis, he had the high cheekbones and dark sunken eyes of his mother's race but there was something of his father in him too: the straight mouth and heavy brows, rather spoiled by dark hair, cut short and ragged.

My father grasped my shoulder with his huge hand in just the same manner as Louis François had done to his own son all those years ago. I could feel the rough bite of his fingernails through the thick shirt. I scanned the faces of each man in the room knowing there wasn't one amongst them who didn't wish himself in my place as heir to the Delacroix empire. My father's shout for silence was little heeded so he began to call out: 'To Louis,' and then desperately tried to recover himself by turning and raising his filled glass towards the painting, 'and Francis, Delacroixs to the end!'

In truth he didn't seem much embarrassed though the mistake was, I suppose, understandable. Throughout the generations the oldest of the Delacroix boys had always been called Louis. So it was my misfortune, being merely named Francis, that I was destined to carry that mantle.

Through the laughing crowd I saw the face of my sister, Lys. She was standing hesitantly in the kitchen doorway, her shoulder inclined against the doorpost, her face now somewhat pale. But of us all, my cousins included, only Lys carried any real signs of our Indian ancestry. Her skin usually had a pale olive blush and her straight hair was bluish-black, unlike my own sandy colour. And although she favoured our mother, daughter of Dutch immigrants, in many features, the eyes gave her away. They were dark and limpid - immensely expressive.

Now as she looked at me across that crowded room the corners of her mouth were only slightly lifted, not in a smile, not even in acknowledgement. To further roars of approval, I raised the gun high so that she should see it more clearly. She followed the movement and fixed on the rifle with those eyes and a great sadness filled them that almost choked the spirit from me. When I looked again she was turning away and the hesitant smile had gone from her lips. Why had she been so sad? I didn't understand, might never understand. And at that moment, I didn't really want to.

****

Recovering consciousness I quickly experienced a sense of horror: my fingers were frozen to the icy barrel of the rifle and the weapon lay even deeper in snow. I looked across the clearing. The wolf was still there under the conifer boughs. It hadn't moved. Perhaps he hadn't seen me, the thick blanket of snow concealing my scent.

More probably I seemed dead already. As if it had read my mind the wolf stood up suddenly, shook itself free of the clinging snow and took a step out from beneath the tree. It stretched out its thick neck. The long grey forelimbs and fur-covered paws splayed across the snow, its body arching until the dusty brown hindquarters were well about the level of its head. I saw for the first time the great thigh muscles which give his race the strength and stamina to follow their prey.

As he relaxed I expected him to turn and come for me. But his great head came up and for a moment he stood upright, clearly exposed against the white of the snow, taking a stance I'd never witnessed in a wolf before: I was so used to their skulking cowardly nature. Now at least I was able to study him as an opponent. It was, after all, the only thing I could do. The wolf's muzzle was broad, narrowing only slightly from his forehead which contained a massive skull. The fur was brindled brown and black though his chin and jowls were quite pale. Across dark shoulders the dense fur was interrupted by two silvery crescents on either side of his body: a pattern I hadn't seen before.

What a prize that pelt would be for someone, properly handled and conserved! But watching the wolf in this singular display of strength I felt uneasy. Something stirred in my mind which I wouldn't acknowledge, even with death, in the form of this wolf, staring me in the face. To distract myself I gazed up at the intense blue of the sky. It was already turning indigo above the distant whitened hills, heralding an early winter sunset. If rescue didn't come soon, it would never arrive and I would die out here anyway.

I'd heard wolves howling before. They called most nights on our hunting trips through Minnesota's densely wooded valleys. So, when the wolf lifted his head showing his white chest to the sky, ears pressed back along his neck, I thought I knew what was coming. I was wrong. It began with a long deep thrust from his throat then the notes came out long and fluting, almost anguished, cutting through the chill air of approaching night. In my whole life I'd not been as close to a solitary wolf nor heard such a strange uplifting, yet terrifying cry.

I believe at that moment I actually admired him. He called for perhaps twenty seconds, then twice more, each phrase longer than before. But as the last notes faded and his head dropped I suddenly heard other calls coming from the valley floor. By the rustling sounds a large pack was advancing. Now I understood the wolf's real nature, saw him for the coward he really was: he wouldn't attack until the rest of the pack arrived. The thought sent panic racing through what remained of my senses.

The howling stopped and the male bounded to the lip of the col, where a second wolf was emerging. Immediately they began yelping and squirming, biting each other's fur and tails. Though I steeled myself against it, this did not seem like preparation for the savage attack I feared. The new animal was smaller, its pelt patterned a pale uniform silver. From their behaviour I took her for his mate. Excited yelping echoed from below. The male leapt back to the valley rim. The female ignored him and tracked across to one of the conifers, never even glancing in my direction, and dived into the snow drift at its base.

The male yipped loudly twice then bounded back to her side. The two of them sank down together, dipping their heads into the snow so that I lost sight of them. They were sure to be performing some bonding ritual in anticipation of the kill, so what happened next gave me the greatest surprise of that day.

When the male raised his head his muzzle had a thick coating of blood and there were morsels of flesh clinging to his teeth. The female was slightly lower down the slope. As he choked back the meat she dived in below his chin quickly tearing away some choice morsel. Unconcerned, the male slumped at her side.

His teeth settled around a piece of meat and gristle.

Pulling fiercely at it dislodged the carcass and the caribou's lifeless head lolled forwards. Its antlers were carried out from beneath a buried branch revealing a ruddy bullet hole between the creature's ears. I had killed him after all. Was this the reason I hadn't been attacked?

As the two adults gorged on the flesh of the caribou three more wolves, a yearling and two smaller cubs, bounded over the lip of the col. The cubs streaked side by side across the clearing, scouring their noses through the pristine snow, excitedly tossing at the crisp white powder. One was almost completely black the other had paler silvery fur. Together, they hurtled half way across the clearing getting close to where I lay paralysed and helpless.

My heart raced wildly. Suddenly the male yelped loudly. The two cubs turned away. Snow cascaded over me as they swung back round and chased into the conifers. Their broad tails sent showers of powdery snow down to whiten their pelts as they sank beside the carcass and began to gorge, tearing at the flesh.

Their muzzles came up soiled with reddened snow. The male raised his head sharply and gave the nearest cub a sudden nip on the shoulder. Undeterred, the cub opened his jaws wide in mock alarm then thrust forwards underneath his nose, quickly ripping off more flesh which he gobbled down. The second cub tumbled down beside the female, fended her bloodied jaws away with a paw and began eating.

The yearling hadn't followed the cubs to the carcass. He was large animal, almost as full bodied as the male. I guessed his age at about eighteen months. Instead of joining the others he turned into the shelter of one of the conifers where the snow lay deepest. He moved with extreme stealth, each paw testing the new crust of snow until his leg sank through the looser material onto a solid surface of frozen ground. His head was lowered, though his eyes, instead of being trained ahead, flickered constantly each way, revealing the white crescents of his eyeballs and delivering a decidedly evil expression.

I wondered whether he was an outcast from some other pack, unwilling to test the family's welcome until they grew indulgent after feeding. As he made his way around the clearing the thought that the caribou was not his only quarry sent shudders through my half frozen body. By now he was only ten yards away. I had time to study him. He had the male's broad head and dark colouring yet the silvery sheen running from his neck along his back and filling out the thick animated tail, must come from his mother's line. Most striking of all were the same silvery crescents silhouetted by the dark shoulder fur so reminiscent of the male's patterning.

Suddenly the yearling burst from the cover of the conifers, heading not towards where I lay but straight across the shallower snow of the clearing and up into the midst of the family group. The male stood up rapidly, I thought to defend himself. Instead he had to dodge aside awkwardly. The yearling gulped down several mouthfuls of food then suddenly grabbed the haunch of the pale cub.

In the jumble of squirming bodies it was difficult to follow his actions but it was obvious soon enough that the attack was not sustained. The cub's head jerked up from the carcass and recoiled with open red jaws to grab the muzzle of the yearling. He dodged away. Instead the cub found himself facing his own sibling. A skirmish began between the two of them. Taking no notice of the fight and replete from their meal, the two adults drew aside and began to groom. But now the yearling had torn off a caribou leg bone with some skin still adhering. He shook it over the cubs who were tumbling in deep snow. Immediately both leapt up growling, eyes darting, ready to grab the dangling skin when it dropped close enough.

The yearling danced back, landing just out of their reach, then planted his forelegs flat on the snow and begged the cubs with whisking tail and sagging jowls to attack. They were no match for him. I guessed the younger cubs' age at eight months; they had neither the yearling's experience nor his agility. In their eagerness both launched themselves high into the air, their bodies arched, feet and snow-laden paws splayed out, and plummeted together in a joyous heap on the spot the yearling had rapidly vacated.

They would have played this game before, yet both rolled to their feet and looked around in consternation. The yearling had already dashed beneath the conifer boughs and was half way across the clearing before I could follow him with my eyes. I don't believe I'd ever seen an animal propel itself with such energy and couldn't resist the crazy urge, there and then, to baptise him 'Speed'. It was several seconds before the cubs spied him.

Carrying the caribou leg bone easily in his jaws he entered the first rank of conifers to the left of the col. From the flurries of snow tossed off the lower branches I followed his passage. The cubs may have seen the movement but instead they bounded along the furrow Speed had gouged for them through the deep snow.

When he again lunged down the hill and across the clearing the dark cub quickly spotted him and gave chase. Yearling and cub swept up the hill into the trees. I heard much yelping and snarling before they returned.

The dark cub was now carrying the leg bone. His sibling, already trotting back towards the carcass, got into a tussle with him over the trophy. Soon Speed emerged. He lunged towards them, quickly snatched up the bone, dropped it again as if to taunt them, picked it up as suddenly, then darted off through the snow.

The cubs were still keen on the chase but Speed constantly outran them, leaping with great strides across the clearing. He came nearer to where I lay helpless in the snow. Through half-closed eyes and despite my fear, I felt compelled to watch his skilful progress through the banked snow. Beneath the rippling dark pelt, the huge thigh muscles swung his rear legs forwards in a great arc, the long back feet plunging deep into the snow to catapult him forwards like a coiled spring.

As he raced towards me getting closer and closer, his deep-set eyes fixed directly ahead, his head held high over the long dark muzzle, tail bouncing as he paced effortlessly through thick snow, 'Speed' now seemed to me the true embodiment of a predator. Lean and relentless, I imagined him racing after the long-limbed caribou, keeping the same easy pace hour after hour, skilfully testing the strength of each animal. At the moment of my greatest peril, the recollection that Speed was a savage predator, the enemy of every hunter in the country, was vindicated. Yet now this knowledge grieved me bitterly.

Speed had almost reached the fall of snow where I lay

buried. But for no particular reason that I could fathom, he swung easily round through the snow bank and careered back towards the far side of the clearing. The two cubs were a long way behind, gainfully following in his wake yet making heavy weather of the virgin snow. I found I had to peer through fading light to follow them. The sky was a deep indigo now, the tops of the conifers already lost from view and the distant snow-laden hillside had dissolved in the gloom. But not quite.

I thought I could make out a light quivering above the most distant slope, accompanied by the steady throb of a rotor blade. Only a rescue helicopter would be out this late. But even as I lay with my heart beating fiercely against my chest, hope was already dying. The heavy drumbeat was subsiding, the tiny pinprick of light blinked once more then vanished over the hill together with the remains of the winter sunset. The forest was evilly black, the trees leaning ever closer and the rank scent of wolf had become a tangible thing filling the rapidly freezing air.

At first I couldn't make it out. There hadn't been a breath of wind to stir even one small twig. The forest was deathly still, a cruel hard frost censoring all movement. Yet, there it was again, the breeze that seemed to fade even as it grew and that strange rumbling as if the trees were exercising their great limbs.

I recalled the Indian legends of my childhood: beasts who spent the daylight hours as ancient trees only to transform themselves under cover of night into mystic beasts that took breath from young babies and caused hunters to plunge to their deaths over great waterfalls. Darkness had finally settled across the clearing. I couldn't see the wolves any more but I knew they were there, waiting in the shelter of the conifers. I sighed deeply and closed my eyes, I thought for the last time. I would not see what was to come.

If I dozed it was only for seconds but reality and dream now seemed to coalesce. The storm swept in so violently that the conifer boughs crashed and boomed against each other and light snow flurries turned into blizzards. The sound increased to a steady drumbeat, then expanded into a screeching roar which seemed to blast the wooded sides from the col. Above the appalling racket I heard sounds I'd never expected to hear again, the screeching of an engine, rotor blades beating inside my head and, above these unearthly sounds: voices, angry and excited, voices shouting commands above the devastating shatter of the rotor blades.

Through half closed eyelids, I saw flickering light. The heavy helicopter was already manoeuvring over the lip of the col, it had started to descend into the main valley, its form masking the distant hillside. The side doors were open, I could hear shouting and saw the great searchlight swinging round in my direction. Rapidly it swept towards and over me. They hadn't seen me, I was lost!

Again the searchlight swept the cliffside. There were angry shouts. The machine rocked and the first shots rang out. The swirling snow had settled. I saw the pillar of light catch the wolf family fully in its midst. The female fell to the first ragged volley. The top of her head was shot away, her lifeless body sprawled across the caribou antlers. The male stumbled up the snowbank diving frantically for the cover of the conifers, but the glare of the searchlight silhouetted his struggling body fiercely against the white snow and a score of shots rang out.

Bullets rocketed through the fine shoulders and the silvery crescents were shot to oblivion. The recoil threw him against a conifer trunk. Amazingly he was still upright. More volleys rang out tumbling his lifeless body down the slope. It came to rest below the caribou carcass.

With each volley my chest constricted. Sobs welled up from somewhere deep inside me. My face was wet with tears. I hardly understood why. Mercifully I didn't see the cubs go down. The two young ones lay thrown together in a bloody mound, legs and heads pointing in every direction. Still quivering, yet very dead. When I tried to cry out only huge agonised gasps escaped my throat. I thought I would die at that moment. Somehow I didn't and the nightmare is still with me.

The shooting continued as the column of light swept back across the clearing and hovered over me. The note of the helicopter's engine pitched higher. For a moment the machine rocked backwards and forwards. Much later, I learned that Gary was arguing with the pilot who had refused to land in the shrouded clearing. Suddenly men tumbled from the hovering helicopter. Some ran towards me. Others knelt and trained their rifles into the gloom. In the distant corner of the clearing I saw a wolf tumbling through the snow in the shelter of the thickest conifers. It was Speed and there was a skim of red bloodying the broad head alongside his right ear.

Even as the shooting climaxed, men were racing towards me. I heard my name called again and again, men's voices incredulous that I should have survived. But as they closed around me I sought wildly with tear-filled eyes to follow Speed's progress. He was plunging down a snowbank making his escape across the col.

Someone shouted. They'd seen him. The helicopter lifted suddenly and hovered above him. Speed was moving fast then suddenly the floodlight caught him briefly in its path. Shots pulsed out, it seemed unendingly. I thought he'd been hit but as the light passed he twisted to one side glissading through thick undisturbed snow beneath the trees. It cascaded out from beneath his feet, he seemed to stumble, recovered, bounded back into the forest. Rifle shots crashed through the foliage, hammering trunks and branches.

However fast Speed raced, they would surely kill him. The ruthless clamour of the rifles merged with the helicopter's engine into a terrifying tumult. Men stumbled around me, Gary laughing and shouting, almost crying. Other men digging the snow away. Still others, smelling of medicine, methodically searching for a vein. But even as they huddled around me, as the floodlights palled and night drew across the clearing, I heard my own voice, as if from far away, screaming out one word, No! No! No!

Chapter Two

September in Minnesota Lakeland is an idyllic month. Gone is the sear heat of summer. The air, once dry and breathless, turns fresh and cool and the low sun adds texture to the lake's parched shore. Today was such a day, just a few wispy clouds and a sky the colour of pale eucalyptus leaves, with sunlight shimmering through the bold elongated cat-tails at the distant end of the lake. Beside the jetty, wild rice, still green and lithe, mingling with the browns and greens of the dying algae, bow their heavy seed heads to the slow wash of the current. I stepped onto the dry boards of the jetty, wondering what Pamela's reaction will be when she learns of my decision.

To distract myself I looked up at the surrounding hills, their flanks deeply swathed in dark pine and even darker firs. They seemed hardly touched by the low sun and there will be only shadows on the forest floor. Lower down ranks of birch follow the sinuous shoreline, broken only where boathouse and jetty intrude onto the lakeshore. For some reason, known only to him, my father has permitted no other development here. Our house is set back into the woods, and the other living quarters and the noisy workshops fan out to either side of the dusty approach road.

The sprawling industrial plant which manufactures our precision rifles lies some twenty miles away in the town of Blackheath - out of sight but never out of mind. The lake my father owns outright. The virgin forest, stretching some thirty miles to the north, is leased to Delacroix Enterprises. Quite a sum of real-estate.

A car had stopped some distance away and a door

slammed. I didn't turn right away but waited to hear Pamela's footsteps on the planks behind me, wanting to delay seeing her face, eager as it would be, with our plans and dreams. But I was mistaken. She hadn't arrived. I turned briefly looking along the empty jetty then let my gaze settle back on the lake.

The silver birch are faithful to the water's edge. Fall has yet to strike them with its vibrant colours, but the sun is filtering through their pale foliage, heightening the white trunks and dashing the water with their pallid reflections, so re-affirming its name: Silver Lake.

Throughout the long summer the lake surface warms up, becoming still and translucent, first at the shore margins, then pale fingers spread out coalescing and finally imprisoning the cold waters beneath. With the coming of fall, little squalls ruffle the mirror-like stillness. Small dark pools prise their way towards the light at the very centre of the lake. Most are short-lived. The Indians say this chill dark water will not reflect light even on the sunniest day. Sometimes, one of the dark pools uncoils sinuously, moving like a serpent across the surface of the lake but never closing with the shore. Indian legends call this *Wapitchu*, Dark Serpent, and say it's waiting for the souls of the dead. It's bad luck to row into the serpent as it uncoils.

'Francis..…?

I'd been so lost in my own thoughts that I hadn't heard Pamela arrive. I half-turned, glancing towards my fiancée. She'd come down the back steps of the lodge directly from the dining room and was running towards me along the gravel path wearing tiny beige sandals without backs. It always amazed me how she managed to drive safely in them. She was wearing a pale cream summer dress which set off her coppery hair to perfection. We'd known each other since grade school. She was the only girl I'd ever loved and I wanted to take her in my arms and swear my undying love. But now it would sound trite, she'd quickly sense my true mood.

'Francis, I thought you'd be in the house. What on earth are you doing here?'

There was an edge to her voice, her expression somewhere between annoyance and impatience but a smile played briefly on her lips. Now the time had come I couldn't face her. I gestured back to the lake.

'Seemed a shame to waste such a day. I thought we could go out on the boat,' I dissembled.

'You got me to come all the way from town just for a boat ride, when there's so much to do?'

The irritation was now plain in her voice, she almost pouted then recovered herself.

'I…..we…. need to talk.'

'Haven't we talked enough, why I've…,' then the tone of my voice got through to her. Instinctively she looked down at my hands, a worried frown on her face, 'Is something the matter? Is it …' I thought she was going to mention the scars, instead she asked, 'your father?'

'No…….no.'

Pamela screwed her eyes up at my hesitation. Ripples around the jetty sent little watery reflections up across her body, threading gold through the cream of her dress and setting the coppery highlights of her hair almost to flame.

'No....then what?'

'I thought… that is……'

Half blinded by the sun, she raised her right hand to her forehead and looked at me quizzically. Then she looked around the lake, seeming to see it for the first time that day. Clearly she had sensed my mood. Without any further words from me, she said, 'A boat ride then - perhaps just for half an hour. Last time at the old corral before…,'

I relaxed a little and tried to laugh but it was the last thing I wanted to do. To my relief she stepped towards me, ran her fingers expectantly down my bare right arm then quickly brushed past, stepping easily into the boat and sitting in the bow. At any other time I would have made her laugh, taking those little shoes from her feet, and lifting her in bodily. Instead I followed her wordlessly down onto the bare boards, cast off the line, shoved both hands into heavy leather gloves and settled down to row. Pamela studied me closely for several minutes without speaking. Then she turned her attention to the countryside around us and seemed to relax.

'It really is beautiful,' she breathed 'Thank you.'

'For what?' Knots were forming in my stomach, this was not the time for Pamela's gratitude.

'For making me take this time away from business, it's easy to forget. You know, I'd forgotten how peaceful it is. I thought we'd spend all six months away. But perhaps we'd better come back from St. Paul quite often. Your father will appreciate……'

'I'm not coming to St. Paul.' Pamela took a sudden intake of breath and started a high-pitched laugh which, observing my expression, she cut off mid-flow.

'Not….coming?' she stammered. I suppose she needed time to sort out her thoughts. I could see the questions forming in her mind - how serious is he, what's caused this, has the sickness come back? We were almost at the middle of the lake. I'd stopped rowing, secured the oars and took off the now sweaty gloves. The left one came off awkwardly as it always did. I looked up at Pamela and we both glanced down at the hand.

Apart from the rather stiff thumb and forefinger, it was a sorry mess. The middle finger was a mass of scars from the skin grafting, the other two shapeless rods, the reddened skin corrugated along their length. It's strange how two people can look at the same thing and see something totally different, but my mind had been racing so far ahead. When Pamela reached across and took the injured hand in her own, turning it palm uppermost then leaning forwards to kiss the damaged skin, I almost wept. The doctors had said the feeling might come back across the whole palm but right now I could hardly feel the light brush of her lips. Still holding onto my hand she began to speak but what she said was not at all what I was expecting.

'Just give it a little longer, you know what the doctors said.'

I slipped my hand from her grasp, 'They said there was nothing more they could do. This is as good as it gets.'

I clenched thumb and forefinger together, watching the middle finger form a hesitant arc over them both, the other two fingers refused to move. I convinced myself the pain of the grafts was lessening every day. Pamela sighed, looked at me briefly and shook her head. Not wanting to see her expression I let my gaze wander beyond her. Slightly to the left, one of the strange dark pools had formed. As I watched, it began to uncoil into a long dark line that was moving toward the boat. I shifted the right oar to swing the boat to the left but the serpent came on, sinuously, filling the space beneath the boat.

Something made me hold my maimed hand out over the black water, there *was* no reflection, not even of the bruised red skin. I thought for a moment the Indian legend was right, but there had to be some hard scientific reason for the phenomenon. Pamela hadn't realised my distraction and was talking again, 'I didn't mean…….. About St Paul….. You've been through a lot, it's only natural that….'

'…that I should lose my nerve, like the psychiatrists said. And you think that's why I'm ducking business school … St Paul. It's more complicated than that. You know it is, I thought I'd made it clear months ago.'

'Months ago you were still in hospital, I thought you were better now.'

'But it's what you all thought wasn't it, my father, you, Uncle Gary. Part of the delirium, lying hour after hour frozen in the snow, enough to turn a man's brain, enough to send him mad. Poor sod has lost his nerve, but the doctors'll put him right, the higher paid the better. He'll be shooting with the best of them when the hunting season comes round.'

I raised both hands mimicking and exaggerating the action of a high-powered rifle, and said, 'Well I can still shoot - as well as any man.' I paused, uncertain how to continue. 'Except I don't want……'

But Pamela didn't wait to hear, 'Darling, you must believe the doctors. You just can't let this beat you.'

'It's nothing to do with the doctors.'

She recognised the old argument, one I'd let her win countless times back in hospital. She drew back from me and breathed out slowly, her expression softening. She almost smiled. Give him time, give him time, she was thinking, and I'll bring him back round again. The boat shook slightly as the dark line of the serpent slipped away and sank back into the depths, leaving only ripples behind it. I took up the oars but thought better of it as Pamela continued.

'You just need to gain your confidence back. Look I know it can't be easy, but other people have come through what you've been through. Just think of Jasper, I know it was …'

'Jasper's a wreck'

Jasper Carter was an old time trapper and hunter. Some time in his twenties he had, like me, been caught in an avalanche up in the mountains. He wasn't buried but had lost everything: food, rifle, ammunition, and wandered around in the woods for over a week before he was found. He suffered a fractured leg which never set properly giving him a permanent limp. He was still a good hunter and assisted with the hunting parties. He was a big man too, full of bluster, always swaggering, impressing clients with his hunting stories, a favourite was about slaughtering whole wolf packs for the bounty - hunting them was legal back then.

Even as a child I hated the relish with which he recounted the tale. He was inbred of course, like most of the locals, and he was also a lush. But a controlled lush, and although my father humoured him, something made me keep my distance. He hadn't liked me much either. Pamela quickly saw she'd made a mistake in mentioning him.

'Oh, Jasper was a bad example, I agree. But he's old now, you can't make a judgement on his past. Just think, you've got so many more advantages. Your father's relying on us - on you…..'

'To run his vast new hunting complex?' I asked,

shuddering at the terrible prospect, but Pamela continued, 'You can't let him down Francis. He can't do it without you, he's only waited until you've qualified at management school to start this venture. I think he's been planning this since you were a child.'

'Then you know more about my father than I do.'

'Whatever do you mean?'

'When I was little, after mother and Louis died, I couldn't do anything right for him. I think he resented the fact that I'd survived them.'

'Perhaps he couldn't accept the fact that he'd survived, Francis. Desperate with grief, maybe even guilt, and with a six-year-old child to care for. If it wasn't for you he might not have carried on.'

We had been travelling as a family down to Duluth. My mother was driving, Louis was in the front seat. Neither of them survived the collision with the timber lorry. I thought, grudgingly, that there was an iota of truth in what Pamela said but given my father's temperament I didn't want to acknowledge the hurt and pain he must have gone through. 'You're forgetting Lys, she was only sixteen.'

'And away from home, able to look after herself, you weren't.'

Yes, Lys was away from home at the time of the accident, pushed out as an assistant-cum-domestic in a senator's household when it suited my father and brought back as quickly when he needed someone to care for a home without wife or mother. She was at home still.

'You're assuming by not going to St. Paul, I'm abandoning Dad's business.'

Pamela gave a rapid sigh, relief bursting through her

words as she said, 'Well aren't you, I thought...,' Her hands clasped the wooden sides of the boat, then she suddenly pulled them into her lap, only reaching out towards me at the last minute. She was shaking now and seemed close to tears. 'You mean you're going to stay and run the hunting lodges after all? Why not say so right away Francis? You've let me think…... why, all sorts of things!'

I had to stop her. 'I didn't mean that exactly. I haven't spoken to Dad yet.'

'Then why……?' Her eyes widened suddenly and she pulled her hands back, hugging her chest. I've noticed women do that to protect themselves, men just put their hands to their sides and clench them, ready for an attack.

'It's something I've done then, something... or ….another women, is that why you don't want me at St. Paul with you?' Her eyes narrowed and creased up into a look of unrestrained horror. There was a flare of anger in her voice. But I was angry too, angry that she could even think such a thing.

'No Pamela, never! It was always you, always.'

But she was rattling on, still disbelieving. 'It's that Jacqueline isn't it. Good old Jackie Taylor, always there in the background, always chasing you. She'd do anything to split us up. She'd be happy if she could break your father's hold over you too '

'Stop it Pam, stop this nonsense. Do you hear?'

Pamela had begun to stand up, always a bad idea in a small boat. I took her arms, pulled her back down and shook her violently. The boat swayed in the water and nudged the side of another dark pool just forming. Pamela slumped back on the seat but she hadn't finished. She'd latched onto Jackie Taylor, friend of my childhood and adolescence. Jackie's father, a full blood Indian it was said, had been a Delacroix driver for twenty years and Jackie had always been about the place, the eldest of a family of five other children, all boys aged four to fifteen. She was petite and kind of pretty in that subdued Indian way and although she was always ready with a smile, I thought her rather cool, even calculating.

'It's nonsense you know it is,' I insisted again.

'Oh yes, I'm sure it's nonsense. What about when you were at the hospital? She was always hanging round. Each time I arrived she'd just melt away, but I'd see her in the refectory and as soon as my back was turned I know she'd be up to the ward again.'

I knew I sounded exasperated as I countered, 'See sense Pamela. Mrs Taylor was always sending in fruit and cakes, every day almost. She has all those boys to look after, who else do you expect to bring the cakes in?'

I paused waiting for the anger to leave her face but her expression didn't change so I placed my good hand on her right knee. She brushed it off.

'Pamela you've just got to stop this! There'll never be anyone else for me, never....,'

She let her shoulders slump, smarting from the presumed affront I'd given her. I guessed this was nothing to what was to come, still I couldn't have anticipated the vehemence of her response.

'Then why? Your father, he'll...'

She carried on about my father's business, the grand enterprise he was planning in which Pamela and I were to play principal roles. We would build new hunting lodges in every western state, more through the Rockies, each would be furnished to the highest standards of luxury, the guides and hunters sourced from the best that money could buy. Our clients would be politicians, US congressmen and senators, businessmen, international entrepreneurs, even heads of state - some of the Middle Eastern royal families had already shown interest.

It was a grand scheme. I don't know where my father had conceived the idea but he was preparing to spend billions achieving his aim, most of the money coming from the highly successful Delacroix Enterprises, premier manufacturer of weapons and hunting equipment in the States. After a while I stopped listening and looked over the gunwale of the boat. Three small dark pools were appearing some distance away across the lake but none looked like uncoiling. I concentrated on them and started talking, quietly at first, so that I could hardly hear my own voice above Pamela's.

'Two weeks ago…' My mouth was dry and I couldn't seem to find the words. The confession was going to be more difficult than I had anticipated. I started again, still talking quietly, pausing now and then to check whether Pamela had actually heard me. That she had, soon became apparent from the look of utter disbelief, or perhaps it was disgust, forming on her face.

'I went to St. Paul, two weeks ago to …'

'The doctor, yes I know,' she interrupted, continuing to prattle on.

'No, not to see the doctor. When I was in hospital I met a chap who works for….for the Wolf Conservation League.'

'I heard they'd come looking for you, wanted you to sign one of their petitions. Muscling in on someone else's misfortune. They've no pride.'

Her voice had become highly scornful. I wanted to ignore her, but couldn't. Raising my voice over hers, I said determinedly, 'They have a lot of pride. A lot of courage too. They have to, in the face of the hunting lobby.'

'I'd think they'd be foolhardy rather.' Pamela had at last stopped her tirade. There was outrage evident on her face though for once she was listening. There was nothing for it but to continue.

'I've joined them… the Wolf League.'

My fiancée gave another short, stubborn laugh, clasping her hands to her mouth. Her whole body shook with laughter, then she caught sight of my set expression and the laughter died. She let her hands drop to her lap.

'It's a joke, yes? You've made them think you're joining them. Why?'

'No joke. No ploy.'

'Then, I don't… No, I don't understand you. You've been playing a game with me haven't you Francis, all this…,'

'Pamela, I'm seeing my father this afternoon, about…., well I've had a long discussion this week with Jacob Leason, Director of the League. He thinks…that is….I'm going to ask Dad to turn the hunting lodges over to a conservation programme for the wolves. There're millions to be gained from tourism - people from all over the world, luxury hotels, camping, treks into the forest. Combine it with an education programme and the publicity will be enormous. We'll get sponsorship for research projects not just on the wolves, but…,'

I wasn't allowed to finish. 'Your father knows …?'

I hardly noticed how pale Pamela's face had gone. 'No…' I stuttered, 'I wanted to see you first, to explain…,'

'You're mad, really mad Francis! This isn't anything to do with your injuries? Those blasted people saw a chance because you've been ill, because you've been talking wildly to the newspapers about your ghastly wolf family. Now they've completely brainwashed you. They've seen a chance to inveigle themselves into one of the premier hunting families in the country, maybe the whole world when Louis and you - yes and *you*, put this hunting complex together…And you are going to do it, I'm going to see to that. We'll do it together, me beside you helping, guiding, every grudging step of the way!' She paused breathlessly. Noting my dismay, her voice became tender as she continued. 'But you can't see it can you my dear. They've taken advantage of you just because you've lost your nerve.'

'I haven't lost my nerve Pamela, I thought I'd made….,'

But she shook her head and sneered. 'Why ever did you have to talk to the papers, just because a few wolves were killed?' 'Pamela, wolves are protected by law, you know that.' But she wouldn't be stopped. '…and they would have killed you too. Those lawmakers in Washington haven't a clue how we live out here. You know wolves are vicious predators. You've grown up with them, damn you, seen the damage they do to livestock, and they kill hundreds of thousands of moose and caribou and deer.'

'Not as many as the hunters, and the wolves didn't kill me.' I sighed, reliving the time eight months ago when I had been trapped in the snowdrift. I might have been out of mind, certainly not entirely lucid, but I had learned more about wolf behaviour in those few frenzied moments than I had in all the years before.

'A family of wolves Pamela. Taking no notice of me, eating the caribou I'd killed - so it....' and here there was a lump in my throat '..so it shouldn't go to waste. Kind of ironical don't you think - when we killed the wolves instead?'

Pamela simply stared at me.

'If you could have seen them, eating together, the cubs playing and squabbling just like any human family, even....,'

But Pamela's anger was too much for her. She sneered and looked away, thrusting her hand down into the lake water as if trying to grapple with the Wapitchu.

'Even Speed' I'd wanted to say. Even Speed. But no-one knew about the larger cub. Even in my hospital bed, doubtless babbling about the pleasure I'd gained watching the wolf cubs, I'd always held back from mentioning him. Probably he'd perished with the rest of his family.......probably but not certainly. I'd waited a whole month before questioning Uncle Gary, asking kind of obliquely how many wolves they'd killed. I knew he would have taken the opportunity, albeit illegally, to trade the skins. He'd responded slyly - saying three or four. Three or four - not five!

Pamela pulled herself upright. She drew her hand back inboard and quickly took my right hand in hers. Trying a new appeasing approach she said softly, 'Remember Francis you've been ill. Terribly ill.'

'And I imagined the whole thing. Is that what you're trying to say? Is that what the doctor's told you? Well I'm not mad Pamela, not deranged, you'll see, come with me to the League...'

'Come with you. Visit those people? They're all little people, they can't accept that a man like your father has a great vision. They're jealous of the politicians and cattle barons that come here and want them pulled down to their level, so they can carve up the country for a load of worthless little farmers with no land and no....'

I was aghast at her accusation and could hardly force out the words. 'Is that what you really think?'

When she didn't reply I continued, 'In the colonial days when this land had nothing but small isolated farmers, the caribou and wolf, yes even the bears we no longer see, were living in harmony together. No-one taking too much for himself. But we've changed all that'

'And is that so very wrong?'

'Yes it is - very wrong. If you'd only come with me to the League. You'll see the law conserving wolves wasn't just made by the people in Washington but hundreds of conservation bodies and local societies who are trying to conserve our wildlife before it's too late. Washington signed up for the law, you know they did.'

'And soon they'll un-sign it. Of all creatures why wolves Francis? They're bestial ....I can't understand how you can ever...' Exasperation was turning her voice husky.

'Because I saw them, watched them. I'd never been so close to living wolves before Pamela. All my life, I believed the stories of wolf attack, the rabid, excessive and malicious killing. But if you could have seen them, a whole family....,'

'A family! No I shan't ever see them Francis, and neither did you. Whatever your conservationist friends call them wolves will never be anything but depraved killers. They have to be wiped out. Your father's going to do that, whether you like it or not. The senators for Minnesota and Wisconsin are coming down here next weekend - did you know that, they're putting in a bill to overturn the ban? Your father and I are going to support it all the way down the line.'

I didn't know about the meeting, I'd heard some rumours, but where Pamela fitted into all this I couldn't guess. True, she'd majored in politics at Columbia University, and last summer had worked at Minnesota's senate office, but I couldn't believe she'd let herself be engineered into involving the Delacroix family in this bill.

'You and my father, you and my father?' I asked solemnly. 'Pamela, is it me you're marrying.... or is it the great Delacroix dynasty?'

'What on earth do you mean... I.... I...' she stopped but she'd already given herself away. Still I said, 'I want to marry you Pamela, no matter what......

'Francis you're a fool. Now please row back to the jetty, I want to....'

'Pack? You're still going then? To St. Paul?' She set her face towards the house and didn't respond.

The boat had drifted shoreward's with the current. It took only twenty strokes to get back to the jetty. Pamela leapt from her seat and was up on the dry slatted boards before I could help her. I thought, rather irrationally, that I should give the boards a coat of preservative. I tied up the boat and followed Pamela. The sun was in her eyes, she had to squint to look at me. I noticed there were tears in her eyes. She leant over quickly, kissing my cheek, and moved away before I could grasp her arm. As she looked back her face bore a pitying look. 'I know this will sound cruel Francis, but it would better if you *had* lost your nerve. When your father's finished with you - well, you'll be on the floor.'

With my confidence thus challenged, she left me. I watched her race onto the gravel track, then a door slammed and her car swerved out from the front of the house where it had been hidden earlier. She was already going full pelt when Gary stepped from the scrub up onto a bend in the track not twenty yards from the car's bumper. I suppose in her rage she didn't see him, though I saw him wave, because the car continued to accelerate and he had to dodge to the side as she slewed past him. The tyres churned up the gravel sending clouds of dust into the air. Gary had taken his hat off and was already dusting himself down by the time she passed the big aluminium gates. He was probably four hundred yards away when he looked back at me. At that distance I couldn't really be sure but it seemed to me, despite the dust, that his forehead had creased into a quizzical frown.

Gary soon disappeared into the office complex at the rear end of the house. I'd no wish to be quizzed about Pamela's hurried departure. Probably he was making the routine report to my father before knocking off for the day. The end of summer was an idle time for us. Business would be frenzied during the season though, and Dad would run Gary ragged with his demands.

Again I wondered why Gary stayed at Silver Lake, but I guess I already knew the answer. He was younger than my father by eight years. Dad had kept him back, refusing to pay college fees. Even now, he still held the purse strings. So Gary never had the courage to break free. He must hope that Dad would someday give him part of the business. If that's what he thought then he was a greater fool than I was.

I walked into the long anteroom, welcoming the instant shade, the cool resinous smell of pine. Opposite, the dining room doors were open, the windows giving onto the surrounding trees and yielding a glimpse of the lake water.

It was unusual for them to be open. Most likely Lys was in there cleaning but I didn't want to see her just then and took two steps along to the window facing the driveway. From here I would be able to see Gary leave. The conversation with Pamela had unsettled me. I was tense. I thought I hadn't made any noise so didn't bargain for my sister's appearance.

'Francis…?' Lys came in from the undercroft to the right of the doorway where the kitchen lay and where she had her own kind of sanctuary. She looked around the dark-panelled room, and seemed disappointed at only seeing me.

'Where's Pamela, I was making some coffee, I thought….,'

'She had to go.'

'Oh!'

'And I don't want a drink, not at the moment.' She looked suddenly unhappy, so I added, 'I'm waiting to see Dad. Perhaps later.'

She was shorter than me but with a thin winnowy body that belied her age. Lys was over thirty now and from her reserve, or was it just a kind of peacefulness, she seemed older. All those years, looking after my father and me, all the visitors, it couldn't have been easy. She'd been all the mother to me I'd known. She'd never been mad at me, never lectured, never even scolded me, but be sure my father did enough of that for both of them.

We'd been friends early on but my father had never

let me get too close to her and once he'd proved himself exceptionally cruel. I was in my early adolescence when he found out I was bringing all my juvenile, often physical, concerns to Lys and had shipped me off to military school.

After three years, at sixteen, I returned home but by then I was too shy and confused to revive that closeness. Lys was gentle and kind, though I never really knew what she was thinking, and sometimes, like now, with those deep sad eyes gazing at me, I shrank from her. Perhaps it was just that I was my father's son, cast in the same mould? I hoped not. Right now, before I confronted my father, I wanted to ask, 'Have you stayed here for me Lys, given up some better life elsewhere?'

But it was too late. My father had heard my voice. He came through his office door at the end of the room and simply gestured. Like always Lys melted back into the kitchen and I went to join him. From the open window I could see the trackway. The wind had got up sending waves of dust across the gravel. Gary's back was towards us, he was walking down the drive without a second glance. At least we would be alone.

'Come in Francis, I've something to ask you.'

'Has Gary….?' I asked uneasily.

'Gary? He's just left, did you want to see him?'

'No.'

'Your licences, I need all their certificate numbers, do you have them? Canadian as well as US.'

'The hunting licences. No, well yes of course. They're in my room, shall I get them?'

I turned to leave, astounded at myself for doing so. I hadn't come here to talk about licences, least of all the hunting type.

'No need, just let me have them after dinner.'
'OK I've.….'
'Sure, you and Pamela have a lot to do. Didn't I just see her leaving, in rather a hurry I thought?'

My father missed very little, or was it that Gary had talked after all. I stayed silent.

'Well I won't keep you. You'll be going to St. Paul tomorrow. I'd have done this sooner but the lawyers couldn't get everything together in time. Still at least it's here before you leave. I had hoped Pamela would be here too - I realise how much you two will be working together on the project.'

I couldn't figure out what he was saying, but it was best to let him speak, he quickly got annoyed at interruptions. His desk was piled high with files. He moved some aside, then spread out the plan of a building.

'Our first fully-equipped lodge - all ready for new clients. I was going to call it Francis Lodge, but it's already registered under the Ambrose name.'

'But that's up near Thunder Bay. I didn't know you intended to go into Canada too.'

'Sure it is, but the place came up for sale suddenly - just at the right moment. It seemed too good an offer to lose. It took some time to register. Couldn't do it under Delacroix Enterprises of course, so it's in your name - pure and simple. Fully fitted already, and the very first of Delacroix's new empire. The start of hunting's new era.'

'Our empire?' My head was reeling at the news, the irony of it. I gasped for breath, held myself steady against the desk and choked out the words, 'I can't take it.'

My father never accepted a negative answer. 'It's done, signed and sealed, you've no choice.' He slapped me hard on the left shoulder and turned around to an open drinks cabinet, quickly pouring two shots of whisky into glasses he'd laid out for the occasion. 'A drink to celebrate.'

'I mean I can't take it, not as ….. as a hunting lodge.'

The glasses slammed together as he brought them up between us. Whisky is not my favourite drink, certainly not neat, but I took the drink and swigged the fiery liquid down, watching him swallow more moderately over the rim of my glass. From his fixed expression, he was assessing me, just as he'd done the day I came home from hospital. He'd heard all the rumours of course, seen the doctors' reports, but he'd just stood in my bedroom doorway looking down at me as if he could tell everything there was to know in that one summing look. It wasn't a pleasant sensation, then or now.

'Not as a hunting lodge? That's a strange thing to say.' I tried to deflect him for a moment.

'Pamela was here just now. She said I should tell you, tell you I'd lost my nerve, after the accident and…. '

My father's expression had not changed. He sipped the remainder of his drink showing no inclination to sit down, or even to offer me a seat. 'Well have you, is that what you're saying? For God's sake boy don't let a woman speak for you. If it's the truth then we'll just get in a better doctor, someone who'll understand my family.'

'But it isn't … the truth.'

His nostrils flared. I watched him draw breath into his broad chest as his pupils hardened into black pebbles. 'Then you'd better tell me what this Truth is.' he said.

He spoke the word 'truth' as if it could have a variety of different meanings, none of them explicit.

'I…. I can't run the hunting lodges, I've had a change of heart.'

My father was not a man to quibble. He wasn't interested in my reasons, or the background to my decision, he just dismissed it outright. 'Millions of dollars, billions by the time we set up the whole complex, thrown at his feet and the boy says 'I can't do it.' Well you're going to do it, d'you hear, I've not wasted…,'

'I'm sorry for that…' I interrupted, genuinely concerned, but he seemed not to notice. He twisted half round and placed the glass down slowly, determinedly, on the shelf, then came around the desk to face me. If he had placed his hand on my shoulder like Louis had on his son's in the nineteenth century painting in our lounge, I'd have been able to shrug it off. Instead he brought the whole force of his authority down on me.

'Sorry are you? Well if you're sorry you'll do what I say. And I say you'll put this namby-pamby nonsense behind you and get on with the job. I brought up a son who does what I say Francis and I expect no less. You had better get used to it.'

I hadn't wanted to get angry but I knew he was goading me and responded unthinkingly, 'Get used to it like Gary, like Lys, like everyone else who does what you tell them?'

'Yes.' His reply almost clipped the word in half. 'It's eight months since the accident. In that time I've listened to your doctors and humoured you but I see now that was a mistake. You need to get back into harness. I'll get Jasper down here and we'll start out for Ambrose this evening. You can forget all about business school an' learn the trade as you go along. I'll phone Pamela, tell her the job of manager will be waiting for her when she's finished her course.'

I knew my father was an expert at manipulating people's lives, but here his audacity amazed me. He had resolved to run Pamela's life as well as my own. 'Pamela knows my decision, and she doesn't….,' I started, but he'd swung away from me.

'Get out of my way boy, I've lots to do before we leave.' He was neither upset nor angry, just very determined that I would follow his orders. He had moved on, his mind already calculating ahead to the minutiae of the journey. Folding the Ambrose plans he shoved the file at me. 'Study that boy, when we get there I want you to check the inventory, number of rooms and equipment, we'll also need to sort out the rifles, ammunition, that sort of thing, with the season starting soon we're going to need……'

I'd been stunned before. Now I gave my final answer. 'I'll never come to Ambrose. I'm leaving for Bitter Springs tonight.'

He'd already sat down at the computer keyboard, where the screen displayed his diary, and began to sort through the week's events changing times and shuffling aside meetings.

'Bitter Springs?' He asked with no particular interest. 'Anyhow you'll have to cancel……,'

'The Wolf Sanctuary, it's where….,'

At sixty-five my father had excellent sight, but sometimes when looking at the screen he squinted in irritation. He was doing so now, but as I spoke the expression on his face changed from annoyance to loathing. When he spoke again it was obvious he was having difficulty containing his anger.

'I know what's there boy.' He spat out the words. Though he was still concentrating on the screen his fingers were now quite still. 'What I want to know is what business you have there?' Still he hadn't looked at me.

'I've joined the Wolf League. I talked with them right after the accident, and two weeks ago I met Jacob Leason, the director. We talked a lot and well…. I knew I wanted to help them and there seemed an obvious answer….. ' The room was quite still. I could hear the clock ticking in the lounge. My father hadn't moved a muscle. 'I decided I didn't want to go to St. Paul. We want….that is I want to use the hunting lodges. Not all of them to start with of course and they'll need some converting, but with new buildings that should be easy. And you see there's so much more money in it, tourism, television, research. Yellowstone have done it and……

My father opened his mouth to speak, his parted lips thin as fine wire. If he was seething under his stern exterior I couldn't tell. 'And what exactly have they *done* at Yellowstone?' he asked, his voice icy.

'Reintroduced timber wolves where they've been lost for decades, the tourism industry has….'

'Wolves! The same animal that nearly killed you, would have killed you if Gary hadn't….'

'But they didn't. They didn't kill me, don't you see…I lay there hour after hour and they didn't come near me. I was helpless, unable to move and not one of them even…'

'The caribou, they had the whole carcass,' he said as if this explained everything.

'But they kill for the sake of it, isn't that what we always believed? I was at their mercy, they'd no reason not to kill me but they didn't. And all those stories of adults and even children taken…Jacob told me none of them was true.'

My father stood up from his desk abruptly and gave me an assessing look. 'Your brain's been addled boy.' His words, as much as the vehemence with which he spoke, disconcerted me more than I would admit.

'Just listen to me. The timber wolf is the worst, most evil, vermin ever created. I've heard stories your friend Jacob would never admit to, prime cattle killed by packs with up to thirty wolves. Savaged, eaten half alive then discarded after a few mouthfuls - ask Senator Grimes, Carson Johnson of Wisconsin, and just five years ago, near Duluth, a rabid pack of them ganged up on domestic dogs in Leeworth, tore them to shreds right in front of a little girl.'

I'd heard of the sorry event, and even then had doubted the story. 'Jacob investigates every case. Those were half-wild dogs, probably crossed with wolves. They're far more unpredictable than any wild wolf.' My father's eyes creased into a look of intense loathing.

'This Jacob is very wise, it seems. Hardly up from your sickbed and he's convinced you has he?' And then my father continued, using almost the same words Pamela had used but where there had been veiled malice in her voice, my father's was the full-blown version.

'…..convinced you and brainwashed you. Latching onto the Delacroix family. Trapping the only son of a greatest hunting empire in the whole USofA, when he's half-dead in hospital. Getting him to join in this ludicrously offensive….. offensive *and* dangerous, campaign. When he's delirious and whining on about some wolf family: mother, father, some delightfully playful cubs, that's been killed right in front of him - when he's blabbing like a baby....'

Though I'd never felt shame at the memory, I now felt my face redden. I hung my head but my father mistook the action for acquiescence to his arguments.

'Yes, you might well hang your head, my son.'

'But you're wrong, so terribly wrong about this.' I saw the muscles of his face tighten so I continued with the only argument I thought he would understand. "The tourist industry is booming in Yellowstone, if we set up similar schemes in all our new places - North Dakota, the Rockies, as far south as Arizona, we'll be leaders in the industry and in conservation. Government grants and research projects are only half of it. Just hunting animals to kill them is for the old, worn-out generation, conservation is the key to the future. Having children watch and learn about them, not wiping them out with some high-powered rifle so you can hang a dead trophy on your wall. That's not the way, not the future!'

Wordlessly my father stood up and walked across to the rear wall of his office. I stood back from his desk, my hands were trembling. This was the first real argument I'd had with my father since childhood. Almost detached from his presence, I saw him lift down his latest rifle from its fixing on the wall. Under county regulations it should have been under lock and key, or the firing mechanism removed for display purposes. Instead, as he drew the gun down and cocked it I realised the thing was ready to fire. Slowly, he raised the rifle and sighted along the barrel directly towards me. I tensed.

'The wolf is a depraved, contemptible brute!' he growled, not looking away from the barrel. 'No son of mine is going to nurse any damn wolf cubs. If I had one in my sights now I wouldn't hesitate to shoot.'

It didn't matter to my father that killing wolves was illegal, he had never taken the edict seriously. I'd been too young before to question his actions. My forehead and palms, all one and half of them, were wet with sweat. I'd always seen my father as a cold calculating man, not given to passion. Had I pushed him too far? Surely he wouldn't fire. I raised my hands in a gesture of appeasement.

'You don't mean to use that.' I stepped round the desk. I was only a yard from him when he turned the barrel round aggressively and forced the thing into my open hands. As he glared into my face, spittle fell hot on my cheeks. 'Remember how it feels in your hands…' he barked, 'how good it was when you had a wolf in your sights, that split second after the shot, when you thought he'd escaped, and the sheer exhilaration when he went down, tumbling and dirty onto the ground.'

Tears, of something other than joy, squeezed from the corners of my father's eyes. 'Remember!' He grasped my arms and pulled me towards him. For a moment I was overwhelmed, almost giving way, then I pushed him away angrily.

'No. I can't do this any more.' I let the tip of the rifle barrel touch the floor. It fell with a clatter against the metal fireplace. I turned and walked toward the door but my father edged round the other side of the desk and was there before me. I noticed for the first time that his shoulders were slightly bowed. But although his forehead was creased, his expression was a mask of indifference. He put his hand up towards my chest and said, 'Eight months ago I nearly lost my son. It would have been a blow, but one I'd have weathered …..weathered I say, just as I had to seventeen years ago.' He was breathing deeply and froth had begun to form at the corners of his mouth. 'But you came back, wounded, shaken, but alive - or so I thought. Now I wish you'd died out there instead of bringing this disgrace on the family. You persist in this ….,' here he almost choked, 'madness, then you'd better get out.' He pointed to the outer door. I turned away sourly, reaching for the door handle and immediately felt the iron grip of his hand on my left forearm. His fingers pressed down hard on the skin graft. I winced, but he didn't notice and continued breathlessly, 'If you leave this house now, you'll not enter it again as my son. D'you understand?'

I stared at him in disbelief. 'If that's what you want.'

His grip didn't loosen, somehow I felt he didn't believe his own words. But it was already too late. One by one, I unpeeled his fingers, his face so close to mine I could feel his burning breath. I strode into the anteroom, trying to free myself of his anger. Lys must have heard the raised voices, she stood in the kitchen doorway looking towards us. I heard a stumbled footstep behind me then nothing. Lys' hand was raised to her cheek, she started to speak. 'Stop, Francis you can't….'

Can't what, I didn't learn. An exasperated growl from my father sent the words back into Lys' throat. She recognised the futility her words and ran towards me.

'No,' I begged her, raising my hand. I didn't want Lys involved in any backlash from the quarrel.

'Let me go….please.' She stopped halfway across the room, tears spilling unheeded down her cheeks, and watched me leave by the open doorway.

Chapter Three

For hours I drove aimlessly through the local backwoods, occasionally stopping at places we'd hunted from. But even these wild forested places, with their familiar sounds and scents, hadn't the power to raise my spirits. Eventually I turned onto the Grand Forks state highway. But Bitter Springs lay in that direction. I had no business going there now. I had no business going anywhere.

It was growing dark when I pulled onto the forecourt of a roadside motel outside Blackheath, with no more intention than to call Pamela. I was still smarting from our argument but was in no doubt love would somehow heal the rift. What I was going to tell her about the argument with my father, I hadn't decided. Her cellphone was switched off. I redialled the Jansen's home number. Dan came on the line.

'Can I help you?' he said in a phrase he'd practised in his hotel business and now used as an overture to most conversations.

'Dan, it's Francis, I can't get Pamela on her phone and….,'

'Er.. Francis, I think…she's out somewhere, oh!…,' he sounded hesitant. I heard a woman's voice - not Pamela's - whispering in the background.

'Maddy says Pamela's gone out …,'

'But she said she was packing tonight and….,'

There was no reply then some rustling as though he had covered the mouthpiece. Dan was not a man who found it easy to dissemble and when he came back I knew he was lying. 'That's right, she's packed, er,…..I think she's out now.'

'You're sure, couldn't you go and look?' The Jansens had a long rambling place. It had been converted at the end of the century from a family ranch house built around a central yard. They had no other children at home and Pamela now had a suite of rooms at the most distant end from the Jansen's lounge, her car was usually out of sight in a converted stable.

'Sure, sure I'll ……..oh, sorry Francis, Maddy's talking… ' A muffled conversation was followed by a sigh. I heard a door close, then the phone rustled into life. 'You still there Francis?'

'Sure Dan. I guess Pamela's told you….'

'Look it's all right to talk, I'm in the yard, left Maddy behind in the lounge. She's kind of seething, womanlike.'

'Pamela told you we had a row?'

'Sure, a tiff. People have them. You two've got a lot before you, it's natural you're under a strain.'

'If that's what Pamela said can't you get her to the phone?'

'It's more than my life's worth. Maddy's kind of mad, sent Pamela to bed with some headache pills. She thinks you've broken the engagement, said so right in front of Pamela.'

'I haven't Dan…,' He wouldn't let me finish. 'But you're not going to St. Paul with her are you, staying at home with your father?' Clearly Pamela had only told her parents half the story.

'No. I've left.'

I heard him draw breath. 'Left Silver Lake, why?'

'I had the same row with my father as I had with Pamela.'

'You're not making much sense son. Where are you

now?'

'Some small motel off the highway outside Blackheath, guess I'll get a room for the night.'

'Well I'd like to invite you here of course but……'

'No need Dan.' Suddenly I wanted to cut the conversation, 'I'll phone Pamela tomorrow.'

'Sure.' I heard the relief in Dan's voice just before I terminated the call.

The motel lobby was sparse, brightly lit, but clean. The lobby clerk, a tall lad barely eighteen, stifled a yawn and confirmed there was a room available.

'Any bags?'

'None,' I said, shaking my head. He looked relieved but his lack of interest didn't surprise me. Motels on the state highway must be used to businessmen descending on them without luggage. He handed me the register with a look of total indifference. While I was signing he lifted a room key from a hook, but as I swung the register back round, he looked down and jerked into life.

'Hell, you from the Silver Lake Delacroixs?'

I gave the briefest of nods.

'Both my uncles hunt with the Delacroixs, they're getting me a rifle this fall and I'll be up there with the best of them. You the son or something? '

'Just a relative,' I offered, hoping to conclude the conversation.

'But you hunt surely. I hear all the family…'

'Sure, sure,' I said taking up the key.

'Then I'll probably see……….' The boy had such a broad foolish grin on his face that I wanted to slap it.

'Which way to the room?' I asked curtly.

'Around to the left ….but won't you….'

I left the lobby without hearing the rest. The diner next door was still open with a full range of greasy meals, all came with French fries whether you wanted them or not. When I got back to the motel room I tried Pamela's number again but the phone was still turned off. My watch showed only ten past ten. If I got in the car now, I could be at her home in less than thirty minutes. Not too late. But the impulse died even as I reached for the door handle. I remembered her last words to me: 'better if you *had* lost your nerve .. you'll be on the floor'. What could I tell her now that would change things, that I'd had the anticipated row with my father, that I'd walked out and now had no future either in my father's firm, or anywhere else for that matter.

That the proposed agreement with Jacob Leason relied on my Delacroix name and little else. Why had I been so convinced I could get my father's agreement? But the answer lay in the past eight months. Eight months of pain and recuperation, six and half in hospital, the first months lying flat on my back with a punctured lung, fighting pneumonia, and thinking only of the slaughter of those innocent wolves, of seeing their lifeless bodies in the crusted reddened snow. Those nights in hospital re-living the nightmare, waking in turmoil, my face wet with tears. The nurses had simply plied me with tablets to kill the pain. None of them had understood.

That night my hand ached fiercely. Sleep came in fits and starts and by morning I'd little to show for the night but a light stubble. I had a razor in the car but for other necessities would need to shop soon. After a quick breakfast at the diner I walked into the reception lobby.

An older man was on duty. I offered money, saying I'd keep the room for a second night and turned to leave, only to be greeted by a familiar voice.

'Mr Delacroix, I hoped I'd see you again.' It was the same young lad, casually dressed and somewhat more enlivened than during the evening. He had a bundle of newspapers under his arm.

'Still on duty?' I remarked, unwilling to continue our earlier conversation. I headed quickly for the doorway. A man was just entering. I vaguely recognised him. He was of middle height, with grey balding hair and wore a worn leather jacket, the type with arm-patches, but I couldn't place him. He was heading towards the reception area when the boy persisted.

'It's Francis Delacroix isn't it, your old man's….'

I made a grab for the open door but it swung to in front of me and I saw the man's head come up with a start. I'd left it too late.

'Delacroix?' The man said. 'The Silver Lake Delacroixs? I've been wanting to speak to your lot.'

'Our lot?'

The man, I remembered, was a journalist. I'd seen him at functions in St. Paul with my father but couldn't guess why he'd come all the way to Silver Lake. 'Well… old Louis Delacroix as it happens.'

'Then I won't detain you.' I had my hand on the door handle but he turned with me and began pulling a notebook from inside the leather jacket. 'But if you're his son….. Listen, I'm with the St. Paul News. What's the story on this hunting complex he's putting together? Sounds as though it'll be nationwide, the biggest…'

'I can't help you,' I insisted. We were now outside the door. 'I'm sorry, I have to go.'

Even as I ran for the car I could imagine the headline 'Secret scheme, hunting monopoly scam …. Son refuses to talk…' As I drove away I wondered what he would write if he knew of my own classic betrayal. First the lobby clerk, then the newspaperman. Under present circumstances the name Delacroix was becoming a liability. Two miles down the highway I pulled into a lay-by and picked up my phone intending to call Jacob. It was nearly nine but I knew he went to his office early. The display indicated I'd just missed a call. The number was the Silver Lake residence. I listened ready to hear some irate demand from my father but Lys' voice came over the speaker.

'Francis, where are you?' Her voice sounded thin and strained. 'I thought you'd call … last night. I stayed up waiting.' Poor Lys. How could I phone Silver Lake and risk getting my father on the line? If only she had her own cellphone. 'Phone me please, let me know how you are….where you are…' There was a long pause 'Francis,…' then a longer pause '...please,' her voice nearly broke and the message ended. I nearly dialled straight back only stopping myself just in time. Dad's habit was to start the day walking around the site checking on his staff and their work. He wouldn't settle back into his office before ten. I decided I would phone Lys just before. If she was out, I'd leave a quick message for her with Janice in the office, with an embargo not to tell my father. Janice was the soul of discretion in most things. I thought back to Lys's words and wondered what kind of night she'd had with my father prowling angrily about the place. She'd sounded kind of lost and under a lot of strain, but what surprised me most of all was that she really cared for me.

Jacob was out, not expected in till late afternoon. I was refused his mobile number and left no message. I'd just finished a quick trip to the local superstore which set me up with my short-term needs, a water bottle, toothpaste, underwear, spare shorts, when the phone rang. It was the Silver Lake number and I was relieved when Lys' voice came on.

'Francis, are you all right?'

'Sure Lys. I'm fine, you needn't worry about me. I stayed the night in a motel.'

'Oh, that's a relief Francis, I was worried something had happened to you, and…'

'Stop worrying Lys.'

'Will you come back - tonight?'

'I can't.'

'But what will you do, d'you have any money?'

'I've plenty for the time being. I'll get a job. It's *my* life Lys, things will work out.'

'Will you tell me where you are?' I hesitated. For the moment I didn't really want anyone to know my whereabouts. 'It's probably best if you don't know.'

'How can you say that Francis? I won't tell Dad, you know I won't.'

No, she wouldn't intend to tell Father, but if he wanted to know he would force it out of her. I didn't know what to say so remained silent.

'You think you can't trust me?'

'Lys, you must understand…'

'Suppose something happened….someone should know where you are.'

I couldn't think of an argument to counter this and said simply, 'The Manning Motel, Blackheath. But Lys

I've only booked in for tonight, then…well I don't know.' The call ended but shortly after I realised Lys hadn't mentioned the argument with my father. She must have heard most of it, yet she said nothing. Delacroix Enterprises had been all she'd ever known yet she'd put forward no arguments for me to return, hadn't even spoken of my father's outrage.

From the superstore I drove on into Duluth for no other reason than I had nothing else to do. Close to Lake Superior the road splits, north towards Thunder Bay in Canada, south towards the twin cities: Minneapolis and St. Paul. The very road Pamela would have taken that morning. For a brief moment I thought of following her there. She had my mobile number but she hadn't called. I had no wish to visit Thunder Bay nor Ambrose Lodge, but at the junction I turned north, running along the shoreline beside the vast inland lake. You could drop all Silver Lake's waters into it without causing a ripple.

I wasn't aware how far I'd gone when I saw the blue and white sign enclosing a dark brown border with an irregular figure painted inside it. I slammed on the brakes to the annoyance of the lorry behind me, quickly skittering onto the gravel shoulder. My hands shook on the wheel as I pulled to a halt while the laden vehicle thundered past. I could almost hear the driver cursing. I reversed the car slowly to the intersection and sat there fully five minutes looking up at the sign, while the shaking subsided.

'Ely International Wolf Centre Welcomes Visitors' the sign said, '10 miles down the road on state highway 169'. I realised that the brown border enclosed silhouettes of three running wolves, their legs outstretched, heads low, ears pricked. It was barely eleven and Jacob wouldn't be available for hours.

When I'd settled the car into a parking bay at the Centre I was still undecided. Tame wolves, was that what I wanted to see? Four-legged ambassadors for their own kind, trotted out for schools, for the curious and the well-meaning who remain blissfully ignorant that cattle barons and even state senators are hacking away at their wild relatives.

Yet I was just as guilty myself. Finally deciding I couldn't be party to this cosy image, I switched the engine on again just as a bus drove up and disgorged a party of about thirty old-timers. They'd be from a generation who'd witnessed the wolf's decline They'd know of the wolves' legendary ravages and have come to loathe them. In the end they would surely celebrate their demise. So, what were they doing here? I decided to find out.

They were a lively group, none of them younger than seventy and all talking together as if aware of the short time remaining to them. I followed the group through the entrance handing over my seven dollars to a bemused receptionist. 'You with them?' she asked bluntly. When I shook my head, she grimaced. 'Well unless you want to join in with this crowd the next tour's not for another hour.'

'That'll be fine,' I said nodding as I took my single ticket and reading for the first time the motif written large above her kiosk. 'Teaching the World about Wolves.' It sounded an ambitious claim. I turned towards the old folks, vaguely aware of being watched. A man of about medium height, with slightly bowed shoulders, had screwed up his bright bird-like eyes against the sun and fixed his gaze on me. He had a shock of white hair and small moustache, and was standing beside a woman of much the same age who I took to be his wife. He held out his hand and above the babble of voices in the foyer called, 'Name's Leroy Tucker. You with us son?' in a sing-song voice that might have come from anywhere in the Great Lakes region, or even further south, 'course if you is, you're in for a rough ride, this lot don't know how to be quiet.'

He shot a look at his wife and scuttled towards me conspiratorially.

'But you'll be OK with us - won't he Lindy?' The woman squeezed a long sweet smile out of her lined face and her eyes twinkled. 'Once Leroy gets hold of you, there's no escape,' she tittered. I wasn't allowed time to reconsider. Leroy had me by the arm and was leading me into the midst of the party.

'You one of them there biologists boy?' Leroy badgered. I shook my head. 'No, I didn't think so. Hey everybody, this here's....say, what's your name son?'

My name? Could I admit here in pet-a-wolf country that I was part of a fraternity bent on their destruction, that the Delacroix family was doing its best to carry that out? It was a name that had already got me into trouble twice recently.

'Frank.....Frank Dawson.' The name slipped off my tongue as if I had already cultivated this new persona.

'This here's Frank Dawson.' Mimicking the name as if he'd known me all my life, Leroy bellowed it again to the assembled gathering. I was greeted with shouts of welcome and much laughter.

'He's not one of them young biologists, but he's come

here to…,' I knew the old man was trying to coax information out of me but just then the tour guide entered the foyer. She had to shout above their combined voices to gain our attention. She introduced herself as Janet Jonson and led us into a formal seating area in front of wide glass panels looking out onto a prairie-like field. At a distance of about thirty yards a group of pine trees cast deep shadows on the ground. She began her talk, but Leroy had already spotted three wolves lying asleep in the shadows. In a low husky whisper, he kept up a running commentary alongside her speech.

'These are our ambassador wolves, Sharli, Yarka, and Lepsi, a male and two females, they're sleeping at the moment, but…,'

'There you are son, ever seen anything like that, have you?' Leroy taunted.

'No, I….I'm not a country boy.'

'But you ain't a city boy either,' he insisted above the guide. I was only half listening to the woman anyhow and Leroy's chatter served to distract me from my own thoughts. The three wolves lay motionless as if … I gave Leroy a weak nod.

'Sharli and Yarka are from the same litter, Lepsi came in from Canada, from Manitoba, where there're plenty of wolves unlike some states in the USA and they…,' I stopped listening. I'd heard nearly as much as I could take of this cosy talk and would have walked out right then if Leroy's hand wasn't fixed rigidly on my right arm. Something stirred beneath the trees. A long dark shape stretched out into the bright sunshine and the wolf stared straight at the window. It had light mottled fur with dark patches marking the sides of its muzzle, head and ears, and a long dark tail that almost brushed the ground. Most of the group had already noticed the wolf and there were assorted sighs and grunts of appreciation as the woman explained.

'That's Yarka, the male, he and Sharli were born right here at Ely.' The woman said almost with pride. I was only half listening, how anyone could be proud of raising a wild creature behind bars was beyond me. The wolf settled on its haunches in the dappled sunlight and began to groom as she rattled on. For a long time I didn't register what she was saying. The bright open prairie lit by the autumn sunlight could hardly have been more different from what I'd experienced, hemmed in by snow and pines, only eight months before. And yet the wolf Yarka stood and moved and groomed as those wolves had done and bore all the same canine attributes.

Fed and pampered till they were in peak condition, yet none of these wolves had known a moment outside their pens. We were told Yarka had been vasectomised to prevent him breeding with the females. I felt strangely sad. Did wild wolves have a sharper awareness, a stronger survival instinct because they were wild and living in a changing environment where uncertainty gave them an edge these tame wolves might never possess? I wondered how Yarka and his companions would fare if they were ever released. Even given the dreadful fate of Speed and his family I couldn't help feeling sympathy for these three tame wolves sleeping so peacefully in the shade of the conifers. I came back to the room to hear Janet Jonson talking about hunting. It gave me a jolt and I listened more carefully to her words.

'Wolves are true hunters, they can run at 40 miles per hour, over many hours. They can gulp down about ten pounds of flesh then might not to feed again for another two to three days. A wolf pack can be as small as two mated wolves or as large as twenty-five to thirty.' Here the woman paused, looking round at her now attentive audience.

'How many of you think pack size relates to the physical size of the wolf's prey, from deer to the largest moose?' she asked.

'The bigger the prey, the bigger the pack.' asserted one old man at the front of the room.

'Old Jamie, he doesn't know anything,' Leroy yelled disparagingly.

'Can you do better, you old varmint?' Jamie countered.

'Just two's enough!' Leroy yelled back.

'Leroy, just behave!' Lindy called. 'Let the young woman talk.'

There was a brief pause as the room quietened and the woman took up the threads of her talk. 'Well you're both right in a way,' Janet Jonson said to the accompaniment of jeers from both Leroy and Jamie. The woman seemed unfazed by the constant interruptions from these wily old people and, almost against my will, I felt myself admiring her. Still keeping my eyes on the field where the other two wolves slept on beside Yarka, I began to listen to her more attentively.

'Pack size is often a reflection of food availability. Even though they hunt mainly the weak and the old and take many young deer in the early summer, two or three wolves alone can bring down a fully adult moose, enough to feed a litter of five cubs. But a pack of twenty or more adults needs more food, so one moose will provide only a single meal for each of them, some may even go hungry. So the size of the prey doesn't determine the size of the pack.'

'Just what does then?' Jamie barked. Clearly this information was news to him as indeed it was to me. I'd always believed that large packs attacked any large mammal, cattle, caribou or moose, but it never occurred to me that each single member of a pack would only get a small portion of this food. Where large packs might take large prey, and small packs smaller prey, the amount of food per wolf was the same. The dynamics of the system were mind-boggling but what if humans head in and change things. It stands to reason that if overzealous hunters remove large numbers of caribou or deer, wolf packs turn to the only prey left to them: beef cattle.

I'd always regarded the wolf as an opportunist, feeding on anything in its path and adapted to the chase, unlike the puma which kills by stealth. When a hungry wolf comes across fenced and sluggish cattle, it will chase any animal that runs from them. Hence the, apparently, senseless carnage occasionally wreaked by them, and for which they are condemned. Janet Jonson was right when she said, 'It's a complex world for the wolf, as a cub or adult. The determining factor is often the availability of prey throughout the year. When prey numbers are low, then the pack may split, just for a time, or permanently.'

There was a lot of muttering and many nods of approval. Leroy was nodding too, and clutching at my arm as if seeking my agreement. I began to wonder about his background. The guide was talking again and ushering the unruly party out through wide double doors. Through the glass panels I could see an open area of woodland and some more pens. With one look back at Yarka, who had settled down again to sleep in the afternoon sunshine, I followed Leroy and Lindy through the doorway. Janet Jonson took up the rear and locked the door to the lecture theatre. She gave me a brief wink and hurried after her charges.

'Now if you'd like to wander around the exhibits I'll be here to answer any questions you may have.' She had stopped in the centre of a courtyard surrounded by five huts with attached pens, though no other animals were visible. For a long time I stood looking into the nearest pen without seeing any sign of the wolves. Eventually, I looked back at the shingle-built sheds. Signs announcing the names of the resident wolves were attached to each hut and a wealth of information was contained in notices plastered about the walls. One would think there could hardly have been anything else to learn, but as I stepped towards Jane Jonson, Leroy came up beside me and urged me towards the nearest hut.

'You seem mighty interested in that Yarka fella,' he exclaimed, 'I bet you seen wolves yet you said you wasn't a country boy.'

I could see I would have to be wary of such a perceptive old man. 'They... they just reminded me of a picture I saw as a child.'

'No, that's not good enough son,' he cajoled, laughing to himself. 'I'm betting you know as much about wolves as I do.' And when I couldn't find the words to answer he just prattled on. 'Bet you couldn't guess where I live. No, well I'll tell you, Kansas City. My daughter and one of my boys're down there. But you know for sure I wasn't born there, no sirree. My old dad was from Red River, a bit aways from Grand Forks.'

'Cattle country?' I asked, amazed.

'Sure was boy, only my dad and his dad before him got small spreads, not like those monstrous places them cattle barons run. The Red River runs straight up to Winnipeg Lake, right there in Canada, did you know that?'

I did know but not wanting to hurt the old man's feelings I shook my head.

'And that big old Mississippi that's only 50 miles away, he just turns around and flows the other way as if he don't want to be friendly-like. Well the Red River headwaters was all marshland back in the 1920s, but my grandfather and a group of other farmers, they got in some water engineers, cut canals and drained the land so it dried out plenty good for cattle, it was rich pasture too.'

'So your dad made good.'

'Oh yes, he made good, 'course that meant the wolves made good too,' he said, his voice suddenly all cunning.

'They killed the cattle?' I asked bluntly, ready for the old arguments about wolf culling. But Leroy squeezed my arm tightly. His shock of hair shook bright in the sunlight and a queer grin broke across his face.

'Canny things wolves,' he said quizzically and paused, obviously waiting for my response. When I didn't reply he continued, 'You see boy, the pasture got so good, we was running two or three wolf packs along with the cattle.'

He guffawed and burst out into a fit of exuberant laughter. Beside him Lindy was laughing too. Tears were streaming down Leroy's old lined face as he became aware of my consternation.

'Deer, boy. Deer! We'd so many, they was eating out all the winter fodder, leaving precious little for the cattle, so when the wolves moved in an' started their own cull, well my Dad just put away his gun.'

Leroy collapsed in another fit of laughter and by the end of it was wheezing and snorting over Lindy's arm. I could tell the two of them were enjoying a joke half as old as themselves. But was it possible?

'Is it true?' I asked guiltily, already rehearsing in my mind what I'd been pondering moments before.

Leroy wiped tears from his face with a pink hanky which Lindy had pressed into his hand.

'True?' His body was still shaking. His face popped out from under the pink material, the skin wet and ruddy. He looked me squarely in the eyes and said, very seriously, 'As true as I'm in my eighty-fifth year this fall.'

'Eighty-five!' I gasped, I'd thought him a barely over seventy. 'And I'm guessing you're about a quarter that age,' Leroy said stuffing the hanky into his reefer pocket. I nodded. 'And I can still tell when something's troubling a man. Maybe age gives me the right to ask what that is son.'

The easy grin on his face belied the searching inherent in this statement.

'Maybe it does Leroy, but....,' I had warmed considerably to this jolly old man but that didn't give him the right to quiz me.

'You're not talking huh?' I shook my head.

Janet Jonson's voice intruded, apparently the tour was timed out and we had to leave. The three of us moved with the remainder of the group towards the last pen in the courtyard. On the way Leroy continued in his enquiry and I felt myself getting annoyed.

'I'd been working away from home, as an engineer, some years when Dad sold up. He'd worked the place alone for a while, was doing fine too, till Mum got ill and died. Even with the medical bills the land was doing all right. That's when the pressure started.'

'Pressure?' I asked as we halted outside the exit.

'Half the prairie had already been sold to a few men, cattle barons as they become now, greedy men, wanting all the land they could get - especially prime land like ours. Dad held out, then things started to happen. First it was the fire, a barn up in smoke for no reason, and other nuisances. Then all the deer was mysteriously hunted out and the wolves turned on the cattle, it wasn't their fault. I knew most of the packs on the homestead, seen their cubs born and raised. They'd been no bother, sure they took a few strays, but..., well, myself I think it was half-wild hunting dogs forced onto our land.'

'Leroy, you're saying they were deliberately brought in?' I asked in an undertone.

'Transport wasn't so easy in them days son. If I'd been at home I'd have known, but I was two hundred miles off. I couldn't get home and Dad sold up right quickly afterwards. Not that it'd have made a difference. He was alone see and didn't have the heart to carry on.'

'Leroy, how long ago did this happen?'

'About fifty years back, I reckon.'

'Then why....why are you telling me all this?'

He gave me a summing look and wiped a belated tear from his eyelid with his left hand.

'Because I watched you looking at them wolves.'

For a moment he remained silent and I thought I'd heard the end of his ramblings but he hadn't finished.

'You want to be one of these wolf biologists son?' Almost without thinking, I answered, 'Hell no, the idea's never entered my head.'

'Then maybe it should have!' He turned from me, took Lindy's arm and made as if they would head for the bus. Instead he half-turned and gave a long disconcerting look at my scarred hand then squinted up into my face in the strong sunlight. 'A son can't always follow his father boy,…. just look at me.'

I gasped. Leroy would certainly have been older than me when he left his father to run the farmstead alone. But I couldn't tell what he made of my injury. Had he guessed my name, seen some news report of the accident? I'd probably never know.

'You ever get down Kansas City way… Frank…, ' I heard the emphasis on my assumed name, ' ..you just look us up, we live with my son-in-law Congressman Abe Langer. You ever want an individual of integrity he's your man. He might be a congressman but he was a cattle rancher like my ol' dad and there's no side to him. You come and see us sometime, we're on Chesapeake Highway, right out in the sticks, bordering on the Missouri River, but we call the place 'Red River'.' He laughed sardonically.

I remained staring at the place where he'd stood as the bus drove onto the highway, and a voice behind me said, 'Well I think your old folks enjoyed the trip, Mr…?'

'Dawson, Frank Dawson,' I said almost instinctively. Well perhaps Frank Dawson would achieve what Francis Delacroix could not. Janet Jonson was a pretty girl, not too tall and with a warm smile, she was probably just three years older than me and already a fully-fledged zoologist.

'I hope you'll bring them again Mr Dawson.'

'Sure,' I responded coolly, but I wasn't really listening to her any more.

I drove the hundred or so miles back past Superior and Duluth, thinking about what Leroy had said, and as I turned towards the motel forecourt I knew I couldn't face the pokey little room. Instead, I drove down a side road into a parking bay overlooking the tiny Swan river. There was no-one about. Shrubs crowded the banks but the gravel-strewn bridge gave onto boggy marshland. For a while I watched the happy antics of a dozen twittering swallows as they caught insects above the open pools, then turned to the phone. This time there was no delay in getting through.

'Hi Francis,' Jacob sounded relaxed. 'Did you call earlier today?'

'Sure I did,' I answered rather querulously. 'They're a cautious lot at your office, wouldn't give me your mobile number.'

'They have to be, Francis. I thought I'd made that clear.' His voice had become serious and I remembered the warnings he'd given me before. The League had lost offices to unexplained fires and vandal attacks, people's lives had been threatened. Linking it with the Delacroix name might have helped prevent such outbreaks.

'Sure Jacob, I'm sorry.'

'Well what can I do for you. Have you some news?'

'It's not good.'

Jacob didn't come back with a lot of futile questions. 'Tell me then, in your own time.'

I couldn't tell him the whole story, not about the split with Pamela or the row with my father. All he needed to know was the bare facts.

'You know Francis, right from the start, I didn't think this would work out. We were too ambitious.'

He really meant that I'd been far too resolute, thinking I could win over my father so easily.

'I know, you warned me often enough. I don't know how I could have been so self-deluded.'

'It happens, with the best of us. Where are you now, at home?'

'No.....No I've left.'

'For good?' he asked knowingly.

'I guess so.'

'It's worse than I thought.'

'I'm at a motel over near Blackheath. Jacob, I started out on the Thunder Bay road today, saw the sign for the Wolf Centre.'

'At Ely? You visited the Centre?' he quizzed, sounding astonished.

'Yes. I couldn't take all that stuff about ambassador wolves, not after what I experienced. But I just can't forget that family of wolves. It's convinced me more than ever that I want to work with them. That hasn't changed Jacob.'

There was silence at the end of the line. A Delacroix in his organisation, that would have been a feather in the Wolf League's cap. A token which people would look up to and admire - nationwide. Now the cast-out son would simply be a liability, ex-hunter, ex-entrepreneur, ex-wolf-killer. I could hear his brain working, seeking some way to let me down lightly.

'I'm going to get a job.'

'Ah!' He sounded relieved. 'Where, what will you do?'

'I'll do something, it doesn't matter what. Bar-hand, labourer.'

'Sounds dodgy, do you have money?'

It was a mark of the man that he could think of me

even after our grand plans had come crashing down so violently. Maybe he was used to such disappointments. I didn't know him well enough to tell.

'For the moment, yes. Look Jacob, one way or another I've got to do this. Otherwise it will all have been for nothing… for nothing. Do you see?'

I waited long moments giving him time to think up more excuses but was already preparing to put the phone down on the silence when he offered.

'Look Francis I'll have to think this through, can I phone you tomorrow morning?' The arrangement sounded tentative, unpromising.

'OK I'm not going any place. But Jacob…,' I added almost as an afterthought 'I might just put myself through college.'

'The Business School? I thought…,'

'A zoology faculty. I want to study animal behaviour - if I can.'

'You mean it? Did you study zoology in high school?' His voice was quiet, disbelief evident.

'Only the basics. I can still learn.'

'I guess you can Francis. Look if you're serious in this……well there might be something I can do for you. Do you want to come downtown tomorrow morning?'

'Try and stop me,' I gasped enthusiastically.

'I'll see you then, about 9.30. But Francis don't get your hopes up, I'm not making any promises.'

'No promises.' I agreed and put the phone down hopefully on what promised to be a new era in my life. But the enjoyment quickly vaporised when I remembered I still hadn't heard from Pamela.

The diner looked less attractive than at breakfast. I

gathered up my purchases and headed towards the chalet intending to shower quickly and seek out somewhere in Blackheath for a meal. As I passed reception the young clerk came through the doorway, obviously intent on intercepting me. His face bore a sheepish, embarrassed look.

'Mr Delacroix, I'm sorry, the lady said it was important.' He paused and licked dry lips, then continued hesitantly, 'I asked her to leave the bag for you, but she insisted….. on going to your room. There wasn't anything I could do.'

'Pamela? When was this?' At that moment I felt cheerful, imagining the news I would give her, that it didn't occur to me to berate the boy for letting a stranger into my room.

'Just a few minutes ago, she'll still be there.' I glanced around the car park seeking out the familiar convertible. If Pamela had driven back from St Paul - but then it hit me. Pamela didn't know where I was. Only Lys knew and there were no cars that I recognised in the front lot. The disappointment must have been evident on my face as I opened the door and Lys got up from the bed.

'Lys, why did you come?' I asked insensitively.

She stared at me for a second then gestured wordlessly to an old case of mine which lay on the bed. 'I wanted to make sure you were all right. But I can see you don't want me here Francis. I'll go now.'

She made as if to leave the room but I took her arm in my good hand and said by way of explanation, 'I thought Pamela was here.'

'Oh!' Lys still sounded upset. She lifted her eyes to mine, the pupils blue-black in the half light, and tried to pull away. 'It's best I go.' I loosened my grasp. 'Perhaps so, you shouldn't be seen with me. There'll be trouble if Father finds out.'

Bizarrely she moved back into the room.

'What if he does?' she exclaimed angrily. 'I'm used to that kind of trouble.'

'Lys, he hasn't hurt you?' I asked savagely.

'No, he wouldn't, it's just…,'

She was shaking now. I thought she might collapse.

'Sit down Lys please.' She sat down gingerly on the end of the bed beside the small case. Unzipping the bag she drew out neatly laundered clothes: sets of my underwear, shirts, a favourite jacket of mine.

'I'm sorry I wasn't more welcoming Lys, you've gone to such trouble. It's just …,'

'Just what Francis?' She sniffed and took out a tissue from her sleeve. I realised that the events of the past twenty-four hours had taken their toll on her.

'When the boy said there was a lady waiting for me, I just thought, that is I expected it to be Pamela.'

'Have you spoken to her?'

'No, I couldn't get her on the phone. Why?'

'Well I didn't tell anyone where you were, I thought you must have told her.'

'Oh, yes I see. No I haven't spoken to her, she won't return my calls.'

A look of uncertainty crossed Lys' face, then she had control of herself again. She got up as if to leave. 'Did you know she's coming back to Father's meeting with the senators at the weekend, I heard him on the phone to her last night.'

'Last night?' I tried not to show my disappointment. Lys didn't know of my argument with Pamela and I didn't want to discuss it with her. 'I know there's a meeting but…,' I'd forgotten what Pamela had said, now her words came back to me. 'I'll see her Saturday then.'

'At Silver Lake?' Lys asked hesitantly.

'Not there no, I'll sort something out.' And then I wondered what things were like at home, adding, 'Is everything going on OK, between you and Dad?' Lys shrugged. Her face turned pale, her expression almost vacant as she said, 'I see to the house, all his guests, with a little help of course…,' two girls from town occasionally helped her with the rooms and the stream of visitors who came for business meetings. Many went on long into the night. 'Sometimes I think he wouldn't notice if I wasn't there.'

'You do yourself an injustice, Lys.'

'No, no I don't. He orders me around, expecting things to happen. I often think he forgets I'm not his wife.' It was a strange thing to say but Lys went on with a rueful expression on her face. 'But then it works two ways…,' She smiled at me, tears glistening in her eyes. 'Just as I sometimes forget you're not my son.'

A tight knot formed in my stomach at this strange declaration. I opened my mouth to speak but no words came. 'No, No. Don't speak little brother.'

Lys slipped her hand beneath my chin, held it there for only a second, then gave me a gentle hug. I felt inadequate, almost unmanned. Perhaps this explained why Lys put up with father's tyrannical behaviour. To stay close to me, she had stayed with my father. Her next words were almost a confirmation of this. 'I have some money saved, not much. It's yours if you need it.'

'Don't be a fool Lys, you've your whole life before you. You'll need that money.'

She gave me a disturbing look. 'What have I to spend

it on. Nearly an old maid and….,'

'Don't talk rubbish,' I said but at that moment I suddenly felt very selfish. If I could earn or get money some other way I would but…..'

'I must go now.' She had the door open. Sunlight streamed in.

'I didn't see your car in the lot.'

'It's round the back out of sight of the road, I thought it best.' She gave a brief sigh.

'Lys you think of everything.' We laughed conspiratorially and I gave her a hug. 'Won't you stay for a meal?' She glanced at the colourfully painted diner. 'No not over there, in Blackheath.'

'I can't Francis. Father will be waiting for his dinner.'

'Father!' I said irritably.

But Lys wouldn't be drawn. I walked her to the rear lot, recognising the battered Delacroix Ford behind a shrub border bright with flowers. Lys had never owned a car of her own. 'You know you should spend the money on a new car Lys, have a bit of a show.'

She made no comment, opening the door and slipping into the driving seat. 'Dad can pay for one if this conks out.' She laughed, sounding happy. I had my left hand on the window frame. She switched on the ignition. Before driving away, she laid her hand carefully on my injured fingers. All the laughter had gone from her voice as she said, 'Francis, promise me you'll take the money - if you need it.' She seemed determined in this, so I answered softly. 'If I really need it - yes, I promise.'

Chapter Four

I set out for Jacob's office on Tuesday with few hopes and a lot of trepidation, but by Friday morning I was travelling in his car up the long winding road leading to Bitter Springs, my future already mapped out for me. It was a future I hardly recognised, as I hardly recognised myself. The intervening three days had been hectic. Most of Tuesday I'd sat in Jacob's office while he made call after call to Friars University, Bemidji, some miles south of Bitter Springs.

All the faculties were on summer recess. After many attempts to contact the zoology lecturers, Jacob got through to a registration department whose staff were frantic with arrangements for the new term. I couldn't but admire the man's tenacity and after nearly a whole morning, he had one amazing success.

With me listening at his side Jacob discussed my application for a place on the University's conservation course starting in October, with John Dean the faculty head. From the tone of Jacob's voice the conversation had been difficult. Even given Jacob's offer to stand as my personal sponsor, the man had not liked being pressurised into enrolling an unknown candidate so close to term commencement, especially one who had no previous background in animal behaviour studies.

But when he came off the phone Jacob jubilantly told me that the offer of a place had been granted, conditional upon my passing a brief examination and a formal interview with a senior lecturer. Things happened rapidly thereafter. By mid afternoon I'd made a provisional registration, divulged my various grade school and college records, discussed fees, arranged a medical. The rest of the day and most of Wednesday, I spent in the local library cribbing what I could of the biology I'd learnt before the age of sixteen. It was a hard task but the more I read the more interested I became, and the more convinced I'd made the right decision. That evening, I travelled the eighty-odd miles to Bemidji.

At twenty-three I still suffer from examination nerves. I had to rack my brains trying to remember everything I'd learnt. The college psychology course came in useful as behaviour figured highly in the questions. I thought I'd failed abysmally. But if the exam was bad the interview was worse. The zoology lecturer, named James Thompson, was a brute of a man. Tall and elderly with receding grey hair and hunched shoulders, he was clearly hostile from the start. Whether he resented being called back from holiday during recess or whether something else was driving him I wasn't sure.

When he asked about my decision to take the course I told him simply that I'd recently met Jacob, that it was his enthusiasm for wolves that made me want to change from business studies to animal behaviour. I made no mention of my accident. It was obvious Thompson didn't consider this a legitimate reason for taking the course at such short notice. At one point he even stopped discussing the demands of the course and looked me straight in the eyes for several seconds before saying, 'Delacroix's a big name in these parts. Your Father's business empire, his wide hunting interests are well known, why I even understand he's expanding his business nationwide….'

He paused, obviously expecting me to respond.

When I didn't he placed his hands casually behind his head and breathed deeply taking time to continue. 'That doesn't seem an appropriate background for your animal studies and what I'm asking myself, Mr. Delacroix, is why someone like you should want to do this course.' He was ascribing some ulterior motive to my application, so I told him quite briefly about the split with my father and finished by saying that I no longer considered myself a member of the Delacroix family. That seemed to placate him. Soon after my test results were brought through. Here at last he smiled, nodding ironically over my poor effort and concluding, 'Not bad.' He looked up and smoothed his chin with his hand, 'but not particularly good either. You'll have a lot of work to do, a lot of revision.'

'I'll work hard, do whatever's necessary.'

'Mr Delacroix, if I may still call you that? These courses are designed for people working part-time at outreach sites such as the Wolf League's Sanctuary. The course demands one hundred hours a term working with animals. You'll have your course studies and the revision so you're obviously going to need a lot more time than the average student. Most have to fund their way through college, but you will have precious little time left for paid work, Mr. Delacroix. Precious little time, unless you have other funds available.'

He'd obviously been leading up to this point for the past few minutes, wanting me to reveal some latent connection with my family. He even seemed disappointed when I replied, 'I have my own funds.' I hoped, fervently, that I wouldn't have to call in Lys' offer. But this news appeared to satisfy him. Somewhat mollified, he confirmed my acceptance onto the course with a rueful smile, concluding the interview shortly afterwards and even assigning a lecturer to aid my revision. There would, I learnt, be a fee for the service.

At Jacob's suggestion I'd kept on my room at Blackheath but it was from a lonely motel room in Bemidji that I spoke to Pamela on Wednesday evening. She'd been on the verge of going out with colleagues from the business school and the conversation had been brief, not to say cool. She agreed to meet me at her parents' place on Saturday afternoon before the meeting at Silver Lake.

Jacob picked me up at Blackheath early on Friday morning. To my surprise, he turned towards Duluth then headed up the Iron Range road to pass across the watershed where many rivers start their long journey to the sea, and where the Swan and Prairie rivers, major tributaries of the mighty Mississippi, have their source. Only yards wide, they wind aimlessly, even sluggishly, through low valleys and shallow lakes as if unaware of their great destiny. An hour into the journey, Jacob surprised me by pulling the car into the carpark at a tourist viewpoint. It was mercifully empty. The site offered a panorama of blue hills and dark secluded valleys of virgin forest but I didn't think Jacob had stopped to admire the view. He was silent for a few seconds and it was obvious he had something on his mind.

'Something wrong?'

'Let's get out and walk.' I nodded anxiously, unwilling to leave the car and face whatever he had to say.

Jacob was heading across the clearing towards a lookout bay.

I got out but remained by the vehicle eventually

yelling after him with a sinking feeling.

'Jacob if you're having doubts about my part in all this...then I'd just as soon turn the car round and head back for Blackheath.'

Jacob ignored me. He stood on the promontory for a few moments then called back, 'Magnificent isn't it?' The wind had caught his hair, tossing the brown strands across his face and pulling at the light jacket he wore. I felt its cool touch waiting beside the car and moved away to kick at the gravel at my feet. When Jacob didn't return I slowly made my way towards him. He must have heard me draw breath to speak. Without turning he spoke in a low chiding tone. 'I wonder Francis, have you thought this all through? Really thought it through?'

My heart sank, he was coming to the crux of the matter. After all his efforts on my behalf those misgivings I'd first noticed on Monday were resurfacing. I knew he was going to let me down. How could I have been so wrong about this man? I hardly listened when he began speaking again.

'Delacroix. It's a name they'll be familiar with at Sanctuary. I'm afraid it'll make trouble for you.' He twisted around to face me, his lips taut, his expression almost sorrowful.

'I can cope with that sort of trouble, if that's what you're worried about.'

'But Sanctuary can't, Francis...,' he paused to let his words sink in, 'The wolves deserve our fullest attention, any disharmony among the helpers, it will affect them, and our work.' I was stunned. It took me several seconds to spit out my answer. 'So you're turning me down Jacob, after everything....' The anger in me was coming to the surface. 'You've made me look a fool, all that business with the University, the test, the interview. How you must be laughing at me!'

'No, Francis, no. You've got it all wrong, I was just trying to put the case to you...' He raised his arms almost in a gesture of exasperation. I took it as a dismissal. 'I've heard enough, you've made yourself quite plain Jacob. No matter how strong my convictions, no matter what I've been through, a Delacroix is unwelcome, persona non grata, at Sanctuary. Untrusted and untrustworthy, is that it?'

I strode away from him heading back to the car, then thought better of it and headed towards the road. I'd damn well walk all the way to Blackheath if I had to.

'Don't be so rash, Francis. Just think beyond yourself for a moment can't you....There is a way out of this,' Jacob called after me.

'Yes, there's a way out Jacob. And I'm taking it.' I turned my back to him and began jogging. He must have been fit, for all his fifty years, because he caught up with me before I'd got to the tarmac, grabbing my arms and spinning me round to face him. I took a slug at him with my right fist which he dodged expertly and we fell to the ground in a tussle. Before I could struggle to my feet he grasped my shoulders with both hands. Our faces, wet with sweat, were close together as he gasped, 'I didn't mean for this to happen.' I shoved him from me and tried to rise. He had hold of my foot. I would have had to kick him to get free but I couldn't do that no matter how I felt about him.

'Use another name. You can be Francis Delacroix everywhere else, just not at Sanctuary......That's all I'm saying.' I kicked myself free and went to stand. Instead I fell back onto the gravel. I began laughing, fitfully at first, then so much that my sides ached. Jacob must have thought I'd had a fit.

'Francis?' He knelt over me, and pressed hands dusty from the gravel onto my chest as if to still the convulsions.

'You want…you want….Oh no, it's too stupid.'

'What Francis, what do you mean?' Jacob began dabbing my face with a cloth. I pushed his arm away and, at last, said, 'You want Frank Dawson to come and work for you instead.' I continued laughing at the joke.

'Who's Frank Dawson, Francis? How can he…,' he cried, consternation crimping his features.

'Frank Dawson, AKA Francis Delacroix.' Jacob sat back on his haunches and stared at me bemused.

'It's a name I made up at Ely, when someone asked my name. Like you said, Delacroix's a name not favoured of wolf-lovers. If you wanted me to use another name why didn't you say so from the start?'

Relief was spreading over Jacob's face. I got to my feet, drawing him up beside me. I put my arm round his shoulder. Dust clung to his face and hair as he said, 'I didn't know how to ask Francis, a man's name…. it's very personal, it wasn't something I'd had experience of.' He was displaying genuine embarrassment.

From that moment my regard for Jacob Leason increased. As we continued the journey, travelling on through various country ways, I was still laughing to myself. At Togo we headed due west towards the Red River catchment, before skirting the south side of Lower Red Lake. Just before we turned back east into forested hills I had a brief glimpse of a broad valley and distant plains. Leroy's family farmstead, with its neat fences, had been down there somewhere; now the land stood out as one vast tract of open country empty of everything except cattle and dollars.

I was mulling over what he'd told me, when Jacob announced, 'Bitter Springs, Francis. What d'you think?'

We had just turned off the tarmacked highway and were driving up a sloping gravel road bounded on one side by a collection of lonely shingle-clad houses and on the other by a dry streambed stretching back into the eastern hills. Here in the lower street, almost all the houses had shingles missing from the roofs and gaping empty windows but as the road climbed and twisted through the pines more houses appeared and the creeping decline diminished. A group of about fifteen houses, well-kept and painted, crowded a small plateau below dense stands of oak and ash intermingled with conifers. They appeared to mark the end of town. The road had no place to go beyond their little picket fences. I wondered at the absence of people until I opened the car window. A fierce midday heat rushed into our air-conditioned cell.

'Pretty rum place, easy to see where it got its name.' I'd seen no signs to the wolf sanctuary and guessed he'd other reasons for driving into the town.

'You're right, I should think the early settlers relied on the stream we saw below. Probably it ran dry in the summer months as many of them did. The sandstone outcrops up in the hills would have been the only source of water for their animals,' Jacob said as if he had researched the town's history. He kept on driving, but every moment I expected him to stop in front of one of the houses.

'So... where's Sanctuary?' I asked at last.

'Patience. I wanted you to have a good look at the place, you'll be seeing a lot of it. See that house there.' We were passing a house with its front door painted red. A long veranda encircled most of the building. Apart from a few garments flapping on a long clothesline stretched between the back veranda and a huge pine, it appeared devoid of life.

'Josh Benson lives there. He's an engineer, anything wrong with a car he'll fix it.'

'He works for Sanctuary then?'

'We work on a slim budget Francis. The men make use of Josh. We can't put him on a retainer though he's always willing to help if we have any mechanical breakdown. The people in Bitter Springs know us pretty well. It kind of helps with security too.'

'It must be pretty secure. Just where is Sanctuary, I've not seen any signs, and the end of the road's…'

'Just here.'

We were approaching one of the last houses in the town. It was set back from the road and overhung by a huge fir that must seriously darken the rooms of the upper storey. The car slewed onto a dirt track running alongside the picket fence and we were immediately lost in the deep shade of the trees. The track was full of potholes that would stream with water or be packed with snow later in the year. Now the air was filled with dust, drifting pine needles and dry leaves.

It took us fifteen minutes to negotiate them and emerge into a clearing where our way was barred by a huge wire fence and gate. Inside the fence but a little way from it were two huts set at right angles so they masked the view beyond. On the nearest hut was a notice simply stating the name of the place as 'Bitter Springs

Sanctuary', with no mention at all of wolves. Below it was a zigzag danger sign indicating that the fence was electrified. I must have been gaping stupidly at the fence as Jacob turned to me.

'Not like the centre at Ely is it?'

'More like a prison.'

'A prison to keep people out. It's something we've all had to get used to. You will too.'

I stared at the high mesh fence and wondered how long it would take me. Jacob had made no move to get out of the car and in a few seconds a man emerged from one the huts to unlock the gate.

'Here's Charlie.'

Beaver! Dark nose and whiskers, dense brown pelt, but there the resemblance ended. The creature's broad forehead was pale grey barred with darker brindled crescents that curved above the amber-gold eyes. Deeply set in their sockets these last were rimmed in pale fur. Above a nearly white muzzle, the exaggeratedly large ears sported crisp white hairs bordered by a fringe of mahogany fur. The long powerful dusky-brown body was supported by four muscular legs which carried him rapidly across the clearing. A huge brush of dark tail swung out behind the animal as it reached the fence, halted and fixed me with a intense gaze. Beaver was undeniably a wolf!

I turned to Charlie Sleeman with raised eyebrows and saw amusement crossing his face. He was a hulk of a man, tall with broad shoulders, yet he was dwarfed by Sanctuary's broad acres stretching up the hill behind him. There must be fifteen fenced pens in view and only a few empty. Each broad compound, hidden in this mellow season beneath tall yellowing prairie grass, was furnished with its own stand of conifers and low bushes. Shallow conical mounds rose from within the grass, each surmounted by low wooden platforms constructed as viewpoints for the captive wolves, wolves who, through crippling injuries, advanced age, or behavioural problems, could never be set free.

Beaver's pen was the last I would visit that day. Higher up the slope Charlie had already drawn my attention to the bunkhouse and beside it a frieze of denser woodland which obscured another massive fence reinforced with metal shafts. In this more secluded compound were housed several wild-born wolves recuperating from injuries. Upon recovery they would be released into the wild. Any wolves in need of veterinary treatment, Charlie told me, were housed in small pens below the bunkhouse where they were under constant supervision by staff and veterinarians from Grand Forks.

Charlie had heard Jacob calling him from the office window. He turned away from the pen, squinted into the sun and waved an acknowledgement. He gestured me to follow.

'So what's wrong with Beaver?'

'Nothing.' Charlie was already trudging up the hill. I looked back at the pen where Beaver, having lost interest in me, was racing after a pigeon that had unwisely settled on the logs of his lookout. Long legs stretched before him, tail flying, head bobbing rhythmically under the influence of a strong bounding gait, he looked the picture of health and vigour.

'But…?'

Charlie stalled on the steepest part of the hill, waiting

for me to catch up. He was breathing heavily from the exertion yet there was a distant look in his eyes.

'Kind of gets to you doesn't he?'

I nodded, waiting for some explanation.

'Been brought up with dogs from a young age. About two years old now, and still thinks he's one of them.'

'Then how did he get here?'

'Became too boisterous. At eight months he fought with one of them pedigree chows, broke its tail. An old story.'

Charlie resumed his slow walk up towards the office, he reached the set of concrete steps and stopped. I tried to ignore Jacob who was standing by the open window beckoning at his watch. It was nearly time for us to go but I couldn't leave without hearing the end of Beaver's story. Charlie glanced at me. He looked kind of sad.

'He was less than a year old when he arrived. We got him put on the state re-training scheme straight away, they took him up-country. Beaver and a second wolf were released later that year . We chip all the releases. When we heard nothing we thought it'd been successful.'

'But it wasn't?'

I looked back at Beaver's pen. He was crouched down low on the platform, half hidden in the yellow grass. Pale grey feathers danced in the sunshine above his head.

'Know what the darn fool did? State team took him up near the Canadian border, other side of Red River. Three hundred miles and eight months later he was back. Imagine, full grown wolf, and he thinks he can move back in with the family. Caused quite a furore. Might've got himself shot too. Sod's been here ever since.'

Charlie sounded angry, but his wry grin confirmed an

unspoken fondness for the errant wolf.

As Charlie ushered me into the office Jacob called out, 'Ah Frank, I want you to look over the rota.' Completely forgetting my new alias I turned back to see who was behind me, only checking as Charlie's bulk intruded in the doorway.

'Something up pal?' he enquired jovially before squeezing through the door in front of me. Jacob came to my rescue.

'I've looked at the shift rota for Frank, Wednesday seems a good day for him to start.'

Charlie looked over Jacob's shoulder at a clipboard he was holding and nodded. 'Looks fine. Jenny and Albert'll be here too. Both thoroughly experienced.' He looked up at Jacob and became businesslike. 'You shown him the bunkhouse yet?'

'No that's next on the list.'

'Well suppose we get over there. He prodded me between the shoulders and all three of us went back out into the blazing sunshine. For a moment I couldn't see anything against the dark conifers masking the entrance and just followed Charlie's gravelly voice to my left.

'It's straight twelve hour shifts, students do three on and two off, but once you're here you don't leave the site again for sixty hours.'

'What about the university classes?'

'That's all taken care of in the scheduling, and 'case Jacob hasn't told you, you'll be working all them twelve hours. If it's daytime you're checking the pens, often sorting the feed and there's all the maintenance work about the place. Night-time you and two others take turns looking round the pens. Thankfully the veterinary cells are empty now but if we have any new arrivals, injured ones, then you all take turns watching them too. We can always call in more volunteers if need be. That all clear?'

'Sure, only....' The magnitude of the task of provisioning the place and caring for more than fifteen wolves along with the staff had only just begun to dawn on me. The responsibility was staggering too.

'Say, don't look so worried Frank...,' here he paused and slapped me on the shoulder. 'You won't be working alone. We've some pretty good people, you'll shape up quick enough under their guidance. Now here's the bunkhouse.'

The building was larger than it had looked from below and proved to be rather better appointed than its traditional namesake. For one thing there were separate bedrooms reasonably well furnished with bed, separate shower, lounger, but no TV. Upstairs were apartments for Charlie and his second in command, Mike Delahay, who I'd yet to meet. One of them needed to be in attendance the whole time whether sleeping or on duty. Shift workers and volunteers came and went to a regular pattern and the computerised duty roster was maintained by a member of staff who only came on weekday mornings.

All staff meals were prepared in a small canteen alongside the office and it was a standing rule that no food was permitted near the wolf pens. Beyond the ten or so bedrooms, a wall separated the body of the bunkhouse from the viewing area overlooking the veterinary wolf pens. Charlie led us into this room which was furnished with several video screens and computer terminals. The external glass screen was tinted and mottled making it impossible, I was told, to see in from outside. From where I stood the inside of the three pens and adjoining huts were clearly visible.

One man, dressed in shorts and a loose white T-shirt with a wolf's head emblazoned on the back, was seated in front of a console in the far corner overlooking the nearest pen. His attention was fixed on a screen broken into four hazy black and white images. He didn't look up immediately.

'Hi, Pascal, ' Charlie intoned as we entered. 'Want you to meet a new recruit, Frank Dawson. Frank this is Dr. Pascal Yolande, head of research at Sanctuary.'

Seated, Pascal had not looked very tall but as he unfurled himself from the desktop and strode towards us I guessed he must be well over six foot. A mop of thick dark hair and dark flashing eyes confirmed the Mexican ancestry suggested by his name. He smiled briefly and nodded to Jacob. Hardly acknowledging Charlie, he grasped my hand quickly and in one fluid movement returned to his workstation and re-folded himself into the padded chair. Obviously a man with a mission, he quickly fixed his attention back at the screen, saying, 'You a volunteer, then Frank?'

Charlie spoke for me. I thought his voice sounded slightly resentful, 'Frank'll be studying at Bemidji Uni, Pascal.'

'Animal conservation course, part-time,' I added.

Pascal nodded over a clipboard where he was making notes. His long black air obscured his eyes and face from my view. 'Better come and look at this then Frank.'

I glanced at Jacob, 'We got time?' Jacob nodded, 'Sure, no problem.' I heard Charlie mutter something under his breath which I did not catch.

Pascal motioned to a chair beside him. Hardly waiting for me to sit down he pointed to a section of the screen and began tapping away at the keyboard.

'There, what do you see?'

The screen changed from views of four sunlit meadows into a blur of shadowy infrared images showing a cluster of bushes bent over in a strong wind. The tangle of branches bounced wildly. Slowly from beneath one of them came the figure of a crouching wolf. The animal was clearly stalking prey, yet I could see nothing in the darkened compound which would warrant his attention. A second later, the wolf had sprung up into the air, stretching his paws into the mêlée of tossing branches before landing firmly on the ground with the body of a squirrel clenched between white fangs. With a toss of his head, the wolf killed and consumed the unfortunate squirrel. Then he slunk back into cover.

'What do you think, Frank?' Pascal asked.

'Not something you expect.' I stammered.

'Exactly,' he exclaimed excitedly, slamming the clipboard down on the desk. He brushed the dark hair from his face. 'Four nights ago, I watched a squirrel clamber into pen number four and race into the trees. Whether this is the same one I can't tell, but I watched the wolf for three nights and last night this happened.'

'Is it unusual?' I asked naively. Pascal lifted his head and fixed me with his dark eyes. I felt his hand settle on my arm, the fingers tense and strained.

'That's what we don't know, Frank. You can find twenty books telling you wolves take only large prey, and another twenty telling you the opposite.'

I didn't quite know how to respond. My experience

with wolves hardly qualified me to debate a wolf's dietary habits with this earnest young man.

'Are you writing a book?' Pascal shook his head and looked back at the screen. His grasp eased and I could feel his enthusiasm melting away.

'In another year or more,' he said rather morosely. His fingers flashed over the keyboard, other daylight images rose on the screen and Pascal recommenced the note taking which our entry had interrupted. I felt myself dismissed.

'Don't mind Pascal,' Jacob laughed, gesturing towards the bunkhouse door. 'Pascal spends so long studying his wolves he sometimes forgets how to be human.' Charlie was already waiting in the corridor. 'That's true enough,' he called back into the room. But Pascal ignored us. A scowl moved across Charlie's face rather than the smile I'd expected.

On the way home I questioned Jacob about Pascal's work.

'He seems very intense.'

'He's working pretty hard for us. Spends all summer at Sanctuary but his real work's done in the field. We were lucky to get him.'

'I kind of got the feeling Charlie resents him.'

'They jog along together well enough. Charlie's plenty knowledgeable on animal husbandry. He's more'n twenty years field experience with wolves and bears, but he's got no formal qualifications. When we advertised the post of head of research two years ago we didn't expect many other applicants, what with the low salary. Charlie kind of assumed he'd be appointed. He's doing great work at the place, nobody better, but he just can't accept that we need Pascal's type of research too.'

'Where else does Pascal work then?'

'Up in Canada mostly, some in Alaska too, studying wolf packs through the winter, they're easier to track in the snow…,' here Jacob wavered. '… but I guess you'll know that.'

'Sure,' I agreed, not wishing to pursue the subject.

Two-thirty Saturday afternoon, an unusually cool breeze blowing from the north. I was sitting in the Jansens' front yard with the car windows down enjoying the freshness of the air and watching whiskers of dust spin down the windscreen. The car would be visible from the main living area. Pamela would know I'd arrived. She must know too that I didn't want a confrontation with her parents, especially Maddy.

But if Pamela wanted to see me she was in no hurry to put out the welcome mat. Ten minutes passed with no signs of life in the place. I began to think it was empty. I got out of the car and headed across the gravel to the front door which was approached by a shallow stone stairway. As I did so a deep blue land-cruiser raced from the rear of the property and headed in my direction. It was the latest model, with high wheelbase and darkened windows you couldn't see in.

Pamela's parents had a coveted light blue 1980s station-wagon, she herself a modern convertible. I stood back to let the thing pass but gravel spun beneath its wheels and the vehicle ground to a halt with the passenger door beside me. The window purred open and Dan called my name from inside. I peered at the window straight into Maddy's eyes. As soon as she recognised me she grimaced and looked away. She ruffled the collar of her blouse with her hand and fixed her gaze on something far in the distance.

'How do you like the new machine?' Dan called.

'What've you done with the station wagon?'

'Back at the traders - if you want it.'

Despite the awkwardness of the situation I laughed and patted the new metallic paint on the hood. As I did so I felt Maddy's gaze settle on me.

'I'm surprised you can laugh Francis Delacroix, in the circumstances. How can you even show your face here - after what you've done,' she burst out.

'Aw' let the boy be Maddy,' Dan insisted, but I wasn't ready to let Maddy off the hook.

'Why Maddy, what have I done?' I asked, moving nearer to her window. She shrank away from me and was lost in the shadows thrown by the car roof.

'Upset Pamela.... Isn't that enough?'

'If I have, then I've come to apologise.'

'What about your father then, the firm? No-one even knows where you're living.' Maddy's interest in my father's business struck me as rather too intrusive.

'What's between my father and me's no-one else's business Maddy.' I said caustically, then remembered I was talking to my future mother-in-law. 'Sorry Maddy. You're right, Pamela and I have some things to sort out.'

'Pamela's waiting for you son, she only got in early this morning so she's a bit tired. Why don't you go on up to the apartment,' Dan interrupted across his wife.

'I don't want you upsetting......' Maddy's voice was lost in the sound of churning gravel as Dan gunned the car off the drive. The dark window closed over her irate features. I was suddenly woefully aware of Pamela's likeness to her mother.

The door opened to my touch and Pamela's voice echoed from the distant apartment, she had obviously been waiting for me. 'Come on up Francis, coffee's brewing.'

I followed her voice through broad pine-clad rooms full of the type of frontier-style furniture fashionable in Dan and Maddy's youth, and emerged on the first floor where Pamela had her rooms. The smell of coffee mingled with a heady fragrance I already knew was Pamela's own - Wild Orchid I think they call it. As I entered the lounge there was no sign of her.

'Pamela?'

She came hurriedly through from the bedroom, a hesitant smile on her lips. What she saw on my face must have reassured her for in a second she was in my arms. We kissed briefly without passion, then she hung back saying, 'I've missed you. It's been almost a week.' She spoke breathlessly. The auburn hair was swept back away from her forehead revealing deeply set eyes masked with blue eyeliner that made them appear deeper still. She had chosen to wear a loose turquoise shift caught about her waist by a matching ribbon, and long white calico trousers that somehow emphasised her small stature.

'Seven days.... a lot's happened Pamela.' I'd intended to explain myself before things went any further but I couldn't take my eyes from the trailing ribbon at her waist and the soft swell of her breast. I pulled her gently towards me, struggling to untangle the thing.

'Francis, ...can't we talk...first.' Her hand settled on my own, preventing further movement.

'Do we need to talk?' I felt the ribbon fall open of its own accord.

'I think so... yes Francis, we do.'

'Can't it wait?'

She looked at me steadily and for a moment I thought she was going to resist. A half-determined, half-petulant look crossed her face.

'Well perhaps....'

Our lovemaking was not as languorous and caring as it often was, but hurried and with a kind of desperation in the final frenzy of desire. Afterwards I lay, as I often did, with her beside me looking through the broad window to the branches of an agéd lime tree. The wide green leaves had begun to change colour and in the afternoon sunlight showed bronze against an ice blue sky. Was this a sign of a bad winter to come? Certainly it brought a wintry feel to my heart. I turned to Pamela, intending to dispel the image by caressing her breasts and excite arousal once more but she slipped to the side of the bed and reached out for her clothes.

'Getting dressed, so soon?'

She gathered my slacks and underwear from the floor and flung them at the bed laughing as she said, 'You too. Coffee's waiting.'

Coffee and a lot else were waiting for me in the lounge. Pamela had brushed her hair and caught it into a pleat at the back of her head. It wasn't a style I liked, it made her look altogether too business-like and cool. Perhaps this was what she intended. She sprinkled one spoonful of sugar into the black coffee and handed me the cup.

'Just as you like it.' She laughed up at me.

'I'd have liked it better if you brought it to me in bed.' Her mock grimace was followed by a long searching look as I sat down opposite her. 'Where do we go from here

'You know what it'll mean, you working for him, for the hunting fraternity, what it'll mean to us.'

'I was hoping you'd see sense. Honestly Francis you can't go on like this, you'll ruin yourself.

'Ruin myself in my father's eyes, is that what you mean?'

'I... Francis, if only you'd give up this crazy Sanctuary business. You can't let a few unfortunate wolves come between yourself and a magnificent future.'

'A few unfortunate wolves have a right to live Pamela. And if this splendid future you talk of means unlimited killing, then I don't want anything to do with it, ever.'

She jumped up. Pushing the table away she came swiftly to my side. She took hold of my arm, sobbing onto my shoulder, her words muffled but audible. 'Francis, you can't mean that, you can't. Don't you see it's only the malady talking.'

I turned and took her in my arms. 'Don't do this Pamela, don't do this thing, it'll pull us apart.' I tried to draw her towards me but she was straining for release. Her gaze steadied on me. Looking deeply into my eyes she said, 'But he wants you back, Francis. When I saw Louis last night, he implored me to get you back, he'll doing anything....' Something in the way she spoke aroused my suspicions then and there, but I wouldn't give a name to them.

'He's asked you to talk to me? You've seen him?'

'I was there last night, we had a lot to discuss with the senators coming, then he started to talk about you and.....'

'You saw him last night, but Dan said you only got in this morning. How late were you there Pamela, how

Francis… we have to decide.'

'I've already made my decision Pamela, I've been hoping you'd come to…....'

'….understand. Is that what you hoped? That I'd understand you throwing away your future, *our* future?'

It was the first time in a week that I realised she would be as much affected by my action as myself. Somehow I believed she would find another outlet for her talents than my father's business.

'I'm sorry about that Pamela. You'll continue with the business school won't you? Perhaps we could set the wedding for after you finish there?'

At the word 'wedding' a quizzical expression crossed her face that I could make nothing of. 'I'm going to work for your father Francis,' she said determinedly.

'But how can you….. ah…..you mean in six months? Do you think he'll still accept you after everything that's…,' she cut me off briskly. 'No, not in six months, he needs someone right now.'

I hadn't seen the betrayal coming, it hit me unexpectedly and I dashed the coffee cup down on the bare table, spilling the grounds across a magazine laying there. Pamela saw that she had shocked me. 'Francis, he needs someone now you've deserted him. With so much at stake, his biggest venture ever, and his only son turns against him.'

'If you think this little trick, this blackmail's going to make me change my mind and come back then you've seriously misjudged me.'

'Perhaps I misjudged you all along, Francis.' Her lips curled in a cruel twisted smile.

'You think I've let him down.'

'Well, haven't you?'

late?' I demanded.

'Late enough, there was a lot to prepare for this evening.'

'Lys made up a bed for you?' She blinked rapidly, obviously disturbed by the question.

'Lys…? No, Lys was baby-sitting at the Taylors.'

'So you were alone with him, all night… God Pamela, he'll do anything you said, does that apply to you too, did you sleep with him, did you actually sleep with my father?' I burst out appalled.

'What if I did, Francis,' she shrieked back at me 'You've deserted both of us, turned away from the future we planned and schemed and slaved for. What do you expect me to do, come crawling after a loony no-hoper who's lost his nerve, some crazy wolf-lover …,'

Her hair came loose from the tightly-coiled pleat and swung wildly in front of her face. I'd had enough. I pulled her towards me and slapped her face, not once, but twice. She screamed in horror. Tears poured down her angry face and two red wheals flushed her cheeks where I'd hit them. I looked at her aghast at what I'd done. She clasped her hands over her face and screamed through them. 'Get out, get out of here, I never want to see you again.'

'I'm sorry, so sorry…' I cried, slipping uncontrollably to the floor beside the sofa. Too stupefied to react, I watched her tugging at her finger until she'd pulled off the engagement ring I'd given her ten months before. She leapt away from me and threw the ring across the floor.

'Take your ring and get out now, before I call the police!' Her voice was a high-pitched wail as she raced into the bedroom and slammed the door.

I'll never know how I made it out of the house. I was suddenly in my car tearing across the noisy gravel and heading along the Duluth road. I didn't stop until the car ran out of petrol and crawled to a halt above Lake Superior's rocky shore eighty miles away.

Chapter Five

Six days later, at the end of my first three-day shift at Sanctuary, I was sipping coffee in the bunkhouse canteen and contemplating the drive back to my lonely digs in a small town ten miles outside Bemidji. Waiting for me there was the whisky bottle which had sustained my nights and the piles of biology books which had filled my days. I'd turned my back on the whole ghastly hunting world, on Pamela, on my father, and let all phone calls go unheeded.

Though dead beat when I arrived at Sanctuary three days ago, I'd thrown myself into all the physical work they offered: hewing and chopping wood for the boiler, whacking in fence posts, repairing buildings and even clearing and toting garbage from the canteen. The only positive result was the beginnings of renewed strength in my left hand.

In truth I wasn't much company for anyone, hardly able to talk above a simple grunt of acknowledgement for fear of breakdown. What my workmates thought of my brusque manner I neither knew nor cared. I avoided contact as far as possible, working alone for long hours and crashing out in my cot at the end of a shift, exhausted and thankful for a dreamless deep sleep.

I guess it was only that day, the day the wolves were fed, that I'd returned to something resembling life. Carting heavy loads of food down to the wolf pens had seemed a thankless task. I loaded the heavy joints from the store, placing them into the chilled meat buggy and lugged them out for Sammy Kitson, one of the experienced volunteers, to feed directly to the wolves.

Sammy was in his fifties, unemployed and seemingly unemployable. He had been a civil engineer until five years ago when he was badly injured in an accident on a building site. He'd almost lost his left leg and walked with a severe limp which gave him a lopsided look. Sammy's limping figure was almost a constant presence among the wolf pens. He was divorced with no kids. So Sanctuary was his whole life. He'd developed a keen awareness of wolf behaviour and was an excellent teacher. I learnt much from him, but on that day he showed another facet of his character.

Sammy followed a strict routine throughout the food run. In the corner of each of the large pens was a small wooden shelter with a concrete base. Once he'd established that the wolves were not in this area he worked the pulley which closed the inner gate connecting it to the main grassy paddock then entered the pen carrying a haunch of beef, leaving it on the concrete, retreating and reopening the gate.

Sammy said the precautions were necessary. Although the resident wolves were habituated to humans, they were fed at irregular intervals to keep them from boredom. They might quickly become irritable, even dangerous. Observing the way in which each wolf reacted to food was an education in itself. Sammy's great tenderness towards them was obvious from the way he described each wolf in turn, so that I need only listen and watch to learn a great deal.

'Now Jude here, she's blind in one eye,' Sammy said as he entered the first pen in the circuit '…she's pretty cute though. We do the food rounds in a different order each time and if she thinks she's going to be last she'll hide up on the lookout with her head low in a sulk, pretending she doesn't see you, won't even come down until you're back at the store. But sometimes when we're early, like now....' He'd just re-closed the outer gate and was looking back across the rustling prairie grass 'Look.' his voice became a whisper 'there's your food girl.'

The thick grasses parted briefly near the gateway, a dark muzzle and jaw, long pale nose and almost white ears pressed between the grass stalks. Jude's left eye was bright and moist. With it she watched us warily. The right was a white globe without pupil or iris. Jude was small for a wolf, smaller than most adults I'd seen, and her fur was a pale, dusky white, as if she'd been dipped in dry flour. She'd be exceptionally well camouflaged in the hazy maturing grasses but here in the concrete compound she knew she was at a disadvantage.

Her head constantly moved from side to side, each paw moving hesitantly forwards until she reached the chunk of meat, then with a sudden great lunge she'd grasped the whole thing in her jaws and staggered backwards pulling it towards the safety of the grasses. I knew each parcel of meat weighed about ten pounds for I'd laboriously shifted fifteen of them out of the store half an hour since, but Jude made short work of the task, pulling the bloody, bulky haunch awkwardly back through the gate and disappearing into cover within seconds. I could hardly believe she'd even been there and shook my head. Sammy was laughing gently at my side.

We followed the same routine with Luke, Jade and Jasper, three wolves whose injured legs gave them a lopsided look as they came down into the concrete compounds for their food. Sammy was an adept, always forecasting the manner in which they would act as he approached their pens and delivered the food. Luke was a huge dark male, bold and canny, with a crooked back leg that appeared to cause him only minor difficulty in bounding towards the meat. Invariably, as today, he stayed in the compound consuming huge quantities of meat before carrying the remaining bone back into the forest of grass to rest.

Jade and Jasper, two dusty brown females, had pens side by side. Both were missing a front leg, yet they spent long minutes pulling and hauling the carcass portions out of the concrete compounds before attempting to feed. Jade, the smaller of the two, even returned to lick the bloody pool from the concrete floor before disappearing to gorge on her prize. We stopped at cage after cage yet each commentary from Sammy had me reeling. I was amazed at his insight into the character of each wolf.

Finally we had come to Beaver's cage. Here, I detected a strange reserve in Sammy's attitude. When we reached his pen Beaver was bounding along the outer fence following us down the aisle which led to the wooden shelter, just as he had when I first saw him. Sammy got hold of the pulley handle and barked out a warning.

'Get back, back you varmint!'

The wolf pricked his ears at the sharp tone of Sammy's voice. He plunged his paws deep into the grass, suddenly twisted sideways and sprawled against the fence with his head low, wet tongue lolling from his mouth. Keeping his eyes disconsolately on Sammy, he watched every move my companion made from closing the inner gate, to entering the pen and depositing the meat, and finally through to closing the outer gate.

When Sammy returned, I expected him to give his

usual effusive commentary but the man just stood beside me watching the wolf's slow, tentative entry into the small pen. Beaver's eyes had glanced just once in my direction and for a second I'd seen the old warmth return, but when he looked at Sammy it was as if a veil had come down. Both of us watched the big healthy male edge towards the chunk of meat.

Beaver leant down, quickly grasped it securely between his jaws then lifted it bodily at the first attempt. I watched the dark fur over his shoulder muscles ripple and tighten. His haunches steadied to balance the weight of the meat. He stood quite still, for perhaps two seconds, while he and Sammy glowered silently at each other across the open ground. Then Beaver turned easily and jogged through the grass, quickly reappearing on top of the wooden lookout with his haul intact.

'He's a fine animal,' I commented in an attempt to lighten the mood.

'Fine…?' Sammy turned towards me, the easy manner of the morning gone. His face was a hard mask. 'Shouldn't be here by rights!' His voice turned savage. 'Those other wolves, they can't ever leave. Beaver's had his chance of freedom. I can't forgive him for that, just can't….' Sammy's voice trailed off resentfully. I watched him rub unconsciously at his own injured leg. It came to me that he saw the injured wolves as being in need of care, his care - they couldn't leave Sanctuary, any more than he could go back to his old life as an engineer. But Beaver was fit, active. He'd been given a chance of freedom and failed. Sammy could never forgive him for that. I remember thinking that such an opinion might cause friction with other Sanctuary staff, friction I'd sought to avoid by my own change of name.

I was down to the last dregs of coffee and contemplating a bleak future without home or loved ones when I heard my alias called. 'Frank!' Jenny Dracott stood in the canteen doorway. She was a buxom girl of more than average height, the full body squeezed into tight jeans. But everything about her was neat, from the trim T-shirts, clear peach and roses complexion and sunburnt skin, to blond hair scraped into a tight ponytail. She had a quick precise manner too. In her final year of veterinary college, she was Sanctuary's next best thing to a fully qualified vet. But this didn't prevent her from helping in any task that wanted doing, even the most trivial. In the three days I'd been there I'd had nothing to do with her but she was always in the background, guiding the other volunteers, tapping away at the computer keyboard for hours, or just overseeing the activities as a kind of second-in-command to Charlie.

We had never been close enough for speech, even if I'd been capable of conversation, though occasionally I'd seen her watching me from a distance. Once, after hauling and preparing wood posts for a new pen, I'd been ramming a pole down into the ground with the sweat pouring off me. I'd stood up, smeared a cloth over my face and taken the briefest of rests. Earlier I'd seen her moving about the upper part of the hill, occasionally scribbling with a pencil on a clipboard she had in her hand. But just then she was standing on the upper steps, the pencil lodged against her lips, her gaze fixed on something just beyond me. She didn't smile or even seem aware of me, just dipped her head as if agreeing with some private thought then bent over the board. When I looked up again she'd gone.

Now Jenny was looking around the canteen as if disappointed to find me as the only occupant. I'd seen Mike Delahay heading towards the outer pens with another student and the two new shift members were already at work on the fences at the base of the hill. My shift was near its end. Soon I would leave too.

'Better get yourself cleaned up.'

I'd come into the canteen straight from working, dirt was smeared along my arms and probably my face. I hadn't realised her tight regime extended to mealtimes, but I'd misunderstood her.

'Quickly, you're wanted. There's an emergency and I need your help. Meet in the computer room in five minutes.'

'I was going off shift and …,' I began, but she'd gone from the room.

What kind of emergency would call for greater cleanliness than I presented just then I didn't know. I hurried to my room, sluiced quickly under the shower and was heading towards the computer room with wet hair when I heard wheels tearing up the gravel just outside. Vehicles were not normally permitted in that area. Jenny was seated at one of the consoles. At this sound she sprang up from her chair and came careering out from the room.

'Quickly!' She grabbed me by the arm, turned me in the direction of the courtyard and sped through the outer door in front of me. Dust flew into our faces from the wheels of a 4x4 that had pulled in hard against the outer wall. I was just in time to read the words 'Grand Forks Sheriff's Department' emblazoned on the side before I felt Jenny's hand on my arm. 'This way Frank.'

She hurried around to the rear of the vehicle as the

occupant stepped out. A tall lean man of about forty and wearing a broad stetson, the sheriff rapidly lifted the rear door and leant inside. What he pulled out surprised me. In his hands was an old blanket, dusty with age. It was doubled over in his arms yet he leant gingerly with it towards Jenny and I saw a brush tail flop from one of the inner folds.

'Is the vet here yet?' he asked. Jenny folded the blanket more securely into his arms so that it again covered the inert tail.

'Suzanne's on her way. How bad?'

'Probably a road accident, might be a couple of bullet wounds though. Hard to tell, not much blood.'

'Frank'll take him off you,' Jenny gestured towards me.

The western sun was shining directly across the bunkhouse, almost blinding him. He squinted at me and said, 'Best if I take him straight down, don't want to disturb....'

'OK.'

Jenny raced towards the outer door at the rear of the computer room. She flung it open and led the way into the veterinary clinic. I'd never been in there before.

'You know the way, Hal. Frank see he doesn't stumble.' He edged forwards, gingerly carrying his load through the door and following Jenny down a long corridor. I saw her open a doorway and the smell of chemicals came strongly through the air.

'Come on down, Frank.'

I was just closing the outer door when another vehicle tore through the gate in the outer fence which had been left open, presumably for this new arrival. The car came to a halt beside the sheriff's vehicle.

'That'll be Suzanne,' Jenny's voice echoed down the corridor. 'Help her in with her equipment can you Frank?'

The woman beside the grey convertible was only a little older than Jenny. She was tall and spare and was already bending over a mass of equipment in the trunk. Brusquely and without looking up at me, she pulled out two stout plastic boxes and thrust them into my hands. A third she swung at her side and nudged me forwards. 'Well go on, go on, I can manage these.'

I'd never been in the veterinary rooms but the clean clinical precision of the equipment flanking the walls and the harsh smell of pharmaceutical chemicals were not what shocked me. Sheriff Hal had just unfurled the blanket he'd been carrying and I could tell from the rich colours that it was not dusty and unkempt as I had thought. Inside, covered with dust and dried blood were the ragged remains of what might once have been a mammal of some kind. The four limbs were bent anyhow in the folds of the material and the head and tail lay flat and inert, the dark pelt without lustre - or life. Certainly the state of the creature did not seem to justify the bustle and activity that I became involved in.

'Is the autoclave on, Jenny?' The vet brushed past me. 'Here, put the cases here,' she ordered peremptorily, indicating the wooden benches set against one wall.

'Been on since Hal's call,' Jenny replied.

'Quickly then, get the table prepared.' The vet took bottles from the windowsill and began pouring chemicals into bowls set alongside the benches. I stood back away from her and caught the sheriff's eye. He watched me as the two women bustled around us. His expression said we weren't much use to them but then Jenny said, 'Frank, I know you've had no training, but you're going to have to help us.' She pulled two plastic aprons from a drawer, wrapped one around herself, then advanced towards me. She'd pulled the neck cord over my head, wrapped and tied the waist straps behind my back before I'd had time to object.

'Put these gloves on too, we need to swab the table and let Hal have his blanket…Then I'll show you…..'

I followed her instructions, cleaning a second table with strong chemicals then slipping clean plastic sheets under the comatose animal before moving it gently across. I saw at last that it was a wolf, one that looked so close to death as to resemble the real thing. This worried neither Jenny nor the vet.

Over the next half hour, time stood still. I was vaguely aware that Sheriff Hal had left the room, complete with blanket, but what followed was a blur. Jenny instructing me in the use of the equipment, the autoclave, the chemical bottles, careful disposal of used chemicals, then all I remember is her standing with Suzanne alongside the operating table and the rhythm of their voices talking softly to each other or asking me for implements or materials.

I know we got through a lot of gauze and swabs, but at last the job was done. Sometime during this period I heard the metal container beside Suzanne rattle as she dropped first one then a second bullet into it. The 'road accident' would be reclassified as unlawful killing, if the wolf died. After the operation Suzanne gave the wolf an injection and inserted a needle into its front leg where a saline drip was attached. Jenny and I together lifted him from the operating table into a cage in a tiny room set alongside the main veterinary room. Behind us Suzanne hurried about cleaning her equipment and storing it away in her cases. We set up the drip bottle at the top of the cage.

'How long?' I asked, closing the door and re-setting the secure padlock.

'We'll have to keep him sedated for a while. Suzanne'll come back each day to check on him.'

Suzanne wasted no time packing up. We followed her along the corridor and across the courtyard where Jenny received her final instructions. As Suzanne drove away I realised that another vehicle had arrived and was tucked in neatly behind the Sheriff's car. It was already dark. I couldn't make out the logo on its side. I sighed. It was time I headed to Bemidji though I desperately wanted to shower off the chemical smell. Once I saw my bed I knew I would be tempted to stay on overnight.

'Guess I'll get my car keys and head out.' I turned away from Jenny.

'I forbid it Frank, you've been working hard, now you're dead beat. At least stay for coffee.' At first I resisted the urge to give in. She saw my indecision and taking me by the arm, encouraged me towards the canteen. There she punched in two strong black coffees from the machine and headed into the computer room.

'Say, where are you….?'

'Hal's waiting for us. And there's someone else here you should meet.'

Sheriff Hal Strader, as I came to know him, had collapsed into one of the console chairs. At first I thought him asleep but he was only nodding over a mobile phone held to his ear. Alongside him another man was flipping through the pages of a document laid out on the central table. He was wearing a uniform of a crisp green material with darker mottling. His collar was open and a tie tucked awkwardly into the shirt pocket bearing a logo I knew. I froze. My hand shook, coffee spilt onto the table as, at Jenny's insistence, I sat down beside him.

'Frank, this is Jack Michelson. Jack works for the Minnesota Wolf Patrol.' The man looked up disinterestedly from the document and only nodded. If he recognised me he gave no indication. The Wolf Patrol was charged with investigating the unlawful killing of wolves. Its overzealous operatives were the bane of my father's life, often dropping in unannounced on our business, including the scheduled hunts.

'Jack, Frank here's one of our newest recruits. Helped us out with the operation.'

'How's the wolf?' was all Jack said. He looked tired and careworn. He was about fifty, with a ragged crew-cut of dark hair turning grey at the temples. At any other time I might have said he had a pleasant face but his expression was fixed and he showed little surprise as Jenny set her coffee down and drew from her pocket the plastic bag in which she'd placed the two rifle bullets.

'Alive. Hopefully he'll be fine now that we've got these out of him.'

'So he was shot?' Hal asked, taking the bag from her and shaking the long narrow bullets into his palm. 'Some bullets,' he remarked turning them over in his hand.

'That's high calibre material,' I ventured looking at the long pointed projectiles. 'Kill a moose at 300 yards.'

'That's a mighty distance. You think the hunter was after caribou instead?'

'You'd use a specialist rifle for downing a big male. Shoot straight through the chest to the heart, no stopping it if you've got the range right.'

'So how come something as small as this wolf wasn't blown to pieces?'

I hesitated, uncertain whether I'd be revealing more of my old life than I wanted. 'That's what I'm trying to decide.'

'You're thinking it was done deliberately.'

'Deliberately yes, but….from a long way off - far too far off to be certain of your target.'

'Couple of chance shots from a moving car maybe?' Jack asked.

'Maybe…if the wolf was found on the roadside.' Hal nodded agreement.'

'You know a lot about hunting, Frank?' Jack asked more as a matter of courtesy but I knew I would have to be guarded with my answer.

'I've done a fair bit of caribou hunting in my time, I like to think that's behind me now.'

Hal continued to turn the bullets over in his hands. Jack Michelson leant over and took one of them to examine.

'Looks the same as last time.' Here he turned to me and said, 'Killed outright, not as lucky as the one you operated on here. Do you think we can do anything with these, Hal?'

'Not much chance. Even if you can ID the bullet you've got to find the gun. To find that you have to know whose it is and get a warrant. And to get a warrant….'

He left the words hanging and the two men nodded to themselves. For a few moments nothing more was said. The whole thing was too dangerous for me to offer any more information. I knew only too well my father's collusion in suppressing enquiries about wolf kills through county and district judges. Only the little men ever got prosecuted, the big hunting leagues never got anywhere near being indicted.

'Where d'you find him Hal?' Jack asked at length.

'Just outside Agassiz, down along the road to Thief River Falls.'

'Near the wildlife refuge again. Can you give me the details, I'll get down there first thing tomorrow?'

Agassiz was well west of current Delacroix activity and I found my voice again. 'What will you do?'

'Go searching for witnesses, talk to people, find out who's hunting so close to the reserve. You'd be surprised what people tell you, sometimes without even realising it.'

'You say this isn't the first time you'd had wolves shot at Agassiz. Wouldn't it be better to talk to members of the hunting groups, a little PR and education might go a long way.' I could hardly believe what I was saying. In just ten days I'd come an awfully long way from Silver Lake.

'A lot of that goes on already, Frank, Wolf Patrol's just the final weapon we have. Blunt, often ineffective, but something of a deterrent all the same.' I could see the man was saddened by his own failure.

'Still, I would have thought...,' Jack was shaking his head and yawning. Jenny seemed intrigued by my interest.

'Why don't you take Frank with you Jack. He's more than a volunteer, he's enrolled in Bemidji Uni majoring in animal conservation, the experience would be good for him.' Jack blinked and pulled at the corners of his eyes. He remained silent, so Jenny addressed me instead. 'What about it Frank? Term doesn't start for two weeks, you'll have plenty of time for studying later.'

Jenny must have read my thoughts. The days stretching away till my next shift at Sanctuary, had seemed emptier than ever. I'd already contemplated asking for more shifts, using the excuse of the injured wolf. I was musing over what to say when Jenny continued, 'It would be useful experience for his course. Won't you consider it Jack?' Jack looked at me with weary eyes.

'Grateful for the company.' He nodded, looking towards Jenny. He stood up and gave her a wry smile. then glanced towards me questioning, 'Seven-thirty outside Agassiz entrance. Never could resist you, Jenny my girl.' She rose and gave him a quick kiss on the cheek.

So that was how it began, a simple conversation late at night between four exhausted people that changed my life and those of the people dearest to me in ways I couldn't then imagine.

Minutes later I retired to the little bunkroom, set the alarm for six a.m. and slumped down in bed. I knew nothing more until about half-past five. Quickly swigging down a glass of water, I grabbed a cereal bar for my breakfast and was unlocking the car door only moments later. The morning was clear and bright, with a slight autumnal chill which on other occasions I would have described as stirring to the blood. Now I felt only loss and uncertainty at the approaching winter.

'Frank, you're about early.' I swung round at the sound of Jenny's voice, dropping the car keys in the process. I saw that her hair was swaying loose about her neck and the neat red T-shirt was crumpled and not tucked neatly into her jeans as it usually was.

'Could say the same for you.'

Stooping to pick up the keys she laughed. 'Going so soon?'

'I have to meet Jack and….'

'And…..' She laughed again. It was a light high sound, fitting for the morning freshness.

'Nothing really.'

'Then you've just time to look in on Eighty-Seven with me.'

'Eighty-Seven?'

She looked up at me with a kind of childish amusement playing on her face. 'Eighty-Seven, that's the number we logged the wolf under….,' she looked down at the keys and placed them in my open hand saying, 'kind of sad isn't it?'

I could only gasp. 'You've had eighty-seven, no eighty-six other casualties? In how many years?'

'Almost four years, most are road casualties of course. But that's not the total number, they were only given names before, now we're into a real numbers game. Come on…let's see how he's doing.'

She opened the door and preceded me down the corridor.

'Have you been up all night?' I asked.

'No, I managed some sleep. I looked in on him twice, the last time about three a.m., then I slept some more.'

'I guess I woke you then?'

'No, don't think that, Frank.' She turned towards me, shaking her head. 'I'd have got up again with the dawn. Suzanne will want my early report before her rounds, in case Eighty-Seven's condition's giving cause for alarm. Let's see how he is.'

In the morning light the little cage in which we'd placed the wolf looked woefully inadequate. The creature's legs were bent up against the wire in the careless abandon of sleep and his muzzle was pressed so close against the double-gauze of the lower wall that I wondered how he managed to breathe. Yet breathe he did. Through the wire barrier I could see the deep chest rhythmically rising and falling, the thick pale fur of his stomach undulating and flattening with each inhalation.

Except for the bandaged area on his chest and the catheter inserted in his front leg, we'd made no attempt to clear the caked mud and trickles of blood from his fur. Stricken and dirty as he was I could see the wolf was hardly older than a yearling, with slight limbs and narrow shoulders which had yet to develop the breadth and strength needed to chase big game. Apart from the light belly, his fur was so dark it was almost black. Jenny was changing the saline drip container above the cage.

'I'll need to check his heart.' She pulled a stethoscope from a nearby drawer and I began to unloop the chain holding the cage door closed.

'No, wait.' She placed her hand over mine.

'Is it unsafe, he looks deep asleep?'

'He needs another injection. That cabinet's got needles and drugs.'

She leant across the bench behind me, deftly unlocking the cabinet with a key on a fob at her waist. I stepped back from the cage and observed the wolf's twitching ears. Perhaps he wasn't as deeply unconscious as I'd thought. Jenny held a drug ampoule up to the light, then slipped the new syringe out from its sterile container. She held the needle up to the container then shook her head and looked across at me. 'Something wrong?' I looked away from the cage directly into her eyes. A vague uncertainty clouded her face.

'Would you like to give the injection, Frank?'

'I've never done…that is…..'

'You'll have to learn sometime. It's far easier when the animal's out cold - like he is.'

Jenny nodded across to the cage, a tender smile fleetingly on her lips. She guided me patiently through the regime for breaching the sterile seal of the ampoule, filling the syringe and checking the level against the millilitre rule.

'Now just give the plunger a slight push to clear any air from the needle.' I did as she instructed, amazed how easy it was to eject the first droplet from the fine needle. She unlocked the cage and pulled the door open. The animal's head rocked gently to the side but otherwise he remained still. 'Take hold of the scruff of his neck, just like a mother dog will do.' I'd been around dogs most of my life, Jenny couldn't have found a more apt example.

'Like this?' It was the first time I'd actually handled the animal and I was amazed at the soft, almost luxurious, feel of the fur.

'Pull the scruff up a little more so that the skin's away from the neck, then gently insert the needle.'

Fur and skin proved no barrier to the tiny sharp needle. It manoeuvred easily into the hollow I'd created in the skin above the creature's spine.

'That's right. Now press slowly but firmly down.'

I did as she said, easing the plunger shaft until it would go no further.

'Done?'

'Yes, I think so,' I gasped in amazement at this small achievement.

'You need to be even more careful now. Hold onto the scruff and pull the needle right out before you let go of the skin.'

I did so and eventually withdrew my hands from the cage, more pleased than I would even admit to myself. Jenny quickly checked over the animal's chest with the stethoscope, nodding to herself at intervals and afterwards we closed the cage together.

'You did well.' Jenny beamed.

'And Eighty-Seven?' I asked.

'His heart's good, a little slow perhaps. But that injection will give him a boost.'

'What was it?'

'Antibiotics, and a protein booster, help him rebuild the muscle damage quicker.'

'I should think these young ones heal quickly though, if you build up his strength day by day.'

Jenny looked at me quizzically.

'Yes they do.'

'He'll be in the outer pens for some time will he?'

'You're looking a long way ahead, Frank.'

'It's just... well I won't get back here for some days.'

'And you want to follow his progress.'

'Yes.'

'I'll have a word with Charlie, if he agrees you can do the food rounds with him in the release cages.' I nodded. 'I'd like that.'

Jenny cleared away the syringe, locked the drugs cabinet and stuffed the stethoscope back in its drawer but I was still looking down at the young wolf when she came back to my side.

'Don't get too fond of him Frank.'

'You think… he won't survive?' She must have seen the look of horror on my face.

'Not that, no. That's depends on Suzanne and his own stamina of course. But if he recovers in a week to ten days he'll be on the release rota and you'll never see him again. If he doesn't… well….'

Here Jenny looked down and placed her hand on my left arm. Her touch was light, almost comforting, with a hint of warmth as her fingers gently probed the crimped skin of the wounds. During my lonely visits to the canteen I'd heard Jenny spoken of with affection, both by volunteers and students. An inner circle of favourites classed themselves as 'Jenny's lads'. I now felt I'd been admitted into the same fraternity. As if to dispel the brief moment of familiarity Jenny withdrew her hand.

'I've been watching you Frank, you've worked hard since you came here. But you're not like the other students. Most of them are quite fazed the first time we do an operation, all the hospital stuff and the chemicals. You're different. You see the whole animal, just as if you were looking at him in the wild.'

I didn't know what to say. It was too soon to mention my feelings about Speed, even to Jenny.

'It's just that I….'

But I was interrupted by the door of the operating room opening. Mike Delahay entered the room.

'Ah there you are Jenny, I hear you've a casualty to….. ' He paused catching sight of me in the doorway of the side room. He seemed surprised to see me and a grimace passed quickly across his face as Jenny explained. 'Frank helped with the operation.'

'A bit unusual for a trainee,' he started, the grimace

lingering, then continued '....but if you approve, Jenny.' He put a hand lightly on her shoulder which I noticed she shrugged off without embarrassment.

'Well, you'll want to hand over now, and get some sleep - the two of you look as if you've been up all night.' It was meant to be a light-hearted joke, but I couldn't take it as such, in any case Jenny seemed as loath as I was to relinquish responsibility for the wolf we knew as Eighty-Seven. If Jack Michelson hadn't been waiting for me I might have asked to stay on.

'Guess I'd better get going.' I glanced at the side room with a heavy heart then proceeded into the corridor leaving Mike and Jenny going over the wolf's after-care.

Chapter Six

It was about 80 miles to Agassiz. I covered the distance in under an hour and a half, breaking the speed limit several times on the freeway. Still, I hadn't arrived soon enough for Jack Michelson. At precisely four minutes after half-seven I drove into the Refuge carpark only to see Jack's car heading towards the exit. I sounded the horn and he brought the heavy patrol vehicle to a juddering halt.

'You're late.' He called across from the open window.

'Sorry, I…'

'Best park up and get in.'

I parked right up close to the exit and ran over to the Minnesota Wolf Patrol vehicle, unable to conceal a wry smile as I turned the door handle. Jack didn't speak, just thrust in the gear shift and took us away from the park and onto the Thief River Falls road. When I could stand the silence no longer I asked, 'Where we headed?'

'Been speaking to the Ranger back at Agassiz. He's got a theory about the wolves.'

'The wolves that have been shot?'

'Partly.' He paused, changing the shift to take a turn towards to the east. The Falls road where the wolf had been shot lay due south, but I'd already learnt that Jack Michelson could not be hurried into replying and kept silent.

'He thinks they're young animals dispersing out from Voyageurs on the Canadian border down through Red Lake Wildlife Management Area and kind of spreading out south and west. Agassiz is too small for them, just a stopping-off point but somebody's real scared they're here to stay.'

'Why are they moving out from Canada. Isn't it safer there?'

'That's a mighty big question mister...eh, Frank. Seems they've been having trouble along the border, even right through to Thunder Bay. We used to take the releases up that way, kind of unofficial of course but we reckon they'd have a better chance if they could get through to Canada. More wolves up there too.'

'More wolves but they've a hunting quota. From what I hear they stick to it, all official,' I said, repeating what Canadian hunters had told me in the past.

Jack slowly shook his head. 'Used to be that way.' His voice was muted and kind of angry.

'You heard of some trouble?'

'Lots of wolf kills up across the territory west of Thunder Bay, some of our releases as well - two good young females.' Here Jack whistled bitterly through his teeth. 'Rumour is some big estate up there's been taken over. No-one knows who owns it but it looks like they're clearing the country of wolves for some big hunting league.'

'Not.... ' I hesitated, but couldn't stop myself from asking ' ....the Ambrose place?'

'Sounds familiar, might be, you know the place?'

'No, I just wondered.'

'Well, if you got any leads be sure you pass them on.'

But I kept my thoughts to myself and we travelled on in silence for some ten miles eventually turning north towards Roseau. The territory was marshy and covered with small slow-growing pines with little evidence of deer or even cattle. It seemed an unlikely area to find wolves. Jack pulled in at the next service station. He didn't stop at the pumps and drove the vehicle round the side of the kiosk. He put his hand on the door handle then thought better of it and leant back towards me.

'You still game for this?'

'Sure.'

'Then we'll start here, don't expect it to be easy though. I'm not the most popular man in the district.'

I took his grunt for a form of laughter and followed him out of the patrol car and round to the back door of the kiosk. Before he entered the place I asked naively, 'Why start here?'

'Got to start some place...' He spat on the dusty gravel.' I got some insider knowledge from Harrison back at Agassiz.'

There wasn't time to question him further before we were inside the kiosk. The conversation he had with the forecourt attendant formed the model for the other conversations Jack had with three gas station attendants during the course of the next hour. First he introduced himself to the attendant, but you could tell that the logo on his vehicle had preceded him.

'Jack Michelson's the name. I'm enquiring if you seen anyone out on the highway with a gun or rifle in the last few days?'

'Nope.'

'You know it's illegal to travel about the highway with a loaded rifle, someone might get injured.'

This declaration was followed by a further deadpan 'Nope'.

'You got any hunting pals, do a bit of hunting yourself maybe?'

The man nodded warily. He was chewing avidly on a piece of tobacco and spat brown saliva straight out of the open doorway missing Jack's sleeve by inches.

'Well here's my card.' Jack placed the card down on the counter. The man simply looked down at the Wolf Protection Patrol logo without making any attempt to pick up the card. 'Got a bit of a problem with some unsavoury characters shooting at wolves. Killing them's against the law. But I guess you fellas all know that.'

'Strange law that one.'

'Strange?'

'Protecting predators against law-abiding citizens, especially them with livestock.'

'Strange or not that's the law. You know anyone who's lost cattle you just direct him my way. There's a good compensation scheme in Minnesota - the best, no-one's turned away.'

The man extended a greasy hand to pick up the card. He stuck it awkwardly on the grimy wall just above the cash till.

'Nice doing business with you.' Jack extended his hand and met the man's palm with equanimity. We turned to go.

You would have thought from his approach that Jack was following up a simple misdemeanour or traffic violation. Later after visiting a third service station, I realised what he was up to and questioned him about it. He grunted and his mouth twisted into an uneven smile.

'No harm in letting them know we're around. Prevention's better than cure.'

After that visit he drove off the forecourt and parked on a patch of sandy ground barely two miles down the road. 'Best get to the real business of the day.'

'The real business.....?'

'What you've seen's just the icing on the cake. Those

guys will have been networking their chums by now, getting them stirred up, making them a little bit scared 'case one of them talks.'

I began to look at Jack Michelson in a new light. His tactics looked just a shade unsavoury. 'You've been deliberately goading them?'

'Sure have, now when we start the house-to-house we'll have the edge on them, someone might be nervous, let something slip. Just reach me that list of hunting licences from the dash.'

I pulled a clipboard from the pocket near my knees, and sat looking at it for some moments. It contained sheet after sheet of lined paper printed out with people's names and addresses and the number and status of their hunting licences. The addresses ranged across several counties. 'This something you always carry with you?'

'Nope, got it wired out from the office in St. Paul, first thing this morning. Mighty useful this new technology.'

'Jack, were you ever in the police?'

'Twenty-five years, man and boy.'

I gave an involuntary laugh and for the first time Jack's face creased up into a hearty grin. I began to feel that I could like the man after all.

'Remember Frank....' Jack said, before we set out on a mammoth survey of licence holders, 'We'll be dealing with good, law-abiding citizens - most of them. Got to treat them right.'

And he was true to his word. We must have called on over a hundred households in town and hamlet during the day and Jack became the most polite, most friendly man you could wish to meet, nodding politely to pensioners, tolerant of childish screams, so affable with even the most taciturn of people as he probed into their movements over the past forty-eight hours that I forgot the boorish man who'd earlier quizzed the petrol station attendants with such severity.

It proved to be an exhausting day, broken only by a brief visit to a diner along a deserted highway up near Baudette regional airstrip. The Wolf Protection Patrol van stood out in glorious isolation on the forecourt. Not another vehicle turned onto the dusty gravel the whole time we were there. I was sure I heard a muted sigh from the staff as we rose to leave.

Jack dropped me back at Agassiz at about seven in the evening. I'd started the day optimistic of tracking down, or at least getting some hint of where, or who, the wolf's assailants might. But we had little to show for a long tedious day's work. I'd given up all hope and said so to Jack. He was more hopeful. 'Always another day.' I had to be content with that and watched him head down the Grand Forks road.

I awoke with a start. Somewhere a doorknob rattled, paused then rattled again more stridently. I was lying on a broken-down settee in the two-room apartment I'd rented, the remains of a TV dinner strewn across the small coffee table and a half-full can of beer, which now smelt stale and unappetising, on the floor. I hadn't got as far as the bedroom when sleep had overtaken me. In any case the bedstead was strewn with university books. The flickering TV in the corner just three feet away was the only illumination in the room, for night had fallen long since.

The doorknob rattled again. I clutched at the back of the settee to pull myself up, then sank back. The caller could not possibly be for me. I'd given no-one my address, no-one except Jacob and he would have phoned if he wanted to contact me. Maybe he had. I hadn't switched on the phone for a week now. The rattling of the doorknob became more insistent, knuckles drummed against the thin glass pane. Sleep still clouded my mind as I fumbled for the light switch on the wall and a dim yellow glow shone down on the dowdy leaf-green carpet. I pulled open the door and peered out beneath the overhang of the half glazed porch.

'Jacob?' I asked expectantly.

There was no porch light, the nearest street light was two houses away and the yellow glow barely penetrated the darkness beyond the glazed window. I was aware of a long black car parked against the verge, its shiny metal softly reflecting the glow of passing headlights. The car looked vaguely familiar in an unsettling kind of way but the lights weren't on. I couldn't see into the interior. Something, or someone, moved in the pool of darkness to my left.

'Who's there?'

A woman came forward into the glow of the electric bulb though her head was still shrouded in shadow. She wore a long brown textured dress topped by a colourful braided waistcoat, the embroidered sort with tiny stone amulets threaded through with feather which the native Americans fashion. Soft black hair hung in loose coils about her shoulders. She had a slip of paper clasped within her fingers. I thought she was going to shove it into my hand. I looked at my watch.

It showed ten-thirty, rather late for a fund-raising call, then I realised that the paper, though much crumpled, bore some scribbled handwriting in blue ink. It was disconcerting that I couldn't see her face. I grumbled irritably and turned back towards the doorway but the woman's hand came at me out of the shadows, the long thin fingers on my arm somehow familiar yet threatening at the same time. As she spoke her face was suddenly in the light, a tearworn face ridden with care. Lys' face!

'Francis, Oh Francis, thank goodness you're all right, I made Jacob give me your address but…..I couldn't, you see I didn't …'

The words exploded from my sister's mouth. She seemed so upset that at first I wanted to pull her towards me. Instead I stood in the doorway sensing some unseen danger.

'I didn't want to come…..,' Lys gasped again. This time I took her hands to draw her towards me. As I did so, footsteps sounded on the pathway behind her. She shivered and half-turned looking back across her shoulder. 'He made me, he….. ' Sobs replaced her words as she twisted from my grasp and backed away. Suddenly she was lost in the shadows and my father's tall figure appeared in her place.

'Get back to the car girl.'

Lys' shadow did not move.

'Get back, your business here is done!' he growled angrily.

With a stifled sigh, Lys moved away.

'Don't talk to my sister like that!'

I tried to push past my father but his body filled the narrow porch. For an instant I wanted to shove him away, but Lys was in his thrall. It wouldn't do her any good to antagonise him further.

'Keep your sister out of this,' he barked, 'I've a matter of business to discuss, then we'll be out of here.'

In the darkness I saw Lys stumble towards the black saloon. She stood beside the vehicle shaking uncontrollably but she made no attempt to enter it. She looked very small and her face was a pale orb against the darker shadows. I made one brief attempt to push past my father but his big hand was pressing against my chest. 'This won't take long.'

I gave in to his uncompromising arrogance as I'd given in so often before, pulling back to let him pass and drawing the door closed behind me. I watched him enter the room and survey the tawdry scene. He stood bolt upright before the sagging settee as I swept the remains of the meal into a rusty metal waste bin. Almost inevitably the beer can slipped from my grasp, toppling over and spilling the contents on his polished shoes. The hem of his trousers became dappled with beer. His comments were no more than I expected. 'This is a pitiful existence - but it's your choice Francis,' he mused ironically. 'Seems you've made your own life and….'

'Yes, it is my life ….'

He sat down stiffly on the settee, raising a hand. 'I'm not here for arguments boy, what you do now doesn't concern me. It doesn't concern Silver Lake, or Lys, or Delacroix Enterprises any more.'

'Then what are you here for?'

He sighed heavily and ordered. 'Sit down boy.'

I shook my head, preferring to stand where I could look down on him. It would be hard for him to look up through the weary yellow glow and detect any weakness in me, for he surely wanted something from me and whatever it was I knew I was going to refuse.

'As you wish.'

Since he'd arrived he'd been clutching a soft leather

document case under his arm. Now he grasped a piece of newspaper, wiped the table clear of any remaining grease then laid the bulging case on the cleaned surface. The zip gave him some trouble but eventually he had the thing open and papers unfurled across the table.

'Some unfinished business that needs clearing up.'

'I've no business with you.' I announced quite calmly.

'You're right, I should never have burdened you with it. Still the lawyers have sorted it all out, you only have to sign.'

He drew out the slim Parker pen which he always carried. It was a keepsake, rumoured to have been given him by my mother. He gestured with it towards the topmost papers. 'It'll rid you of the responsibility. Doubtless that'll make you happy …' He looked round the room again. '….seeing as you're doing so well for yourself.'

'I am…,' I insisted, 'I am doing well for myself. I've enrolled in Bemidji University.'

'Have you now…. have you now.' He nodded to himself and waggled the pen in my direction once more. His disinterest had begun to anger me.

'Don't you want to know what I'm studying?'

'If you want to tell me.' He gave a brief stilted laugh. 'But it's of no consequence, once you sign these forms you'll be free of Delacroix Enterprises altogether.'

I shrugged at mention of the Delacroix name. 'I've no idea what you're talking about and since you've no interest in what I'm doing….'

'Ambrose, the estate. What else could I be talking about boy. Just sign here and……'

'Ambrose?' I asked aghast.

'Yes, our lawyers have convinced the Canadian

taxation authorities the Delacroix Enterprises claim is legitimate, there'll be no trouble about the American ownership. Now if you'll just sign.'

'Sign away Ambrose, you must think I'm mad!'

Up to that moment my father had seemed unaccountably calm. Now he looked quite shocked. 'You must realise signing the place over to you was only a business arrangement.' He looked up at me with clear blue eyes, his gaze all candour and innocence.

'Oh, yes, a very convenient business arrangement. Do you know what's been happening up there - but of course you do, you instigated it. You must have been planning this for months, even before the sale went through…'

'There were some difficulties, I had to be sure of the state of the place before I made the final bid.'

'And killing wolves was part of the plan, was it?'

'The place was overrun with them. We just took out the Ambrose quota, it's all quite official.'

'Before you even owned the place?'

'Well yes that was a small problem.'

'But your people scoured out the wolves thirty miles outside the estate boundary, right down to the international border. I suppose you know two reintroduced animals from Minnesota were killed.'

He chuckled to himself and bent down towards the table. 'You'd do the same if you were running Ambrose as a going concern.'

'Would I?……Would I Father?' I was trying to keep tight hold of my temper. He still had no understanding of my actions. Then something in his overconfident manner got to me.

'Your killing squad's still up there isn't it?'

'What if it is, Ambrose is almost ready to go but for a few rogue wolves. We'll dispense with them, then Ambrose will be Delacroix's flagship. Imagine 50 rooms, all doubles, people are falling over themselves to come. And that's just the beginning……..'

'You've no right to do this.'

'I've every right. Now if you'll just sign.' He was hunched over the papers, not really listening to me.

'I'm not going to sign, now or ever, you'll have to clean your people out and ……'

He looked up quickly, a jagged smile crossed his face.

'But you have to sign, everything depends on…..why the whole enterprise…..' He stood up, glaring at me, conflicting emotions crossing and re-crossing his face. 'I order you to sign, Francis.' He jabbed the pen into the air, his breath short and catching in his throat as he said, 'You'll do as I say in this.'

'No Father, I won't. Now take your Ambrose rubbish and get the hell out of here.'

I swept the papers off the table crushing them anyhow into the wallet and shoved them towards him. When he didn't respond I yanked open the door and threw the lot out onto the grassy front yard. You would have thought I'd stabbed him. He came at me then, his big hands tearing at my throat. We crashed against the porch window, shattering the thin glass. I rolled sideways managing to free his grasp briefly but he lunged at me again and we went tumbling together down onto the pile of papers and shrubs. I struggled to free myself, pushed him aside and managed to crawl back towards the wall to pull myself upright. But he was close behind me. As I turned to fight him off he grabbed my shoulders and shouted, 'You'll sign boy, you'll sign.'

His face was only inches from my own and in the thin light I could see that his eyes were bulging almost out of their sockets. 'Ambrose is mine, d'you understand?' he screamed and pushed me backwards. My head crashed against the brick wall. I sensed a trickle of blood running down my neck. He was trying to crush the breath out of me but it was all I could do to keep upright.

'Not to kill wolves with. Not to kill anything…' I gasped.

His grip tightened again. He was a big heavy man, 'You're soft Francis, soft. Always were a bloody nuisance, but you're not going to beat me in this. I'll have my way d'you hear!'

I tried to push him away but that made him angrier still, I could hear his teeth grating in his jaw and his fingers tightened around my throat. Short of hitting my father there was little I could do to save myself. Suddenly I saw Lys' face behind him. She was screaming at the top of her voice.

'Stop this, oh God, stop it.. …both of you……..'

'Get away girl.' My father growled, spitting saliva into my eyes. 'This is between your brother and me.'

'But you're killing him……'

'He'll wish I had when I finish with him.' He made the point by head-butting my face. My head cracked against the wall. I was losing consciousness.

'No….' Through a haze of sweat and saliva I saw Lys' hands reach up and claw at our father's face. He bawled out some crazed oath, jabbed his elbow into her face and let fly with a blow to her shoulder. Lys screamed violently and went staggering back onto the pile of damp papers. Her screams got through to me. Instinctively I'd felt inhibited from hitting my father, even in self-defence, but an assault on Lys I could not condone and he had crossed that tenuous line. I lashed out with my right hand catching him full on the jaw. He staggered from me towards the pavement, almost tripping over Lys as he went, but he didn't fall, just stood on the flagstones staring at me and holding his jaw. Silently he watched as I knelt down beside Lys trying to comfort her.

'Lys, Lys,' I cried. 'Are you all right, shall I get a doctor?'

She was crouched into a ball, her shoulders uppermost, her face hidden in the folds of her long dress. She gave a muffled 'yes' then lifted her head. Her face was all concern for me. Her eyes were watering though I couldn't tell whether from tears or pain. She looked up raising a hand across my shoulders and probed the bloody mess at the base of my skull.

'I don't need a doctor Francis, but *you* have to get one for yourself,' she wailed.

'I will Lys, I will, only stay here.'

'I can't, Francis, I mustn't.' She pulled herself up with my help, then leant against me to steady herself. She looked across at our father. I was amazed to see him shuffling about on the grass collecting up wet papers and trying to stuff them into the leather wallet. Feeling her eyes on him he seemed to come to himself and said quite simply, 'In the car.'

Lys stepped away from me, but I clung to her.

'No Lys, you can't go with him.'

'I must Francis, it's better this way. I can't leave him as well, not now, not yet. I'll be all right, you'll see.' She was whispering at first then she looked over at the man who was our father and said in broken tones but loudly enough for him to hear. 'He'll not hurt me again.'

It was five-past ten when I phoned Silver Lake next morning. Lys came straight on the line as I hoped she would. I gave her the briefest of instructions and told her where to meet me. Now I was waiting for her to appear.

Even if my head hadn't been thumping most of the night I would have slept badly. In truth, sleep had hardly touched me and I'd risen just as dawn was breaking, made my plans while the anger was still hot inside me, then had driven the hundred miles back to Blackheath. The battered car drove into the motel's rear carpark next to my own and Lys ran straight into my arms.

'Oh Francis, I woke up this morning thinking last night was a terrible dream... but it wasn't was it, it's real?'

I held her back from me and observed the red flush to her cheeks and the dark bruise forming just below her left eye. She would be lucky if the mark didn't spread to the lower eyelid. I held her tightly by the arms, and looked down at all five feet four inches of her. Last night's dress had been replaced by workman's jeans and beige jerkin, but the feathery ornaments of the Indian waistcoat poked out from beneath her rough waterproof.

'It's no dream Lys,' I said sardonically.

'Your head, did you see a doctor, is it....?'

'No, it's a slight headache, nothing more,' I lied as another wave of pain shot through my head, clouding my vision. 'Have you brought the stuff?'

'It's in the trunk.'

'Good, I'll take it now, then you can get off home, better you're not seen with me again.'

Lys gave me a puzzled frown but didn't reply. She moved round the back of the car and opened the trunk. I rummaged through a vast pile of old clothing.

'Hell Lys, I only wanted stuff for a couple of days.'

'I mixed it in with clothes for the homeless refuge, in case anyone asked.'

'Did you see anyone then?'

'No, only......no, no-one.'

'You don't seem very sure,' I said hardly concentrating and becoming quickly exasperated when I couldn't find what I sought. 'Where's the rifle and ammunition?'

'I had to be careful Francis....' I stared at Lys, wondering at the quizzical expression on her face.

'You did bring them?'

I began to think Lys had seen something malicious in my bluff. 'You're not working with the Wolf Patrol are you Francis?'

'It's not what you think Lys, I shan't.... I've no intention of hurting Father.'

Lys clasped my arm as I plunged again through the clothing and my fingers grasped the smooth barrel of the precious rifle. I pulled it free and sorted through some of the clothing I'd need. After Lys' explanation I wasn't surprised to find this included some of her own clothing, but then she said, 'Francis, I know you wouldn't.....You're going to Ambrose aren't you?'

Startled, I stopped sifting the clothes and asked, 'Ambrose, how did you guess?'

She shook her head. 'The argument last night.... Francis I'm coming with you.'

'Lys I'm going up there to let them know who owns the place, that's all. I may have to dismiss some of Dad's people. It could get nasty.'

'That's what's been worrying me, ever since you

called. I'm coming with you, if they see a woman…'

'Don't be a fool Lys. Think what trouble it'll cause for you if Father hears about it - and he's sure to. You're better off at home.'

'Home, I'm not sure where that is any more.' she said enigmatically

'Is there something you're not telling me Lys? Did he hurt you again?'

'No Francis…' Lys lowered her head. 'Not in the way you mean.'

I'd wrapped a bunch of old clothes around the rifle and the pack of ammunition I'd found beneath them and had transferred them discreetly across to my car, when a sudden cold feeling clutched at my heart. My head was aching fiercely and my vision swam. I couldn't really make sense of what my sister was saying.

'Then how?' I demanded.

Lys looked straight at me, sensing my pain. 'It's nothing. We're wasting time,' she said quickly gathering up some of her own clothing and pulling out a small vanity case. These she carried across and installed in the trunk beside my own gear. She seemed very determined as she opened the side door and slipped into the passenger seat.

'You planning to stay overnight?' I asked glibly.

'Probably.'

There didn't seem any point in arguing. 'OK but if things get nasty I'm sending you right back.' But I had no intention of taking her up to Ambrose. The appearance of a new owner at the hunting lodge could more than cause dispute, it could be downright dangerous. I didn't tell Lys but I planned to drop her off at the next possible moment, the border crossing might be just the place.

We travelled in silence for a long time, through the Duluth outskirts, following the signs to Thunder Bay, past Two Harbours. Soon, when Lys saw the signpost for Ely Wolf Centre with its brown silhouettes, she asked, 'Have you been there? What's it like?'

I had a sudden feeling of optimism that Lys might be encouraged to detour and visit the Centre. I could lose her there without worrying. Plenty of buses pass the place and she would have little difficulty in getting back to Silver Lake that day. 'Yes. But you can't get near the wolves.'

'You don't sound very enthusiastic.'

I should have been more guarded. 'It's OK. You want to make a trip, we could turn off now?'

But Lys had already seen through the ruse. She shook her head.

In another fifty miles we reached Grand Portage and the international border. I'd already bought plenty of food and drink from the motel diner, stowing them away under the rear seat. Although it wasn't strictly necessary, I drove up to the customs office to declare the rifle and ammunition. A uniformed Mountie approached. Ostensibly sifting through my pockets for the hunting licence, I turned and lied to my sister. 'We'll need some food and water for the day, there's a store over there. Why don't you get some food in.'

Quite unsuspectingly, she got out of the car and walked towards the store. I waved the licence at the bored guard, got his approval to pass and in two seconds was gunning the accelerator, heading towards the open road and Canada. 'Sorry Lys,' I called out almost to myself but she must have heard me or realised the car was speeding away from her.

She turned at the entrance to the store, a look of horror crossing her face and was instantly flying back towards the car. I realised she was on a collision course with the left headlamp. The waterproof jacket tossed behind her as I veered away, then somehow flapped along the front wing and Lys' fingernails were tearing at my left arm through the open window.

'Stop Francis, you can't….,' she screamed.

I gasped at the sudden pain, my foot slipped off the accelerator pedal and the car juddered to a halt. I tried to sweep her hand from my arm and quickly fought to gain control of the car but it was too late. Lys had tight hold of my arm and wasn't going to let go, even if I tried to accelerate away. I couldn't risk injuring her.

'Francis, take me with you, you must take me…,' Her hands folded around my arm. She was gasping for breath as she leant down towards the window. 'You have to take me…I can't go back today. She's there…,'

'She? Who are you talking about Lys?'

But Lys rambled on almost to herself and I became concerned for her sanity. The car was slewed around in the middle of the tarmac apron not fifty yards from the border patrol office and one of the Mounties had begun walking determinedly in our direction. I saw him gently ease the holster at his hip.

'I didn't sleep, the whole night. I told you I had bad dreams didn't I, but it wasn't true.'

'Lys what are you talking about?'

'Pamela. She moved into Silver Lake the same day….the same day that, well everyone knows about your quarrel.'

'She's working for Dad,' I said, not really

understanding Lys' concern.

'She asked for a room to be made up, said she'd be working late most days. I didn't think anything of it.'

'Why should you, I guess it's the truth. That's no reason not to go home.'

But Lys ignored me, 'And last night....... last night she was still up, waiting for us almost...almost vulture-like, though it was well after two a.m.'

Tears brimmed in her eyes, the bruised cheek looked more prominent than ever. The Mountie was now only twenty yards away. I pushed the car door open and eased myself out to show him I meant no harm to my sister. I edged her round so that the bruised cheek was away from him and said, 'She must have known what Dad wanted from me, perhaps she was just anxious.'

'Anxious enough not to go to her own room last night. It's the last one along the balcony, you have to pass my own to get .....'

My head throbbed abysmally and I tried to wipe away the mental picture forming in my brain. I was shaking my sister's arm violently ordering, 'I know the room Lys, what of it?'

'Her bed was never slept in, I checked this morning. Francis I don't know what happened between you and I don't want to know, but….'

'…she's sleeping with Dad, I know.' A look of stunned shock passed across my sister's face.

'You know Francis, but….' I waved across to the Mountie, smiled and shook my head.

'Get in the car Lys, we're going to Ambrose.'

Chapter Seven

We skirted Thunder Bay City, taking the country route, and came out on Canadian highway 11 but it was after Kashabowie that we first sighted trouble. The hoardings were unbelievably large and flamboyant, proclaiming an almost infinite variety of prey: caribou, moose, white-tailed deer, brown bear. But there was no mention of wolves until we turned off and ran the last few miles down to Ambrose on the Quetico Provincial Park road. I stopped the car at the first of six temporary plastic banners fixed to box scaffolding arrayed on the right hand side of the road. The first triplet read *'Wolf - Free - Zone'*, the second, a further hundred yards off, read *'Guaranteed - Caribou - Bag'*. I'd seen a boundary marker a mile back down the road and guessed the signs were on Ambrose property.

'I've had enough of this,' I said getting out of the car and unpeeling the hunting knife I habitually carried. Lys had been dozing fitfully in the car, catching up on the slumber she hadn't had the night before. I'd let her sleep. She was suddenly awake as I slipped through the fence.

'Francis what are you doing?' she yelled.

I reached up to the first placard and began sawing at the guy ropes. Lys pushed the car door open and leapt out wildly.

'Doing what I should have done back down the road,' I declared.

'But you can't, you'll get into trouble.'

'Look down the road Lys.' I pulled the first lower corner of the banner free and gestured with the knife blade. 'See that marker, the blue one on the fence post?'

'No, I don't.'

'You're looking too close, there down near the conifers, two hundred yards off.'

She was looking into the east and had to shade her eyes against the fierce morning sun.

'The …blue bars on the post?'

'That's it. All these signs have the same two blue bars, I guess we're on Ambrose land right here. My land, Lys.'

'Are you sure?'

'As sure as I'll ever be, but Lys…these signs are coming down anyway.'

Lys gave a quick, rather childish, snort.

'Better be hung for a sheep or a……wolf.' she said her voice stilted yet kind of playful.

'Cut the next rope, I'll grab hold.' And so I laboriously hacked and sawed at the guy ropes holding each plastic-coated placard. Lys took them from me, folding and laying each one on the rear seat of the car. Considering what happened after we reached Ambrose, it might have been better to have stowed them in the trunk but I wanted quick access to the rifle. In any case there didn't seem a need for secrecy, not then. We'd caught a few strange looks from passing motorists, but no-one challenged us and after about thirty minutes we'd taken down all the offending signs and left the scaffolding looking stark and useless behind the boundary fence.

As it turned out the placards had been positioned only four miles from the Ambrose entrance. Tall stone pillars with the Ambrose name chipped out in gold, supported iron gates set wide open to the road. We drove straight down a long avenue lined with conifers which gave way to individual oaks then solid glades of aspen and came out onto a gravelled crescent fronting the lodge. I slowed the car and whistled. At my side, Lys gasped. There was no-one about and no other vehicles parked there.

'I didn't know what to expect, but it wasn't this, it's pretty impressive.'

'Imposing, more like,' Lys' voice wavered.

I pulled to a halt in front of a massive brick building fronted by huge pillars of mellow pine set on the broad veranda. Just two storeys high, the long line of matching window frames gleamed in the sunlight, and a slatted staircase of the same wood rose gracefully from the gravel. There were twenty or so windows fronting the courtyard. The left hand side of the building was obscured by a cluster of dark green pines. Some had reddened needles as if suffering from blight. We sat and looked at Ambrose Lodge without speaking. I wondered just how much money my father had invested in the property. Enough certainly to justify the attack he'd made on me. As I gazed at the place, overwhelmed by its sheer size, it occurred to me that it was quite unlike any of Delacroix's other lodges, even the new ones that had been designed for the western states.

'Heavens, this would be ideal for wildlife holidays, nature trails, that sort of thing.'

'Is that what you want Francis?' Lys asked almost matching my growing enthusiasm. I looked down at her sensing the unreality of the situation. 'Don't get too excited Lys. Running Ambrose as a nature park's a big deal, something I'd have to consult Jacob about.' I sighed and looked back at the massive façade. 'Without money my only option might be to sell.'

Right now I had a far more harrowing, possibly

dangerous, task ahead. 'Lys I want you to stay in the car.'

'I'd prefer ......' But I'd already edged the car door open. I went straight to the trunk and drew out the rifle. Lys was soon at my side. She laid her hand on my left arm which still bore the red wheals her nails had made earlier.

'Francis, you won't need that surely,' she implored.

'Best not to leave it in the car unattended.' I could see she was torn between wanting to join me in the house or staying with the car and concealing the weapon.

'I'll stay here,' she offered looking wary. 'Honestly?' I asked. She lowered her head momentarily then raised her eyes saying, 'But I think it's best if we go in together.'

So we did, climbing up the shelving staircase until we stood under the high wooden portico. Two sets of double doors opened off the frontage. The left hand ones standing open to the air and exhaling the scent of beeswax and old mature wood and some other acrid smell I couldn't then identify. Much later I learnt the building had been designed as a health spa by some Victorian Englishwoman who hadn't lived to see it completed. We entered the foyer and wandered across polished parquet flooring.

Behind the brick façade, the interior was almost completely constructed of wood. Massive pine columns soared upwards through the two floors and pine beams criss-crossed above our heads, but the right side of the foyer was obscured by a curtain wall of rough cut pine that cut across the parquet and ran up into the roof. The joinery was poor with no attempt at harmonisation of the new pine with the older timbers. Only one door broke the run of this new partition. I walked towards it hearing the wooden blocks sigh beneath my feet, and turned the handle. The door wouldn't budge.

Opposite the entrance we'd come through was a broad opening screened off by heavy sheets of dark plastic, the sort they use in factories to separate workshops from the prying eyes of visitors. From this direction came the smell of newly-sawn pine mingled with cooking odours and that dense acrid smell I'd already detected. It was a surprise to walk through the plastic curtain into daylight and onto a long wooden veranda bordered on the left by a set of newly-built pine-clad rooms. To the right, beyond a white-painted picket fence, lay an open courtyard planted with low shrubs that had seen better days. A gravel drive ran from the fence round the rear of the house. Another rough track lead into the estate woodlands.

Beyond the courtyard was a second wing of the house with metal vents and aerials jutting from its wall, indicating bathrooms and kitchen areas. Lys was wandering down towards the far end of the veranda looking towards two wooden buildings, the nearest still under construction. Men moved about carrying planks and other equipment. Several vehicles were parked alongside, including various cars and a couple of jeeps. A JCB was engaged in moving timber across to the workshops. Opposite was an older wooden building. It looked like a bunkhouse.

The ground in front of it was mottled with some dark substance that had been churned up by the movement of vehicles and feet. The source of this material wasn't far away. Piled up against the ragged line of pines near the house were beam after beam of fire-blackened wood, the jagged spars often pointing skywards, the crusted half-seared wood already breaking open to the elements. Pines and timber had both burnt in the same fire. Lys was looking at the blackened wood, a questioning expression on her face. Voices issued from inside the nearest room.

I beckoned her to me, lowering the rifle barrel to the floor. A tall rather spare man came out of the first room. He was wearing an old hunting jacket, thick cords and knee length boots, the sort with hidden steel caps. He was nodding into the room with his back towards us at first but at the sound of Lys' footsteps on the new springy pine he swung round, the smile on his face rapidly changing to anger. He must have been in his late forties, with a lined weather-beaten face which, while it had looked affable before, contorted and became challenging.

'Who the hell let you in?' I had barely drawn breath before he continued. He gesticulated angrily towards the distant workshops, 'And if you got that rifle from the store then you'd better take it back right now.'

'It's my own rifle.' I said in a low non-abrasive tone.

'A likely story. If you're some punters coming for a look around, the place ain't open yet. In any case it's booked right up to Christmas. Best get back where....'

It was hardly an appropriate welcome for prospective guests, however unexpected - or unwelcome.

'What is it Talbot?' A man's voice called angrily from inside the room.

'Nothing for you to be bothered about.'

'Is that your boss?' I asked edging towards the door. Lys was holding tightly to my rifle arm. I was trying, surreptitiously, to shake her off.

'What if it is, you won't be meeting him, now give

that rifle over and git.'

'I repeat, this is my own rifle. And I want to see your boss.' Lys understood at last. She released my arm and edged to the outside of the veranda. I raised the rifle only inches from the floor and the man backed away warily.

'OK. No need for that....look what's your name?'

'Your boss's name first.' I raised the rifle barrel just a fraction higher, but he became brave as footsteps echoed from inside the room.

'James Leland, Mr. James Leland to you. He's managing the whole show.....'

Soft, more cultured, tones issued from the said James Leland's lips as he drew open the door. He might have come straight out of a western show, with all the marks of the dandy. His body was tall and solid, he had a long face bordered by neat dark sideboards. His leather jacket was the colour of sagebrush, with elegantly fringed sleeves. But below the showman's jacket he wore black jeans and short black businesslike boots that were creased and hardened by wear. He was probably in his early thirties. His bland expression, vaguely welcoming, changed to one of scorn as the dark brown eyes flickered back to his companion.

'By the 'whole show' Mr Talbot means the most exclusive and most luxurious hunting lodge in the western hemisphere. Now your name sir?'

'Luxurious for who - the wolves, the caribou?' I countered.

A quizzical expression fluttered over his face, then his features calmed again. I watched him closely, expecting a look of abhorrence as I started to give my name. Before I could we were interrupted by the arrival of a small black van which shot around the distant corner of the house, tore up the gravel track and came to a juddering stop just inches from the picket fence.

'What the hell's Joe up to?' asked Talbot.

Dust spewed up from the wheels of the van and a youngish man in paint-blotched overalls spilled out from the door. He looked decidedly angry as he waved the dust away and yelled up to us. Dust and the angle of the sun must have prevented him from seeing more than shadowy figures on the veranda.

'Some bastard's been tearing down the signs.' He pulled off his baseball cap and wiped sweat from his brow with a shirtsleeve. 'Car's out front with them placards all across the rear seat, Mickey's keeping watch in case the jerk comes back. Cut them ropes right off,' he finished, exhausted by his own rapid speech.

'What placards you talking about Joe?' Talbot moved to the side to the veranda right beside Lys. She watched him anxiously, edging back to my side and taking hold of my arm. I could feel the tremor in her fingers.

'That you Mr Talbot, can't see for this dust.'

'You caused the dust man. Get up here and explain yourself.' Talbot moved down the veranda as the man climbed the steps. I noticed Leland had positioned himself to one side and was now standing behind us, effectively blocking us off from the foyer.

'Right out there it is.' The man pointed to the front of the building, I knew there was no escape as he continued 'Cadillac saloon, couldn't get into the trunk, who knows what else they been doing.'

Talbot spun round and gripped the man's arm tightly almost shaking him.

'How d'you learn this Joe, thought you was collecting

145

window frames?'

'Needed fuel on the way back, so Mickey and I stopped at the gas station. His mate Lars comes in and starts spouting about some guy and a woman cutting the cords and tearing down all six signs, you know the ones that say Wolf-Free-Zone and....'

'I know'em, sure I know'em, just cut the cackle. You said they were in a car - outside here?'

'There's no need to badger the man Mr. Talbot, I took the signs down.....'

Talbot jerked the man's arm back at him. Joe staggered against the rough-cut pine of the wall, just managing to keep himself upright. The pine boards creaked savagely under Talbot's boots as he advanced towards us. Leland was shaking his head and tutting.

'You took them,' Talbot almost screamed into my face. 'What gave you the fucking right to .... ' Lys slipped closer to me.

'Every right, I'm Francis Delacroix, I own this .....,' I wasn't allowed to continue.

'I don't care who the fuck you are you've no....' There was a startled movement behind me as Leland spoke.

'Shut up Harry!'

'No bloody showman tells me to shut up...' Talbot raged.

'I said shut up and I meant shut up. Didn't you hear the man, his name's Delacroix. Must be Louis Delacroix's son.' Harry Talbot's reddened eyes flickered to his boss and back to me with a sneer. Still needing something to target his anger he fixed his gaze on Lys. She'd taken off her jacket in the car and the feathers on the embroidered Indian jacket were moving under the influence of a slight breeze or her own shaking, it was impossible to tell.

'And I suppose this little squaw's his wife.' He leant forward and flicked at the downy feathers. Lys drew back towards me muttering. 'No, I….'

But I had to interrupt her.

'Yes, Anna's my wife so leave her be,' I demanded, clutching Lys' shoulders and hoping she would understand as I edged her away from Talbot's weaving fingers.

'You'd better come inside Mr Delacroix, Mrs Delacroix.' I felt Lys shake beside me. For some reason she didn't want to go into the room.

'Talbot, I'll deal with this. You can get back to your work.' I felt Lys relax but Talbot just stood foursquare on the broadwalk and glared at us. Leland ushered us into the room and closed the door on him. It must have been almost a minute before I heard footsteps receding along the veranda.

Although it housed a cot bed and small washbasin in an alcove towards the rear, Leland's room was otherwise laid out as an office, with a cluttered desk and architect's table strewn with blueprints and plans. I was surprised not to see a computer. The only window, facing out onto the veranda, allowed in subdued daylight. A desk lamp, with a long strip-light, was burning over the desk.

'Forgive the domestic arrangements, Mrs. Delacroix. It's all we've managed since the fire.'

'The debris down by the pines?' I asked.

'You saw them, huh?' Here he turned to Lys, drawing a seat from under the architect's table, 'Perhaps the lady would like a seat.' Lys took him at his word. It seemed to me rather as if he was giving himself time to think. He walked to the chair behind the desk and shifted a few papers.

'Perhaps you'd like to tell me why you're here and why you took down those placards… Mr Delacroix, or should I call you Francis?'

'Sure, Francis is fine. When was this fire?' I wasn't interested in his questions.

'Nearly three months ago, the place might have been a write-off. You've Talbot to thank that it wasn't.'

'So my father owned the place even then?'

'Well no, he didn't actually own it, he was just making enquiries. The place had been empty for some time, luckily Talbot was here making a survey for your Dad. He raised the alarm, otherwise more than this wing would have gone up in flames.'

I had a strange feeling that Ambrose might have been luckier still if Talbot had never been near the place, but didn't say so. 'And my father still bought the lodge?' I asked amazed at the revelation.

'Apparently there was some trouble with the insurance, the owner hadn't kept up the payments. He wanted a quick sale.'

'So my father bought at a knock-down price,' I asked rather more caustically than I intended.

'I don't think I like your tone Francis… whose side are you on?'

'His own side.' Lys found her voice at just the wrong moment. 'He's every right to ask, he owns Ambrose now and…..'

Leland looked across from me to Lys, a puzzled questioning expression clouding his features.

'Something happen to your Pa?' he asked, but I guessed he already knew my father had handed Ambrose over to me and didn't much like the idea.

'Nothing. He's signed the place over to me.'

'It's the first I've heard of it.' I didn't believe him.

'Nonetheless it's true. Phone him at Silver Lake if you like.'

'I will, …' here his eyes narrowed. 'But why'd he do that?' I saw him reach for a packet of cheroots lying on the desk. When Lys backed away he pushed them aside.

'That's between him and me.'

'Oh, no young fella, it isn't. I got men working for me, they got half a year's work here, it's their future we're talking about.' Here he shook his head as if puzzling over my motives. 'And just why did you take those placards down anyway?'

'I'll tell you after you make the call. You must know it, but here's the number.' I turned to my sister. 'We'll wait outside.'

'No need for that, let the little lady rest. She looks dead beat.' I glanced at Lys. She looked all in. Whatever Leland's motives he was right. I should never have agreed to bring her.

'There's no need Mr Leland.' Lys began to rise from her chair. She looked suddenly pale and I thought she might faint. I remembered we hadn't eaten since breakfast and it was well past one. I stood beside her and rested the rifle barrel against the top of the desk.

'I'll use the cellphone,' Leland said reaching for the scrap of paper I'd given him. 'Often use it when checking the plans and…. ' He'd already begun dialling. I sat down beside Lys. It took only seconds for him to get through to Silver Lake but a little longer to get past Janice. Leland moved out onto the veranda. I wasn't sure I wanted to hear the conversation, the explosion that would likely come when my father learnt I'd come to Ambrose but I couldn't help myself. I patted Lys on the shoulder and went to stand beside the door.

'Hi Louis, it's James… James Leland, Ambrose…,' he paused and then said, obviously in reply to several questions. 'Yes, yes, it's fine, progressing all the time, it's just…..' My father must have interrupted him again.

'Yes, didn't I say …. yes of course, but something's turned up. No I'm not trying to put you off, only Francis is here.' Leland paused, evidently waiting for a reply. He waited a full minute before asking, in a more conciliatory tone, 'Sure he's here now Mr Delacroix, you want to talk…no, OK.' Leland moved away down the broadwalk so I couldn't hear his next words, in any case the phone on his desk began to ring insistently and a klaxon outside the office started an annoying high-pitched whine. Almost involuntarily I picked the thing up. Leland's face appeared in the doorway, the cellphone still clamped to his ear. To his annoyance I ignored him and answered, 'Ambrose'.

'Hey it's Kevin, you took your time. You got that freezer working?' It seemed an inane question in view of the circumstances. I tried to mimic Leland's drawl and saw the disgust on his face.

'Sure, sure.'

The conversation with my father was getting difficult, Leland's face was reddening. For my part I decided to string the caller along.

'Well I'll bring them in then, two nice ones.'

'Great.' I mimicked, to Leland's obvious displeasure.

'Hey Mr Leland, you sound kind of funny, you sure about them freezers. If'n they ain't working I'll just bury them somewhere in the woods, like before. Be a shame though, young female and her pup by the looks of it. Real nice fur. Got them both in the same trap late last night. Took a couple of bullets to kill the female though.' He could only have been talking about one thing. He'd caught two wolves in baited traps and shot them at point blank range. Disgusted with myself, I insisted, 'Sure, the freezer's working, bring'em in right now.'

Kevin argued that he was over fifty miles out and still had to pick up some other guys, at best he couldn't get back till about dusk. I slammed the phone down on him. Leland looked relieved as the phone toppled onto its base. After a long period of listening to the cellphone he looked at me guardedly.

'Right Mr. Delacroix. I'll do exactly as you say,' he said sharply and switched off the phone.

'Satisfied?' I asked.

'Sure, sure,' Leland said mimicking me. 'Your Pa confirmed your ownership. Said to do whatever you wanted.' Almost immediately I got the impression Leland was humouring me.

'Will you really?' Lys asked looking up excitedly from the desk where she'd been glancing over a plan of the building. 'Francis has such plans, a theme park or...' I glared at Lys. She'd no business discussing anything with Leland. Seeing my dismay, she stumbled over her words and paused.

I patted the telephone. 'It's got to stop!'

'I don't know what you're talking about.'

'You know perfectly well. Right from this moment Ambrose is no longer a hunting lodge. And there'll be no more killing of wolves. If he told you anything my father will have told you that.' Leland began to look decidedly uncomfortable. 'What about my men?'

'What about them?'

'They won't get any other work this late in the season.'

'There may be work for some of them, I haven't decided what…..'

'You haven't decided. You come up here throwing your weight around, tearing down placards, putting people out of their rightful work.'

'Rightful work Mr Leland?' I asked cautiously. I wanted to see how far he would go and how he would explain the two wolf carcasses already on their way back to Ambrose.

'Whatever licences you have, they don't permit killing of wolves in the closed season.'

'You're mad!' He'd been about to sit down but he twisted away from me and started to leave the room.

'Mr. Leland!' I called after him menacingly. My tone got through to him when he'd taken three steps down the broadwalk. When he turned round his face was as black as thunder.

'Yes?'

'I'll need to talk to the men.'

'Sure, you can talk to the men, any time. I'll call them right now shall I?'

I wasn't sure I was ready for a public announcement. Leland had forestalled me. At least it would get the news out into the open. Leland had reached the bottom of the steps. He called Talbot over to him and the two of them started a tour of the workshops and bunkhouses shouting orders for the men to convene by the veranda.

It was a motley crowd of about thirty, that gathered to hear me. Men in overall: builders, carpenters, even saddlers. Most were Caucasians, but there were a few black faces and two Ojibway Indians with long dark hair and black eyes. I quailed at the sight of them all, but stood my ground. I'd hoped Lys would remain inside but she came out onto the veranda to face them. There was a low murmur of expectation among the men. Talbot and Leland had come back silently and were standing together on the lowest step. It occurred to me they had positioned themselves to prevent the men rushing the veranda, or perhaps they simply wanted to be in the vanguard. In the event nothing untoward happened. Leland stole my thunder even before I could open my mouth. I stood impotently against the veranda rail cradling my rifle in my hands listening to him.

'Mr Francis Delacroix's taking over Ambrose Lodge from his father, Louis. There's going to be some changes.' He paused, I thought to let me speak. I wetted my lips but he interrupted before I could draw breath.

'Francis won't be running Ambrose as a hunting lodge, but he hasn't quite decided what he's going to do with it. Sixty guests due in a few weeks, some of them high-class people, senators, businessmen, but Mr. Delacroix'll be running the place as a theme park.' There was a roar of laughter from the men, one or two nudging each other in amusement. All took their cue from him.

'That's not true, Leland stop this.'

'Well what are you going to run the place as, Francis?'

I looked down at the sea of expectant faces. Kevin's call and Leland's subsequent insolence forced from me the only words I felt able to utter. 'As of this minute all of you men are on twenty-four hours' notice to leave Ambrose. I'll honour all your contracts.'

There was another roar of laughter. They hadn't believed a word I'd said.

'What contracts are those Mr. Delacroix? Whenever did men like these, and the trackers and hunters who aren't here, have written contracts,' Leland barracked.

'I'll honour any contracts written or otherwise,' I shouted over the laughter. Lys was clinging to my arm.

'We'll never do it Francis, I just haven't got enough saved…' I turned to her and said briefly, 'Please be quiet Lys. Can't you see he's goading me. He thinks I'll back down.'

'Oh, I hadn't thought.'

Leland took the initiative again. Speaking in a mocking tone he said, 'Mr Delacroix will honour any contracts you bring to him this evening. Now get back to work. You'll need to pack up come the morning probably.' There was more laughter, some of it raucous, then the men dispersed to their various tasks. The building work started up as if I had made no announcement. Leland and Talbot were talking quietly. There didn't seem anything else I could do for the moment.

'Leland, tell the men I'll be back before dark, seven at the latest.'

'Certainly Mr. Francis,' he mocked in return. Talbot turned away trying to hide a guffaw.

'And Mr Leland I presume you are in charge of the hotel accommodation, catering etc?'

Leland scoffed as if the idea was beneath him. 'Not me mister, hired a manager for that sort of thing.'

'Is he here?'

'Rick Tomlinson…nope, won't be here until near opening, runs the Americano Motel down at Thunder Bay.' I knew the place, it was a quick stop-over, no-frills, tourist motel for the Lakes and Ski resorts. Hardly a good apprenticeship for pampering Ambrose's luxury clientele.

'Well phone him, try to get him over here tomorrow morning.'

'Yes sir, Mr Delacroix, sure thing.' Again that mocking tone.

'And I want the keys to the building.'

'In the office desk, top drawer.' He made no move to return so I took Lys by the arm. We entered the office and searched through smoker's debris: empty cheroot packets and discarded wrappers, until we found two keys labelled Ambrose. After that we made a whistle-stop tour of the remaining house, entering by the second of the main doors and taking in the vast deserted kitchens with their empty cauldrons and idle dishwashers.

Then we crossed an elegantly decorated dining room and through into guest room after guest room where mattresses were stacked against old-fashioned flock-lined wall paper. When I thought there was nothing more to see Lys took the stairs to the top floor of the building, exclaiming as she entered a corner room.

'Oh Francis, you must come and see,' she called down across the polished pine balustrade. The room was like all the others, with the furniture piled against one wall. A pair of French windows opened out onto a small balcony where Lys was now standing. I walked out to see what had gained her attention. The dining room and ground floor rooms in the east wing looked out onto a garden courtyard screened from the outside world by a high beech hedge. From the wooden veranda it was now possible to see over the hedge towards a circular artificial lake and an adjoining paddock. In the heart of the field a roe deer and young fawn were feeding on the grass.

'Isn't it amazing. Ambrose Hunting Lodge and a deer with its young right at the heart…..'

'If I'm going to keep the place, don't ever say that Lys,' I chided. Lys started and stood back.

'Whatever do you mean….Oh, Ambrose Lodge - no hunting.' she corrected herself. 'You meant it then?'

'Of course. But it's not going to be easy Lys. Do you want me to take you back to Kashabowie. You could get a bed for the night.'

'Get me out of harm's way, that's what you mean isn't it? No I'm staying Francis, for good or...' She left the words hanging.

'Come on then we'll take a tour of the place and get some lunch.'

'There wasn't a diner on the way down from the highway.'

'No need,' I laughed. 'I've got plenty of supplies in the car.'

'Why you lying…!' She grimaced and launched a mock blow at my shoulder letting me duck away just in time.

Chapter Eight

Against all expectations the car was in one piece with the placards still lodged on the rear seat. I lifted one of the cushions and drew out a box of groceries for Lys to rummage through. We sampled portions of cold meat pie before I drove around the east wing of the house, past the beech hedge. To the right there was quite a drop to the lake, the grassy bank separated from the road by a sturdy white picket fence and some solid looking posts that might have been stonework. The deer had gone from the paddock.

'Why are you coming this way?' Lys asked. 'I thought you'd had enough of the house for the moment.'

'I have but I wanted to check the rest of the place.' This wasn't the complete truth, I really wanted to investigate the rear entrance to the house and see where the track led down to the inner picket fence. It was here I planned to park the car later.

We spent the next few hours driving through an idyllic landscape of hills covered in mixed aspen woodland intersected by valley meadows, passing every now and then by the shores of a small lake half-hidden in rushes and aspen saplings. Several times we saw white-tailed deer with fawns and once a moose disappeared into the conifers followed by two sturdy young. Turning back in the direction of the house brought us to a lake where the shoreline was clear of vegetation and the road came down suddenly onto broken shingle. A small jetty stretched out many yards into the lake. We got out of the car and ate the remains of the pie and tomatoes under rustling aspens, washing the alfresco meal down with lemonade chilled by the lake water. Lys eventually broke the silence. She was looking across the lake at a pair of whooper swans and their growing cygnets.

'Why did you say I was your wife?' she asked, without preamble, although she must have been thinking about this for some time.

'Seemed safer.' The disturbing image of Pamela as I'd last seen her came to the front of my mind. I blinked it away, disinclined to talk.

'Yes, I suppose it was. Are you expecting trouble at the Lodge?'

'Expecting no, preparing for it yes.' I turned away. Across the lake one of the cygnets spread his wings and beat erratically on the water in an abortive attempt at flight. The effort and sudden abandonment caused wide rippling circles to spin out across the lake. It seemed an omen for what was to come. Lys took the hint and asked no further questions. We drove back to the house in silence. It was still light as I drove the car onto the gravel at the rear of the house. I swung it round so it was facing back along the track, and reversed beside the picket fence. Lys looked at me strangely. 'In case we need to get away quickly.' She gasped and shivered slightly.

'Don't worry. But Lys, I want you to stay in the car for the moment.'

This time she didn't comment as I lifted the rifle and opened the car door. As I'd driven in I'd noticed two new vehicles drawn up alongside the bunkhouse broadwalk. The sun was behind the tall frieze of conifers and the vehicles stood in deep shadow. Clustered around them were a dozen or so men.

As I approached I saw there were three men seated on a bench under the bunkhouse window. Two were blood Indians I'd seen earlier: an old man with a seamed face, the other much younger, closer to my own age. There was a certain likeness to them. I wondered if they were father and son. Both wore modern workaday clothes. The shirt of the younger man was partially open. Against his bare brown chest hung a thong with the traditional leaf-shaped Ojibway jet pendant. One lock of dark hair above his left ear had been made into a thin plait in a style I wasn't familiar with.

I was more familiar with the curved knife he was using to whittle a piece of half-blackened pine. Shavings on the floor between his feet were evidence that he had taken off the worst of the black staining, and was now guiding the evil blade round the remaining blackened growth rings so that the dark features stood proud of the yellow wood. The creature forming in his hands could have been a dog - or a wolf.

Next to him was another man I hadn't seen before. Over his working shirt he'd on an old hunting jacket of a style more suited to the dandy - probably it was one of Leland's cast-offs. The man was about the same age as the younger Indian, but he'd the florid complexion that comes either from a life spent outdoors, or from drink. I suspected the latter. A long scar ran down his cheek, puckering the skin. No-one looked up as I approached.

'Which one of you is Kevin?'

The two native Americans looked up slowly. Neither man spoke but older man looked sideways at the third man. He saw the action.

'Who wants to know?' the man said, kind of surly. He looked back down at the floor and sifted the smoky pine debris at the feet of the sculptor. I tried to remember the voice on the phone. 'You called earlier.'

'No mister, you'm mistaken.'

'I don't think so…… Where are they?'

'Don't know what you're talking about. In any case what right you got….'

'Something wrong here Mr. Delacroix?' Leland had come up behind me quietly. I hadn't heard him. I also saw that Lys had disobeyed me and was following nervously in his wake. That wasn't the moment to order her back to the car. I was getting nowhere with Kevin so I tried a full-on attack with Leland.

'Where's this freezer?' I asked angrily.

Leland laughed into my face. 'The man wants a freezer Lionel, see he finds one.' Leland nodded to a room in the bunkhouse behind the man who got up unhurriedly and ambled towards the open doorway. To the jeers of the other men I followed Lionel into a small bare utility room. He went to the back where an old chest freezer was breathing its last beside an equally agéd sink. A modern gas cooker stood alongside them. It was covered in grease as was the worksurface. Unwashed plates were piled up against the wall. Stacks of cans of beans and oily fish lined the shelves above them.

An open, barrel-like, waste bin beneath was brimming with the remains of empty tins. Leland, it seemed, ran a lazy ship. Wordlessly and with sad eyes the old man lifted the lid of the freezer, holding it up so I could look inside. Thick ice caked the sides right from the base to the opening, the only contents a few soggy packets of string beans nestling at the bottom. It was an unlikely place for a wolf carcass even if the packets of vegetables had been thrown in there recently for effect. I backed out of the room and faced up to Leland, very much aware of the curious stares and jaded laughter coming from the men. Lys looked crestfallen at the reception I was receiving.

'OK you've had your joke. Now I want....' But just then Lionel came out of the room behind me. I thought I heard him sigh. He edged unhappily towards the young sculptor who flicked his eyes surreptitiously in the direction of a inconspicuous green-painted and windowless building at the far end of the bunkhouse. It was partially screened by some rambling shrub. I let my gaze wander in that direction and caught Leland in an unguarded frown.

'Well Mr. Leland, you've something to hide after all.' With him close on my heels I strode towards the building. Pushing the low door open revealed a pair of chest freezers, each over a yard long by two feet wide, filling the floor space and leaving only a small walk-in area between them. Both were fitted with metal lugs but only the right hand one was secured by a padlock.

'I'll ask you for the key Mr Leland.'

'You've no right, this is private property.'

'Is that private Delacroix property Mr. Leland?' I demanded. 'The key please.'

He knew he was beaten. Whistling between his teeth he pulled a key chain from his pocket, yanked off a key and thrust it towards me. I was breathing heavily, like him, and I saw he had it in his mind to drop the key just short of my fingers. I carried the loaded rifle uncocked, but when he saw me raise the barrel an inch from the floor he thought better of it, simply dropping the key into my palm. The men who had followed him in my wake, including the man called Kevin, now fell back a pace or two, their laughter quelled. Lys was wending her way between the men. Anxious at what I might see, I motioned her back and fumbled with the padlock.

The bodies hadn't frozen yet and the flesh was still warm from the day's heat. Little flecks of ice sparkled on the soft crusty-brown fur. Both animals had been thrown down hurriedly, that much was clear from the way they lay, a jumble of torsos with the legs lying anyhow and beginning to stiffen. But it was an irrational dread that lead my fingers through the fur of the juvenile down onto the neck of the adult. I eased the silvery body fur gently towards me until I could see the shoulders and assure myself that the animal was a stranger, that it wasn't Speed.

All my instincts had told me Speed was a young male, but I hadn't known for certain. There was no earthly reason that it should be him, we were at least forty miles from Pelican Lodge yet wild wolves are known to travel great distances. Speed was probably dead: I was a fool to believe otherwise. I pulled my hand away meaning to close the lid but as I touched it the freezer wobbled.

Somehow the balance altered. The wolf's body slid down into the shadowy depths at the base of the freezer, forcing the upper part into view . Her ears slipped up into the light and with it the head - or what should have been the head. Instead, I saw an unrecognisable mass of blood and gore and bone and I cursed the butcher who'd brought the young female to such an end. It would have taken at least three bullets to cause such destruction.

I had tight control of myself as I secured the padlock and went back out into the subdued light of the dying day. Only yards away Leland was deep in conversation with Kevin, the hunter. The rest of the crowd had dispersed. Men stood around the bunkhouse in twos and threes, watching and waiting. With intense restraint I walked past them. Lys was quickly at my side. She saw the streaks of blood on my hand.

'Francis?' I shook my head and strode on. She stayed silent and close on my heels as I reached the steps. Here I turned round, controlling my voice just long enough to order.

'Leland, I'm taking over your office. Get any of the men that want to come and see me there. And get me the second key to that padlock.' I thought he would obey without demur. Instead he yelled back mutinously.

'It's in the office drawer - if you've time to search for it.'

'What does he mean, if you have time, Francis?' Lys asked at my shoulder.

'Nothing, a joke.'

Leland had come up behind Lys at the base of the steps. Talbot, who I hadn't seen until that moment, joined him there and proceeded to ogle Lys. Something snapped inside me.

'Get back, both of you.'

Talbot smirked. 'Got a nice little injun there Delacroix, why don't you let us all....'

'Shut up you fool,' Leland demanded, smirking. 'Can't you see the man's upset.'

'What's to upset for - couple of dead, no-account, wolves.'

'I warn you Talbot....If I find out who ordered those wolves killed......'

'Francis, Francis.' Lys screamed. I hadn't realised that I had raised the rifle barrel until it was pointing directly at Talbot. My sister was tearing at my shoulder, almost pulling off my jacket.

'Leland, any spare beds in the bunkhouse?'

'Sure, it's only two-thirds full.'

'You'll be sleeping down there tonight.' His face contorted into a black scowl but he made no reply. 'Now what are these other rooms? No.. no need to come up,' I called down as he went to step up to the veranda.

'Services right at this end,' he pointed to the last room hardly able to control his voice, '.... next's where Talbot usually sleeps.' He spat.

'Little woman can sleep in my bed any time she wants,' Talbot chortled. Leland smiled and let the comment sink in without rejoinder. Lys was holding tightly to my rifle arm. I got the message.

'Tell the men they can come up while the light's on.' But I intended neither to sleep nor to put the light out, that night.

We sat in the office for just under an hour talking desultorily, both of us hesitant and alert to any step on the veranda boards, whether from friend or foe. But none came. At one stage from somewhere towards the rear of the new block, I heard the sound of engines, two cars, perhaps three, one with a deeper note than the others. They appeared to be moving away, heading back round the house. I wasn't particularly concerned. If some of the men chose to leave, it meant all the fewer to deal with come the morrow. When it went quiet again Lys leaned across and asked, 'Will you stay?'

'In this big rambling place?'

'Yes.'

'Right this moment I don't know Lys. I want to phone Jacob, get his advice.'

On the way from the border I'd told her about the

Wolf League and Jacob's part in arranging my work at Sanctuary.

'Do you think anyone believed you about....'

' ...about closing down the hunting? I don't care if they didn't. One way or another it's got to stop, all of it.' I glanced over at Lys. 'You heard what Father said - was it only last night - just a few wolves.'

'I don't understand it all Francis,' she yawned deeply, 'it's too late at night.'

Too late at night and neither of us with a good night's sleep behind us, so we stayed quiet for a long time listening to the rustle of the conifers and the slow easing of wood now the sun's heat had dissipated. Lys was sitting on Leland's cot bed, her eyes were drooping and darkness had fallen long since when I asked, 'You look all in, do you want to sleep. We could make up a bed in one of the guest rooms,' I said half in jest.

'Amongst those empty spooky rooms?' She shook her head. 'No thanks. I'm all right here'.

'You must want to rest.'

'I do, oh Francis I do, but I can't leave you....to, to....' She lost the thread of what she was saying and yawned wearily.

'You can bed down next door, it might be safer.' She was suddenly dramatically awake, fierce tears blinking from her eyes. 'In that awful man's bed! Francis, you mustn't make me.'

'Lys...,' I wondered how much to tell her of my fears. 'I want to take a look around now it's dark. It's very quiet out there and.... well I just don't trust Leland. He's a born ringleader. The mood of the men was too easily quelled.'

'Then why don't we just go, drive out of here and

never never come back?'

It was a tempting choice, one I should have taken. 'Things have gone too far for that.'

'Why, why do you say that?'

'For one thing, I need those wolves' bodies as evidence. I'll never get as far as the cold store and back to the car undetected and they'll simply disappear if we leave now.'

'I could drive you across and wait.'

'And wake up the whole site? Be sensible. I'm sorry, but I meant what I said about looking around. It'll be safer if you go next door and sleep.' It occurred to me, fleetingly, that I was ordering her about just as my father did. 'I'm sorry Lys.'

'You're wishing I hadn't come.'

'Don't start that all over again. I'll come in with you and see you bedded down.'

'I won't sleep in that man's blankets.' She sounded like a naughty child and my heart ached for her.

'Then take these,' I said, roughly pulling the covers from Leland's cot.

Talbot's room contained only a camp bed littered with some old clothes Talbot had tossed down. An upturned wooden crate had a dirty plate and cutlery scattered across it. Otherwise the room was bare; as bare as I judged Talbot's soul to be. I turfed his bedding onto the floor and flung Leland's blankets onto the bare canvas. Lys edged into the covers as if they might bite her. I sat on the crate waiting for her eyes to close. I didn't have long to wait, her breathing became heavy. Soon she was deeply asleep. I turned out the light and crept from the room then cursed under my breath. I'd intended to make her bolt the door behind me.

Now it was too late. I re-entered the office, picked up the rifle and spare ammunition. Forgetting my earlier resolution, my last act was to turn out the light. It was the signal for all hell to break loose. Disorientated by the darkness after the glaring light from the lamp, I heard glass shatter. The window beside me exploded, showering me and the desk with thousands of glass fragments. Men's voices jeered and cat-called from below the veranda. I thought I was safer in the room.

The yelling grew louder, feet thudded along the broadwalk then there was a loud thump as something crashed down on the boards. I had the rifle cocked but still I waited, hoping against hope that Lys would stay in her room. I hoped in vain. I heard a door creak open. Light from a security fixture flooded along the veranda striking through the shattered windowpane, followed by an ear-piercing scream. They shouldn't have done it to her, not to my sister! Lys stood stone-dead under the arc-lights looking down at the body of the female wolf with its head shot away and wailing to herself. Men were shouting and laughing all around the veranda. I swung the rifle up and blasted the air as a warning shot. This only made the clamour greater.

I heard shouts of 'Get out Delacross, get out before we throw you out,' 'send the bugger home with a branding', 'dirty wolf-lover', all of which scared me silly but another call rang out among the throng which struck fear much deeper into my heart: 'Francis Delacross ain't got no wife, so the little injun's fair game, eh? eh? Mr Delacross?' I recognised Harry Talbot's voice and swung round to see him climbing the steps towards Lys. In the glare of the lights it wasn't difficult to make out James Leland's face behind him. He was smiling evilly.

'Keep back,' I yelled, edging myself round the body of the wolf and in front of Lys. For a moment they halted. Yells of ridicule continued from below the veranda. I heard scrabbling at the far end. Out of the corner of my eye I watched two men clamber over the balustrade. They were edging slowly towards us with their eyes firmly fixed on the rifle. I worked the mechanism and had trained the barrel on Talbot, ready to swing to the right if need be. Leland pushed round in front of him.

'What's the meaning of this Leland?' I yelled above the deafening roars. 'Are you out of your mind?'

'That's a good one. I talked to your Pa again, Francis. Seems you're the one losing your mind...how long was you in that hospital?' He turned to face the jeering crowd and raised the fingers of one hand then the other in the air. It was easy to count off six fingers and one bent knuckle for the six and a half months I'd spent at DeTrou hospital. 'Seems he's going to have you sectioned, put away.'

'What the hell are you talking about Leland, my father would never....'

'Spoke to him half hour ago. Seemed right certain of himself. Going to get the courts to give him power of attorney.'

'He's trying to get Ambrose back?'

'That's sure enough what he's planning to do boy and there's nothing you can do about it, so be a good lad and hand over the rifle.' Suddenly Lys came to herself, she looked kind of dazed.

'He's not mad,' she shrieked 'It was a medical hospital, my father's no right....' Somehow she made herself heard above the shouting, to devastating effect.

'Your father - old Louis? Christ, the bastard's fucking his own sister. Get him boys he doesn't deserve ......'
Of course it was Talbot's hectoring voice. The first bullet cracked through one of the veranda uprights and screamed on to shatter a board near Talbot's feet. I was aiming a second shot above his head when the heavy missile smashed against my shoulder. I stumbled, struggling to maintain my aim, blocks of blackened wood rained down. I saw Lys cover her eyes before a sharp piece of burnt wood caught me on the temple and I went down half conscious on top of the rifle. Footsteps thudded along the broadwalk towards us but it was Lys' screams that got me to my feet, raging and half blind.

Talbot had Lys by the shoulder. He was tearing at her waistcoat and spitting as the tasselled feathers flew into his eyes. She was struggling to free herself as he tried to kiss her mouth. They were surrounded by a gang of other men, each grasping at her clothing, running their hands up her slim body and across her breasts.

I wasn't quick enough to raise the rifle as another man came from my right. I kicked out as he came close. He screamed as my foot connected with his genitals and fell beside me with a sickening thud and a cracking of bones just as a second man came at me more warily now but equally bent on attack. I caught hold of the rifle barrel and just managed to stagger to my knees when he was upon me.

Through a haze of blood and sweat I smashed the butt directly into his face and saw nose and cheek shatter in a gush of blood. With Lys' screams growing louder it was little consolation that the face belonged to Kevin, the wolf-butcher.

Somehow I stumbled to my feet. Lys was barely an

arm's length from me. Talbot had torn the shoulder of her jerkin open to the skin and somehow got his face down onto her neck. He was oblivious to my shouts so I yanked at his long greasy hair, pulling hard so he finally knew me, then used the rifle butt to crack down on his skull. Amazement and horror shot across his features, then he was sinking jerkily to the floor, taking several other men down with him.

I caught at Lys' shoulder and shook her until she looked at me. Her cheeks were puffy where the earlier bruise had inflamed them, now more bruises marred her neck. More men were advancing stealthily from both ends of the veranda. I saw an empty space in the crowd just below the balustrade opposite where I'd parked the car.

'Down there Lys!' I yelled, gesturing with the rifle. She looked at me, horrified. The broadwalk could not have been more than four feet off the ground. The jump seemed to present no difficulty, but Lys was only just over five feet tall. Somehow I had to get her over that balustrade but I didn't dare take my eyes off the vanguard of men approaching from left and right. Lys tentatively approached the edge of the broadwalk and looked down. Her hesitation was making me angry. 'For God's sake lean on the balustrade and roll over like you were a child.' Even as I spoke I remembered that Lys's childhood was a complete mystery to me, that she was already 16 years old when she took my mother's place in my life. 'Roll over damn you!' I yelled. I pushed her down onto the rail and something in my voice got through to her. She let herself tumble over the balustrade. I shot out each of the two arc-lights so that she landed on the ground in complete darkness.

'Francis!' She screamed. I jumped down a few feet away. Her hands grasped at the darkness. I grabbed her and half-carried her through the shadows to the car. I'd purposely left it unlocked. Hastily shoving Lys into the driver's seat, I edged her awkwardly past the wheel, then gunned the engine. It started first time. I thrashed the lights on as a warning and swung the car recklessly towards the crowd attempting to bar our way. They parted with howls of protest. Blows and thuds rained down on the car's roof as we tore past, but we were quickly free of them and running out of the rear courtyard.

Too soon I sighed with relief. Suddenly from the left came a screech of tyres, lights flashed and two cars streamed from behind the new building. They were running parallel with us, heading towards the country track which I intended to use. Then I saw what the band of conifers had hidden from view. Stationed at the entrance to the track was a stout jeep.

It looked abandoned. With its high wheelbase and broad intimidating metal fenders it effectively blocked off the country track. I yelled to Lys to hang on with all her might and swung the car back on itself. The nearest car was close behind. The driver had not anticipated the turn, and swung his vehicle wildly to the side. There was just enough road to pass and we streamed alongside, wing mirrors colliding. I saw the whites of the driver's eyes before we gained the shelter of the beech hedge and were heading towards the main entrance.

The driver of the second vehicle had time to compensate for the manoeuvre though. He kept coming. I felt a shudder as his car collided violently with our rear fender. The car rocked from side to side. I concentrated on keeping it steady on the road but metal crashed on metal, there was another savage grating sound as the fenders rode over one another, then a pause as he fell back and tried the strategy again, this time coming up alongside the hedge, aiming for the right fender.

When the two fenders locked he swung his wheel over and tried to force us against the picket fence. I felt a shock as the car hit and flung my hand across Lys to hold her safe. There was a fearful sound of wood splintering, whole spars broke away leaving a yawning gap in the fence and I was painfully aware of the dark mass of the lake below. I fought to get the car aimed along the track but not soon enough. As we hit the first of the uprights I thought to hear wood shatter, instead the sides of the car shook and screeched alongside a stone upright, tearing off paint and trim.

Lys screamed as I fought with the wheel, eventually regaining control of the steering. A straight section of the track showed in the car lights and I accelerated wildly. Lights thrashed along the road behind but the anticipated attack didn't come. Heartened, I drove faster still, the speedometer hitting sixty as I steered around the final corner of the hedge, heading now for the courtyard and the safety of the highway.

They had planned the ambush well. At the entrance to the main track between the confining hedge and the lakeside fence, blocking all exit from the site, sat the vast bulk of a JCB. Turned towards us, its lights suddenly flicked on. I saw the body of the thing shake as it began to move relentlessly towards us. As I slammed on the brakes the inevitable happened. The car behind ploughed down on us, crashing with such force that the car bucked sideways. In a second the front of the vehicle had risen up, crashing down against one of the stone uprights in a battle of strength.

The car lost and toppled over at an angle of thirty degrees, the lights playing across the dark waters of the lake. One more thrust from the car behind and we would be in the water, but the attack did not come from that region. Instead above the grinding throb of the JCB and the screaming engines of the two cars came the shouts and clamour of the approaching crowd. There was no time to struggle free of the tilted vehicle before they were upon us.

Lys was conscious but crying bitterly. She had fallen against me, and was lying along my side. My door was yanked open. I heard the sound of metal grinding as it swung back, then hands pulled me from my seat. I couldn't evade them. I was pulled bodily to the ground and dragged down the bank to a blatant chorus of 'get the bloody wolf-lover' 'have done with the bastard, and other threats and curses. To the pain of bruises and blows gained in the impact were now added punches and kicks and I sensed unconsciousness wasn't far away.

On the bank above, the lights of the three cars beamed down. I fought back the darkness that threatened to extinguish them. Blows continued to rain down. I tumbled helplessly to the waters edge. Mud and water poured into my open mouth. I gasped for breath as yet more punches forced me deeper into the water. I went under, coughing and spluttering. When the shots rang out I'd been pushed under again and was gasping for breath, I sensed for the last time. The shots had momentarily dented the crowd's fervour.

The hands that held me loosened and pushed me

hastily back into the water. I heard Lys' voice screaming as if from a long way away. Lights wavered before my eyes as I peered through red pain up at the lights of our car and was dimly aware of a figure standing erect above the tilted passenger door . Somehow Lys had got out that side of the car. She was leaning on the roof, using it as a support for the rifle that she was angling towards the angry jostling throng.

'Get away from him, get away.' Her voice rose to fever pitch above the continuing clamour, and after long seconds of loud grumbling and dissent, it sharpened still further. 'I'll shoot anyone who touches my brother again. I mean it.' I was half-unconscious but the menace in her voice was clear. Would the violent hostile crowd understand her strength of will?

In any event she was saved from fulfilling her promise by the harsh wail of sirens. The noisy crowd scattered frantically. Without their support I slipped once more into the deeper water, but other, gentler, hands hoisted me up and I felt myself dragged onto the grassy bank. Here a bout of coughing caused pain to shoot through my chest. Finally, I passed out.

I awoke to the increasing clamour of sirens, to an unnatural silence beyond and had a sensation of being carried away from the lake. The beech hedge loomed up, was lost in the shadows again, then Lys was at my side, hurrying ahead along a veranda. Lights illuminated the dingy room, Talbot's room. Why here? I asked through the pain. Hands lowered me onto a bed and wrapped covers over me. Then, remembering the office had been showered with glass, I lost consciousness.

Lys' soft murmuring woke me. Someone was securing a

bandage round my chest. Naked, with muddy wet clothes lying around on the floor beside the bed, I was encouraged to lie down. The dry blankets folded round me. But the hands were not Lys' and the face looking down at me had the wisdom of age etched on its sad features - Lionel! Two other people were talking at the far end of the room. Their conversation stilled as I looked up beyond the old man.

'Lionel, Lionel he's awake, oh thank you, thank you.'

Lys sank down beside me, one hand clasping the old man's shoulder in gratitude, the other on my forearm.

'Francis, the ambulance is waiting… only Lionel, he said it would take too long to get here. He's given you a poultice and strapped you up better than any nurse.'

'Poultice?' I asked hesitantly looking at the old man as he stood back from the bed, then almost immediately felt the warmth of the herbs and ointments he had placed under the wrappings.

'If you can't speak…..' but Lys didn't wait for a reply. She looked towards the darkened doorway where the faces of two young interns, their uniforms trim and starched, stared down at me. Blue emergency lights flashed and flickered from the courtyard. 'He's ready, can you take him. Which hospital….?' But I put an arm out from beneath the warming blankets, raised myself painfully and stilled her with a grimace.

'No ambulance,' I whispered. 'I'm staying here.'

'But you can't Francis, you simply can't,' she insisted.

'I feel fine, nothing a little sleep won't...'

'You're talking nonsense Francis. Please let them…. '

'I've got to stay Lys, don't you understand?' Lys looked distraught. Her lips moved to repeat her earlier entreaty, then my tone of voice got through to her.

'You mean ....someone should stay here? Oh no, hasn't this place done enough to you? Can't you leave it - whatever it is you're fighting?' Tears were in her eyes as I shook my head and lowered myself back onto the pillow.

'I could stay,' she exclaimed, wide-eyed.

'When all you want to do is come with me to the hospital?' She pouted, I knew I'd touched a nerve and continued, 'you think I'd leave you here alone, after what's happened?' Almost involuntarily she pulled at the torn sleeve of her jerkin. Her hands were shaking. I saw that the shoulder seam had been wrenched open leaving her right side exposed down to the swell of her breast.

The embroidered waistcoat, now tattered and muddy, barely covered her shoulder. Lying against her skin just above the partially exposed breasts was a jet pendant I hadn't previously noticed. She must have kept it hidden in the folds of the material, now as she clasped the ragged ends the carved stone swung out beneath her fingers. It bore the same Ojibway design the younger Indian wore. He was standing in the far corner of the room silently watching the exchange. Now Lys turned to him.

'I won't be alone,' she said quite emphatically.

I looked at both men, more convinced than ever of the father-son relationship. I concentrated hard to fight a wave of pain and raising myself from the bed said very slowly, 'Let the ambulance go Lys.' Lys didn't reply, just chewed on her lip for a second then gave a wordless nod to the interns. In the silence which followed, I heard them walk off down the broadwalk and later the sound of an engine moving swiftly away. But the flashing lights I'd noticed before didn't move. Lys read my thoughts.

'The police are waiting to speak to us, they're sitting

outside in the squad car.' She pressed my arm and gave me an exultant look. 'Francis, they've arrested Leland and Talbot and some of the men. Most of the others have fled.'

'Leland, Talbot. You're sure?'

'Both arrested, yes. There were some hospital cases too, that's what the police want to ask you about.'

'Let them wait,' I sighed, letting myself subside onto the bed. Fighting waves of pain I looked up at the older man.

'Why did you stay Lionel, you and your....son? Aren't you Leland men?' I asked pointedly, expecting him to dissemble, but the sorrowful face became sadder still. He shot a tender look at the young man.

'You are right, Denzil - Denny as he likes to call himself - is my son,' Lionel countered, ignoring my veiled accusation, 'And we are not a violent people.'

I found breathing painful. I shifted in the bed to ease the bruised ribs and saw a flicker of concern in his rheumy eyes.

'Yet you work....worked for a violent man.'

'Some things are not avoidable.' It was a queer way to express it, as if there were times when avoidance was not a simple option.

'There's no other work?' Even as I asked I remembered the reports of unemployment that had come down to us across the Canadian border over the past few years. Inflation, closed factories, take-overs and layoffs had all taken their toll. Both men shook their heads and I began to feel guilty at taking away their only means of support, a season's work lost at the whim of some spoiled brat they would be thinking.

'You called the police.' Neither man blinked but I

knew from the subtle change in Denzil's attitude that I was right.

'There may be a few days' work, but little money to pay you, perhaps just food and board.' The two exchanged a knowing look.

'A few days may stretch into a week, after a week who knows…..' Lionel was not reproaching me, just emphasising his innate optimism. 'We'll make you a meal.'

A smile creased Denzil's lips, he chuckled and I heard his voice properly for the first time, it was strangely deep and compelling. 'You'd better see the police first, before Dad poisons you with his cooking.'

Lionel made no comment. He simply collected together his potions and bandages into a standard industrial first aid box and the two of them got up to leave.

'Where's the rifle?' I called after them, but Lys had shifted aside to show me the rifle lying on an upturned crate.

'In good hands.' Denzil's lean brown face creased into a brief smile. 'And the safety catch is on.' With that the two men left.

The police came in, two brawny men filling out their Mountie uniforms. Lys moved against the back wall offering the upturned case to the lieutenant. He sat down while the other man, a sergeant, leant against the door jam, notebook and pen ready in his hands.

'Better tell us what happened here,' the lieutenant said. He was a man of about forty with a hard-bitten look about him that would stand no nonsense. I moved awkwardly on the bed trying to rise. He heard my sharp intake of breath as pain shot through my chest and shook his head. The big hands pressed lightly on my shoulder, 'No need,' pausing to add 'In your own time fella.' With a constantly aching chest and sudden pauses as the breath failed me, I told the story right from our arrival at Ambrose to the time when I'd lost consciousness, but leaving out the insults and jibes hurled at Lys and my father's threats to have me sectioned.

The sergeant had written it all down in his notebook. When I finished speaking, he shot a look at Lys. 'What about you miss?' The sergeant asked.

While I'd been talking and probably to distract herself from the horrors of the tale, Lys had been moving about the room surreptitiously picking up my clothes from near the bed, shaking off the worst of the lake mud and hanging jeans, shirt and jacket up on a series of rough wooden pegs ranged along the rear wall.

As they turned to her she was brushing intently at a particularly stubborn piece of mud from the bottom of the jeans using her fingernails. Now she stood looking out from the shadows, her eyes large and intense. I'd briefed her, before the police came in, against offering any unnecessary information. She was to say she had come along for the ride, and knew nothing of my intentions.

'It's as my brother told you,' she said calmly, as if this told the whole story.

'You just got caught in the violence?' The lieutenant quizzed.

'Yes,' she said simply, trying to hold his gaze but eventually looking down at her feet.

The man seemed dissatisfied with her answer.

'You want to press charges ..for rape?' It was a harsh

ugly word, but so near the truth that Lys blushed and clutched at the torn jerkin beneath the spoiled waistcoat.

'They didn't...they...no,' she insisted, so emphatically that the man turned back to me.

'You must have been expecting trouble when you sacked all those men Mr. Delacroix ...' The lieutenant pronounced my name in the French-Canadian way. 'A whole season's work lost. Why didn't you send your sister away first?'

'We didn't expect real trouble, I'd offered to honour the men's contracts this evening. No-one came. But in any case I'd already offered to get Lys a room at Kashabowie.'

'You know a hotel in the town?' the sergeant asked. It seemed a rather inane question but I guessed there was a reason behind it.

'No, but we'd driven through there earlier. I thought.....'

'Why did you really come here Mr. Delacroix?' The lieutenant shot the question at me.

'I own the place, I told you.'

'Ceded from your father, as a hunting lodge, just two weeks ago.' I couldn't fathom what he was getting at. 'And none of the men here knew you were going to close the place down? Seems a little strange coming up here and making an announcement like that without warning. Why d'you do it?' I heard Lys gasp, she wavered and I thought she was going to faint. The lieutenant was quickly on his feet offering her the crate, but she shook him off and leant against the back wall, her face almost white against the dark wood. 'I'm all right, really.'

I wasn't convinced. 'Sit down Lys, please.'

She gave me a long calculating look and eventually sat

down on the offered crate. The lieutenant looked back down at me.

'Well Mr. Delacroix?' he insisted. I sighed painfully and said, 'When my father handed the lodge over to me he intended it as an extension to his own business - hunting, trapping…..killing animals.' Here a painful coughing fit took hold of me, but even as I coughed I felt the lieutenant's eyes on me. As the spasm passed and my breathing steadied to a harsh rasping he waited patiently for me to continue. 'I told him I didn't want anything to do with it. We ..we had a flaming row.'

'You came up here to spite him then?' The sergeant had hardly finished talking when Lys thumped a fist down on the crate and shrieked. 'No, no it wasn't like that. My brother wouldn't….,' her voice wavered and died. The two officers fixed their gaze on her face. She realised too late that she'd made a mistake.

'Then suppose you tell us what he is like.'

'He .. he…,' she began, but I interrupted, fighting down another spasm of pain.

'Leave her alone! I wanted nothing to do with the place - Ambrose, the hunting, but I heard rumours, bad rumours about wolf-killing at Ambrose. Outside the place, not just on the estate. I came up here to investigate.'

'You'd already decided to close the place before you got here?'

'It didn't happen like that.' I was getting angry at his line of questioning. I reiterated Kevin's phone call, the revelation that the wolf carcasses were being processed at Ambrose and continued, 'but Leland, Talbot - the men you've arrested, I didn't like their attitude either, or the type of men they hired to work for them. I decided to sack the lot of them and start again if need be.'

'Start again, I thought maybe you're aiming to sell?' The question revealed the reasons for the intense questioning. I imagined what it must look like to an outsider. They would think I'd arranged the whole thing as an excuse to default on the men's contracts. Wages unpaid, contracts cancelled and I would reap a huge profit from the sale of the estate.

'No no,' I said, rather too emphatically, 'I … I haven't decided yet.'

'You could just give it back to your father.'

'That's the last thing I'd do,' I wheezed, holding my aching chest. 'He knew about the killing, condoned it even.'

'You willing to swear to that in court - a Canadian court?'

I was stunned and didn't know what to say. Without waiting for a reply he asked, 'These wolf carcasses, where are they?'

The question threw me off tack, as he must have planned it would. I was rapidly getting too tired to think clearly.

'The carcasses.. yes, they were in a freezer, a cold house beyond the bunkhouse, at least…,' I remembered Lys looking down at the bloody head of the female wolf and lowered my voice. 'They must have broken in, is…… is it still on the broadwalk?'

The sergeant switched on his flashlight and panned with it along the veranda. 'Nothing there,' he offered. 'Board's got some red staining.'

'Get over there.' The lieutenant inclined his head. I heard an exchange of voices from down in the courtyard then an unsteady footfall on the broadwalk. Lionel emerged through the doorway carrying a tray. Taking no notice of the police lieutenant, he laid the tray containing a covered bowl, water and a crust of bread down on a crate.

'Thought you'd want something light.' I could smell good homemade soup under the cloth. 'Can you sit up?' he asked as the lieutenant backed towards the door. I struggled to rise. The effort completely exhausted me. Lionel lifted me up, helped me lean back against the rough pine planks and placed the tray on my lap. Uncovering the bowl he set the spoon at my right hand. 'No more questions, huh!' He waggled his old head at the policeman. I could see the man was going to argue and started in on the soup.

It was surprisingly good, though the bread was stale and crusty, I hadn't the strength to break it up. Lys came to my rescue breaking the pieces off and dropping them into the soup to moisten them. No-one in the room spoke and I ate slowly though it seemed an age before the sergeant reappeared in the doorway. He was breathing heavily as if he'd been running. He shook his head at his colleague. 'No sign of them?'

'None. Both freezers're clean as a whistle.'

'Seems your wolves have escaped Mr Delacroix.' The lieutenant agreed. 'Of course we've only your word....' He let the sentence tail off while watching me finish the last dregs of the soup. If anything the meal had exhausted me still further. Lionel took the tray with shaky hands as I slowly collapsed onto the pillow. Pain shot through me and I closed my eyes.

'Can't you let him be?' Lys pleaded. Through closed eyelids I heard the man say, 'We'll need to see you both at the station sometime Miss. You going to be all right here? See you got some help.'

'We'll be OK,' I murmured opening my eyes briefly.

Denzil was standing in the doorway waiting to help his father, instead he moved towards the crate and took up the rifle. 'I'll be right outside all night.'

The sergeant nodded. 'You've two good men here,' he offered, patting Denzil on the shoulder, at the same time cautioning, 'Best be careful though.'

'The car?' I asked as they turned to go. 'Moved it aside with the JCB, to get the ambulance through. Probably a write-off.' The sergeant explained.

It was an unhappy end to one of the unhappiest chapters of my life. I heard Lys insisting that a bed be made up for her. I was dimly aware of movement as Denzil carried Leland's cot in and set it against the far wall. I fell asleep to the rustle of blankets and whispers as they made the bed up with fresh bedding Denzil brought from the bunkhouse.

Chapter Nine

All the events of the previous day could not hinder the change of seasons. The following morning, October dawned bright and cool offering the promise of heat, but with the kind of raw dampness that hints at autumnal frosts. Across the paddock, aspens shimmered in the early light, but with each step along the track both injury and doubts nagged at me. I'd met Denzil, or Denny, on the steps of the veranda. He seemed to understand my disinclination to talk. We exchanged nods while he waggled the rifle to indicate an uneventful night. Lying in the cot in the pre-dawn light, watching the shadows soften and fold away, I'd done a lot of thinking about the evening's events.

Sorting priorities too, and Lys was the first of these. I had to get her safely home. Second was the state of the car, for on that depended whether I could get her there. The third and most awesome was Ambrose itself: what to do with it, and when any decisions were finalised, how to go about fulfilling them. It was too big a task for me to tackle alone. I was sure Jacob would help and put aside all thoughts about the place until I could contact him. The fourth worrying priority was Lionel and Denny, I had to be honest with them, I couldn't promise them any sort of future at Ambrose. Fifth and seemingly last, came my university course and the work at Sanctuary. Whatever happened I resolved not to give them up.

The car was an ugly mess. It was lying half tilted against the beech hedge, its front end still in the maws of the

JCB as if being slowly consumed by that yellow beast. The side panels, buckled and stripped of paint, would have done credit to a dodgem car. The rear fender, crushed and completely torn off, lay some distance away under the bushes. Even if the car was drivable it might not be fully roadworthy. Any highway cop worth his salt, was sure to stop me and from now on I wanted minimal contact with the Canadian police.

I sighed, and with every muscle in my body aching, knelt down and peered underneath the vehicle. White scars stood out among the muddied superstructure, but the sump looked unscathed. I got in, noting the sharp angle of the wheel where the keys hung from the ignition. The engine coughed and spluttered for a few seconds then broke into a hearty throb. I selected reverse gear, let in the clutch and edged the front fender out from the JCB.

Metal screamed on metal, there was a slight juddering then she was free and running back alongside the hedge. I changed into first and limped the vehicle back along the track, feeling some resistance from the wheels as if a stanchion had buckled. As I pulled up beside the picket fence, there was little doubt in my mind that I would have to spend precious funds on repairs. That still left the matter of getting Lys home.

As if on cue my sister appeared in the doorway of the office, fully dressed but looking dishevelled with her hair uncombed. She was wide-eyed with fear. I leapt out of the car and saw relief spread across her features. Almost involuntarily she swept the fingers of her left hand through the dark mane of hair, smoothing out the tangles and pulling it away from her face.

'Francis, I saw the empty bed... I didn't know what

to think. When you weren't in the office…..' I realised from the slight wavering in her voice that she had been panicked by my absence.

'I'm fine Lys, a little sore in places…Can't say the same for the car though.' I laughed but she didn't even attempt a smile. I wondered whether she had slept much and felt guilty for having involved her in my problems. 'We have to get you home, Lys.'

The look of relief turned immediately to dismay. 'You don't want me here.' She'd been close to tears before, now the drops spilled from her eyelids. She lifted her right hand to her cheek in an uneasy attempt to brush the moisture away. She was clutching some object in her closed fist. She saw I'd noticed. Opening her hand on the balustrade and carefully displaying a small wooden carving, she said, 'It was lying beside my bed.' I recognised the object as the 'wolf-dog' Denny had been carving the previous afternoon. 'He must have dropped it.'

Denny didn't strike me as the clumsy sort. I ignored the comment.

'They'll be worried about you at home, we have to get you back.'

'No-one at home cares where I am…..'

'Of course they'll care about you. Father will….,' I opined, but Lys interrupted, 'I left a note.'

'A note?'

'I said I was visiting a sick friend, that I might stay over.' I sighed with relief, but it was a strange thing for her to do. When I had phoned the previous morning she must have guessed my plans and made her own accordingly. Still her disappearance would seem odd to father, coming as it did so soon after my fight with him.

'I've never known you stay away Lys, all these years, you should get back before he realises you're with me.'

Lys looked amused and a smile crossed her features.

'Francis you forget how much you've been away, at school, college. Father won't guess I'm with you, he won't think I've got it in me, if he thinks about me at all.' Lys was painting a sorry picture in my mind of a very lonely woman. 'Won't you let me stay and help?'

'Lys…. I don't even know what I'm going to do. Right now I can't even get myself home, the car needs fixing and….'

'I've got cash, I'll go to the bank …' I stood beside the balustrade, looking up at my sister wondered what I had done to deserve her and only said, 'We'll see.'

'Then I can stay?'

'Until we can get transport. I don't want father knowing you're here. Besides I might need you at home for other reasons.'

She looked suddenly hopeful.

'He's going to try to get me committed.'

'Oh Francis, he wouldn't, he…..'

'Lys, Father has more riding on this than just Ambrose, new hunting lodges all across the USA. I want to know what his plans are now. If you're back at home, you could find out what's happening.'

'If they let me,' she said rather forlornly, and then 'Of course I'll do what I can Francis. But about the money….'

'That'll wait for the moment….,' I was going to say that I'd still some money of my own from trust funds set up before our mother's death, when footsteps sounded on the distant end of the veranda. Lionel had appeared out of nowhere. He was carrying a tray laden with coffee jug, two mugs and a plate loaded with buttered toast. The smell sent spasms of hunger through my stomach. Lys exclaimed, 'Lionel, how did you guess, I'm famished?'

'We both are,' I laughed, 'I hope there's enough for four.' His lined face creased in a knowing smile.

'Just two, Denny and I, we eaten long since.' he quipped.

I trudged up the steps holding my side and moved to take the tray from him. Lys' thoughts were ahead of my own when she said, 'Francis, can we eat out here, I don't want….'

'Sure, Lys, sure. Can you hold on Lionel, I'll bring a case out here.'

I spent a few seconds freeing the packing case from the bedside and was pulling it awkwardly through the door when I heard Lys whispering behind me. Lionel had put the tray of food down on the boards and she was attempting to give him something. At first I thought it was money, but she was trying to give him the little carving. Lionel had listened in silence then said quite clearly, 'Oh no, missy, if Denny left it for you then the little thing's yours.'

'But…' Lys started, as Lionel turned away heading for the steps. The old voice called out behind him in a genuine French-Canadian accent, 'Bon appétit.'

Before I could settle down to eat, Lys was at my side. Self-consciously folding back the torn shoulder of her jerkin she asked,

'Francis, I know the back of the car looks a mess but ….could you get the trunk open do you think, I want to change out of …'

I stopped her right there, eased myself carefully over

the balustrade, unlocked and tugged at the lid of the trunk. It opened with a slight grinding of metal where the lid caught on a buckled side panel. At Lys' direction I handed her up a couple of blouses and the vanity case. She disappeared into Talbot's room. By the time I'd walked back along the broadwalk she'd already changed into a new open-necked blouse the colour of cornflowers, although she still wore the damaged waistcoat around her shoulders, and had combed the worst of the tangles out of her hair.

She smiled wordlessly, her expression lightened. We sat down to eat on chairs I'd pulled from Leland's office onto the veranda, munching toast and drinking coffee which, that morning, tasted like nectar. For the moment neither of us spoke. Finally Lys leant across to take my empty cup. She hadn't buttoned the blouse right through to the top and the jet carving peeked out from behind the lapels.

'That's Ojibway isn't it, where d'you get it?' I asked simply.

Lys raised her dark eyes to me as if seeking approval. For a full five seconds she slowly fondled the leafshape ornament as if deciding how to reply.

'It's a tribal symbol,…….. there's a group in Dorma Wells.' She'd named a town five miles east of Silver Lake where she did most of the marketing for the lodge. I asked, with more insight than I'd shown in recent days, 'You've joined it, this Ojibway group?' Lys nodded.

'I made some enquiries a long time ago. But after …. after you left, I joined.'

Her voice had dropped at the end of the sentence. Now she lowered her head and was looking out at me from beneath the dark hair.

'Well if it's what you want, was there a ceremony, did you have to…..'

'A little ceremony, I'm only an initiate, you have to be full-blood for full membership.'

'Ojibway are a peaceful people. Has it been so very hard for you Lys, living up to the Delacroix image, the hunting and…..' Lys looked at me with soulful eyes.

'Quite hard,' she said and looked away, her face hidden in the folds of hair. I knew it was all she would ever say about my father's business or the last seventeen years she'd spent caring for me. A pang of guilt ran through me. Somehow I'll make it up to you I promised. We sat in silence for several minutes then I reached across and squeezed her hand. The little wolf-dog carving lay in her lap, a present it seemed, from another Ojibway.

It was already past eight when we'd finished eating. Still too early to phone Jacob but I had a lot to occupy myself. Accompanied by my sister, I carried the breakfast tray over to the tiny bunkhouse. We found Lionel in a small kitchenette. It was separated from the grubby area we'd seen earlier, and thankfully far cleaner. She began chatting with him so I left her there after enquiring Denny's whereabouts. I found him busy chopping wood behind the cold store. Apparently he hadn't heard me coming and was in the act of cleaving a piece of wood when he spun around, an evil look on his face. The large axe was poised threatening in his left hand and my rifle, I noticed, was lodged against the pile of wood nearby.

'You come up mighty quietly,' he said almost in accusation.

I put up my hands in a gesture of supplication and a

broad embarrassed smile broke across the threat so evident on his face.

'Sorry Mr. Delacroix, must be a bit jumpy……after last night.'

'Francis, Frank if you like,' I added, thinking I was getting used to the shorter name. 'Francis then,' Denny said, trying to get the feel of the name. He nodded. We were of an age yet his life and experiences differed greatly from my privileged background.

'D'you know a good garage? Car's going to need some work.' He set the axe down on the chopping block, rubbed shavings off his trousers and fixed his gaze full on me. Like his father he was not to be hurried. 'Sure, Bert Gregory's place in Kashabowie. Old firm, reliable. Give you a good price and won't sting you like some others.'

'What's Kashabowie like, as a town?' He gave me an odd look that told more than any answer he might give.

'Mostly OK, bit run down, and….,' here he looked back across the courtyard to where my sister had come into view. The new blue blouse showed off her dark glossy hair to perfection. She was laughing at something Lionel had said and was fingering the jet pendant with her left hand. 'And they don't like Indians much.' By this I understood him to mean Indian women in particular. Clearly Kashabowie wasn't a place I should allow Lys to visit alone. Most probably Taylor and other members of the workforce I'd sacked came from the town and not a little resentment would have built up over the loss of their jobs.

'D'you drive Denny?'

'Sure, truck's over there with the rest.'

He pointed towards the rear of the new block. A

group of cars parked at various angles almost filled the space. The only empty lots were near the entrance from where the two cars had chased out the previous evening. The men would come back soon to retrieve their vehicles and belongings. I wondered how long it would take Leland and Taylor to get themselves released.

'Which is yours?'

'Can't you tell, the old pickup.' He pointed to a battered green truck nestled under the conifers.

'We're sure to have visitors soon. Best get it over near the house. Anyone turns up we'll let them take their stuff.' I looked purposely down at the rifle. 'If any of them speak to you, tell them I meant what I said about their pay and contracts. If they want to they can come up to the house and I'll see them alone. Otherwise leave them be and give me their names later, if you know them.'

'You're not expecting any more trouble then?'

'I'm trying to avoid it. Best give me the rifle though.'

There was a stubborn look on his face as though I'd insulted him.

'No need for that.'

'Denny I'm grateful for what you've done, for what you are doing, but I'm not paying you to act as a guard, in fact I'm not paying you at all - yet.'

'There's no need for payment. You need someone on guard Mr … Francis, there's no knowing…..'

'Look I can't take that responsibility Denny.'

'I could get another rifle out of the gun store.'

'There's a rifle store?'

'Sure thing. The end of the new block.' He pointed to the nearest door, the windows were sealed with tightly-fitting shutters. 'He fitted it up as a strong room soon as this section was finished.'

I stepped across to the closed door and tried the handle. It was locked. I pulled at the shutters but they were firmly bolted from the inside. I tried several of the keys Leland had given me. None fitted. Denny was still watching me.

'Mr Leland's... he kept the keys up there in the office.'

'That was going to be my next question. I'll need to find them.'

I picked up my rifle leaving him to finish chopping the logs and, to soften the blow, said, 'Denny, there is something else you can do for me.'

'Sure, anything.'

'I may want to get my sister away from here in a hurry, I'll need someone to drive her home.' His face brightened as I'd hoped it would. 'Just say the word Francis, if she doesn't mind travelling in that old box.' He was more relaxed now, the laughter freer.

'One more thing, I'll need to see you and Lionel later after I've made some phone calls.'

He nodded, a little more anxiously now and turned back to the wood pile. I wondered if he would bother to move the pickup. As I passed the bunkhouse Lionel was working away, humming to himself, but he was alone.

'Where's Lys?' I demanded.

He looked out into the bright sunlight and seemed surprised. 'Why, she was here just a minute ago.'

'Lys,' I cried out anxiously, and again 'Lys, for heaven's sake where is she?'

'She can't have disappeared.' I couldn't agree with him. I didn't know what dangers still lurked within Ambrose grounds.

'We'll have to look…' I began, then growled with relief '….Hell, there she is….'

Lys had reappeared from the rear of the new block. She gave me a quick smile but looked intent on crossing to Denny. Instead I called her over imperiously and she came with only a glance at the young man. I took her savagely by the arm demanding,

'Lys for God's sake, I don't want you wandering around alone. You've just walked past all those cars, men will be coming back for them, do you understand what I'm saying….' I was angry at losing sight of her so quickly.

'Francis, let me go you're hurting my arm.' She wriggled free.

'But it's still very dangerous Lys, I thought you'd have realised.'

'All right, all right. I'm sorry, I didn't think. It's such a beautiful day, I caught sight of the lake and….,' her words tailed off. She was remembering the events of the evening before. 'Am I forgiven?' she asked softly. I didn't feel contrite, she'd given me a shock and she knew it. Already my earlier resolution to indulge her was in tatters.

'I need to find Leland's store keys.' I beckoned to the store while stepping up onto the broadwalk. 'And I'll need to phone Jacob soon. You can help me sort things out in the office.'

I led the way into the office pulling Leland's chair in behind me and sat down in front of the desk. I checked the safety catch on the rifle and carefully lodged it against the desk in easy reach. Lys followed meekly behind. She stood looking down at me. My anger dissipated when I saw her sorrowful expression.

'What do you want me to do?'

I smiled and looked across at a metal cupboard set against the side wall. On top were piled a number of folders and card index boxes.

'You could sort through that lot, might contain personnel information.' As she started to sift through the files I rummaged through drawer after drawer of Leland's desk. It wasn't a pretty sight, cheroot packets and pens all mixed up with loose papers, most of them bills or invoices which thankfully had been marked with paid stamps, but there weren't any more keys. I began to wonder whether Leland carried the store keys with him on his key fob. Lys hadn't spoken, she was silently reading through the files and staking them up in neat piles. I cursed and slammed my hands down on the desktop in exasperation.

'No keys?'

'None that I can find. The drawers are such a mess.'

'Why don't you take each one out and tip the contents on the desk,' she said. I glanced at her thoughtfully then pulled out the topmost right-hand drawer and turned it over. She came over and together we sifted through the debris returning each item into the drawer. We did this with all three drawers then turned to the left side. We had no luck. I pulled out the first drawer showering the desk with cheroot packets, pens, all the same type of paperwork we'd already seen. We'd finished putting it all back when Lys, who was now standing back from desk, observed, 'Look this drawer's shorter, it's only just half the width of the desk.'

I looked down gauging the length and saw what she had seen.

'I think you're right Lys, I wonder if….'

I felt into the empty slot, spreading my fingers out. As I pressed against the wood at the back there was a slight click and another small drawer slipped forwards. It rattled as I pulled it towards me.

'I think we may have something here Lys.'

Into view came a small drawer containing a collection of keys, and a slim cardboard box. I looked, thankfully down at the keys, but the contents of the box provided an added bonus. I slid it towards me and laid it on the desk expecting nothing more than some personal keepsakes of Leland. Instead the box contained money, not just a few dollar bills, but multiple denominations, the whole probably totalling several thousand dollars. Tucked in behind the cash was a chequebook for Ambrose Estate.

'Wow! What do you think, a little private stash Leland was keeping to himself?'

'He's just the type,' Lys agreed.

'There's enough here to sort out the car and some....hell!'

'What's the matter?'

'The car, I need to phone that garage Denny mentioned. Have you seen a directory anywhere?'

'Not yet, I've not looked in the cupboard.'

'Could you look now, while I count up this stuff?'

I'd hardly got started when Lys exclaimed, 'Francis, there's a safe in here.' She drew the cupboard door open so I could see inside. 'More cash you reckon?' Partly hidden in the shadows, the safe was an old fashioned sort with no combination wheel and only one keyhole.

'You'd think he would keep the payroll in there rather than leaving it in this drawer,' I said, picking up the bunch of keys I'd found. 'Let's see if we've got a match.'

I separated one long key from the bunch and got lucky right away, the lock cranking open. Inside was a disappointment. Several folders contained contracts with builders, two bankbooks, and a small unlocked cashbox containing some coins and three hundred-dollar bills. Beside them was a ledger with a list of thirty or so men's names and records of pay they'd received. But underneath was another surprise.

I pulled out a sheaf of papers, the topmost of which was a recent bank statement entitled Ambrose Estate. It had a balance of $1,200. On 1 September a credit payment of fifty thousand had been deposited from Delacroix Holdings followed by debits to various builders reducing the balance markedly. The final withdrawal appeared to be a monthly cash float drawn just recently, presumably for the payroll, but it totalled nowhere as high as the sum in Leland's own drawer. Other statements dating back three months carried similar information.

'Unless that cash is for some other bills, and why not write cheques, then it certainly looks as though Leland's been salting money away for himself.'

Lys stood at my side thumbing through earlier statements.

'These go back three months, each time at the first of the month there's a payment from Dad's holdings. I don't suppose…..,' she mused looking up at me. 'That he'd allow the October payment to go through,' I finished for her. 'No, probably not.' There seemed nothing else to say.

'Better get all this stuff locked away again, including Leland's cash.' I carried the cardboard box full of cash to the safe. 'What's that stuff you've been looking through?'

'Names and addresses in here,' she said indicating the card index boxes '…the rest's just lists of timber and supplies.'

'Let's see if there's anything else interesting.' I went to close the safe door and rested my hand on top where a telephone directory lay.

'Ah, time to phone the garage.'

I made three phone calls while Lys alternately sifted files or stopped and listened. The garage people agreed to come to Ambrose to collect the car but they had no spare car available to rent. I called another garage in Kashabowie and arranged a quote. In view of what Denzil had said, I didn't want more strangers coming to Ambrose and said I'd be in to collect the car late afternoon, though I'd no idea how I was going to get there. The third call I made to Jacob's cellphone. He'd given me the number when he'd arranged to ferry me to Sanctuary. I got through straightaway, but the conversation proved rather more difficult and stilted than I could have imagined.

'Jacob Leason….,' he answered abruptly.

'Hi Jacob, it's Francis Delacroix, AKA Frank Dawson,' I said laughing, but there was no equivalent laugh at the other end of the line.

'What can I do for you?' He sounded aloof, disinterested. The phone rustled as if he had covered the mouthpiece, but I heard a voice in the distance asking 'Delacroix?'

'It's rather urgent….. kind of an emergency.'

There was a pause at the end of the line, I heard more shuffling, then Jacob's voice at some distance from the phone. 'How do I know why he's called…says it's an emergency.' Another male voice said, 'better talk to him.'

I could only guess that Jacob was at a meeting. Acting as if I'd heard nothing I asked, 'Is it convenient to talk, Jacob?'

'Sure Francis, how come the emergency - where are you?'

'It's a long story Jacob, I'm at Ambrose Estate in Canada, I need to see you and pretty soon.' He gave an explosive gasp but was quickly back with a question, his voice sounding agitated even aggrieved.

'Ambrose, what the hell… ? No, no, I can't just…,' the words were spoken to someone else. 'Francis what're you doing at Ambrose of all places? Have you gone back to hunting, has your father's …?' He was decidedly angry. I couldn't understand why, and quickly gave him an outline of the past twenty-four hours' events: about the conversation with Jack Michelson, how I'd found the wolf carcasses in the cold store freezer. When I told him briefly of the attack by Leland's men, ensuring I glossed over the extent of my injuries, he remained silent.

'You see I sacked the lot of them. From the hunting boss right down to the carpenters.' Jacob's unrestrained laughter now echoed down the phone line.

'Say that again Francis, what have you done?' I heard rustling and I realised other people were listening.

'I sacked the whole lot, 'cept for a couple of regular Indian guys.' Incongruously, laughter burst out all around Jacob. I didn't understand what was going on but knew once I'd started that I had to get my message across. I shouted down the phone to make myself heard.

'I need some help Jacob, good help sorting out what to do with Ambrose. If I sell the place it'll only go for hunting and ….well I thought you might be able to help.'

I heard a whispered discussion then Jacob came back to the phone. 'Sure, Francis, we'll come right up, shouldn't take too long to reach you.'

'More than three hours I'd say, but I hope this doesn't mess up your day.'

'I'm at Thunder Bay, Francis, we should be with you in less than an hour.' This was such surprising news that I didn't ask who he intended to bring with him.

'Why are you at Thunder Bay......?' I asked but the line had gone dead. I turned to Lys. 'Jacob's at Thunder Bay, he's coming right down.'

'Why's he there? I thought he was based in the States,' Lys asked.

'Heaven knows, but it's pretty good news, said he was bringing...'

I wasn't able to finish. Lys shrieked, 'Francis, look out!' She was looking towards the open door and backing into the corner beside the cupboard. Light from beyond the veranda flooded into the room silhouetting the figure of a man. I couldn't see his face. In his right hand he was holding a wide-brimmed hat but the left hand was hidden from view. I grabbed wildly for the rifle. In one movement I'd released the catch and trained the barrel on him, yelling, 'Who the hell are you? How did you get in here?'

The hat fell to the ground accompanied by a sheaf of papers the man had been carrying. His hands shook slightly. 'Rick ... Rick Tomlinson.'

The name rang a distant bell at the back of my mind, but I couldn't place it and I wasn't really interested. 'How did you get in here?' I was reminded of Talbot's challenge to us the previous evening and didn't much like the comparison with my own behaviour.

The man gestured to his left pointing along the corridor. The movement brought him further into the room. I saw now that he was young, probably no more than twenty. He was nattily dressed in a type of safari suit that's the rage with the younger members of the hunting brigade, though he looked more like a lawyer, or debt-collector.

'The front door, it was open. I called but no one heard, so I....,' he said as if challenging me.

'Hell!' The front door wide open? As it had been when we arrived yesterday afternoon, as it must have been all night and as it was now. 'Then you'd better state your business.' I heard Lys draw in breath but she was wise enough to stay silent.

'I heard your conversation... just now,' the man gestured towards the phone. I still had the rifle trained on him. He didn't sound fearful, just dispirited. 'So I guess you won't be wanting me anyhow.' He leant down to gather up his papers and hat.

'Stop there.' I still didn't trust him. He could have hidden anything among those sheets of paper. 'Hand me those.' I swung the rifle barrel towards the window which he would have to pass if he made a break for it, and put out my hand. He leant forwards very gingerly handing over the papers then stepping back against the wall. I looked down at them; they consisted of examination certificates, the top one made out by Wyoming Hotel Bureau to one Rick Tomlinson for distinction in hotel catering. Now I understood the reason for the man's arrival.

'You're the hotel manager Leland hired.' I relaxed my grip on the rifle and lowered the barrel slightly.

'Sure, Mr. Leland, he phoned......yesterday, said to

come over this morning. Sounded serious. The job sounded too good to be true, I knew that but…..'

'Leland's in jail, he was arrested here last evening.'

'Well I guess that's it then.'

Lys had moved to my side. I heard her say very gently, 'Francis I'm sure you can drop the rifle now, I don't think we've anything to fear from Mr. Tomlinson.'

I edged the rifle down, first clicking on the safety. 'I guess you're right. As you heard I've closed Ambrose. Now if you have your contract...' I said coldly. Despite the man's relaxed appearance I didn't trust anyone Leland had hired. I laid his papers down on the desk and thumbed through them.

'There wasn't a contract, Mr Leland …he said we didn't need one as the work was seasonal, he said I'd be paid monthly and there'd be a fat bonus in Spring - if things went all right.'

'That sounds like a rum deal, is it normal in the hotel trade?'

'Aw look Mr…,'

'I'm Francis Delacroix, this is my sister Lys.' I tapped my fingers on the desk rather than take the proffered hand but Lys was more cordial. She came forward and took his hand, gesturing to him to sit down. He edged onto the front of the chair obviously still unsure of his welcome.

'I'm sorry Mr. Tomlinson, you'll have to forgive us. There was some bad trouble here last night. We're both pretty jumpy.'

'Rick…' he said taking her hand in both of his and shaking them. 'Guess I understand. You're talking to Rick Tomlinson, motel manager long term, never likely to progress.'

'Is that why you accepted Leland's offer?'

'Sure, prestigious place like this. You don't know what it's like Mr. Delacroix. You make a job application with only Mid West motels on your CV and your application's out the window. Might have made a big difference, managing this place. Mr Leland said I'd be given a free hand to run the hotel side, I'd big plans.'

I thought I understood Leland's strategy. He'd hire ambitious young managers, pay low wages with promises of major perks later. If Ambrose a success, Leland would demand greater effort. After a while his ruse would be exposed. They'd confront him. But without written contracts there was little they could do. Eventually they would simply leave, poor but wiser. And if, exceptionally, Ambrose wasn't a success, Leland would sack them, hire another ambitious 'Rick Tomlinson', and pocket the promised bonuses. I wondered how much my father really knew about the man.

'What about all these examinations. Don't they count for anything?' I thumbed through the papers.

'Just paper, that's all they are Mr. Delacroix. Everyone's got them, but the big hotels .. they want high-class experience.'

'And you can't get high-class experience while you're a motel manager?' He nodded and got up to leave. 'Still I'll take them and get out of your hair, I guess you've got things to attend to.' Lys bade him farewell. He'd got as far as the door before I called him back.

'Wait!' I was mulling over an idea in my mind. Rick looked round eagerly. 'Are you going back to the Thunder Bay motel?'

'Sure thing. Another week's work then start the rounds of the agencies.'

'Just a week, but I thought you weren't starting here for some time.' He gave me a queer look, obviously unsure of himself. 'I was coming here next week, help with the setting up.'

'Unpaid?' He blushed and looked down at his feet. 'Just board and lodging.'

'I'm sorry I can't offer you anything Rick. There's someone I have to see this morning. It's important I talk to him before we make any decisions about Ambrose, d'you understand?' A thought struck me as he nodded. 'Are you a good salesman?' Lys looked startled.

'The best.'

'Would you be interested in some short-term work, just while you're looking for a new job, since you're going to be free for a while?' I asked not feeling at all guilty about taking advantage of him.

He nodded, vigorously this time.

'OK but I can't promise anything. Either I phone you this evening, or…..'

He finished the sentence for me, '… or there's no job, and I start writing my applications.'

Lys and I saw him as far as the outer doors and watched him drive away before I threw the lock and hauled on the bolts to secure them. As we walked back to the office, I explained, 'Whatever Jacob suggests there's a lot of work to do, contacting all those people who've booked rooms for one.'

'And paying back their deposits,' Lys said wryly.

'Sure, sure. And seeing the bank manager and lawyers….and the police if I'm unlucky.' Father too I thought, and couldn't wait for Jacob to arrive.

Chapter Ten

As Jacob stepped from his car he looked across admiringly at the Ambrose building and put out his hand to grasp my shoulder. A second saloon car, stark black in contrast with Jacob's red sedan was drawing up onto the open courtyard in front of the house. I'd rushed there from the back yard only moments before at the sound of vehicles arriving. Beside Jacob stood another man. He was tall with a florid complexion. I guessed his age at about thirty-seven or eight.

'This is Larry Carter, from the Wolf League.' Jacob didn't give the purpose of Larry's visit but the man was beaming from ear to ear as if at some private joke. He shook my hand.

'Very pleased to meet you Mr. Delacroix, very pleased indeed.' I couldn't imagine what was amusing him.

Another man got out from the second car. He was rather short, soberly dressed and looked like some kind of administrator.

'Here's Ralph Lyall, Acting Chief Constable of RCMP Manitoba, currently attached to the Wildlife Service, we were at a meeting together at Thunder Bay.'

'The Mounties…?' I gasped. The RCMP man nodded politely.

'You sure put the fly in the ointment Francis.' Jacob offered, laughing. 'I've been working with these guys for weeks trying to set up a surveillance project on these wolf kills at Ambrose. It was the first meeting today and you walk right in and blast the whole thing wide apart.'

Lyall wasn't really listening, his gaze wandered over the Ambrose façade and along the roadway past the east wing. I'd gasped at the news, astonished and too unsure of myself to speak. When I found my voice it was to offer an apology.

'Chief Constable I've led you on a fool's errand. The wolf carcasses have gone missing. I thought, at least I hoped, we might get a conviction. Without them….'

Lyall drew his attention back slowly from his scrutiny of the estate, giving me a long cool look before saying, 'We may yet find them. I'll be seeing the local police when I leave here in any case. That track, where does it lead?' He pointed to the eastern end of the building.

'Goes round the back of the house and into the estate. I was going to suggest we drive round the back. I've just locked up the front doors, they'd been open all night, bit late I know….'

Lyall nodded noncommittally. He got back into his car while Jacob, Larry Carter and I got into the red saloon and drove off followed by Lyall. We skirted the lakeside with its shattered fence. Before we reached the picket fence, I noticed Lyall pull his car round right in front of the new storerooms. Jacob alongside my wrecked car. When Jacob and Larry got out they stared in amazement at the damage. Jacob asked sympathetically. 'You got out of there without injury.'

I held my ribs involuntarily, the ache now quite strong. 'Got out then got beaten up, it was Lys saved me. Lys and the police I guess.'

'Lys, your sister, she's here? You didn't say on the phone.' Jacob sounded genuinely concerned.

'Sure, she's….'

'Right here Francis.'

Lys appeared out of Leland's office. She was holding a sheaf of paper and when Jacob reached up to take her hand a sheet fluttered down in front of us. Larry dived to pick it up.

'Jacob Leason Lys, glad to meet you. This here's Larry Carter.'

Carter neatly handed back the sheet and took Lys' hand giving her a broad smile.

'Seems you two have had quite an adventure.' She frowned, saying, 'It's not the sort of adventure I'd want to repeat.'

As she was speaking Lyall came up silently beside me. He nodded briefly while I introduced him then asked, 'Mind if I take a look around?' He gestured back towards the end of the bunkhouse. 'That green building, without windows, that the cold store you told Jacob about?'

'Sure thing,' I replied impressed by the man's insight.

'I'll need to see the freezer, maybe some samples I can take.'

'I'll take you down there. I haven't checked the gun store yet.' I pulled from my pocket the set of keys we'd found in Leland's hidden drawer.

'Gun store?' I could have kicked myself for mentioning the place. My ribs ached again as I drew breath and turned back to Jacob. 'I guess we'd all better take a look at this. Lys do you want to….'

My sister grimaced and shook her head. She'd had enough of guns. Clutching the papers to her chest she watched us head back towards the courtyard. As I fumbled with the keyring, trying to find the right key to the new pine door I gestured towards the cold store but Lyall had lost interest in it. At last I found the right key but the door scraped on the floor as I tried to push it open. I gave the bottom a kick and it opened with a crash.

The three of us looked inside and gasped. The rear wall and one complete side wall had been fitted with purpose-built racks, shiny mahogany rifle stocks, all bearing the famous Delacroix 'D', and gleaming barrels filled them from floor to ceiling. Along the third wall under a window was a long cupboard. I stepped in and pulled at one of the doors. It wasn't locked, and opened to reveal crates of rifle ammunition. Each crate bore the same 'D' symbol, and the Blackheath address.

'The place is a veritable arsenal,' Jacob offered.

'Not seen anything like this since before the 1980s when the new hunting laws came in.' Larry announced.

Lyall made no comment, his face bore a bleak disturbing expression.

'I'd sure like to get rid of these,' I exclaimed.

'There's an agent I know, should be able to help.' Jacob pulled his mobile phone from his jacket, but Lyall gestured him to put it back and became very businesslike. 'With your permission Mr. Delacroix, I'd like to take these in for checking.'

'You think they've been used to hunt wolf?'

'I don't know what to think yet, there are some tests we can make, say as a precaution.'

'Well you can have them any time you want.'

'May I suggest you lock up the place and wait for my call.' Lyall turned away and was already heading for the cold store. The three of us followed him and I saw across his shoulder that the lids of both freezers were wide open. The buckled remains of a hasp hung from rivets on the one where the wolf carcasses had been stashed. The broken padlock lay against the rear wall. From a pocket Lyall pulled out some latex gloves and a bag. He teased some bloody hairs from near the broken clasp and then leant over the open freezer obviously searching for more samples. The picture of the female wolf's bloodied head came into my mind. I turned back to my companions.

'That where you found them?' Larry asked. I nodded and found myself wondering about his role in the Wolf League.

'A sorry business,' Jacob agreed as Lyall's face reappeared behind him.

'I'd like to take that look around now Mr Delacroix?'

'Sure,' I started to say, but he was looking towards the rear of the new block. 'Those cars belong to the men you fired?'

'Yes, except Lionel's old pickup.' As I expected Denny had not moved the vehicle. 'The men will be coming back for them then.'

It wasn't a question, more a statement of fact.

'Are you going to press charges?'

'No, I…' I began to say that I'd sacked a lot of working men and didn't want to alienate the local community any further, but Lyall seemed to understand.

'Then they'll probably be released soon. I'll get onto Kashabowie, see what their plans are, in the meantime I'll carry on with my search,' I nodded.

'D'you need any help?'

'Best if I work alone, I'll start here with the bunk-houses.'

Just then Lionel poked his head out from the kitchen. I'd seen him working inside as we passed by earlier.

'Lionel, this is Acting Chief Constable Lyall of the RCMP, I guess he'll want to ask you and Denny some questions, where's…?' But Lyall interrupted. 'Not necessary at the moment Mr Delacroix, I'll need to check the police report first.'

'Denny's sorting out some wood to fix the broken fence,' Lionel offered as if Lyall hadn't spoken. It was a job Denny had apparently taken upon himself to do. I hadn't asked him to fix the fence.

'I'll get on then,' Lyall said bluntly, entering the first of the rooms. I left him to it and with my companions walked thoughtfully back to the house and up onto the veranda. I wasn't looking forward to our discussion and was grateful to hear Lionel calling after us, 'I'll make you a pot of coffee.'

At various times over the next hour and a half, while Jacob and Larry, Lys and I, sat talking over the Ambrose problem I saw Lyall wandering around the site. Often he would emerge from a room looking down as if deep in thought and sometimes he would be talking avidly into his mobile.

Once, early on, Denny came around in front of the bunkhouse. He was carrying a couple of newly-hewn fence spars and I heard him call to Lionel who brought out a workbox. They were carrying the box and spars between them across the courtyard when Lyall saw them and beckoned to Denny who patiently laid the wood down and followed him to the side of the store.

Lyall had a book in his hand. Looking down at it he pointed several times towards the car park and listened to something Denny said. Once or twice Denny shook his head. From the look of it Lyall was getting him to identify the cars' owners. Denny came back from the conversation shaking his head, he nodded to Lionel and merely picked up the fence spars. The two of them disappeared down the track and out of sight.

Jacob and Larry were seated awkwardly on Leland's cot bed. Lys and I had settled into the only two chairs. At some point Lionel brought in a second tray of thick strong coffee. This time there was no milk, just some sugar to sweeten the brew and make it palatable. I don't think any one else even noticed. When he'd gone Jacob offered, 'You'd better tell me the best and the worst of it Francis.'

For Larry's benefit I told them of my father's demand that I run Ambrose as a hunting lodge, my rejection of the offer and about the row we'd had the previous evening. I concluded with the strained events of yesterday evening. I also told them of the claim Leland had made that my father wanted me sectioned. Up to that moment Lys had remained silent, now she exclaimed, rather bitterly, 'He can't do that to Francis can he, he can't....' She stifled a sob.

'Not if I have anything to do with it. I'll speak up for you as one of the sanest men I know.'

'That's very generous Jacob,' I said, 'but hardly the truth.' I tried to laugh but failed dismally.

'None of which solves the problem of Ambrose.' Larry had sat patiently throughout my narrative and I think we were all discouraged by his comment.

'It will if my father's successful,' I answered morosely. Lys reached across the desk and took my hand. She shook her head.

'Larry's right, just where do we go from here Francis?' Jacob said.

'If I knew that Jacob, I wouldn't have called you in.'

'D'you want to sell up, use the proceeds somewhere else?' I heard Lys gasp. Somehow I knew we'd separately considered and both rejected the idea.

'To another shooting fraternity, so they can carry on hunting? I don't think so.'

'You could sell it to some charity, but they'd probably want an endowment to run it. There'll be no profit for you.'

'What about the Wolf League?'

'I don't know Francis, the idea's tempting but we couldn't run the hotel. You'd probably have to sell it off, or lease it out long-term.'

'Looks at though it still needs some work done on it before you could do either,' Larry said. Lys agreed with him. 'And we've no money for the work, or even to pay anyone. While you were out talking to the chief constable I found this accounts book with a printout of the guests' deposits. As soon as we cancel we'll need to pay back about $3000.'

'Leland's nest egg,' I said. Jacob gave me a puzzled look and I explained about the secret drawer.

'But you've the car to pay for, the men's wages and what about this building work, Francis,' Lys interrupted, 'you'll have to use some of my money.'

'No, it's too soon to think of that Lys.'

Jacob ignored our discussion, coming straight to the point by saying, 'Sounds like you need to talk to a lawyer and an accountant before you can make any decisions. Do you have the deeds to Ambrose Francis?'

Did I have the deeds? Last time I'd seen them was in my father's hands outside the tawdry apartment at Bemidji. There'd been a scowl on his face and the night air had been blue with suppressed emotion.

'No.'

'Seems to me you need a good bank manager,' Larry quipped. We all three looked at him. 'There's one solution perhaps. Reminds me of a similar situation I came across up in Alaska.'

'Alaska, you've worked there?'

Larry nodded across to Jacob who spoke for him.

'Up to last month Larry was chief tour organiser for Alaskan Wildlife Enterprises. He's just come back. I snapped him up for the Wolf League.'

'Alaskan Wildlife Enterprises, didn't they corner the market in bespoke wildlife tours a few years ago, wildlife spotting as well as kayaking and camping way out in the sticks, that sort of thing?'

'Weeks and months out on the trail with just the bears, seals and wolves, through drought and snowstorm.' Larry smiled.

I mused over the idea and knew it was the kind of wildlife spotting I'd only ever dreamt about.

'And you've given that up?'

Larry replied shamefaced, 'No more disappearing for months on end, got a young family to consider now, twin girls nearing school age.'

'So you're working for the League, at Blackheath?' Larry gave Jacob a questioning look. Jacob nodded in silent agreement saying, 'The League was, has been, a purely States outfit. You're the first to know that we're starting up a Canadian Office with full support from Manitoba state government. It's not widely known yet so keep it under your hat. Larry's my deputy here in Canada.'

'And we're going to need an HQ, somewhere appropriate to progress the League's aspirations and philosophy. Somewhere deep in the country with easy access, somewhere we could be proud of.….'

I could see that Larry was leading up to a proposition

and couldn't help myself. 'Somewhere like Ambrose?' I burst out.

'Now hold on Larry.' Jacob seemed mildly angry. 'That's a step too far....'

The two of them bickered for another minute or two over the siting of the new League offices. Lys busied herself studying some of the accounts book, while I looked out of the window. Several cars had just driven rapidly down the track. All slewed into a turn and stopped near the far end of the new block. Doors were thrust open. Three men tumbled out and raced behind the building. In another few seconds I saw two of them reappear from the car park. They were moving hurriedly towards the bunkhouse. Both stopped abruptly and turned in our direction. They were looking not at the house, but at Lyall.

The Mountie stood foursquare in the courtyard, his hands behind his back. I got up to leave but Lyall began talking to them. The earlier looks of anger and resentment faded from the men's faces, they shrugged, talked between themselves then casually entered the bunkhouse, each reappearing with an eclectic assortment of clothes and personal belongings. One man trailed an electric cable. The third man appeared and was given the same treatment. Later all three disappeared behind the new block and the cars sped away. Lyall wandered to the side of the courtyard and drew the notebook from his pocket. As he did so he caught sight of me and winked. I nodded back. He'd given an impressive performance.

Back in the room I heard Larry's muted arguments draw yet another exasperated sigh from Jacob. I pretended not to notice and looked back at the courtyard. All was quiet now although I could hear an occasional thud from the eastern end of the building where Lionel and Denny must be working. Instead of the abandoned bunkhouses and sordid ammunition store I was seeing quite a different picture and the words of Rick Tomlinson came tumbling into my mind. This time I cut through the conversation. Directing myself to Larry I asked, 'What were you saying about Alaska, some similar situation?' Both men looked uneasy. Larry was clearly embarrassed. 'Well,' he began. Jacob meant to interrupt, but I talked him down.

'Whatever I do here Jacob, I have to make my own decisions, I can't do that unless I know what all the options are and what I'm up against.' Jacob looked awkward. Before he could disagree Larry began.

'An old chap died up there. His grandfather had struck lucky in the Yukon and bought a huge hotel. It was successful enough for two generations to live on the profits. The old man was the last of the line.'

Larry paused here to see if he would be interrupted but Jacob remained silent.

'When he died he deeded the place to Alaskan Wildlife. They didn't want it. But apparently the old man was quite irascible, had always hated the hunting lobby, and put a clause in his will that it shouldn't be used for hunting. Alaskan Wildlife couldn't sell the place.'

'So what happened?' I asked eagerly. Larry grinned. 'It was too big and expensive for their own offices, but one of the staff, John Tavener, had been in the hotel trade. He offered to take the hotel on as a concession. Fifty percent of the profits, if there were any, would go to Alaskan Wildlife. That was five years ago.'

'And was it successful?'

'More than anyone expected, the hotel provides a

base for Alaskan Wildlife operations, and provides accommodation for clients passing through on the way to the wildlife tours. John also turned the basement over to a spa, with clients coming all through the year.'

I looked from one man to the other, then winked at Lys.

'Three months. Suppose we gave the League free lodging 'till Christmas?' I counted on my fingers without embarrassment. 'We could run the hotel on a trial basis, all we need is a good salesman.'

'You mean Rick, don't you?' Lys declared. I nodded.

'Who's Rick?' Larry asked. I told them Rick's history and the scheme Leland had dreamt up for him to run the hotel.

'I can tell you feel sorry for him Francis, but that's no basis for trusting him, especially if he was fool enough to fall for Leland's scheme,' Jacob countered.

'And where's the money going to come from to run the hotel anyway? I doubt if even my savings would stretch to that.' Trust Lys to think of more domestic matters.

For the moment I was crestfallen. My mind had run on ahead, imagining a huge poster of Ambrose with the words 'Home of the Canadian Wolf League' emblazoned across it. 'You're right, there's no money.' I mused, looking round at my companions. 'And there's no point in getting into debt.'

'I guess that's the one thing you want to avoid.'

'What I want to avoid most of all is for Ambrose to go back to a hunting estate. If I build up any debts and the place was a flop I'd have to sell and lose complete control of it.'

'You could lease the hotel.' Strangely the suggestion

came from Jacob. 'There's a whole lot of wildlife resources round here, Voyageurs for example.' He meant the large natural park in the States lying south of the international border, it was given over to adventure holidays for families, right through the year. 'Most of them offer outdoor living, camping and the like, there must be room to offer a more luxurious style of wildlife watching.'

'And Quetico provincial park's pretty close,' Larry observed.

'Runs right along the western edge of the estate.'

'I know a couple of reliable local guides would be grateful for work close to their homes. The hotel could offer weekend wildlife breaks.'

'I guess it wouldn't be bad for the League either. We could offer training sessions - maybe at reduced rates.' Jacob gave me a wink, I could tell he was warming to the idea.

'Training sessions and in my free time I could offer lectures to the guests - if the League council doesn't object,' Larry offered.

The atmosphere in the room was like a melting pot, ideas bubbling up from all sides, yet it was Lys who brought us all back down to earth. 'If you leased the hotel out you'd lose control of the holidays they offered.'

The room fell silent, there seemed no solution to the problem of Ambrose and we'd been discussing it now for nearly two hours. The sound of an engine intruded into my thoughts and I walked out onto the veranda as much for the fresh air as to greet the garage mechanic. Bert Gregory's logo was on the side of the tow truck and the person standing gazing at the shattered remains of my car was the man himself. He turned at the sound of my footfall and thrust a burly hand up across the railings saying in a marked southern accent, 'Bert Gregory's the name. You the owner, Mr. Delacroix?' I nodded.

'What d'you think?' I asked. Leisurely he chewed on a wad of tobacco and turned away to spit out a brown stream of saliva.

'You got full insurance?' My heart sank at the question. I nodded and guessed what was coming.

'Then I reckon you got yourself a write-off.'

'Can't you just patch it up?' The burly hands came back onto the wooden balustrade. Bert Gregory's mop of red hair shook from the silent laughter that was creasing his sweaty face. 'Time I done that there'd be nothing left of the original, just welds and seams.'

'But it would be roadworthy?' I did have full insurance but I doubted the insurance company would pay out more than a few hundred dollars.

He shrugged. 'Roadworthy if Bert Gregory has anything to do with it, but it's not something I like doing.'

'Can you do me an estimate?'

'Sure I can, even contact the insurance people too, if'n you want?'

I knew I was fighting a losing battle. One way or another the insurance company would have to be told about the damage. If they classed it as a write-off and I bought the car off them I'd be back where I started and without valid insurance.'

'Sure, do what you think fit.'

I deliberately stayed out on the veranda watching as Gregory and another mechanic wound the car up onto the back of the lorry and drove away. Lys slipped out to take the coffee tray back to Lionel. Jacob and Larry were still talking in the office. I turned back to the courtyard, I didn't want to hear what they were saying. There was no sign of Lyall yet his car was still parked alongside the bunkhouse. When Lys came back along the veranda she slipped her hand through my arm, laying her head against my shoulder. She didn't speak.

'D'you think Dad knew?' I asked. She knew what I meant. Her hand tightened on my arm. She didn't reply. My feelings of depression grew deeper. 'There's no way out is there? Sell or don't sell, either way he's beaten us.'

I heard footsteps behind me. Jacob and Larry emerged from the office. Larry winked. 'As long as Ambrose is under your ownership Francis, and if you want us, I've decided this will be the home of the Canadian Wolf League.' Jacob patted me on the back. 'You know you gave me a mighty scare when you said you were at Ambrose. I thought I'd misjudged you completely, nearly said so to Larry. Well, aren't you pleased?'

'Might be a pretty short-lived home.'

'We'll deal with events as they unfold. The first thing to do is announce the new Canadian League at Ambrose and put an entry on the website. That should give you a media boost for whatever you decide to do.'

A lump rose in my throat, I caught Larry watching me but couldn't speak. The trust Jacob had placed in me might be ill-founded but here were two men who understood and applauded my intentions. Somehow I had to live up to that trust.

'I have to get back to Blackheath for a meeting this afternoon. If you need anything just let me know.' Jacob put out his hand and I took it in true friendship. Next he gave Larry a knowing glance and shook him by the hand, saying rather mysteriously. 'Don't forget what I said.'

My next task was to persuade Lys to go with him. 'Blackheath? Then you can take Lys.'

'Oh no, Francis I don't want to go, please don't make me!' Lys clung to my arm. I prised her fingers away and took her hand in mine. Looking down I reminded her of our earlier discussion.

'Lys, you know what we discussed.'

'I know, but I'd be happier here, helping you.'

'You'll still be helping me Lys, like we said. Besides it could still be dangerous here. I want to know you're safe at home and I can't stay here for long myself. I have to get back to Bemidji for the first University tutorial in a couple of days.'

'But how can you leave, who's going to look after Ambrose, you can't leave it to Lionel and Denny, it isn't fair on them.'

'I'm quite happy to stay, my home's only a few miles away, just this side of Atikokan,' said Larry.

'You'd do that Larry?'

'Sure, why not. This is my new office, I'd better get settled in. Besides I've already talked this over with Jacob.'

Something in his manner deterred me from asking quite what he'd agreed with his boss.

I helped carry Lys' few possessions across to Jacob's car and had another battle with her as she closed the door. I'd leaned in to ask Jacob to take her straight to the house at Silver Lake.

'But Francis, someone's sure to know Jacob's from the League. It'll look suspicious if I arrive with him and Father will know I've been with you.'

'Then Jacob can drop you at the entrance and we'll

take the risk.' But Lys was still ready to argue.

'You've forgotten Francis, my car's at Blackheath. I have to go back there first.'

'When you two stop bickering, I've a meeting to attend. I'll take your sister to her car Francis and she can phone you from home when she gets there safely.'

I had to settle for the compromise. They drove off and I turned back to Larry who was still on the veranda. 'We'd better find you and the League some office space but first I'll check that Denny's still around, I want him to take me into Kashabowie to pick up the hire car.'

'I can get you into town.' Don't ask me how he did it but Lyall had managed to creep up quietly behind me. 'I was just going in myself. Seems they're about to release your manager and I want a word with him first.'

'Leland? Then the sooner I get into town and back the better.'

'The Kashabowie police would like to have a word with you I understand.'

'Am I under arrest, is that what you're trying to say?'

'Certainly not, I just….'

'Then if Leland's going to be released soon I want to be back here when he arrives to get his car. I reckon he's got some keys that belong to me, among other things.'

'Then we'd better get on our way,' he answered brusquely.

'You coming Larry?'

He shook his head. 'I'll take a look around, find that office.'

'Then you'd better have these.' I handed him a set of hotel keys. 'Don't part with them for anyone.'

I had a sudden thought and raced up the stairs into the office. Bringing out my rifle I held it towards Larry.

'You might need this, as a frightener.' I heard Lyall draw breath behind me. 'Unwise.' he said, soberly.

'For protection only.' I insisted. Larry looked unsettled. He hadn't taken the proffered gun. I stepped back. 'Surely you know how to use it?'

'Oh, I know,' he said taking the thing and training a professional eye along the barrel. 'I also know when not to use it, if that's what's worrying you Chief Constable.'

Lyall appeared satisfied. We left shortly afterwards, turning onto the main highway after a brief word with Lionel and Denny who were hard at work mending the fence. Two of the four broken spars had already been replaced.

'You're doing a fine job Denny. I'm going into Kashabowie with Chief Constable Lyall, be back shortly.'

'You not under arrest then?' Lionel passed a pair of nails to Denny and chuckled to himself. I didn't feel amused and ignored the comment.

'Any supplies I can bring back?'

'Anything but beans and tuna,' Denny quipped.

'Could do with some milk 'n bread, and some fresh coffee, you'm already eating me out of house an' home. Still, there's all that food Mr Leland got delivered to the hotel kitchen.' It was Lionel again.

I was surprised at his words, on our tour around the hotel neither I nor Lys had thought to check for supplies.

'He's stocked it up already?'

Denny was busy hammering a nail into one of the few wooden posts and didn't comment.

'Two great lorries of frozen stores, some other stuff too, just three days back. That's why our freezer's practically empty. Mr Leland he drew on them supplies every week to keep us going.'

'Then I'll take care of it when I get back. Anything else?'

'Reckon the local paper might be a good idea, if'n we're going to have to look for work,' Lionel said pointedly. I nodded to Lyall to drive off.

It took me an hour and a half to get into town and back to Ambrose with the hire car, an ancient Ford. Under persuasion from Lyall, I'd gone to the Kashabowie police station with him. Since I was not pressing charges they agreed it was fine for me to write and sign a brief statement for their records, which I did. I collected Lionel's supplies and a few more besides and made an appointment to see the bank manager. Finally I picked up the hire car from a garage near the edge of town and drove back to Ambrose.

When I got there the two Indians were still working on the fence so I took the supplies into Lionel's kitchen and headed along the veranda towards the office carrying a fresh pizza for Larry. It was already past two and he must be feeling hungry. I'd grabbed a sandwich for myself in town. I was pretty tense, already bracing myself for Leland's return when a figure burst through the web of plastic sheeting protecting the inner hall. For a moment I didn't recall giving Larry the run of the place. I glanced into the office and scowled in annoyance. The loaded rifle was lying unattended on the desk. I was outraged by his carelessness.

'You left …,' but I didn't get any further.

'Wait till you hear what I found.' Larry hurried down the broadwalk towards me, a huge grin on his face, then he noticed my anger and looked hurriedly into the office.

'Sorry, I heard the car 'n was only gone a minute.'

'A minute's all it takes,' I barked, 'You should be more careful.'

'For heaven's sake, I saw you pass the front window. Once I knew it was you I didn't hurry back, you see I've made a discovery, the ideal place for the League's office.'

'Just what are you talking about?'

'Come this way and I'll show you,' he insisted gesturing towards the plastic shrouded doorway. My anger had not abated. I shoved the hot pizza down on a chair, picked up the rifle and followed him. We passed through the foyer Lys and I had entered yesterday morning. So much had happened since, it was difficult to believe it was less than 36 hours ago. Apart from the closed doors the broad vestibule looked as it had done that morning with the main double doors locked and barred, the small door in the partition still secure. To the right was another small door, marked 'Private'.

Guessing it was simply staff cloakrooms, Lys and I had not bothered to investigate further, yet it was towards this door that Larry was heading. He held it open and beckoned me into a small corridor. There was a cloakroom all right with two cubicles but the next room off the corridor was set out as a small kitchen cum diner with a storeroom alongside. A second door opened directly into a long room with windows on two sides, one looking out onto the gloomy conifer hedge, the other with a good view of the front courtyard and road, an ideal place from which to watch visitors arriving.

The room was fitted out as an office, with a desk, filing cabinet, two easy chairs and a coffee table. The desk was empty and the filing cabinet still sealed with the tape often used to transport them. I couldn't believe my eyes. Why hadn't Leland used this as an office? Larry read my thoughts. 'All this stuff is brand new, your man can't have had time to move in here yet,' he announced. 'And that's not all, wait till you see upstairs.'

'Another storey, where are the stairs?'

'Just turn right out of here, it's a bit dark.' He sprung a light switch and pushed open the nearby panel revealing a narrow flight of stairs which twisted up above our heads. 'Neat huh? This all looks like it was rebuilt recently. I reckon this Leland guy must like his privacy. If you go on up you'll see there's an ensuite bedroom.'

'You don't think this apartment's meant for the hotel manager?'

'Unlikely. There's another computer office across in the main part of the building.'

On reaching the top of the stairs, I vaguely remembered seeing a couple of computer screens in a room alongside the main dining room. Larry was behind me as I pushed open a doorway and looked in. A new double bed, as yet unmade, vanity furniture and small couch took up barely half of the spacious bedroom. Leading from it, its door partly ajar, was a shower and toilet area. The side windows showed just the tops of the pines remaining after the fire, beyond them distant hills formed a long blue pillow for the westering sun. The front window looked straight out onto the entrance courtyard. Beyond the tract of gravel, aspen trees wove their magic above a lush green pasture of unmown grass. Apart from the faint but rank smell of burning the room was idyllically situated.

'Leland was sure looking after himself. Hell ..!' We heard the sound of a vehicle at the same moment. Larry turned and rushed down the stairs ahead of me. We arrived at the hall window just in time to see a police car disappearing around towards the east wing.

By the time we had raced down the stairs out onto the broadwalk Leland was standing beside the police car. He was leaning on the open door, nodding and laughing with the police driver, his attitude exaggeratedly casual, but as he glanced towards the veranda his expression hardened into one of ill-concealed resentment. 'Still here Delacroix?' He mocked.

I didn't give him the satisfaction of a reply. Behind him Harry Talbot poked his head out of the rear car window. Leland opened the door for him and bent down to mutter something I couldn't hear. The two of them laughed. A coarse loud sound I didn't like. The cop must have been aware of the growing tension. He got out of the car and stepped across so he was directly below the veranda.

'Mr Delacroix?' I nodded, keeping my gaze fixed firmly on Leland, my hand becoming sweaty and ill at ease on the rifle which I'd dived into the office to retrieve.

'The Chief Constable said Mr Leland and the others should get their gear,... if that's all right with you?' It sounded like a question but Lyall must have meant it as an order. The cop glanced down at the rifle. 'He said he didn't expect no trouble.'

'There won't be any.'

The cop nodded towards the car saying, 'It's all right boys, get your stuff and move out', in what I thought was an over-friendly manner. Clearly he knew the men well. Talbot and a third man who had just got out of the car hurried towards the bunkhouse and disappeared into one of the rooms, Leland remained at the foot of the veranda steps, obviously intent on coming up.

'Mr Leland, I don't think…,' the cop began, but Leland interrupted.

'It's all right Chris, got some things of mine in that office.' He put his hand on the railing, his foot on the first step. The cop saw me waggle the rifle in that direction and rushed to bar his way. Leland only laughed and tried to press forward. The cop was no diplomat, he clearly didn't know how to handle the situation. Larry was standing behind me. I felt his hand press lightly on my shoulder and shrugged it off.

'It's OK, Mr Leland can come up and collect anything that's rightfully his.'

A quizzical rather scared look crossed Leland's face which was quickly replaced by the earlier jaunty expression. 'Won't take a moment, I dare say, Mr Delacroix.' This time he exaggerated the last syllable so it sounded like 'ox'.

As he reached the office door I stood back for him to enter. The smell of slowly congealing pizza wafted through the open doorway. In a movement that struck panic in the cop's face and made him to run three breathless paces along the broadwalk, I'd rapidly changed the rifle to my left hand and held my right palm in front of Leland, demanding, 'I'll thank you for your spare keys.' At these words, the cop stopped in mid stride and shoved the half raised pistol back in his holster.

Leland had not been expecting the challenge so soon. 'Sure, but……well I've a few things I need first,' he said, quickly recovering himself.

'It's OK, we found the payroll cash and the Ambrose cheque book. I guess you were in too much of a hurry to lock it all away. You needn't worry, they're stashed securely in the safe.'

Leland blanched. He knew he'd been caught out. He fumbled inside the pocket of the familiar cowboy jacket, drew out a set of keys and unwillingly handed them across. 'I... I.... there was some money of my own.'

'Fine, like I promised the other men, if you let me have a copy of your contract and details of the money owed you.'

'I didn't mean salary....'

'What precisely did you mean?'

'Most of that money belonged to me personally.' He was growing brazen and rather too sure of himself. It was time I slapped him down. Loudly enough for the cop to hear so he could recount it to his superiors I said, 'Mr Leland, five thousand dollars in cash together with an estate cheque book, were found on Ambrose property in possession of the manager, you to be precise. Clearly it's reasonable to presume it's Ambrose money? Someone of your standing would surely have your own bank account, or is it that you don't trust banks?'

Leland hesitated but he hadn't finished. 'That money's mine d'you hear.'

'Make a case in court Leland, and you can have the money, until then it stays at Ambrose.'

'Damn you Delacroix, I'll get you out of here yet, see if I don't.'

The cop was watching us closely. I made sure he was listening.

'I own Ambrose fair and square, Mr Leland. No underhand tricks from you or my father are going to change that. Now get your things and get out.'

The man shrugged and turned to look at the cop. Chris just stared him down offering no assistance.

'Better get your things like the man said, James.'

I thought Leland's pride would prevent him from entering the office, that he would simply walk away. Instead he stalked inside and began rummaging in the desk pulling out cheroot packets and tossing the empty ones on the floor. I didn't comment even when he took up a valuable-looking metal paperweight holding down a set of plans on the architect's desk and shoved it in his pocket. Probably it was a personal item anyhow. Larry stood behind me in the doorway as Leland retreated along the veranda and headed across to the bunkhouse. Wisely he hadn't spoken during the whole episode, now he said, 'You handled that pretty well.'

'You know I wasn't even sure he had a spare set of keys.'

Larry whistled. 'Still it was a fair bet.'

I grimaced and began to relax. In contrast the cop's attitude became suddenly more professional.

'You want me to stay around for a bit Mr. Delacroix? Mr Lyall said to, if…..'

'No need.'

'Well, I'll be on patrol up the highway for a time, just call the station if you need help, I won't be far away.' I shook my head. It was meant kindly, I knew Leland wouldn't risk any further trouble with the police around. But I noticed the police car only moved away after Leland, Talbot and his companion had driven their own cars down the track heading off Ambrose property.

'There's a half-cold pizza on the chair if you want it, you must be hungry.'

'I'll take a bite or two before I go.'

'You're leaving?'

'Kate's going out this evening, wants me home to

babysit. She'll be here to collect me in about forty minutes.'

My ribs had been aching fearfully all through the confrontation with Leland. Now a pang of fear hit me in the stomach, I'd anticipated taking a rest for an hour or two in Talbot's cot.

'I'll be back at first light with my gear.'

'Sure,' I agreed, suddenly remembering all the things I had yet to do that would keep me awake, like phoning all those unsuspecting hotel guests. But the fatigue must have been showing. Larry saw through my subterfuge and said, 'D'you want to get your head down for a bit?' I nodded anxiously.

When I awoke, almost two hours later, Denny was standing over me with a pot of coffee, the rifle cradled in his arm. I looked through the open doorway of Talbot's room.

'No good you looking for Mr. Carter, his wife came to collect him about an hour ago.'

'But…. I heard nothing.'

'You was out cold Mr. Francis, Mr. Carter reckoned you needed the sleep and I volunteered to look out for you. Said he'd be back right early tomorrow.'

I slowly eased myself up from the cot trying to adjust to the new situation.

'It's all right Denny.' I could smell Lionel's strong coffee and saw that this time there was a pot of milk on the tray. 'Take the coffee next door will you, I want to take a leak.'

I found Denny back at the office pouring out a thick brew of coffee. I took a sip and exhaled, slowly testing the damaged ribs; a dull ache had replaced the earlier crippling pain.

'Want me to heat up the rest of that pizza? Mr Larry left you some.'

'No need. Thanks Denny, you can get back to… that is if you've got any work,' I questioned.

'Always work to do in a place like this.'

Always work to do but was handyman's work Denny's true job? 'You seem to turn your hand to anything Denny, but aren't you a tracker?'

He set the barrel of the rifle very deliberately against the side of the desk.

'I do whatever my dad's done before me,' he said pointedly. 'He's old now and what he can't do I does, if that don't suit you…'

'No Denny don't get me wrong, your help here's been invaluable. But if you were …are a tracker, well you can surely follow wildlife, not just game, anywhere.' His face brightened.

'Snow's the best time, everything white and the tracks pearly clear. Big animals no problem but the snowshoe hare, he's mighty canny, runs rings round you. And the raptors, you'd think they'd leave no sign in the snow but they need food as much as anyone.'

'And the wolves?'

'Now look Mr. Francis, I wanted no part in killing any wolves, out of season or in, only..' I guessed the rest.

'Leland?' Denny nodded, I thought rather sadly.

'After the hotel closed down, Dad had no work and I was scarcely making a living. Mr Leland took on the two of us as a job lot, paid us 'bout the same as one man's wages, board and lodging included.'

'That was about three months ago?'

'Uhuh! I was tracking for them. I swear I'd no idea

what they intended. When I complained after the first wolf kill, Mr Leland said he'd tell the police I'd done it. Said I'd be thrown in jail and Dad would lose his job.'

'You had no choice then.'

'I had a choice - for myself. I could have walked away, instead I've been party to more than fifty wolf kills over the last eight weeks I reckon.' The number was astounding, more than Jack Michelson had estimated. I tried not to show my surprise, or disgust.

'Party to.. but not killed.'

'I'm a tracker Mr. Francis, just a tracker,' he sighed and looked very unhappy. 'You going to turn me in now Mr. Delacroix?' Fear had made him lapse into the more formal address.

'You'd be a mighty good wildlife leader. But no Denny I'm not going to turn you in, nor have I any right to offer you a job either. I thought it would all be so simple but Ambrose has become one big headache.'

'Mr Larry said he was sorting it all out for you, said he was setting up an office for this Wolf League.'

'That's purely short term. The hotel's the problem. I don't want to sell it but I can't afford to run it.' Denny made no reply. I sipped at my coffee and he took it as a cue to leave. The sight of the cold pizza on the nearby chair made me suddenly hungry. I pulled on a slice and began chewing but the food tasted sour. I quickly lost my appetite. The piles of paper on Leland's desk were begging for attention but the discussion with Denny had unsettled me.

How could there have been so much killing without anyone knowing or objecting to it? I'd succeeded in stopping it for the moment but I knew in the wider world my efforts would at best be ineffectual. The only recourse seemed to be to forget altogether about Ambrose and get back to my studies and Sanctuary.

There at least I had a chance to change hearts and opinions. I spent another few minutes sifting through the piles of bills and invoices without really registering anything significant and soon gave up on the attempt. Instead I took the new set of keys and went in search of the computer room which Larry had mentioned. I unlocked the door to the partition and spent an eerie few minutes wandering first through the empty dining room, past a closed door labelled laundry which smelt faintly of washing products, and then into the vast kitchen area.

I found the food store easily enough. The huge metal door was locked but juggling the rifle and hotel keys I soon had it open. Racks to one side held a varied array of dry fruits, flour, coffee, and the like, while the other side held two large freezers packed to the brim. At the back the door to a walk-in cold room, full of joints of meat, took up the rest of the available space. I noted a selection of goods to take back to Lionel's kitchen then went in search of the computer.

I've never been good at understanding the insides of a computer and once it goes wrong I want nothing more to do with it. The same applied to the Ambrose computer. It was a state of the art model with a new flat screen and flash printer but I couldn't talk to it and it wouldn't talk to me. When I switched the thing on it began to purr, there was a swishing noise from the printer - aligning itself or whatever it is they do, but the sole indication that the computer was alive was a flashing symbol at the bottom left hand corner of the screen and beside it just one word: 'Password'. I'd had little classical education but in thinking of Leland I instantly typed in 'Machiavelli'.

The purring stopped while the computer digested this. An instant later 'Password incorrect' shot up in large bold letters, then the screen returned to its original configuration and the purring started again. I tried 'Ambrose', then 'Ambrose hunting lodge' and many more alternatives on the same theme without success. I looked around the small office for inspiration. On the wall opposite was a calendar for the year 2000, its edges peeling around a picture of a snowy forest. At its side the current calendar had the months scored across through to March, when I presumed the hotel stopped trading.

Next to the computer console was another desk, its surface empty except for a couple of phone consoles and a mug and plate with a scatter of dry dusty crumbs - the last meal of the previous manager perhaps. I pulled a phone towards me, noting that the number was different from Leland's in the back office. I lifted the receiver, heard the dialling tone and prompted merely by curiosity, pressed 'redial' instantly hearing a ringing tone.

'Silver Lake, Louis Delacroix speaking.' I gagged at my father's gruff tones, unable to speak, even if I'd wanted to.

'Who's there?' When I didn't reply and silence extended down the line, he asked with an intuition I hadn't known he possessed, 'Francis?' I said nothing.

'I know it's you boy. Been hearing about your exploits, didn't know you had it in you. Are you still at Ambrose?'

This time I couldn't deny him. 'Yes.'

'Got some new allies I hear, friends of the wolves or something, but you'll not stay. You'll find I've withdrawn all funds from the estate, you'll never run the place as a hotel.' I suddenly felt very depressed.

'I'll find a way.'

'It'll cause you a lot of heartache and it'll all be for nothing. Look I'm feeling generous, I'll settle twenty thousand on you the day you sign Ambrose back to me.'

'I thought you were going to get me committed?' The line went silent. When he spoke again my father's voice was quiet and coercive just as I'd heard him talk in meetings when he wanted agreement on some proposal or other.

'Ambrose is our new focus Francis, our keynote venture, you have to understand - luxury hotel, staff following you around looking after your every need, and the hunting......' here he continued with the same old jaded arguments but it came to me, as he was speaking, that I didn't actually need to run Ambrose as a hotel, I could lease it out as a conference centre then sit back and wait for the money to roll in. The scheme was so simple and the irony of it was that my father would never know he had prompted the idea.

'Sorry, I've other ideas.'

'Francis, listen to me.....Francis.....' He sounded exasperated and continued to rage even as I put the phone down on him.

The cold light of logic dawned on me as I lifted the phone again. Conferences needed specialist facilities and modern venues. I doubted Ambrose could offer these. I got the Thunder Bay motel number from the directory enquiries only after a massive amount of prompting but Rick came on the line loud and clear.

'Richard Tomlinson, Manager, American Motel....' He sounded so enthusiastic it was a pity to cut him short.

'Cut the spiel Rick, this is Francis Delacroix.'

'Oh!' he said, then 'Oh,' so excitedly that I hurried on with my news. 'Mostly bad news, I'm afraid.' I gave him a brief rundown of my financial affairs. 'So there's no money and no job for you.'

'Well, it's only what I was expecting.'

'If you're out of pocket ....'

'I got a few savings and there's always openings in ..'

'... the motel trade.' I finished the sentence for him continuing, 'Look I know I shouldn't ask but there may be a couple of things you could help me with.'

'Sure, anything,' Rick replied but his enthusiasm had lost its edge.

'I still haven't cancelled the hotel bookings yet, I think all the information's on a computer down here but I can't get into the thing. It's asking for a password, I've tried the obvious Ambrose hunting lodge that sort of thing.'

'It might be case specific.'

'Case? I hadn't thought of that. Let's try again.' I pressed down the capitals lock and punched in AMBROSE HUNTING LODGE without success then Ambrose Hunting Lodge, finally I tried all lower case, the purring went into overdrive and the screen danced with figures.

'Rick, you're a genius.'

'Glad to be of service. Was there something else?' I heard him yawn. A glance at the ticking clock on the wall told me it was only seven in the evening.

'Just one thing, but....'

'Go on, it's pretty quiet here this evening.'

'D'you know anything about the conference circuit?' There was something like an explosion at the end of the line.

'Do I, majored in it for my last course. The big Canadian companies are crying out for conference venues. Say is that what you're going to do at Ambrose?' His voice rose to almost fever pitch.

'Rick, I don't know what I'm going to do with Ambrose, without money…'

'But you won't need any cash. There are firms willing to furnish the place 'n run it for conferences, they take most of the profit off you, that's the catch.'

'There's another catch Rick, I've offered the Wolf League offices at Ambrose. Do you think that'll go down well with any of these firms?'

'I never had much to do with wildlife Mr. Delacroix. But these companies …..you could sting them for their tax concessions. It's what I'd do, every conference puts a percentage in the League's pot, part of their charity work. Might even sponsor the League direct.'

'Did I say you were a genius before Rick? But …,'

'I could put some facts and figures together for you and come down there early tomorrow, I've a late shift. Might even help you with those cancellations,' he hurried on.

It was time I sounded a note of caution. '….there's no guarantee this will work Rick, and you'll still be out of a job. I can't afford to pay you - not yet.'

'I'll see you tomorrow, got to rush.' The line went dead and I was left stunned at the pace of the conversation. Clearly Rick Tomlinson was destined to go places, even if Ambrose Estate wasn't one of them.

Chapter Eleven

I tried to attend to the computer files but there were dozens of them that I could make nothing of. They would have to wait until Rick arrived next day, if he kept his word. I retraced my steps to the kitchen to collect Lionel's supplies. Carrying these incongruously into the empty entrance hall, I imagined the bare imposing space full of intricate, coloured stands while a host of delegates milled round video presentations between talks and buffets, the guest rooms brimming over. It gave me an uneasy feeling, one I quickly banished. I wondered how Lionel and Denny would adjust to the changed circumstances.

I found them in a room at the nearer end of the bunkhouse set with several rough wooden tables and uncomfortable plastic chairs. Two empty plates lay before them. Lionel was sucking contemplatively on an empty corn pipe, though neither man looked at ease as I carried the hoard of foodstuffs into the room. Lionel simply nodded and carried the load towards the kitchen. I'd already sat down when he returned. In the uneasy silence which followed, both men watched me anxiously.

'How long since you were paid?' I asked.

'Almost a week.' Denny looked uneasy as if expecting dismissal. He must think I'd reconsidered our earlier talk.

'How much?'

'About two hundred dollars, and some.'

'Two hundred dollars. And some, supplies you've bought?' Lionel nodded but Denny only looked down at his empty plate.

'Come up to the office and I'll…'

'We getting our marching orders after all?' Denny asked. I was disappointed by his lack of faith in me, but I guess he had the right.

'I stand by what I said, Denny. I've no right to ask it of you and Lionel, but I'd like you to stay, for the moment at least, until Ambrose's future is certain. That's all I can offer you.'

'Young man like Denny, likes to feel secure, not like us old ones who've seen a bit of the world and know there's nothing secure.' Lionel grinned and I laughed with him at the irony of the comment. I was gratified to see Denny's features soften into a smile.

'Larry will be back tomorrow. He's setting up an office for the Wolf League in that separate suite at the west end of the house. Do you know what it was used for in the past?'

'Just store rooms and the housekeeper's room. Fire got to it. Leland had it stripped out. I understand he's made a grand apartment in there for hi'self. Calls it the hunting manager's suite.' Lionel moved to spit on the floor, then remembered himself. 'Rather too full of himself from the very beginning, I'd say.'

'I'd say so too.' I paused, remembering Leland's threats and his recent conversation with my father. My own future was uncertain. I had to be honest with these two honest men.

'If my plans fail, if Leland should succeed in getting back control - well you won't have done yourselves any favours working for me.'

'Indian faces a storm when it arrives, not before.' Lionel said chewing on his pipe.

'An old Ojibway saying?' I asked. Lionel chewed harder, and shook his head.

'An old Lionel saying he's just dreamt up.' Denny offered with real humour.

'Better come and get your cash.' Lionel remained seated and began humming some tune I didn't recognise. I cocked an eye at Denny. He got up without comment and walked back to the office with me. I took three hundred dollars out of the safe and placed it into his hand.

'Too much.' He tried to hand me back a fifty dollar bill.

'For supplies.' He understood and returned my grin. 'And for whatever Leland's underpaid you both.'

When he'd gone I went out on the veranda and watched the beginnings of the sunset across the bunkhouse roof. Copper coloured clouds raced erratically across a pale sky, threatening a change from September's settled weather. I was contemplating the ugly new block with its raw pine planks and corrugated roof, when images of the bed in Leland's plush suite pushed achingly into my mind. I looked back at the tumbled blankets on Talbot's cot and felt the inevitable longing for a good night's sleep.

I gathered up one of the unused blankets Denny had taken from the store, locked the office door and found myself trudging wearily up the dark stairs and into a bedroom flooded with evening sunlight. It seemed a good omen after what had been a ghastly few days. Just before I turned in, I remembered that Lys still hadn't called. I wasn't overly concerned, knowing Jacob had taken her the best part of the way home, but it gave me pause for worry just the same. The trouble was probably that my cellphone was in need of charging. I went down to the hire car, got out the charger and returned to the bedroom. When I plugged it in, I got a voice message from Lys timed only half an hour before. It seemed she had spent the time shopping in Blackheath for her own cellphone. I noted the number and settled down to sleep as dark clouds folded across the sun.

'Francis, Francis you up there……?'

Lionel's bandages came off sometime in the night. The bruises were fading in tandem, leaving only a slight ache. Now, I was sluicing away the night's shadows in one of the hottest showers ever. Larry's voice intruded from downstairs. My watch showed only six thirty. He'd been as good as his word.

'Be with you in a minute,' I yelled over the splashing water. I dressed in a mixture of grubby clothes and some fresh underwear, rescued from my car before it had been taken away, and hurried down to the ground floor. The office door was wide open. It wasn't Larry's face that greeted me, but a stranger's. I froze. A man of about sixty, with grizzled hair showing under a worn stetson and a face half hidden beneath an untidy moustache, stood silhouetted against the window. He was casually dressed in a corduroy jacket, navy shirt and jeans, but against his right hip, half-hidden under the jacket, was a holster and six-shooter. Involuntarily my empty fingers grasped for the rifle I'd left upstairs. It had been securely within reach all night. Now I felt defenceless.

'Who the hell…?' The man lowered his right hand pulling the jacket close to his side in an exaggerated gesture which confirmed, rather than hid, the weapon.

'Security guard - for the League. Didn't the man tell you?' I felt stunned. No, Larry hadn't told me, but just then the far door opened and he appeared in the corridor. He was carrying a laptop and leads which he struggled to set down on the desk. I was ready to explode and hardly able to wait until he'd untangled the thing before speaking, but he beat me to it.

'You two met already?'

'What's going on Larry, I didn't sanction any guard?' I was trying to calculate how much wages for a security guard would reduce my impoverished resources.

'Jacob figured you - we - could do with a bit of assistance here.'

The 'guard' in question was staring fixedly out of the window at the nearest fire-scorched conifers, ignoring the heated conversation of which he was the subject. 'But I can't afford…., look I'd better phone Jacob.'

I moved to the doorway but Larry took hold of my shoulder. 'Francis, there's nothing to pay, they're League men, volunteers.'

'They? There's more than one?' I asked. Only half of what Larry said got through to me.

'Francis, we'll go outside and talk but I'd better introduce you first. Simon Harrison, this is Francis Delacroix.'

The man nodded across, a bemused expression on his face. Not a little uncomfortably, he moved back into the room, settling himself uneasily on one of the office chairs. I followed Larry onto the veranda and, for a moment, stood looking at my jaded empire. Lionel and Denny were crossing the courtyard carrying yet another spar to finish repairing the fence. The earlier violence was receding into memory. I felt I had betrayed all the men who'd been working there, just by being at Ambrose.

'It's a mess Larry. The whole thing's a mess. I can't

wait to get back to Sanctuary and away from all this.'

'These aren't the words of a man who stopped a gang of wolf killers single-handed.' He laughed, not giving me the chance to answer, 'Let me tell you about Simon Harrison. For twenty-five years he was in the US police force. His parents retired up here and Simon moved his own family here to be near them. This may sound crazy to you, but he'd been a hunting man, until he joined the Mounties' wildlife team.

'That was back in the nineties when people were openly flouting the new laws curbing off-season hunting. He worked on wildlife crime, snares and pitfall traps and the carnage wreaked by poachers who left wounded animals to suffer. Gradually his love of hunting waned. When he retired he joined the League as a volunteer. I've only known him a few months, but his reputation in the League is outstanding.'

'Yet you hire him as an armed guard.'

'If he wears a gun then that's because it's second nature to him, but he's unpaid, all the guards are, people with histories like his who've seen the worst men can do to wildlife, who've come to understand our aims and now want to redress the balance.'

I thought back to conversations I'd had with his boss. 'Jacob said there'd been a lot of trouble recently, offices sacked or burned.'

'I know there've been several incidents these last few years. As the League grew more popular, conversely it became a greater target for some unsavoury members of the hunting brigade.'

'Yet you convinced Jacob into bringing the League HQ to Ambrose, where we're so isolated and….and vulnerable.'

'You can be just as isolated and just as vulnerable in a big city Francis, and Thunder Bay isn't for me or the League.'

'I don't know what to say, when I saw Simon's gun something snapped inside me. I thought not again.'

'Men like Simon are free to wear their own guns if they wish, but they're more for protection than confrontation. The League doesn't sanction the use of firearms and the volunteers are only used in surveillance, as Simon is here at Ambrose. At the first sign of trouble his instructions are to send for the police.

'All the same, I don't know if I like taking responsibility for other people's lives.'

'You won't be responsible, the League is and right now Ambrose is *HQ* for the Canadian Wolf Protection League,' he smiled, 'courtesy of the proprietor.'

'The proprietor's a little unused to his trade.'

I helped him carry the next load of computer equipment and supplies from his limo into the office and there, seeing the man in a new more accommodating light, shook hands with Simon Harrison. After the third and final load of boxes bulging with Wolf League literature, Simon asked leave to explore the Ambrose site. We left Larry sorting the materials and I took Simon out onto the sunlit veranda. Apart from Larry's car drawn up alongside the veranda steps there were no new vehicles visible.

'Did Larry drive you here?' I asked.

'Met him down the road a bit, you've a sort of car park behind that new block, my jeep's there beside some old pickup.'

'That'll be Denny's, likely you'll have seen him and his father, they're out front mending the fence.'

'Indian types, yes I saw them. Larry said they helped you the other night.'

'We had a bit of trouble, I was hoping that was all over.' I turned to look at him. He'd taken off his hat earlier and now stood idly fingering the stetson as if anticipating what I had to say.

'I have an apology to make, seeing you, an armed man, in that office - well, it kind of threw me.'

'You've been through a lot recently, it's understandable. But if the gun worries you then....'

He leant over to unlace the holster from his leg. I stopped him. 'No, wear it if you prefer, in any case it's up to Larry....'

He shrugged.

'I'll need a place to sleep. That the bunkhouse?' The question came as a surprise, I'd expected Larry to stay on site for the next few days, while I was away. Now I could see that was unreasonable. He was a family man with many other calls on his time. I nodded. 'Lionel will sort out some bedding.'

'We're expecting another guy, name of Bill Merrick, colleague of mine, he'll need digs too. Be on site around the clock like Larry says.'

Larry, I decided, was a man of hidden depths - and foresight. I wondered whether he saw the Wolf League or Ambrose as being in most need of protection.

'Sure, sure. I'll see to it,' I said trying to keep the surprise from my voice.

I watched Simon Harrison, complete with gun and stetson, which he now wore pushed back on his head, move off down the veranda. Soon he was poking around in the bunkhouse and studying the new store, scrutinising, it seemed to me, every plank of wood and every windowpane. Later he headed down the track with the probable intention of seeking out Lionel and Denny. I unlocked Leland's office and spent a few weary minutes putting invoices, bills and bank statements into some sort of order for my visit to the bank later that day. I was at the safe, when I heard a step behind me. I spun round, the keys gripped tightly in my hand, only to hear Lionel tutting at me. 'Your nerves're sure in need of some good food Mr. Francis, and I got just the thing.' He pushed a loaded tray onto the piles of paper saying, unapologetically, 'Two scrambled eggs on rye, plenty of toast, the best honey this side of Lakeland, an' my best brewed coffee.'

'How do you do it Lionel?' I was asking as Larry passed on the way to his car. My stomach was already churning as he asked, 'Smells mighty good, got a spare cup?'

'Sure have Mr Larry, but there's only one breakfast and it's for Mr. Delacroix.'

I could see Larry was about to ask for a share of the food but checked at the different modes of address which Lionel had used. Clearly Lionel had a great regard for me, though I couldn't think why, I was hardly the ideal employer. Larry bit down on the words. But he'd already glimpsed the two mugs on the tray.

'Coffee'll be fine, Lionel, grateful for it.'

Lionel plodded away down the veranda.

'Think he'll get on all right while you're away?'

I gestured Larry in. 'I'll tell him and Denny the set up before I leave.' I sat down and rapidly demolished the food. Larry sipped his coffee.

'Simon says you've another guy arriving, he wants rooms in the bunkhouse.' I was mopping up the remains of the honey with a tail end of bread. It tasted as good as Lionel promised. I wondered if he knew the local bee-keeper.

'I hope you don't mind. It seemed the wisest thing.'

'You won't be staying yourself?' I knew I'd no right to make it sound like an accusation, but he took it as such.

'I meant what I said. I was prepared to stay, but when I got word Simon and Bill were free it seemed to solve Ambrose's security problems. I'll still be here during the day, and most of the evening, unless Kate starts complaining.'

'I'm not objecting. I'm expecting another visitor myself. Chap who was going to be manager.'

'You had to sack him didn't you?'

'I did, he still thinks there's a future for him at Ambrose. We're going to explore the idea of setting up a conference centre, but the finances are a bit risky, to say the least.'

'He know about that sort of thing?' I nodded wryly. Rick's lack of experience still bothered me.

'How you doing in the office?'

'All set up with the net. Of course I'm only using radio links at the moment. I made a few notes for the website last night, should have something to show Jacob for the launch pretty soon.'

He got up to leave. I shifted the tray onto his chair and went to get the personnel records from the safe. Leland's five thousand dollars wouldn't go very far after the wages of twenty-odd men and bills for building work had been paid. What I really needed was an accountant - a no-fees one at that!

Rick arrived thirty minutes later and stopped me from

getting bogged down in a morass of finances I couldn't easily resolve. He was out of his car in a rush, greeting me with a broad grin as he raced along the veranda. I quailed, quite unable to match his enthusiasm.

'I was up half the night pulling off quotes,' he said drawing pages of printed material from a briefcase. 'Fontaine's the best of course, but they're not the cheapest, then there's Lorenz, and…'

'Rick, calm down I don't know who you're talking about.' His expression was suddenly that of a naughty boy caught out in some lie. We were standing on the open veranda with a breeze building up from the north that rippled and tore at the pages he was holding.

'Why, Fontaine's the biggest conference organiser in the two nations, and…,'

'Rick, if I'm to study this stuff we'd better get along to the computer room before it rains on your research.' He was taken aback, realising I was serious.

I took him along to the computer office and sat him down. Deliberately placing him before the console, I made him punch in the password before I agreed to do anything else. This time there was no delay and the screen displayed files for hotel bookings dating back five years. Rick glanced briefly at the lists of files and turned aside to spread the fruits of his research on the desktop. But I'd just noticed another file which gave me a worrying few moments. Under similar entries for the preceding years, it read simply 'Staff 2007-8 season'.

I groaned. Rick thought, wrongly, that I was annoyed at him. He grasped the top sheet of paper listing the Fontaine company and several others he'd mentioned, holding it urgently under my nose.

'Mr. Delacroix, did I do something wrong, you told

me, at least you agreed……'

'The hotel staff, the catering people, all of them expecting to work here,' I said bitterly. 'We have to contact them too, tell them we've nothing for them….nothing.'

I pushed my chair away from the desk in disgust and stood up. I couldn't understand why Rick settled back in his seat, apparently unconcerned at my outburst.

'No, they won't,' he said, his face wooden but reddening slightly.

'How can you say that, all these people out of work because….'

'The hotel trade doesn't work like that Mr Delacroix. Most of the staff are from agencies, part-timers who fit in with their families and any other work that's available. The agencies are pretty efficient, they'll have contacted everyone by now. Most will probably be offered alternative work, there are always people going sick or on leave. I know, I've been there.'

I stared at him unable, almost unwilling, to believe him. Something in what he'd said jarred, but I couldn't put a finger on it until a thought struck me.

'How could these agencies know about Ambrose closing down Rick?' It must have sounded like an accusation.

'I called them, right after I left yesterday. You had a lot on your plate, and… that is, I thought…' His voice almost died as he looked up at me. At first, I was astonished, even horrified, at his presumption. 'As manager of Ambrose, you see. I hired these people, knew which agencies to call,' Rick added by way of explanation.

'You did all that - for me, for Ambrose?' Relief

flooded through me.

'I know I should have asked you, but it'll work in our favour you see. We've given the agencies plenty of notice. When we want to hire staff ourselves they'll know we're being honest with them.'

I couldn't help laughing. Rick still seemed disturbed as I echoed him.

'Oh yes, when we want to hire…ourselves.' He stayed serious, unable to enjoy the joke until I offered, 'You'd better tell me about your research.'

'Sure Mr Delacroix, I've done my best…there's just one thing. The chef who was going to work here, Jacques Moreau, he's a friend of mine, French Canadian….'

'And you promised this Jacques the job at Ambrose?'

'He was a cordon bleu chef at a big hotel in Montreal, gave it all up and moved out here a couple of years ago with a young family, him and his wife had enough of the rat race, and…well he's doing all right, private functions, that sort of thing, but not the steady work he's used to, this job would have set him up.'

'Rick, if ever Ambrose has need of a chef and I've anything to do with it, then I'll certainly consider hiring Jacques. Now who do you suggest I appoint as manager?' He gave me a quizzical look, then relaxed, giving me a broad grin.

'I wouldn't like to presume.'

We spent the next half hour going over quotations from the various conference firms. Most of them contracted to set up a venue and take a percentage of the conference fees in exchange. Some would run the conferences outright with no input from Ambrose but I put them aside for the moment. Others wanted varying degrees of managerial and catering assistance from the hotel. They all offered different options after the initial six months, with some going for renewal on the same terms, while others wanted you to buy their conference equipment. Rick advised against this. Projection systems, he said, were advancing as quickly as those for computers, many being out of date well before six months.

There were two snags that I could see: firstly I wanted to bar any possible connection with commercial hunting and a clause would have to be inserted in the contract to that effect; secondly I wasn't clear what would happen if Ambrose Estate wasn't successful at attracting clients. When Rick left the Thunder Bay motel in five days, he would come straight down to Ambrose ready for the big sell.

I was content to leave all the arrangements with him and agreed to return to Ambrose in under a week when I would have a clearer view of my own finances. A third consideration and possibly the most crucial, was Ambrose's connection with the Wolf League. I advised Rick to mention this in any approaches to the four firms we eventually selected. I couldn't yet see forward to a day when Ambrose itself was a major wildlife centre, but I guess this hope was at the back of my mind throughout our discussions.

When I at last got Rick interested enough in the hotel bookings for the current season, we divided between us the guest list we'd found on the computer and began phoning. Those we couldn't contact directly by phone were sent emails. To my mind this was the most satisfactory, telephoning was a soul-destroying business.

Many of the men had been coming to Ambrose for the fall hunt for the last five years, all doubtless keeping to the state quota. Many expressed disappointment, some anger. Even claiming change of ownership as our excuse was not enough for one or two of the men I spoke to. Both were US senators. They became downright rude at not being given enough advance warning.

We kept the Wolf League arrangement to ourselves, though I was often tempted to give them the news, just to see what they would say. When I couldn't take the strain any longer, I left Rick to finish the job. Throughout the calls he'd been more diplomatic, often inviting the men to visit what he christened as Ambrose Wildlife Conference Centre, with their families. A few even promised to take him up on the offer.

I headed through the empty foyer, but a light rain had begun to fall. I wanted some space to myself, so unlocked the main door and walked out into the courtyard, letting the large single raindrops wash away the frustrations of the day. Storm clouds were brewing to the north and I would likely have a wet drive back to Bemidji. Instead of using the Thunder Bay route I had decided to head west from Kashabowie, down through the badlands at Big Falls then south towards Bemidji. Even then, the journey would take nearly four hours.

'Enjoying a soak?' Larry called from the office window. 'I've something you might like to see.'

I raised my face to the rain which was growing heavier then raced into the building. He met me at the door to the apartment, holding a towel, a mock grimace creasing his features.

'You'll need this before I let you into my office,' he said pointedly, so I dried off my hair before joining him.

Directing me towards the screen of his laptop he asked, 'What do you think?'

What I saw there filled me with a surge of elation which later carried me through the awkward meetings at Kashabowie and the long hours journeying back to Bemidji. It read:

AMBROSE WILDLIFE ESTATE
lying directly north east of Quetico Provincial Park,
is situated in more than 200 000 acres of rolling parkland,
hardwood forest, and softly vegetated lakes
This beautiful estate is home to the newly formed
CANADIAN WOLF PROTECTION LEAGUE
associate to its long-standing partner
THE WOLF LEAGUE in the United States
Wildlife Training Courses
in preparation for the Fall 2007
Visitors Welcome
Membership concessions to all visitors to the estate
Guided Tours available

Interleaved and beneath the text was an array of brilliantly coloured images showing not just wolves but all Canada's large mammals against their natural surroundings. Season followed season down the page, with images of crisp white snow giving way to spring flowers then hosts of aspens in full autumn finery. There was even a photo of Ambrose façade glowing softly in the early morning light.

'All the website images will be animated of course,' Larry offered.

'You don't let the grass grow under your feet do you? Where did you get that photo of the building?'

'This morning as I drove up, wonders of digital photography.'

'That's a pretty good shot…'

Unbeknown to us, Rick had come through the office doorway. He stood to one side looking at the screen, his mouth open in admiration.

'Can you send me a copy? Pictures like that'd entice most conference organisers, if I'm any judge.'

Soon afterwards Rick went back to Thunder Bay and what remained of his day job, Larry's promise to send him the website photos filling him with almost more enthusiasm than when he'd arrived. Standing on the veranda with the rain streaming down in torrents, I briefed Lionel and Denny about the security guards and about Larry's position as Ambrose's temporary custodian. They took the news in their usual phlegmatic way, without comment, though Lionel looked down his nose when he realised I would be away for several days. I'd been planning to leave the rifle with Denny, as much for his protection as anything else, but remembered Lys' warning against burdening the men with too much responsibility.

In the end I stuffed it into the empty trunk of the hire car, closed the lid and left Ambrose security in the hands of Larry's volunteer guards. I gave Larry the second set of keys, bade him farewell and headed for Kashabowie and the bank. I can't say I didn't leave Ambrose with feelings of relief. I'd taken on more than I could cope with, that much I knew, and I was very much aware that people were now depending on me for direction and livelihood.

The rain had almost dried up and little glimmers of

sun played on the town's shabby buildings as I entered Kashabowie. I decided, first, to drop into Bert Gregory' garage. He was still waiting for a decision on the insurance. After some prompting, he gave me his estimate for the repairs. Once university fees and rent for the apartment were paid, the $1000 he wanted would clean out my current account. I needed reliable transport more than ever now. I thought I might have to cash in some Delacroix shares left in trust for me by my mother, but I didn't want to profit from the very organisation I was in conflict with. It took strength of will to thrust Lys' offer of help into the back of my mind.

In a small town news travels fast, and as I parked on the roadside and headed up onto the broadwalk in front of the bank, Leland was already standing outside the building. The wooden boards smelt warm and damp, redolent of autumnal decay and the promise of winter. Somehow it seemed appropriate for him to be there. As if on cue he put up his hand and pressed it forcefully against my chest. 'My men want their money, Delacroix.'

'Your men?'

'I've been appointed as spokesman,' he snorted derisorily, 'you hand that payroll back and I'll see it's properly distributed.'

'I'll want details of what's owing and receipts.'

'This here's a list of their names and the amounts.' In a fierce exaggerated gesture he pulled a piece of lined paper from inside his jacket and jabbed it into my face, much to the annoyance of a pair of elderly women who were passing. They cast horrified glances at Leland and hurried down the steps.

Leland smiled evilly as they moved away. I took the opportunity to grab the page from his hands and saw a list of about forty names, more than I'd calculated from the estate papers. Various amounts were written alongside each man, but only one of them was qualified with an address: Leland's. Oddly enough the total owing amounted to four thousand eight hundred dollars. Not quite the $5,150 we'd found. Leland was playing it safe. Quickly edging to the bank's door, I made him a promise.

'This'll do fine. I'll get the bank to sort out their cheques just as soon as I get access to the accounts, unless…. ' Leland's face had gone quite red. He was trying desperately to contain his anger. 'Unless you want to come in now and write the cheques yourself, I'm sure the manager would be pleased to verify names and addresses.'

By now Leland was seething. I'd called his bluff and he knew it. 'Write your own blasted cheques!' he blustered and stalked off down the broadwalk. Talbot stepped out directly from the barber's shop, as if he'd been waiting there. After a rapid exchange he passed Leland with an angry stare and came forward to confront me. Leland grabbed his arm, Talbot only gestured threateningly towards me before he allowed himself, grudgingly, to be lead away.

I was ten minutes late for the appointment and the bank manager was waiting for me inside the front door. It really was a small town if he had time to wait in attendance on his customers. It was obvious he'd been watching through the glass panels. He was a thin tall man with aquiline features but a hearty outdoor tan, I wondered whether he'd ever hunted at Ambrose. He introduced himself, putting out his hand.

'Neville Chase, manager for Kashabowie bank.'

'Nice town you keep Mr. Chase.'

'You're not the most popular man in town Mr. Delacroix.' He ushered me past the bank counter and directly through an open office door.

'I see you already knew my name.'

'This is a small town, Ambrose Estate provides …has provided a lot of work for these people.'

'If it was such a going concern why did it close down?'

Although there was a large desk and computer to the side of the room, Neville gestured towards a leather couch behind a broad coffee table. 'Won't you sit down?' Somehow I felt uneasy edging behind the low table. Considering the type of business I had to transact, I would rather have sat opposite the man with the desk between us. When we were settled, he chose to answer my question.

'It wasn't the business that folded but the man, there were debts and later the fire of course.'

'What was his name - the owner?'

'It would have been on the deeds.'

'I haven't had access to them yet.'

'Well I suppose there's no harm in telling you, his name was Jeremiah Hackett.

Hackett was in his fifties, Neville said, when he inherited the hotel from an unmarried brother who had died suddenly. With little money of his own, Hackett had, nonetheless, been a sort of local philanthropist for the town, but inheriting such a prosperous hotel changed him. He moved back east, became an absentee landlord and started spending the profits, with the inevitable results.

'He had to sell up quickly I hear.'

'Creditors were threatening to foreclose, then three months ago there was the fire.'

'Didn't a fire at that time seem suspicious?'

'Not really, the place had been empty for a couple of months, only the prompt action of Harry Talbot, one of Mr Leland's colleagues, saved the property.'

'Leland and Talbot were employed previously by the hotel?'

'Well yes.'

'Leland told me Talbot was making a survey for my father when he discovered the fire. Rather a conflict of interests wouldn't you say?'

'I know nothing of that Mr Delacroix. All I know is that Kashabowie was devastated by the closure. When we learnt your father had bought the property we had high hopes, very high hopes I can tell you, that it would become prosperous once again.'

'Leland was running the place successfully before the closure, wasn't he?'

'Mr Hackett visited from time to time but, yes Leland was effectively in charge. Mainly he looked after the hunting business. He always hired a manager for the hotel. It appeared to be run exceptionally well. He picked bright, young, up-and-coming, people for the job, always from out of town. Though none stayed more than a year. We all assumed they were moving on to better things in the big cities.'

I thought back to Rick's description of Leland's unwritten contract. 'Is it common knowledge that Leland isn't averse to a little sharp practice - feathering his own nest for example?'

'Whatever do you mean?'

I showed him Leland's list and told him about the five thousand dollars he'd left in the office, claiming it as his own. 'It's such a small town, you probably know all the people on that list - if they exist.'

He gave me a sharp look, took the list off me and rapidly ticked off over a dozen names with a pencil. He had to trace back and forth several times before the number of ticks rose steadily to just over twenty. I looked over his shoulder.

'Twenty six, I make it. Out of forty.'

Chase shook his head. 'The rest could be workmen from out of county, craftsman and the like.'

'Maybe,' I agreed but I saw from his look that his faith in Leland had lessened. I finished the task by reiterating my conversation with Rick.

'So that's why they never stayed.'

I tapped the list. 'When I arrived at Ambrose two days ago I found something there that caused me to close the place down. But I made a promise to these men that I would honour their contracts, written or unwritten. I waited in the office with my sister until late but not one man came forward. Leland probably engineered the attack to disguise his own illegal activities, but now….' I gestured towards the list of names '…. there seems little doubt.'

'Those are strong words Mr. Delacroix, but you'd already sacked these men. Just what was it that you found at Ambrose?'

'Hasn't that bit of news got through to you?' He shook his head. When I told him about the wolf kills and the corpses I'd found in Ambrose's freezer he shook it more sadly and very slowly.

'It seems I owe you an apology Mr. Delacroix. I'm a

hunter myself. Though I don't necessarily agree with the new hunting regulations I'd never condone such actions. You were right to sack those men - though I wouldn't like that admission to go beyond these four walls.'

'It won't.' Assured by my reply, he became more businesslike.

'I wonder…' he mused '…. wasn't it a little rash to close Ambrose down completely?'

I told him the whole story, the handover of Ambrose, my father's belief I'd run it as a hunting lodge, about my rejection, and about the wildlife course I was taking at Bemidji university. Finally, I added emphatically, 'I've broken completely with my father. I wanted nothing to do with Ambrose, not until I heard about the wolf kills. I only came up here to investigate.'

Chase nodded sagely. 'And afterwards, will you go back to Uni and forget about us up here?' There was a wry smile playing on his lips. I met him on his own terms.

'I think you know I can't do that.'

'You've plans?'

'Plans, ideas, pipe dreams, but no money.'

'Ah!' It was a bank manager's expression, expectant of financial gain. Whatever the future of Ambrose Estate turned out to be, he wanted Kashabowie bank to have a share in it.

'And you won't sell?'

'If I knew the estate wouldn't revert to a hunting reserve, yes I probably would sell, as it is…'

'So what is it you want from me?'

'In the short term, a re-ordering of Ambrose's finances, an idea of what's owned. This is all the information I found in Leland's office.'

I drew out the sheaf of bills and invoices I'd collected together at Ambrose. Chase looked them over, quickly shuffling through them.

'Well that should be fairly simple, do you have the Deed of Transfer with you?'

'Deed of Transfer?'

'I'll need a note of transfer from whoever holds the deeds before I can act for you.'

'That'll be my father's lawyers. Suppose they prove difficult?'

'They have a legal obligation to provide that information. I could phone them right now if you wish….. of course there'll be a fee for the consultation.'

'Go right ahead.' I gave him the name of the firm in Duluth.

'This may take some time, do you want to get yourself a coffee and come back in say, twenty minutes.' It was four-ten. Kashabowie's high road was empty as was the coffee store. I sat in the window keeping a wary eye out for Leland. He never appeared. I re-entered Chase's office at the appointed time to be greeted by disappointment as well as some welcome news.

Chase was seated primly at his desk.

'Your transfer will take about seven days to come through.'

'Why the delay?'

'Legal niceties, that sort of thing……' here he grinned,' and one of the partners is away.'

'No trouble then?'

'Anxiety, but no trouble. They want you to go to see them, confirm your address, that sort of thing.'

'Did they mention my father?'

'Not in as many words.' I felt he wanted to say more.

'But he still wants Ambrose back, did they mention he was trying to get me committed?' Chase didn't wince, the news obviously came as no surprise.

'I believe he's been advised against it,' he said.

'You've some other news?'

'I've totted up the figures currently owing, based on these bills and the men's wages - assuming this list to be accurate.'

'Which it isn't,' I insisted.

'Be that as it may, the total adds up to nine thousand dollars, give or take a few dimes.'

'Well there's the five thousand dollars back at Ambrose and your latest statement…' I said. Chase had placed the papers I'd given him in a pile at the corner of his desk. I sifted through them trying to find the bank statement. 'In effect the current account would be one thousand three hundred dollars in the red,' he said, adding, 'but there are also some funds in the top-up account.'

'What's that?'

'A system used by firms with large deposits but where money is rapidly moving out from the current account to which it's tied. The banking system automatically tops it up. It earns a little interest too, not much, but….'

'Leland's idea.'

'It's not an uncommon arrangement, but yes.'

'In his own name?'

'No, that wouldn't be possible, it has to be linked.'

'That's a relief. Well, don't keep me in suspense, how much?

'Enough to cover your bills with a little left over.'

He drew a statement out from a folder and pushed it across to me. It showed a balance of twenty-three thousand dollars. Relief swept over me. 'That's my immediate problems settled then. I can go back to Bemidji with an easy mind.'

'And Ambrose's future? The bank may be able to help.'

'We may use it as a conference centre, I've someone looking into it. There are firms which will set the whole thing up and take a cut.'

'Sounds an expensive way to run a business. Why not take out an assured loan based on the property and run it yourself?'

'I've no expertise in that field, in any case I want to avoid any loans. If the project's a failure, as it may well be, then I'll have to sell and I want the freedom to choose the buyers.'

'Well, that's a disappointment, but I can see your mind's set. However, I would advise you to come and see me before you make any final decisions.'

'I'd probably welcome your advice.' Then as an afterthought I added, 'One other thing you ought to know, you'll hear about it soon enough. The new Canadian Wolf Protection League are going to use Ambrose as their temporary HQ, it's an offshoot of…' Chase raised an eyebrow.

'I think I'd heard something of the sort.'

'The grapevine again?'

'Don't knock it.'

On that we parted. I got in the car and headed off to Bemidji. As the miles slipped away behind me, one image filled my mind - the words '*Ambrose Wildlife Estate*' from Larry's website. The name had a good feel to it.

Chapter Twelve

The journey, through late evening and into the night, took almost four hours with a single stop just north of Big Falls service station for coffee and to gather essential supplies. Soon after dark, the rain grew heavy, drenching the dark native forest that stretched from below the international border hundreds of miles into Canada's wildwood and up through the wooded taiga zone into the arctic. A kind of primeval forest with tall trees which looked black and menacing through the thrashing wipers. I had difficulty staving off sleep. When I reached the apartment, not long after one, I crashed into bed and slept soundly until nearly ten.

That morning I was scheduled to visit the revision tutor, Anna Jameson. She proved to be a woman possessed of a lively intellect and intuitive mind. She had a mop of unruly crinkly grey hair which she frequently brushed laughingly aside from her face and her shortness of stature was emphasised by a loose fitting trouser suit. I would have put her age at about fifty, though I'd already learnt she was in her mid sixties. She was recently retired from full-time lecturing, but it was easy to respond to her enthusiasm.

We settled into a lecture room off the foyer of the main science faculty. There she tested my zoological knowledge, often pulling me up short on particular aspects of science and conservation. But she was kind and considerate, coaxing me back expertly through my errors. It was an exhausting few hours and my knowledge of zoology was in tatters by the time we finished. But Anna wasn't displeased with my progress.

As we left the lecture room a group of young students passed us. Freshers arriving for their first days at university, young men and women newly out of high school. They were shouting and laughing, enjoying the freedom of a new life temporarily without responsibilities. For a brief moment I envied them their innocence. As if reading my thoughts, Anna turned her small face up to mine. Shaking away the unruly curls, she touched my injured hand, and said, intuitively, 'You have perseverance Francis, while you have that you can do anything.' Next evening, after hours cramming in the university library, I drove back to Sanctuary with Anna's words still echoing in my mind.

Cellphones aren't allowed inside Sanctuary's main compound. After I'd taken a load of books and clothes into my room, I went back to sit in the car to check for messages. It was almost eight, a few minutes before the beginning of my shift. There were no further messages from Lys. It was too much to expect her to have mastered the craft of texting yet, so I dialled her direct. There was no reply and when the message-minder kicked in, I left a brief message. 'All's well, I'm back at Sanctuary and won't be off shift until morning, love Francis.' As I spoke, Sammy Kitson was passing the car. He gave me a queer look as I gave my name. I joined him in the reception area soon after and was trying to decide on a suitable explanation, when Jenny came through from the office. She greeted us both.

'Hi, Sammy. You're down for the evening feed run in the main compound, as usual. Mike's already at the cold store. D'you want to go on down?'

'Sure. You coming Frank?' He gestured for me to

follow him. 'See if you can guess how Jude's feeling today,' he said with a laugh.

'Hold on Sammy, Charlie's taking Frank down to the release pens.'

Sammy gave me a cold stare. 'What's Charlie want him down there for?'

'Eighty-Seven? He's down there already?' I asked, but Sammy hadn't finished. 'It's time you let me down to those pens again, Jenny,' he said brusquely.

I couldn't tell what was upsetting the man.

'Frank was there when Eighty-Seven was operated on,' Jenny said diplomatically, 'Charlie wants him to see how the wolf's doing.'

'But Frank - or whatever he calls himself …' this with an evil glance at me, 'he's just another volunteer isn't he?'

Jenny gave me a sideways look. 'Frank's studying at Bemidji Uni, he's only here a short time, just like the release wolves. You know no-one can build up the same kind of rapport you have with the captive wolves. They depend on you Sammy, just as we depend on your help with them, month on month.'

This was not the response Sammy was hoping for. He wandered towards the doorway but as he reached the door he turned and asked grimly.

'Student or not, why's a man need two names?'

Before I could reply he'd disappeared. Jenny looked worried. 'Two names?'

I thought quickly and said, 'My sister has a lisp, always calls me Francis, started in childhood. Sammy heard me leave a message for her just now.' I laughed awkwardly at the lie.

'Good, that's a complication we don't need. Now I'd better take you along to Charlie.'

I was growing increasingly worried about the fraud Jacob and I had inflicted on Sanctuary staff. I wished I could have told Jenny the truth, there and then.

Eighty-Seven lay on his left side on a small promontory surrounded by short grass. Through the green mesh fencing it was possible to see that his ears were pricked but unmoving, the gold rimmed eyes arrested by the progress of the meat wagon which we had towed down into the sheltered avenue that was separated from the main compound by tall conifers.

Here, in the light shade of aspen and larch, wild-born wolves recuperated from their wounds and were prepared for release. Each pen was isolated from its neighbours by a double fence with a layer of green mesh between them so the wolves couldn't see one another. In this way, though by scent and sound the wolves could hardly be unaware of each other's presence, aggression and anxiety were lessened.

There were six pens in all but only a few were ever in use together. A wolf's hearing is exceptionally sharp and Charlie communicated to me by signs what he intended to do. We stopped outside the entrance to Eighty-Seven's pen. Charlie lowered the gate to the inner compartment, just as Sammy had done in the main compound. Once it was safely down, he opened the outer gateway and I could see that this area too, was shrouded in green mesh. Charlie lifted a joint of beef, carried it into the compartment, and placed it in a one-way chute.

I was watching through the main fence as he did so. The wolf got up with a start. From the way its muzzle was twitching he could already smell the meat but fear made him wary of moving towards the chute. Charlie came back into the avenue, quietly secured the outer door and gestured to an overhead camera. I shook my head, I wanted to observe Eighty-Seven's behaviour for myself, not watch him on a grainy video screen.

Charlie nodded amiably and we settled ourselves alongside the outer fence. It was many minutes before Eighty-Seven raised himself in an ungainly fashion. His injured leg splayed awkwardly to the side. Finally he stretched both front legs forwards, then limped stiffly down towards to the food. His pelt was now clear of dust and dried blood and it was possible to see just how dark the fur was. As he neared the fence, I made out the shaved skin on his leg. Suzanne had done a good job. The two bullet wounds looked only tiny punctures.

Eighty-Seven had just reached the block of meat when another wolf howled briefly. He looked round anxiously, then knelt down quickly and tried to scoop up the joint. His strength failed him and the meat slipped from his open jaws. The long red tongue flickered round his jaws, licking off blood. The wolf howled again. Eighty-Seven tried to pick up the joint a second time, staggered and dropped it again. At last his appetite got the better of him. He cocked his ear and listened but the other wolf had gone silent. In a rush he knelt down and began to gnaw voraciously on the joint.

In seconds he had gulped down most of the loose flesh, leaving only the knuckle bone. This he grasped securely in his jaws. The injured leg steadied as he rose and limped alongside the nearest fence, finally disappearing over the knoll on which he'd been sitting earlier. Charlie looked at the camera and beckoned me back to the centre. But now the sky had darkened into night and when we reached the office the video screen showed only dark shadows within the grassy compound.

I spent the majority of that night patrolling the grounds and checking on the fences with Sammy. Equipped with only a flash lamp and walkie-talkie, which crackled occasionally when we checked in with Jenny, we did the rounds in near silence. Once, one of the more wakeful wolves howled long and low, setting off a lively chorus from the others, but otherwise the night was quiet and dark with a slight drizzle falling near dawn.

The new reserve in Sammy's attitude hadn't lessened. Through the night we rarely talked. We took our breakfast silently in the small canteen, heating up microwave meals. Steak pie and chips seemed an unlikely breakfast but at five in the morning any hot food is welcome. Without his precious wolves in sight, nothing I could say would draw Sammy out of his shell. I wiped my plate clean, only too grateful to see Charlie enter. He came for a coffee but we'd been so quiet, he must have thought the room empty. He stood in the doorway giving us a quizzical look, then took a cup of coffee from the machine.

'You two are pretty quiet, had a good night?'

'Pretty uneventful but I think I'll do another round,' Sammy offered, getting up quickly. I rose with him but he snatched up the flashlight I'd been carrying. 'No need for you to come,' he added and was out of the door before I could object. Charlie watched the exchange without comment. Now he sipped at his drink, set the coffee cup on the table and sat down opposite me. 'You two not talking?'

'Seems that way.'

'Any reason?'

It was too risky to mention the phone call so I said, 'He's very fond of his wolves, the captive ones, but he seemed to resent it when you invited me down to the release pens. I'm just a newcomer, perhaps he feels excluded.'

Charlie sighed heavily and took up his cup again. He seemed relieved rather than concerned.

'That old story. He knows how important he is to the captive wolves, we tell him often enough.'

'Does he never work with the wild wolves?' I asked, trying to understand Charlie's strategy.

'The trouble with Sammy is he won't accept wild-born wolves shouldn't have any human contact. Time and again we've found him talking to them through the wire. We had to stop him working with them. If he feels excluded, why it's his own fault.'

'How long before Eighty-Seven is released?'

'Good young animal like that - week to ten days.'

'That's sounds pretty quick.'

'We feed those wolves every day, builds up their resources quick. Soon as they're released they'll need all their strength.'

'There was a wolf howling earlier, didn't sound like it came from the main compound.'

'We've got two more wolves due to go out in a couple of days.'

'Where will you take them?'

'That's up to Jack Michelson. He tries to take them back where they were found. '

'You say they go out in a couple of days, that'll be at the end of my shift period.'

'Friday. Why, what you thinking exactly?'

'I'd like to go with them, see how it's done.' Charlie

gave me a summing look, then appeared to come to a decision. 'Jack's often grateful for extra help, but you'll need to talk to him.'

'What time you expecting him?'

'Friday, after lunch sometime. Suzanne has to anaesthetise the wolves first, then Jack's team come in 'n crate them up. Takes a while. Guess you'll get in a few hours sleep before…. ' I didn't say so then, but sleep wasn't a top priority. If Jack agreed, this would be the first release I would witness. It was too good an opportunity to miss.

I spent the next few hours reading about releasing animals into the wild, I didn't want to appear a fool in front of Jack Michelson. Then I slept for a solid eight hours. After a brief meal of toast and fried eggs I went out to the car. Sammy's old Ford was nowhere in sight. Unlike us students he was free to leave the site when not on duty. But before I switched on the cellphone I checked no-one was around. As soon as the signal registered, the phone rang. There was a message from Lys, made early that morning. Her voice was wavering and upset and she wanted me to call her. The call had been made from the Silver Lake landline instead of her new cellphone, she would probably have a reason. I dialled the number anyway.

'Lys, can you talk?'

'Oh, yes……' I noticed she didn't give my name. 'Wait, I'm in the kitchen with Rita. I'll go outside.' Rita's father worked as a tracker for us. She was eighteen, waiting to go to teacher training college and happy to earn some money assisting Lys. I heard a door slam. Footsteps pounded on wooden slats and Lys came back on the line breathless and almost tearful.

'Oh Francis, there've been such arguments about you and about Ambrose and last night …..'

'Calm down Lys, just tell me what's happened.'

'Dad invited Gary and the family here for dinner. Of course Pamela was here too… she's always here.'

I didn't want to hear about my ex-fiancée. 'Lys, get to the point.'

'I heard Pamela arguing with Dad the day before, he…..well, he's still trying to get you committed, Pamela was arguing against it, not because…that is she said it would be bad for the business.'

'I admire her pragmatism,' I said under my breath as Lys rattled on.

'But he wouldn't be swayed, I heard him on the phone yesterday nagging the lawyers, but then last evening, Gary ….well it was terrible.'

'Lys, do you want me to come up there?'

The question brought her up short.

'Oh no Francis, I didn't mean you to….no you mustn't come,' she said finally.

'Well I'm listening Lys.'

She told me then. My father had drunk several glasses of wine, was topping it up with whisky when the real battle started. He threatened to go to the Canadian courts to snatch Ambrose back from me. Gary's wife Sandra went home then, saying 'she'd had enough of their nonsense', but Pamela and Gary had formed an unlikely alliance, telling my father what an idiot he was making of himself. Gary protested he wouldn't be party to declaring his nephew a lunatic, no matter what I'd done. I could hardly believe what I was hearing.

'Oh Francis, they came to blows. Gary was standing

up, yelling across the table. Jeff and Carl tried to hold him back but he managed to strike out at Dad. They both toppled over and fell against the coffee table, it broke under them, you know the antique one with the ornate....'

Frustrated at her emphasis on furniture, I shouted at my sister. 'I know it Lys. But what happened, are they both all right?'

'A couple of bruises only. I think the fall brought them to their senses.'

'And....?'

'I've never seen Gary in such a rage or so ready to argue with Dad. I thought Dad didn't know what to make of it, that is......'

'He didn't sack Gary then?' Uncle Gary's behaviour was astonishing.

'No, that's the strange thing. The two of them were lying on the floor, when Dad started laughing. He patted Gary on the shoulder, telling him what a great guy he was. Gary didn't understand. Dad kept saying the same thing, then suddenly they were both laughing. Jeff and Carl wanted to get Gary home but Dad pushed them away. He got up on his own, dragging Gary with him and the two of them staggered into the office. They were still laughing as they closed the door. They didn't come out until after I'd gone to bed.'

I'd been thinking hard. There was something about my father's actions that seriously worried me. 'Lys, after they went into the office, did you....well did you hear anything they said?'

'They closed the door, Francis, I couldn't hear. I.. ...I thought you might want to know, so I made some coffee to take in. Pamela took the tray off me and went in herself.@

'Did she come out right away?'

'No.'

I asked the question I should have asked my sister before. 'Do you want me to come and get you Lys, I could take you to Ambrose …'

'I thought you wanted me here, Francis,' she said rather too quickly.

'I do Lys, but….'

'Then I'll stay. Besides, Pamela's been busy today arranging an urgent meeting in a week's time.'

'With the state senators, like before?'

'I don't think so. She usually gloats horribly when any politicians are coming. She hasn't this time. I managed to looked in Dad's diary, it mentions Devil's Lake. Isn't that in North Dakota? '

'It's the first of the hunting lodges Pamela and I were going to develop. Was there anything else?'

'There was another entry, a long Indian name I can't remember.'

'Lys you've done very well, I can't ask you do any more, but….'

'But you want to know what the meeting's about, don't you Francis?'

I sighed briefly. 'Anything else you discover could be useful, but Lys ... when you want out for heaven's sake just call.'

'I will Francis. Now I'd better go finish the dinner.'

The conversation with Lys had unsettled me more than I would admit. I couldn't get out of my head the idea that my father had staged the row to test Gary's loyalty. Though why he'd done it, I couldn't fathom. Even with

Lys there, the goings-on at Silver Lake would have to remain a mystery for the time being. Thirty minutes remained until the start of the shift. I badly needed a coffee, but wasn't inclined to talk to anyone, much less Sammy who had just driven into the compound. I dialled Rick at Thunder Bay.

'Hi, where are you?' he gasped, obviously in a hurry.

'Bitter Springs, I won't be back for a few days.'

'That's a shame. Already got two firms coming down to view Ambrose on Thursday, they couldn't resist those photos I sent them.'

'You'll be there to show them round, can you handle it?'

'No problem. Look I'd better go, trouble with some guests.'

'Rick, we're going to want full specs before we consider any proposals,' I cautioned.

'No trouble Francis, I've already explained the set up. Got to go, speak to you soon.'

I went in search of coffee, regardless of who might be in the canteen. I needn't have worried, the place was empty. I was on my second cup when Charlie came to fetch me to the release pens. Eighty-Seven was asleep on his grassy knoll when we approached. It might have been my imagination but his reactions seemed faster, his leg less stiff than the night before. Charlie placed the meat in the pen. The wolf stirred, eyed the ration, and made his way slowly down the field. I felt sad that this wild animal had become dependent so quickly.

In two days time, another pair of recuperating wolves would be released. Over the following days I intended to watch Eighty-Seven fight his way back to health. And shift or no shift, I meant to be present at his release.

What I hadn't been able to do for Speed at Pelican Lake or Yarka at Ely, I would do with a full heart for the wolf named Eighty-Seven.

My shifts, that day and the next, blended into one. There were no more unsettling calls from Lys and no further contact with Rick. I let Ambrose and Silver Lake melt into the background of my life and pursued the process of familiarisation with the wolves. Between patrols with Sammy who remained as taciturn as before, I was glad to spend long sessions with Jenny viewing videos of wolves that had passed through Sanctuary. She was a good teacher. I learned as much from her as from watching the wolves themselves and Friday morning arrived too soon for me. I ate a hurried breakfast, spent a couple of hours studying until the text began to blur, then laid my head on the pillow.

I thought I was too keyed-up to sleep, but soon Charlie was knocking indignantly on my door. It was already late afternoon. Sanctuary's quiet routine had been replaced by bustle and excitement. Suzanne's car trundled into the compound closely followed by two open-backed 4x4s, the first driven by Jack Michelson. The three men he'd brought with him scrambled into the back of his vehicle and wrestled a pair of large crates onto the gravel. These were sturdily built with wooden supports and strong metal sides you could see through. All three men were dressed in the drab green of the Minnesota Wildlife Patrol.

My assistance wasn't needed. I stood back against the office wall as Charlie and Jack discussed the practicalities of the release with Suzanne. At last, I heard my name mentioned. Charlie's gaze darted between Jack and the vet. Eventually Jack looked across at me, his eyes dark beneath the stetson. He nodded briefly and I knew I would be part of the release team. Unreasonably happy, I followed them down towards the pens.

Jack carried a rifle adapted to fire darts to anaesthetise the wolves. We passed Eighty-Seven's pen and came to a halt further down the slope. As Charlie wound down the inner gate we all looked through the green mesh, searching for the wolf. Suzanne saw her first. She was lying half-hidden in the rough grass against the left hand fence. A female with dusky-coloured body and dark head. The dark pointed ears were pricked, her golden eyes ranged along the fence.

Jack parted an overlapping portion of the green filament and took aim with his rifle. Several seconds passed before the rifle snapped and the dart with its coloured ID tassel plunged into the wolf's left thigh. The animal yelped and leapt up on all fours. She spun round, feverishly biting at her haunches, searching out the source of the pain. Her head was dramatically lowered, her tail pressed down beneath her belly. The spasm lasted perhaps a few seconds, then she ran frantically along the fence bushing her left side against it trying to dislodge the dart but the coloured feathery end remained in full view. After a few seconds she collapsed and stopped moving.

We left her there for the moment and went on to the second cage repeating the procedure with a sandy-coloured male wolf who proved less resistant to the drug. He went down in under three seconds. Jack summoned his teams. Suzanne inserted an identity chip in the neck of each wolf, took blood samples and proclaimed the wolves ready for release. We wrapped the wolves in blankets and placed each one in a crate, all the while working in silence. As we passed Eighty-Seven's pen on the way out, I made him a silent promise, 'Your turn next'.

The crates were hoisted into the back of the two vehicles and covered over with blankets. Jack invited me in the cab beside himself and another man, David Lawrence. I asked Jack where we were headed but he wouldn't say, just drove off in his usual taciturn manner. It was left to David and myself to make conversation. He was a tall man, about thirty years of age. When I learned he was a trained wildlife biologist, I badly wanted to ask his advice about Ambrose but, for a Delacroix, this was a taboo area. I felt easier talking about my studies at Bemidji and the work at Sanctuary. When he asked my name so he could follow my progress, I stumbled over the reply. Frank Dawson, I said, wondering how long I could keep up the pretence.

Suzanne's car was ahead of us. Jack followed as she turned west towards Baudette. I guessed we were heading towards Lake of the Woods but in another hour we passed the main entrance to the park and continued towards the border. At Warroad we turned off the main highway into Lost River State Forest. It was over two hours since we'd left Sanctuary.

We bumped down an unmade forest track for another twenty minutes and when I looked into the back of our vehicle I saw that the blanket had come loose and the female wolf was stirring in her crate. She was half-crouched, the golden eyes bewildered by unfamiliar surroundings. The track narrowed and became overgrown, further progress was impossible. We drew in under the overhanging branches of an aspen. Suzanne jumped from her car to check on the wolves. When she nodded, Jack announced wryly. 'Just another two hundred yards, lads.'

After some light-hearted groans we lowered the crates to the ground and lugged them into the forest, hauling and pulling them over fallen logs and across streambeds slippery with sphagnum moss. It was past seven and getting on for dusk when Jack called a halt. We laid the crates down awkwardly on the uneven forest floor. Jack was carrying a rifle, a lethal one this time.

'Are the wolves dangerous? I asked.

He shook his head. 'Have to carry it. Regulations.'

He glanced at his watch.

'We give the female a couple of minutes start Suzanne?'

'That'll be about right.'

It occurred to me to ask why two unrelated animals should be released together. 'They probably are related,' Suzanne answered. 'They were injured within a day of each other on that stretch of road back there.'

'Accidents?'

'Or someone giving chase. Wolves often follow the same route across roadways in their territory.'

'But running them down - is that possible?'

'If someone hates wolves badly enough, yes it's possible.'

She turned away and instructed us to stand out of sight. The doors were positioned facing into bushes less than three feet away. She pulled on the door until it was fully open. Apart from the wind rustling the trees above us, there was utter silence. Then came a mad scramble, claws rasped against the wooden floor of the crate and the wolf shot from the doorway in a blur of dark fur. The bushes in front of the crate parted, shook and came together again. That was all there was. No warning growl. No bark of fear. No thanks. Only a wild animal slipping without a backward glance into its natural home. It was such an anticlimax that we were stunned into silence. A lump rose in my throat and foolish tears started in my eyes. I looked around at the other men with me. All hardened in the ways of wildlife, they were in much the same state. I laughed through my tears and wondered if I would ever get used to the sudden surge of emotion, or the inevitable emptiness which followed.

'Better release the male,' Jack said.

When Jack drove back to Sanctuary it was past ten so I spent the night there sleeping fitfully and listening to the tall conifers rustling irritably under a changeable autumnal sky. Occasionally a wolf howled, the sound long and low in the darkness. When dawn broke I would have liked nothing better than to wander down among the wolf pens and watch the animals moving through the early light. The day was calm and dry, promising warmth. It was ideal too, for walking in the shadowy forest surrounding Sanctuary, which I'd yet to explore. Instead, I forced myself into the car and turned it with a heavy heart towards Ambrose. The place had brought me nothing but trouble and worry, and threatened to stay that way for some time. As I took the northern route past International Falls retracing my journey of five days ago, I couldn't shake off the notion that I should rid myself of Ambrose altogether. By the time I was passing Quetico I'd finally made up my mind. I would get a buyer who would respect Ambrose as a wildlife refuge, maybe one who would even accept the Wolf League as a tenant. If I did, this might be the last time I drove there.

But Ambrose was not to be cast off so lightly. It still held a few surprises. The first was a garish notice hoisted high over the gravel trackway. It read 'Canadian Wolf Protection League Welcomes You to *Ambrose Wolf Day*: *Sunday 8 October*'. Sunday was next day. Unsettled, I continued down the aspen-lined track, noticing how their leaves had been transformed from modest greens and yellows into rainbows of gold and copper-bronze that flickered in the sunlight and sent kaleidoscopes of colour down onto the long grass beneath.

I opened the car window. A light breeze moved the tree tops, red-encrusted aspen leaves fluttered down over the car. The gravel too blazed with colour, not from the aspens but from a scatter of brightly illustrated posters pinned to several tall wooden posts. They danced and fluttered in the breeze. The posters closest to the entrance repeated the welcome motif but beneath each one there was a different illustration: some featured groups of wolves, some portrait-like images, others packs of wolves hunting moose.

I'd intended to drive to the back of the house, but three other cars, two saloons and a dark people-carrier, were parked in front. Curiosity made me pull up beside the nearest vehicle. It was a new model, bright green with a flourish to its looks that made me think one of Rick's contacts must be visiting. Still, Saturday seemed an odd day to view the property. Both sets of double doors stood open to the air. I walked up the steps into the left-hand foyer and was greeted by further surprises.

Light and colour filled the ten square yard space: bright multi-textured stands plastered with posters and information snippets, paraded across the wooden floor; nestling among them and piled high with leaflets, stacks of paper and pencils, were groups of plastic tables and chairs. But close by the entrance, so that the eye was immediately drawn to it, was a diorama designed to transfix and amaze. It was a huge board depicting a bull moose galloping through a tapestry of forest and meadow; beside the image, on a mound of imitation turf and apparently pacing alongside the moose, were three, very life-like, mounted wolves.

Expertly prepared, the three wolves appeared to leap forward with a bounding gait. There was nothing in the lithe curve of their bodies to suggest anything other than life and vigour. I gasped involuntarily. A female voice behind me echoed my thoughts.

'Hard to believe they're not alive isn't it?'

I spun round. Emerging from between two temporary stands was a woman I didn't recognise. She was about thirty with brown hair cut in a stylish bob. She wore a city suit and a brightly-patterned blouse which emphasised the healthy glow of her skin. Sensible flat shoes completed the picture.

'You're early for our Wolf Day but you're welcome to look around,' she said, an amused smile on her lips. She looked through the open doors, obviously searching for my car. The people carrier hid it from view. 'Bring your children in? There's plenty to see.'

'No children, and I didn't come …' I noticed a name tag on her lapel, it bore the Logo of a leaping wolf but she was too far away for me to read the writing. 'You're with the Wolf League?'

She looked mildly embarrassed. 'I'm sorry, I should have said. Avril Saunders, Education Officer, if there's anything….'

She was interrupted by a loud clatter and some shouts from behind the partition wall. I didn't understand what was going on at Ambrose. Suddenly I wanted to know where Larry was, and cut her off abruptly.

'Where's Larry?'

Her eyes widened. She searched my face and asked, 'Who are you?'

'I own this place - for my sins.' I put out my hand then quickly withdrew it as further crashes rang out. 'Frank…that is Francis Delacroix, and I'd like to know what the hell's going on round here?'

I expected some form of apology, instead Avril beamed at me disconcertingly. A look, almost of worship, played across her features.

'Mr Delacroix? Oh, I'm so pleased to meet you. Larry's told us what you did for the wolves. He said you might be along this weekend.' It would have been churlish not to take the proffered hand. Her palm was cool and dry, her grip light but determined. 'And you needn't worry, Rick and his friend are preparing food for tomorrow.'

All this was news to me. 'Well there's a lot here I don't understand Avril.' She still had hold of my hand as if trying to distract me.

'Didn't Larry phone you Mr Delacroix, he promised….?'

'It's Francis, and no he didn't, but,...' I pulled out my cellphone, I'd turned it off during the wolves' release. I switched it on and waited for it to register. There were no messages.

'It's been off for a while.'

Avril gave a small sigh. 'Admin's not Larry's strong point, out in the field that's another matter.' It was said with resignation.

'You've known him a long time?'

'A group of us spent our college summers helping Larry with his surveys in Alaska.' I tried to picture a younger Avril wearing cagoule and jeans camping with other college students. It was an image which didn't sit easily with the stylish woman before me.

'What were you studying?' It was the natural question to ask. The answer surprised me.

'I majored in animal behaviour, though you'd never think it now.'

She gestured towards the tiny office behind her. 'Would you like to sit down? I guess in Larry's absence you're due an explanation.'

'Couldn't we talk outside, I need to find Rick.'

We moved out through the double doors and loitered in the late morning sunlight as Avril began to speak. Together she and Larry had set up their new website depicting the Canadian Wolf Protection League's new headquarters at Ambrose. Enquiries didn't exactly flood in so they decided to organise an open day on Sunday though they'd known an event fixed at such short notice would be unlikely to attract many people.

Then Larry's wife landed a bombshell. She was a teacher at the same junior school their children attended. The school's outing to the zoo at Thunder Bay scheduled for Sunday had been cancelled at short notice. In order not to disappoint the children, Larry switched the venue to Ambrose. League personnel had gone into overdrive arranging events for forty junior school pupils.

Face-painting sessions, treasure hunts and other competitions had been organised and when Rick arrived that Friday morning he was presented with an order for forty-plus burgers, chips and hot chocolate. In a short space of time he had called Jacques Moreau and was now setting up the kitchen. As we came level with the second doorway, Avril explained that Lionel and Denny were arranging nature trails and pond-dipping around the lake. Minibuses had been hired for the day in which Simon Harrison and Bill Merrick would ferry groups to a wildlife campfire. Other League volunteers would shepherd children around.

As Avril concluded her list of activities, a large open-backed lorry drove out from the lake road and shuddered to a halt. The cab window was open. The driver waved happily at my companion, yelling, 'All set up Avril, be back prompt Monday morning.'

'Can't thank you enough Martin,' Avril called back, equally relaxed.

'All set up?' I queried, as the lorry accelerated away.

'They've been setting up a yurt at Pearl Lake.'

'Could you say that in English.'

'They've put up a yurt - it's a kind of skin tent, for the campfire. The children are only young, they have to have somewhere to shelter.'

'But that lake, are you taking the kids down at Quetico?'

Avril glanced at me curiously. 'Larry found some old plans of the place. All the lakes have names, we've used them for the Open Day. Pearl Lake is only a few miles away, there's a jetty and….,' Avril must have noticed my eyes glazing over. 'Don't you know your own place?'

I felt control of Ambrose was slipping away from me.

Unable to restrain my anger, I replied, 'No I don't. I arrived here today intending to sell the place.' Avril's face paled, she bit her lip and asked, 'You don't mean that, surely?'

'I don't know what I mean any more, Avril!'

Ambrose had become like a galloping horse. I couldn't guess what repercussions might follow if I decided to pull on the reins. I turned through the doors and went in search of Rick. I found him, not in the kitchen where the bare work surfaces had disappeared under a jumble of plates and food baskets, but in the dining room, setting out lines of trestles tables and covering them with oil proof sheets. In the depths of the unlit room, I saw that the usual dining room furniture, the elegant chairs and tables, had been stacked along the outer wall. Instead a series of low wooden benches were scattered across what now seemed a vast space.

A lot of work and organisation had gone into this transformation and I began to experience a grudging admiration for Avril. For a moment I stood in the doorway, silently watching as Rick set out the tables. Working alongside him and talking half in French, half in English, was another man dressed in a chef's white jacket over old blue jeans. He was short and squat but had a jaunty air about him. Rick finished arranging the tables. He reached into a trolley and brought out sauce bottles and serviettes.

'No Rick. Pàs là-bas, ici, only at the end, we will be serving this side,' the chef directed Rick towards the furthest trestle.

'But won't we be serving at the tables?'

The chef shook his head sagely and watched as Rick picked up one of the sauce bottles and tossed it to and fro between his hands like a tennis ball.

'For heaven's sake, Jacques you're not at the Hilton…..'

In spite of myself I couldn't help laughing at Rick's expression. He heard the laugh and peered through the shadows in my direction. Surprise broadened into recognition. He slammed the bottle down on the tabletop where it rolled to the edge and threatened to topple over. Racing around the table, Rick caught the bottle then thrust out his hand.

'Mr Delacroix, am I glad to see you. I've got so much to tell you.'

He twisted sideways to place the bottle back on the tabletop. I took his hand in friendship trying to keep the reserve in my voice. 'Good to see you Rick.'

He studied my face, struggling to contain his native enthusiasm.

'I've got everything set up in the office, that is if you…..'

'Can you be spared, looks like tomorrow's a big day?' I spoke without intended irony yet it was there on my lips and in my heart.

'I'm sure Jacques can cope without my help,' Rick said, rather too eager to be free of Jacques' tyranny. They appeared close friends, but it's a brave man who disagrees with a chef.

'I will get on very well without you, my friend.' The man responded in a deep long drawn out phrase, his accent so thick he might actually have been speaking French. 'Although you must first introduce me,' he spoke with the arrogance of a man very much aware of his own worth.

'I'm sorry, this is…' I could tell Rick was about to

introduce Jacques first, then he thought better of it, 'Jacques this is Mr Delacroix, he owns Ambrose.'

'Pleased to meet you Mr....,' I paused and Rick interceded rather anxiously. 'Moreau. You remember Mr. Delacroix, I mentioned....,' I gave Rick a warning look. I didn't want to discuss my affairs in front of this man and manoeuvred the subject away from dangerous ground.

'Tell me about tomorrow, what are you planning?'

Both men spoke together.

'Jacques is cooking, there'll be........'

'.....food for forty children, maybe more if we count the parents.'

'Did you find enough food in the store?' I directed the question to Rick but it was Jacques who replied.

'The Wolf League has been very generous Mr Delacroix, but we are certainly grateful for the services of your freezer and kitchen.'

'The Wolf League are paying for everything are they, including your salary?' I glanced over at Rick warning him to remain quiet. I wanted to know from Jacques' own lips what arrangements had been made about his fee.

'But Mr Delacroix, I am happy to do this for Rick, and for the children. 'Zere *is* no salary to pay.' His accent was more marked than ever.

'And he's made you no other promises, about working at Ambrose?' I asked unapologetically. Rick gaped in amazement. Jacques looked at me sadly, deep furrows forming above eyes which had been dancing with amusement before.

'Rick has told me of your difficulties Mr Delacroix. I can't deny I would have liked to exercise my culinary skills at Ambrose Hotel, it would be a post that suited my…..how d'you say, style, but I know that is not to be. When I moved out from Montreal, I never expected to find such a prize here in the provinces, but there is much business in Ontario, my family and I are doing quite well.'

'I'm sorry, I meant no offence. I just wanted to be sure Rick had told you the score.'

Rick looked strained, I thought for a moment he would speak, but he remained silent. I decided I would have to add diplomat to his other talents. Jacques too seemed aware of his reserve, he turned to his friend and said, 'Now you have work to do Rick, and I must get back to the kitchen.'

I stopped him and put out my hand. 'It's nice to meet an honest man, Mr Moreau.'

He took the hand willingly, the tension gone.

'And if you should ever find yourself in need of a chef, Mr. Delacroix…' Jacques added, a twinkle in his eye, 'you won't forget me?'

'I'll let you know after I try the burgers tomorrow.' It was a measure of this man - a skilled, high-class, chef - that he merely laughed. Rick let out a long sigh.

Closing the office door behind him, Rick asked, 'Don't you think that was rather unfair, I'd already told you about Jacques' situation?'

'I'm sorry I've a lot on my plate - as you observed once before.'

'You gave me the impression you didn't trust me.'

'If I did that I'm sorry, I don't even trust myself these days. Rick I'll come right to the point. I've decided to sell Ambrose. I made up my mind driving here today.'

You would have thought I'd hit him. He sank down

into a chair completely deflated. I stood by the door watching him flip sadly through files piled a foot high on the desk. At last he said, 'You haven't even asked me about these.'

I felt suddenly very tired and forced myself to ask, 'What are they?'

'Quotes from the conference agencies. There's three of them, all falling over themselves to get the place, came in by email late yesterday,' Rick's claim sounded like gross exaggeration.

'Aren't you letting your enthusiasm run away with you?'

'Mr Delacroix, Francis, they were only down here Thursday. I arranged the appointments a couple of hours apart, but word had gone round. They kept asking me what I wanted and what facilities their competitors were promising, what type of contract they'd offered, what timescale we'd be happy with ....' Here he gulped. Tears glistened in his eyes. 'We could have written our own contract.'

The accusation that I had failed him was so evident that I turned away.

'What I want to know, what I've a right to know Francis, is why you've changed your mind.'

'I never made any promises Rick, you know that.'

'But why - just when we were making progress?'

'Too many factors, Rick. When my father deeded me Ambrose I wanted nothing whatever to do with the place. I only came up here to clear out the people who were killing wolves. I succeeded. But that wasn't enough. And it's not enough just to sit here and defy my father. I can use the money for the Wolf Sanctuary, maybe endow a wildlife foundation. My father threatened to have me sectioned to get the place back, did you know?'

Rick stared at me in disbelief. He looked down at the desk and shook his head. 'So you're giving in to him?'

'No. Not giving in. If I sell Ambrose to a wildlife-friendly company he won't ever get it back. Rick, with Ambrose I'm almost bankrupt, without it I'll have the money I need for the wolves at Sanctuary.'

'You could set up a foundation right here and - the conference centre…it could be such a success.'

'What do I really want with a conference centre Rick? I've no experience of running such a business and anyhow my future's not here, it's back in Minnesota.' I was beginning to get angry.

'And what about my future?'

'What about your damned future?'

But I didn't wait to hear his answer. I'd had enough of Rick's arguments. I moved hastily towards the door but he pushed angrily out of his chair, forcing himself between me and the door. 'Sell me the lease for a year!'

'Lease?'

'For Ambrose Hotel. I may never have another chance like this Francis. You've got a winner here, either you're a part of it or you're not. If not then sell me the lease for a year. I'll take the business on myself.'

'But you've no money,' I shouted, astounded at the bizarre proposal.

'I'll get it from somewhere, beg, borrow, mortgage myself up to the hilt. I'll pay you a good rate.'

'A year's lease, you'd take that risk?'

'Yes, but we'll have a clause inserted in the contract. If it's a success after a year we split the profits and I take the lease for another five years, if not you keep the rent and Ambrose and I get nothing. I'll take that chance.' He spoke as if Ambrose possessed its own life-force.

I stared at him in amazement. 'Have you really thought about this Rick, or is it just a spur of the moment idea?'

He gave a shake of his head. It was not really an answer, 'Promise me you'll think about it, Francis. Promise me!'

The room had become intolerably warm. I opened the door, grateful for the fresh air which flooded in from the foyer, 'I'll think about it,' I said and left.

I went in search of Lionel. It was after one o'clock and I found him and Denny in the bunkhouse canteen eating a meal of cold meats and mash fries. Lionel got up quickly scraping his chair on the wooden floor. He headed towards the kitchen saying, 'Glad to see you Mr Francis, got just the thing you need.' He reappeared with a plate of food and a can of beer.

'Looks mighty appetising,' I took a swig of beer. It was nicely chilled, 'You've been busy I hear.'

Both men chuckled.

'Forty kids due tomorrow and their parents. Mr. Larry said you wouldn't mind.'

There was a glint in Lionel's eye.

'I didn't know about it until today. He paying you?' Lionel nodded, 'Two days, says it's the weekend rate.' Denny appeared agitated by his father's admission.

'You won't want to work for me any more,' I said, half-heartedly.

'That ain't true, Francis, we know we're beholding to you.'

'Not true Denny. I wouldn't be alive if it wasn't for you.' Denny's face reddened under the deep brown skin.

His father collected up their empty plates and bustled into the kitchen. Denny took the opportunity to ask, 'You coming back here to stay Mr Francis?'

'I don't think I can, Denny.'

'But ain't things getting better, what with them Wolf League people here? Mr. Rick too, he's been saying he's gonna set up this conference business.'

'Rick's been talking too much,' I said sourly.

Lionel returned with three plates of ice cream. Denny took a mouthful but he'd lost his appetite. He pushed the plate aside and got up. 'Gotta finish the fencing round those nature trails.' He went out without a backward glance.

Lionel stared after him, sensing an atmosphere. I dipped my spoon into the ice cream.

'Something troubling you, Mr. Francis?'

'Nothing at all Lionel,' I lied. I couldn't look him in the eye just then and tell him I was selling Ambrose.

I spent the afternoon in the office, ploughing through mail that had arrived at Ambrose during the week. Letters and bills were collected together in a beige folder labelled Post. I thought I saw the hand of Avril in the arrangement. After browsing through the bills, I opened the thick envelope from Kashabowie bank. It contained a long letter from Neville Chase and a sheaf of papers, many being bills and invoices I'd left at the bank. A statement of account was attached.

Neville had been inordinately active on my behalf. But I suppose the manager of a small town bank has little enough to do, especially when that town is stagnating. In the letter he told me as much. The copper mines which had brought the town into being had failed years before. The timber mills, which sustained it for decades had also recently closed, leaving the town with no industry. Families moved away. Those that remained were often prey to people like Leland. Neville wrote:

'I tracked down the men on Leland's list. As you suspected several of them don't exist or left town well before the Ambrose fire. Most of the men who worked for him say they were hired on a daily basis, with never a mention of contracts. Most irregular. But if anyone complained, Leland swiftly laid them off, sometimes without pay. Even so, many are still loyal to him and have a lingering feeling he was a good employer. This might well explain the attack you suffered.

Your authority to run the Ambrose accounts came through yesterday, (the letter was dated Friday). *Would you like the bank to handle the outstanding payments to the men you sacked?* (He could have said 'released', but Neville was nothing if not blunt.) *'I can certainly arrange for this to be done, that way you might avoid further unpleasantness by coming into town. The total would come to about $4,000, and I have accounted for this in my provisional statement.*

It may interest you to know that many men now working away from town still have wives and families here and a hardship fund was raised for them over a year ago. By paying the men the monies owed you will be wiping the slate clean and the townspeople can have no further hold on Ambrose. However, if you were willing to donate a small sum towards this fund it would go a long way towards soothing passions in the town.'

If Neville had been present at the attack, witnessed its ferocity, he could hardly have written in this vein. The trauma to Lys alone was sufficient to reject this suggestion. I'd done enough, I thought, for Kashabowie by not pressing charges against the perpetrators. Nevertheless, I was considering his appeal when a voice asked, 'Busy?' Larry stood in the doorway.

'I didn't expect you till tomorrow.'

'Avril called.'

'Ah!'

'Seems Rick's been bending her ear as well. You've made up your mind to sell Ambrose?'

I nodded down at the desk, not wanting to face him.

'Want to talk about it?'

'Not really. I don't think there's anything to talk about.'

'I think there is. Care for a ride?'

I was sick of Ambrose paperwork and badly wanted a break. Larry's car was parked round the back. I got in, not particularly caring where we went. He took the trail into the estate. We travelled through thick aspens, the red-gold leaves brushing close against the doors and in about ten minutes ran out into an open glade of tall whispering grasses. In the distance sunlight flickered off a body of water surrounded by tall conifers.

As we drew closer I recognised the small lake and jetty where Lys and I had our picnic that first day. The waters of the lake looked tranquil. A family of swans glided with perfect reflections. In the shallows, ducks nibbled at the dry heads of wild rice which dipped and bobbed along the shoreline. But the full shore was no longer exposed. A strange brown structure composed of skins and wooden poles stood before us on the jetty. Larry drove off the track and stopped the car beside it.

'This the yurt Avril told me about?'

'Sure, I need to check it out before the kids get here tomorrow.'

He got out of the car leaving the door open, and disappeared behind the yurt. Warm air wafted through the car doorway. A light breeze tossed the bone-dry grass heads and wove shadowy patterns down between their stems where grasshoppers screeched and bees searched out late autumn flowers. Beyond the distant pines a loon called his long, low, enervating chant of farewell. Soon I'll follow you, I promised. Larry reappeared from behind the yurt. He had taken off his jacket, was open-necked and in the act of rolling up his shirtsleeves.

'Come and see.' he called. 'It doesn't look much but it's pretty big inside and the paintings…'

I had no particular interest in the yurt but Larry's enthusiasm was contagious. Grudgingly, I got out of the car. 'Paintings?'

'Inside, but…' We were walking towards the yurt. From the way they pressed against the heavy skin from within you could see the walls comprised a lattice of wooden struts criss-crossing each other. Longer spars stretched the roof into a cone some ten feet high. It would have taken many tens of deer skins to form the covering.

I'd thought the brown parchment-like surface bare of ornament, but as we approached I made out small, faded images of bison and moose lost in a landscape of dark trees and hills. Running beside them were stick-like figures armed with bows: native American hunters, painted as they had lived two hundred years before, their bodies picked out in tans, dark ochre and sooty black. I stretched my hand out to touch the strange forms as if I might learn something from them. It was Larry who spoke first. 'D'you think they could be original?'

'Perhaps they are.' The skin was coarse beneath my fingers. It had been roughly cured. I traced out the running figure of a hunter no more than seven inches tall, an ochre breechcloth around his loins, bow ready in his hands, the arrow never released. We mused a moment then Larry beckoned me inside. 'You'll be surprised.'

Surprised yes. Instead of the subtle images outside, the parchment walls were awash with garish colours to mimic the interior of a tipi. Poles, spears and flails ranged around the wall - all painted but quite lifelike. Baskets, animal skins and rush bags stood out against dioramas depicting various scenes: hunters around a campfire, brightly-clad women bent over looms, campside curs snarling over bones, children playing. One powerful image inevitably caught my eye: it was a herd of bison chasing through lush prairie grass pursued by a pack of wolves. The action so frenzied I couldn't help laughing. Larry was chuckling at my side.

'Think the kids'll like it?'

'How could they not?'

'We've arranged craft demonstrations, weaving, fletching arrows, that sort of thing and later in the day a sing-song around the campfire.'

'This the sort of thing the League normally gets involved in?'

He became suddenly serious, 'For children yes, there are many ways to stimulate their interest,' he nodded to the doorway. 'Let's go outside.'

We went out into the face of the westering sun and walked in silence along the jetty. The sun was dipping lower in the sky and the surface of the lake shone milky-white. Where a gentle current rippled the water, it glowed and shimmered with a pearl-like iridescence.

'Pearl Lake?' I queried, already knowing the answer.

'Well named.'

'Is this what you wanted me to see?'

Larry leaned against the rickety railing, 'Ambrose has many lakes, last count I made it twenty-three…. Denny still hasn't finished showing me round yet.' He gestured back to the car. 'I'd like to take you to a special place we found - if you've time.'

'It's Saturday, I've nothing else to do.'

Nothing, except write up Ambrose's particulars for the property agents, and pack my few possessions.

We'd been driving for more than half an hour in a south-westerly direction. The sun was blindingly bright. Larry stopped the car to put on sunglasses but neither of us spoke. I guessed we must be close to Quetico's northern boundary. Suddenly he turned the car northwards onto a track leading uphill. It was almost lost in long grass. The car bumped and leaped alarmingly from side to side as we gained height. Larry was concentrating on driving but he chose this moment to speak. 'Jacob speaks highly of your work at Sanctuary.'

I was thrown against the door as the car hit a rock and grasped wildly for the windowsill. 'Jacob's not been there, not since I started.'

'Nonetheless he thinks of you as a sort of protégé.'

'I thought he saw me more as a responsibility,' I said.

'That's not what he said when I spoke to him today.'

I began to get suspicious, 'Today? That why you came back early to Ambrose?'

'That and other things.'

'Well Larry, if you think you can dissuade me from selling Ambrose you'd better turn back now. I've decided to use the money to support Sanctuary, their work is so important,' Larry sighed heavily. We had been travelling all the while uphill, now the car jogged and slithered until it was almost stationary in front of a huge crusty-orange sandstone bluff. The track, now only a narrow line of washed-out gravel, led round it.

Undeterred, Larry drove on past a little tree-filled col and came out onto a small plateau where the track finally disappeared beneath willow scrub. The climb hadn't been that long, the change in height barely discernible yet the solid sandstone cliff on which the car rested dropped away perhaps a hundred feet. Below a picturesque vista of forest and lakes, prairie and marshland stretched into the west.

Sunlight glinted on a myriad lakes. At the foot of the bluff, water sparkled on the nearest lake where a breeze tossed the surface into flickering shoals and scatters of light. A spit of land wreathed in red aspens jutted into the water where a moose and two calves browsed among muskeg pools, weed trailing from their lips. In the distance a stream trickled from the cliff falling into a grey-green meadow where deer grazed off the summer's growth. It was impossible to tell how many animals there were. Larry drew the car to a halt on a patch of yellow gravel, outwash from aeons of erosion from the cliff above us. The landscape beckoned. I could only stare at it in silence.

'Ambrose?'

Larry nodded. 'Tell me about your work at Sanctuary, Francis.'

I hesitated at first, unwilling to break the spell cast by the spectacle before us. But when I found my voice I couldn't stop talking, 'We released two wolves yesterday,

I can't tell you how that felt.' But I did tell him, about the build-up to the release, that sudden feeling of euphoria as the wolves sped away, and about the wolf Jenny called Eighty-Seven, which I'd promised myself to release when the time came. He knew about the dedication of the staff and all the volunteers too, but I told him anyway.

'So you see,' I concluded, 'I could do so much more if I sold......' but a lump came into my throat and I couldn't finish. I pushed open the car door and stood beside it looking down at the green translucent water of the lake. A car door clicked open behind me. Larry's shoes crunched on the gravel. He stood beside me, not speaking. I was aware that he had glanced down at the lake, then he slowly lifted his hand to shade his eyes from the sun. He steadied his gaze on the distant hills.

'What if we brought wolves back to Ambrose, turned it into a national refuge?'

His words could not have been more tempting or more compelling, yet I flung up my arms, railing against the vast landscape before us. 'And how the hell are we going to do that?' I yelled.

Larry stayed calm, unruffled by my outburst, his voice strangely confident as he said, 'Appeals, subscriptions, donations - a conference centre.'

'You're one hell of a joker Larry,' I shouted. But I knew I was beaten. I slapped him on the back and the two of us clasped arms and embraced, laughing until sweat and tears filled our eyes. When I finally pulled away I asked, 'Is this really all Ambrose land?'

'Most of it ..... OK some of it, the boundary goes on down to that gorge about twenty miles away, then turns back south to Quetico. There's plenty of land for wolves and their prey.'

'I can see I'm going to have to watch you closely from now on Larry.'

'Par for the job.'

As Larry drove down beside the picket fence, Simon Harrison was standing at the door of the bunkhouse squinting out from beneath his stetson. He had dispensed with his jacket and his right hand sat easily on his hip, the six-shooter clearly visible. When he recognised the car he simply tipped his fingers to his hat, waved and went back inside.

'You'll want these. Avril will have gone home by now.' I took the set of Ambrose keys from Larry. I started to get out of the car, aware that the thick plastic sheeting was shaking and furling in the breeze. 'She thinks we should have a new door,' Larry said.

'Aren't the locks to the office good enough?' I joked. But she was right, of course. I made a mental note to mention it to Denny. I hadn't been in the office more than a minute when Lionel scuttled in asking what I wanted to eat. I didn't feel particularly hungry. We settled on sandwiches and coffee, then I went in search of Rick. The double doors were locked and the garish display lights switched off. Even so I wanted to know who was about. I wandered through the maze of stands, past the ever-leaping wolves and looked into the courtyard. The people-carrier had gone. Only Rick's car, an old silver Chevvy, and the sporty number remained. Avril had three children, the people-carrier was probably hers. That meant Jacques must still be here.

I searched through the cluster of keys to open the door in the partition. I could have gone outside and knocked at the rear entrance to the kitchen, but I didn't want Rick thinking I was spying on him. I strolled through the foyer and peered into the dining room. It was dark now that the setting sun had gone behind the conifers. All the trestle tables were wreathed in coloured cloths ready for the invasion next day, the contentious bottled sauces and napkins duly arranged on the most distant table. I looked through the porthole-like windows into the kitchen. A faint glow glimmered over the shiny equipment towards the rear.

I pushed open the door. Low murmuring issued from behind a small partition: a terse French voice mingling with the subdued tones of an English speaker. The men were seated at a low table, a substantial proportion of a meal of spaghetti bolognaise still on their plates. Both of them glanced up as I edged around the partition. Jacques tried to maintain a neutral expression but I detected mild disgust in the way he nodded and turned back to his food. Rick wasn't so successful, his lips tightened and he let his eyes fill with rage before he had control of himself.

'Mr Delacroix!' He went to stand up then thought better of it. 'I should be going,' Jacques offered, stirring in his seat.

'I'd like to see you Rick…. when you've got a minute.' I nodded down at his half-finished meal indicating there was no hurry. 'I'll be in the outer office. And bring those files along would you.'

The two men looked at each other. I didn't wait to hear Rick's gasp of astonishment and Jacques' buoyant laughter. I slipped out behind the partition and headed towards the empty foyer.

Chapter Thirteen

Lionel had piled a load of beef and tomato sandwiches on a plate which sat on the desk alongside a bubbling coffee pot. I poured myself a cup, it was rich and dark and I took it without milk. There was far more food than I could eat in an evening, but by the time Rick entered with his bundle of files, I had munched my way through a goodly portion of the meal.

I thrust two sheets of paper before him, one labelled Accounts on which I'd outlined my ideas of the various items we might need just to maintain the estate and pay any staff, but the second which I'd labelled Management was more important. It dealt with control, specific types of conference clients who were acceptable and those who weren't, questions and ideas on where the ultimate control would lie for the whole conference enterprise. I made no mention of our earlier quarrel. It would already be apparent to Rick that I'd reversed my earlier decision.

I let Rick digest the contents of the sheets before saying, 'It seems to me we are going to have to decide on two very important points,' I tapped the Management sheet. 'Whether we retain and manage all Ambrose ourselves, placing a heavy load on the manager. Or give the whole thing over to one of these firms with a guiding brief but no managerial input.'

'And you'd dispense with my services entirely?' Rick asked despondently.

I nodded. 'There'd be a fee for what you've done already - a type of consultancy.'

'I've done too much work to want it that way Mr. Delacroix, and I think you'll find none of these agencies want ultimate control. They treat each conference as a package, contracting out everything except what they need for the actual event.'

'And pay less for the privilege.'

'The rent would be less of course, but we would charge more for meals and accommodation. We'd have to work within their budget of course….,'

'And still make a profit?'

'Mr. Delacroix…,'

'Francis will do, Rick.'

'Francis, at CanadaStates Motels we organised our own budgets and kept to them. The profit margin wasn't just a target, it was something to be beaten. We had to maintain standards but we were also in competition with the next hotel down the line, in our own group and the whole market. It was life on the edge. If you were no good you were fired.'

'But admit it Rick, you've never had ultimate managerial control. Of course if you want to go for that lease and run the whole show yourself - subject to the same conditions?' I quizzed.

Rick steadied his gaze at me. 'I would have done it, so help me I would.'

'And probably gone under trying.' He grinned, the same innocent grin he'd given me on the day I first met him. 'You know I've studied for all the right management exams Francis, you've seen my certificates, I thought you were willing to take a chance on me. Mr Leland was and….,'

He knew right away he'd made a mistake by mentioning Leland, but I let him down lightly.

'Rick, Leland employed a succession of keen young managers from out of state over the past few years.

From what I hear Ambrose was a success. But it was a fragile operation built on the backs of gullible people. He made all the managers the same promises he made you: a year on low wages with a promise of a share in the profits. All of them worked damned hard, yet not one of them lasted the year, probably saw none of those profits either. Did you know that?'

'I'd heard there were difficulties, rumours I could never get to the bottom of.'

'You needn't blame yourself Rick, you weren't the first of Leland's victims and you wouldn't have been the last.'

'I know it sounds as if I'm feathering my own nest Francis, but if you give up managerial control, you'd lose control of the site too. The agency would abide by your original conditions but you'd never really know how the place was being managed.'

'Good point. So what do you suggest?'

'Greatest input, greatest output, Highest Standards Maintained.'

'A snappy motel maxim Rick?'

'I just thought it up actually.'

I laughed. 'I think I'm going to enjoy working with you Rick. Now we'd better get down to business.'

We thrashed out a strategy for approaching the three companies who had made firm offers to run the new Ambrose Wildlife Conference Centre. None of them wanted ultimate managerial control. Finally we set out our requirements for a meaningful contract. I intended to ask Neville Chase to visit Ambrose as soon as he could to mull over our ideas, probably he would be able to suggest a good local accountant too.

My knowledge of law firms was slight. For that

reason alone I made the seemingly anomalous decision to approach my father's lawyers to take care of the legal business. Thompson & Thompson were an established firm with a history going back over a hundred years. They had a reputation for honesty and integrity.

At about eight o'clock Rick took his pack of files and calculations back into one of the hotel guest rooms. Having commandeered the hotel manager's room next to the computer office, he had also discovered a set of hotel keys with which to let himself in and out of the locked building. Jacques had left long since. Looking back I realise I had no real notion whether Rick's plans would bring in any profits for Ambrose Estate. It seemed enough then just to keep the place afloat and out of the hands of the hunting fraternity.

I went back into the foyer and unlocked the door to the apartment, returning to pick up the remains of the food and half-cold coffee pot. I needed several things from the car and though I could have easily unlocked the double doors to retrieve them I retraced my steps and went out through the back. Lights were on in the bunkhouse and I could hear voices: Lionel and Denny musing over a backgammon board but I didn't intrude on them. The evening air was cool and refreshing, I wanted to walk alone with my thoughts.

As I passed the new half-built store, dew was seeping into the new pine which smelt both sweet and rank. I rounded the track where all evidence of the car crash had been cleared away and sturdy wooden spars now barricaded it off from the lake. A strange meandering contraption had been built alongside the lake which in the half light I could make nothing of until I remembered Denny's reference to a nature trail. Small triangular flags hanging from the guide ropes moved in the breeze, tilting into a pale ghostly mist which was rising from the lake.

From somewhere behind the beech hedge came the sweet smell of blossom, honeysuckle perhaps? Lys loved its fragrance. Over a year ago, when Pamela and I were already dating, Lys had planted two shrubs of the stuff against the back wall at Silver Lake. It would make a private arbour for us, she said. Ironically Pamela would never sit there. She complained the fragrance was too heavy and drenching. I wondered if she ever sat there now.

Thoughts of my old home made me realise I hadn't heard from Lys for several days. I got out the cellphone and flipped to her number. It just rang and rang. There was no intervening message, no indication even if the thing was switched on. After about twenty rings I turned it off. As I passed the end of the hedge the figure of a man stepped out from the shadows. I thought I knew the familiar heavy shoulders and tall outline. I froze. The last thing I was thinking about was James Leland. He knew Ambrose well, choosing a corner for his ambush which was out of sight, both of the bunkhouse and the hotel. There was no chance of summoning help. Then the man stepped forwards offering a beefy hand.

'Bill Merrick, Mr. Delacroix. Seen you around.' The voice was gruff but friendly enough, though it took me several seconds to relax. 'You gave me quite a fright.'

'Twenty-four hour security, that's what Mr. Carter asked for and that's what he's getting.'

I was now calm enough to ask. 'You'll be up all night?' He nodded. I thought back to my conversation with Larry. I couldn't remember making any arrangements to communicate with these men.

'Do you have some means of communication, walkie-talkie that sort of thing?'

Merrick pulled a contraption from behind his back and held it up in front of my face.

'Best not turn it on an' get Simon out of his bed.'

I was impressed but still pursued my concerns. Merrick and Simon might have volunteered for the Wolf League but ultimately it was my property and my life they were guarding. I had a responsibility to see they were protected in return. 'And a cellphone?'

'Naturally, and a whistle 'case you ask.' He put a blunt square of plastic to his lips and gave a short whistle which split the night air and caused the ducks on the lake to babble their displeasure. Blown forcefully enough the thing would probably pierce a person's eardrums. I left him to continue his rounds and went towards the car. When I drove back round past the lake there was no sign of Bill Merrick or anyone else.

I went up to the suite and headed for the bed without bothering to switch on the light, so I didn't know it had been made up. I tipped my knapsack onto what I thought was a bare mattress and tumbled onto the bed ready for instant sleep. Instead the soft feel of a duvet brought me quickly awake. I switched on the light, readied myself to pull off my shoes, and instead saw the folder Anna Jameson had handed me when I left Bemidji. It was poking out of the knapsack and contained a request to complete a 2000-word essay on quarantine regulations.

I groaned. After the releases I'd completely forgotten

her request. She wanted the essay by Tuesday, only three days from now and I had enough other work to do on Monday. Added to that, there was likely to be a lot of disturbance from the Open Day tomorrow. So I set to at half-past nine to write the essay. I finished the final draft just before two in the morning.

'Mr. Delacroix, Francis you should wear one of these.' Avril's voice echoed along the corridor behind me. Other lisping sounds issued from the foyer. I spun round as Avril ran out from the office. Even in the shadowy doorway I could see she was nattily dressed in green blouse, green dungarees and black high-heeled boots. On her right arm was a yellow armband labelled Wolf Guide. She carried another in her hand. Slightly out of breath she said, 'Here, put this on.' She pulled my right arm towards her and thrust a band round my upper arm. I hadn't the heart to resist.

'I'm surprised you weren't awake earlier. It's been like bedlam here.'

Rather bemused I asked, 'What are you talking about?'

'The children, they're here already. It's past eleven.'

I explained that I'd slept late. 'Did you make up the bed?'

'What? No Kate must have done it.'

'There any breakfast?'

'Better ask Jacques - if you're brave enough.'

'What d'you mean?'

'From what I hear he and Rick have already got customers. Fancy a burger for breakfast?'

'No way!'

I went through into the foyer. The place was quiet

and empty except for three very young children seated at one of the plastic tables opposite the mounted wolves. They were scribbling avidly at crayon shapes that more resembled very arthritic lions than wolves. Looking on and admiring every line was a teenage girl with short spiky hair. She looked up at me and gave a brief embarrassed smile revealing a perfect silver brace. The child beside her wailed as his crayon tumbled to the floor. She bent down to pick it up, brushing the child's tears away and didn't look up again.

I got as far as the double doors before full realisation came of what the day had in store. Avril had been almost right, but bedlam wasn't a strong enough description of the scene in the courtyard. A haphazard jumble of cars, minibuses and several school buses were discharging their cargoes while others were driving around in half circles trying to extricate themselves from a sea of children. Toddlers to early teens wandered or ran erratically between the vehicles. Several people with Wolf Guide armbands were attempting to bring order out of this chaos, without evident success. Screams, both of laughter and pain, emanated from all corners of the car park and reverberated on Ambrose's proud brick façade. Unless I was mistaken there were far more than forty children already in the courtyard. 'Bloody hell!' I bellowed.

'Francis, not in front of the children.'

Avril stood right beside me, her mouth half-open evidently transfixed by the scene. I spun round, and hissed again through clenched teeth so that none but she should hear. 'Bloody hell!'

'Ssssssh!' she cautioned raising a finger to her lips, amusement evident in her eyes.

'Why so many, forty kids he said, and a few parents?'

'Siblings, friends, toddlers who can't be left - grandparents even.' She looked down at an elderly couple passing by with twin girls.

'Avril I don't think I'm ready for this,' I pleaded.

'Oh you will be, Francis. By the end of the day you will be!' She laughed hilariously and had her attention drawn away by a small boy who had got up from the table and was insisting she look at his drawing.

'Yours?' I asked. The child looked up at me innocently from beneath a mop of ginger hair, his freckled cheeks aglow with pride.

'Mine are too old for this sort of thing.' Unless she'd been a child bride, I must have badly misjudged Avril's age. She laughed again, dismissing me to take the boy back to the table. I felt a movement by my side. A young girl about eight years old, dressed in some kind of animal costume, definitely not of the wolf genera, stood there. She was holding the hand of a very much younger boy who was tugging at my faded jeans.

'Where's the toilet mister, Jimmy can't wait,' the girl implored.

Toilets? I had no idea where the public toilets were. All the guest rooms I'd seen at Ambrose were en-suite. But I'd been a small boy myself and known the fleeting pressures of childhood incontinence. I panicked, expecting an accident any minute, and tried to bustle the child toward the office doorway. He hadn't gone two steps when Avril came to my rescue.

'Can you take him ... ,' I began but she wouldn't let me finish. She touched my shoulder and giving me the sweetest of smiles gestured into the courtyard. One of the school buses had managed to extricate itself and was moving towards the entrance track, revealing two large grey lorries parked side by side in the colourful shade cast by the aspens. They were identified in large bold letters with the words 'Boys' and 'Girls'. A short wooden ladder led up into each one.

I pointed the girl in that direction. She must have thought I was going to take the boy there myself. She looked at me reproachfully. Eventually she took the boy's hand again and guided him down the steps and onto the gravel. Against my will I watched the children's tottering progress towards the lorries. A young man with a Wolf Guide armband met them half way and guided them between the mêléc of people and cars. Avril stood beside me watching their progress, a frown creasing her forehead. She and the girl must have shared the same thought.

'I'm going to kill Larry when I find him!' I promised.

Of the remainder of that day I remember very little: a visit to the dining room where Jacques and Rick argued noisily about relish amid a gaggle of hungry whining children and agitated parents; a retreat to the bunkhouse where even Lionel's tiny kitchen was besieged by parents wanting drinks for thirsty children straight from the nature trail, for the day had turned hot and sultry; a less hectic trip in a half-full minibus out to the campfire and yurt late in the afternoon where a group of hushed ten-year-olds were listening earnestly, their eyes glazed and dreamy, to one of Denny's Indian legends.

Then by six o'clock the crowds mysteriously dispersed into the cars and buses which whisked them away under threatening storm clouds. The hourly throb of the latrine lorries was replaced by grinding wheels as they manoeuvred out from the aspens and headed with their organic loads down the track and out of sight. Larry and his wife and two young children bade us goodbye not long after. And when all the willing volunteers retreated to their homes, and after Avril and I with the two chefs had cleaned the dining room and the kitchen, leaving them sparkling fresh and eerily quiet, we sat together on the open veranda as raindrops began to fall and thanked our lucky stars the day had been dry.

Two days later, having been closeted most of that time with Neville and Rick, thrashing out our needs and securing a draft contract on-line from the Lafayette Conference Agency, my own choice out of the three who'd sent estimates, I left Ambrose and headed directly back to Sanctuary. Jenny had called to say that Eighty-Seven was about to be released. In the interim, Avril volunteered to type up my essay and it had been emailed to Anna Jameson. We had similarly emailed the draft contract to Thompson & Thompson who had, after an initial reluctance on the part of their senior partner, agreed to act for me. Lafayette's legal department promised to send them the full contract by post at the end of the week.

I only intended to be absent from Ambrose for a few days, the time it took to release the wolf and attend a couple of tutorials at Uni. But, just before I left, I surprised my colleagues by signing an authority at Kashabowie notary department authorising Neville and Rick to act jointly in my absence on any matters to do with the new Ambrose conference facility. It may have seemed a rash decision in view of the tenuous nature of our negotiations. Whether I saw it simply as a way of spreading the weight of decision-making or through some foreboding, I'll never know. In fact nearly three weeks were to elapse before I saw Ambrose again. By that time its status, and that of its owner, would be changed for ever.

With the knowledge that our plans were heading towards fruition, I drove through the gates at Sanctuary at noon next day with an easy heart. Neither Suzanne's car nor Jack's pickup had arrived and I took the opportunity to phone Lys. Again there was no reply. I wasn't unduly worried, Lys would surely phone if she had any news or if she needed me. I put the phone down and saw Sammy wandering out of the main entrance. He had a cup in his hand and had just lifted it to his lips when he saw my car. I waved. He returned my gesture with a vicious stare, dashed the plastic cup to the ground, spilling the remains of the drink across on the flagstones, and dived back indoors. His action was furtive, not to say cowardly.

Minutes passed without anyone else appearing. I grew impatient and decided to go in search of Jenny. I entered the building and walked down the corridor past the bunkrooms. Apart from the hum of the computers and a low murmuring of voices in the computer room, the place was relatively silent.

Strangely, the door to my own room was standing open. As I entered I felt a sudden pang of fear. On the bed lay my Uni enrolment form alongside a plastic folder I didn't recognise. Someone had rifled through my things! A door opened in the corridor. Footsteps approached steadily from the next room. I shoved the form into my pocket, carelessly picked up the folder and got the shock of my life. My own face was staring up at me out of the front page of the St Paul-Minneapolis

News. The paper was over three weeks old. A headline, splashed in capitals across the top, read:

DELACROIX MYSTERY, Father and Son in huge Gunsmith Gambit. Flying in the face of international calls to conserve the few hundred wolves remaining of the thousands which once inhabited the United States, senators from Wisconsin, Minnesota and Michigan join forces to organise a lobby against the Wolf Protection Bill. The leading light in the cartel is believed to be millionaire gunsmith & hunter, Louis Delacroix. However, rumours abound that Mr Delacroix is set to launch a series of high profile Hunting Lodges right across the States and into Canada, with sources indicating investment from those same senators. Mr. Delacroix, who has never been known as a philanthropist or animal lover, is believed to be funding.... I couldn't read much more. The article went on in this vein for several paragraphs, ending finally with a series of questions in bold print: *What's in it for you Delacroix? Come clean about your motives. Gullible Senators or Culpable Partners. Who's funding Who?*

Below they had printed a picture of me getting into a car, the background looked like a motel car park. I suddenly realised that Sammy was breathing heavily at my side. I groaned as I read on: *Francis Delacroix, 23-year-old son of Louis Delacroix, interviewed at Blackheath Motel, refuses to confirm or deny the rumours.*

Journalistic licence had been taken to extremes. I wondered how he'd managed to take the photo without my realising. But if I thought I'd seen enough, worse was to come, Sammy jabbed angrily at the underside of the folder. 'Turn over, go on,' he fumed.

I did as he demanded. The folder contained another article dated only five days before. The paper this time was the Chicago Sprinter. The article was headed 'The Slaying of the Wolves' and began by listing various upright citizens and senators, my father among them, who were shown organising a petition against the ban on wolf killing. Photos from around the state showed grinning senators with enthusiastic crowds clamouring to sign up.

In the middle of the article, they had copied the firm's logo. Underneath were the words DELACROIX CLAN TO FUND CAMPAIGN, and another photograph of my father and myself taken more than three years before, in front of Silver Lake Lodge. The photo had been chosen well. I hardly recognised my youthful features, but the naïve enthusiasm with which I brandished my rifle was unmistakable. I quailed. Sammy didn't wait for a response.

'Who's Frank Dawson then?' he jibed, jabbing at the folder. 'Some figment of your imagination or a bloody spy?'

'I can explain.' I tried to edge past him, but he stood foursquare in the doorway barring my way.

'I'll bet you can 'Dawson'! What you doing here, looking for more victims?' He wasn't very tall and I hadn't thought him a particularly strong man. Now he caught me unawares with a vicious punch to my chest. I staggered towards the bed. Pain shot through my ribs aggravating the earlier injuries.

'I don't want to fight you, Sammy…,' I gasped, pulling myself up.

'But we're even aren't we, your hand and my leg? I'm going to see to it you kill no more wolves even if I have to kill you myself.'

I didn't believe him, they were threats made in anger,

nothing more. 'Just let me explain.'

I truly didn't want to fight him. He would come to his senses if he would only let me explain the subterfuge. But he wasn't interested in listening and lunged forward again. 'No good you whining, you bloody cur!'

Dodging his next blow, I held my side and staggered out into the corridor. I was badly winded. I lost my footing and slumped against the wall. Sammy twisted round, using his wounded leg like a paddle, and was on me in seconds, landing blows on my side and back. With each blow he cursed, alternately grunting the names Dawson and Delacroix.

I had no choice but to fight back. I twisted round and managed to get my left hand up to his shoulder to hold him steady then landed the full force of my right fist on the edge of his chin. He yelped in agony and crashed down on the floorboards. His head hit the tiled floor in the hallway. Blood splashed from his torn lip. More blood trickled onto the tiles from his head, then a spasm shook his whole body and he lay still.

I thought I'd killed him. Horrified, I staggered across and fell at his side, calling out his name. Immediately his eyes opened. He was instantly alert. Breath came harshly from his chest, pain and anger mixing in his expression, yet he managed to yell out the words. 'Son of a bitch!'

Rough workman's hands clawed at my head and face. He pulled me down on top of him, suddenly had tight hold of my head and was trying to bash it against the wall. I had fallen on my side, my right arm was trapped under me. I couldn't free it in the confined space of the corridor. The only target left to me was his chest, my only option to rain down useless punches with my weakened left hand. If I heard shouts or screams of horror from the women I was by now immune to them. Hands grasped at my shoulders and my arms were pulled almost out of their sockets.

Someone rolled me over. I sprawled forward looking for something to hit then I was pushed onto my back and immobilised by strong arms. Waves of pain shot through my chest and I almost passed out. Sammy was receiving similar treatment but sounded in a worse state, gasping and retching at my side. One of the volunteers had pinned him down but he squirmed sideways, his hands pulling at the air and crying out, 'You don't understand, let me at the bastard, let me at him...'

As I tried to struggle up, my arms were grabbed and held. People stood around us appalled and alarmed, the foyer had grown dark with their shadows. Charlie's bulk filled the remaining pool of light.

'What's all this about?' he yelled, his voice a shattering roar.

'Bloody bastard's a spy,' Sammy yelled. I wondered at his energy. I hadn't strength to speak above a whisper.

'Let me up, I'll ... explain,' I croaked.

Hands reached down and we were both pulled to our feet. Sammy glared at me and lunged forwards again. Charlie caught his arm, twisted his face against the wall and pushed the arm up behind his back. Sammy yelped in pain.

'What the hell's got into you?'

'Ask him!' Sammy persisted through a bout of serious coughing.

'I'll chuck the both of you out of the gates, if one of you doesn't answer.' Charlie yelled.

I looked through the sea of anxious faces back down the corridor. Hands held me tightly. I couldn't move.

Sheets of newspaper lay tossed on the floor where running feet had trampled them. Jenny picked up the sheets and was reading the article. She lifted her head and gazed at me with a look of horror. Whether involuntarily or not, just one word formed on her lips. She didn't speak but I knew the word she'd mouthed was 'Traitor'! There must have been at least ten people around me yet I spoke only to her.

'Jenny, I can explain......those articles they're lies, at least part lies.....'

'One percent lies,' Sammy yelled.

Charlie spun him back round and barked into his face. 'Keep quiet d'you hear.'

He pushed Sammy into the arms of two of the technicians and gestured to Jenny. 'Better bring that stuff here.'

She took a step, then hesitated as if scared to approach. I smiled encouragingly, but she edged along the other side of the corridor as if violence were contagious. I searched for some sign of friendship in her face but it was a cold mask. 'Jenny, please believe me,' I begged.

'We'll sort this out in the canteen. Get them in there.' Sammy and I were route-marched through the doorway. We were made to sit near tables at opposite sides of the small room while Charlie took the middle ground looking down at the sheets of newspaper Jenny had given him. He poured over them while people brought us cups of water. Sammy dabbed at his broken lip with a serviette. I took a sip of water. There didn't seem any point in speaking until Charlie had done reading. Finally he looked up at me. 'Is this true?'

'It's true ... that my name is Francis Delacroix.' My

mouth was too dry, I sipped at the water again.

'You see, didn't I tell you…,' Sammy shrieked from his corner.

'Pipe down Kitson. You'll have your turn. Go on Frank, or …… ' Charlie obviously didn't feel comfortable using my real name. The people around us appeared stunned into silence.

'I broke with my father just over a month ago….before… before ever I came here.'

'Yeah, but I done some research, you and your Dad are avowed wolf killers. Not content with moose or deer, no you gotta go killing wolves as well. Gunsmiths, killers, what's the difference?'

'If you don't shut up Kitson I'll have you locked up!' Two of the volunteers held Sammy down in his seat.

'Why did you change your name and……? ' Jenny was straining forward from her seat. She had positioned herself in the far corner of the room. Her head was lowered. I couldn't see her eyes. '…. and why did you have to come here?'

Ten pairs of eyes gazed down at me. There was revulsion in some, others showed ill-concealed anger, even hatred.

'Just look around this room Jenny. See what the Delacroix name means. Jacob understood.'

At the mention of Jacob, two of the regulars, a technician named Jeremy and Sally, a young zoologist, lowered their heads thoughtfully. Both had been sponsored under the Wolf League scheme, they knew Jacob well. Sammy hadn't registered the lowering of tension in the room.

'Bet you pulled the wool over his eyes too.' Sammy heckled. 'What about those articles then? You saying they was all lies?'

'That photo of me with the rifle. It was taken years ago, you must be blind if you can't see that,' I yelled.

'Why don't you lock him up Charlie,' Sally wailed gesturing towards Sammy.

'No. I think he needs to hear this.'

Sammy's laugh was nervous and uneasy. He looked at Charlie, went to speak then thought better of it. When enough time had elapsed for me to gain sufficient courage I held out my scarred hand and tried to make the fingers into a fist. The two crooked fingers refused to move. Livid scars showed pale under the weak canteen lights. It wasn't a signal for silence but it had much the same effect. I heard gasps from several of the women.

'Sammy's right, I've killed plenty of moose and deer. I've lived with hunting all my life and thought nothing of it. I've killed wolves too, many illegally.' There were more groans. Sammy was so satisfied that he forgot to heckle.

'I knew the rules, the State quota, but I was young. It didn't seem to matter. So Sammy's right, I am a killer - at least Francis Delacroix was.'

'What happened to your hand?' asked Tommy, one of the young volunteers.

'Ten months ago I had an accident. It was my own fault but it changed my life for ever. Not because of this…,' I held my left arm up higher. Sally bit her lower lip, but Jenny's expression remained hard and unforgiving, 'but because I learnt that wolves were not the rabid killers I'd been lead to believe. I was hunting alone in snow, against all the rules. I'd taken a shot at a fine bull caribou but he disappeared. I'd killed him outright but didn't know. I was caught in an avalanche. I was there for hours trapped under tons of snow, my leg, my arm both broken. Often I passed out with the pain. But most of all, I was scared - scared out of my mind.'

Though they must all know about the unpredictability of avalanches, I doubt there was a person in the room who didn't think I'd got what I deserved. No-one spoke. Charlie sat down and stroked his chin. Eventually he nodded me on.

'No-one knew where I was, there didn't seem any chance of rescue. Then I saw the wolves - a pair of adults and two…,' here my voice nearly broke. I felt my eyes rim with moisture. In all the time since the accident I'd never spoken of Speed. It would be a release, perhaps my salvation, to speak of him now. I fought back the tears and croaked 'no three cubs, one older than the rest. Later I named him Speed. I thought they'd come to finish me off…'

I described my fear and then how my instinctive loathing of the wolves turned slowly to admiration. The room was still, people listened eagerly while I described the wolves' behaviour at the caribou kill; about watching the cubs playing; my admiration for Speed's strength and prowess; the way he'd tested the younger cubs. I paused. The room was hushed. No-one moved yet they might have been forgiven for thinking this the end of my story.

Charlie began to get up from his chair. I raised my hand again and he sat back down, a new respect for me showing in his eyes. My mouth was dry, I sipped at the water and when I had summoned enough courage I told them about the rescue helicopter. The fierce lights and shattering rifles were with me as I related the final bloody massacre, and the fleeting glimpse I'd had of Speed.

'Was he killed?' Someone asked too eagerly from the

back of the room. I looked in that direction but couldn't identify the speaker. Jenny was looking directly at me, her eyes glazed with tears.

I lowered my head and looked at the floor. 'I don't know, I just don't know,' I mumbled. Finding my breath again, I raised my head and spoke to the centre of the room. 'It's because of Speed and his family that I'm here. I've done with hunting, I want to give something back.'

When I had finished people shuffled their shoes uneasily on the floor. As if to dispel the emotion I'd generated, Jeremy asked, 'What about your father, where does he fit in all this?'

'I was in hospital a long time. When I came out I told him about my change of heart. He didn't like it. We had a blazing row and I left.' I didn't want to go into more detail, the memories were too painful. I looked down at the papers in front of Charlie. 'It's true I learnt about this campaign before I left home. I didn't think it was anything more than talk. My father had many meetings with senators, it wasn't unusual.' The restraining hands had long since left my shoulders. I left my seat to pick up the article relating to the petition, held it high and shook it. 'I didn't believe my father would do this. But he can't succeed, I know he can't.'

There was some low muttering at the back of the room.

'Sounds easy to say. But why d'you have to change your name, why all the lies?' Jeremy asked again.

'It was Jacob's idea. What we did, we did to protect Sanctuary. He said if people knew a member of the Delacroix family was working here Sanctuary would lose all credibility. How many sponsors do you have? Not too many. How many would you lose if it became known

Louis Delacroix's son was working here? Phone Jacob, if you don't believe me. We even had an argument about it,' I laughed at the memory.

I'd watched people relaxing as I spoke but the tide hadn't turned completely in my direction.

'And now?' Jenny asked. She wiped away her tears and listened calmly to me.

'Now I want to continue with my studies, to work here at Sanctuary. Frank Dawson wants to stay....if you'll give him a chance. If you can't then he'll leave. I wouldn't blame you. After I told my father I was giving up hunting he didn't believe me either. But I've learnt so much from you people: your dedication and selflessness - even the way Sammy talks to the wolves...,'

Nervous laughter echoed around the room. Squirming awkwardly in his seat, Sammy dabbed at his split lip with a bloodied serviette. People began to drift out of the room, returning to work. I heard the sound of engines on the forecourt. Charlie turned towards the door and flicked a finger at Sammy. The man gave me a sour look and scuttled out. Other people filed out leaving only me and Jenny facing each other across the room. She came forwards and gave me her hand in friendship and conciliation.

'I'm sorry I doubted you.'

'Does that mean I can stay?'

'That's up to Charlie .. and Jacob.' A brief smile touched her lips.

I gripped her hand tightly.

'There's something else I have to do.' As if she knew what was coming, she sighed and lowered her head. When she raised it again and met my eyes there was a kind of haunted look to her expression.

'Your father?'

'Someone's got to stop him.'

'But surely those senators would never………' I cut her off.

'He won't stop there Jenny, I know him, he'll go right up to Washington if he has to.'

'But what can you do on your own?'

'I won't be alone, Jenny. I'll have help, there's Jacob and the League for one thing.'

'Your father sounds a hard man, don't get hurt Frank… Francis.'

'No chance of that, Jenny,' I heard the fear in my own voice and turned the subject '…and Frank will do fine.'

She tried to laugh but failed miserably. Her fingers lingered long enough in my hands to give me hope of something better to come.

'You lovebirds got anything better to do or can we move this wolf now?' Jack Michelson glowered in mock anger through the canteen doorway.

Jenny blushed. I slipped the newspaper article behind my back and barked a reply. 'Been ready for hours.'

As Jenny and I accompanied Jack to the forecourt, the day was shattered by a huge crack of thunder. Rain thudded down on the assembled vehicles from dark clouds that had brewed up out of nowhere. People huddled in doorways, Suzanne ran behind us into the hallway carrying her satchel. Jack's assistants got hurriedly into their truck. Jack shot in behind us, his shirt already drenched.

'I don't like the look of this, Suzanne.'

'Is it going to last?'

Lightning flashed through the doorway. A series of devastating crashes rang round the building for several seconds. Rain battered down churning up the gravel surface, the droplets large, heavy and tumultuous. Someone pushed the hall door closed. Hailstones began thudding on the roof above our heads. You could hear them pinging on the metal downpipes.

'I can get a forecast update,' Jenny ran into the computer room. We stood about listlessly in the hallway, moisture oozing from our clothes. A sense of futility hung around us. Suzanne slipped into the canteen and dropped her case on one of the tables. The rest of us, Jack, Charlie and another man I didn't know, drifted in after her.

'What do you think the forecast'll show Jack?' Suzanne asked.

'I heard there was a front moving up from South Dakota. Wasn't supposed to arrive until tomorrow. Looks like it's moved faster'n they thought.'

'I can't go ahead with the release if this continues, can't risk the animal getting chilled.'

'I'm with you there.'

Jenny found us again. She had two computer printouts in her hands, one of which she handed over to Jack. He mused for a bit over what was obviously a weather map then handed the page to the vet.

'Closing in fast. That's it then, no release for Eighty-Seven today,' she said.

'They got any idea how long it'll last Jenny?'

She handed Jack the second sheet, saying, 'It won't clear till about mid-morning tomorrow. Looks good after that.'

'Fine, I'll get back here same time tomorrow, that OK with everyone?' Suzanne asked.

Jack and Jenny nodded. Charlie offered, 'I'll give him

another couple of feeds, set him up proper for the release.'

'How about you Frank? Could do with your help, I'm a man short,' Jack asked.

I hesitated. If I worked with Jack again I would need to tell him the truth. I had an idea the lie wouldn't go down well with him. Charlie answered for me. 'Frank's welcome to help as far as I'm concerned.' I appreciated his show of confidence. Perhaps I didn't need to tell Jack the truth just yet. If I was lucky someone else would explain things to him.

I stood in the hallway with Jenny watching Jack and the vet drive away through the storm. She looked through the deluge at the parking lot where my hire car was parked and asked, 'Still without your own car?'

When I got back to Sanctuary after the attack at Ambrose, I'd told everyone I'd had a blowout on the freeway and the car had been flung against a tree. It also served to explain my cracked ribs. Now wasn't the right time to tell Jenny about Ambrose.

'I called into the garage today. The insurance people want to write it off.'

'That's bad news. Have you got enough cash to buy a new one?'

'To tell you the truth I don't know.'

'If I can help at all…,'

I raised the fingers of my right hand in front of her lips without touching them.

'That's kind of you Jenny but it wouldn't be right.'

'The paper said your father was a millionaire. Did you lose everything when you quit home?'

'Some day Jenny, I'll tell you how much I lost, but not now.' The image of Pamela, tears streaming down her face as she threw off my ring, floated before my eyes. I was surprised how dim it had grown, though the pain still gnawed. Jenny saw my unease and turned the subject.

'Will you stay here tonight?' It was a simple enquiry, not an invitation, though I could have wished otherwise.

'I've arranged to attend a lecture early tomorrow, probably best if I get down to Bemidji tonight and do some swotting.'

'You *will* be back here tomorrow afternoon?'

'Try and stop me.' I pushed open the door. Raindrops hurtled through the small gap soaking the doormat.

Jenny was speaking again but I could hardly hear her voice above the growing tumult. 'Frank, what you said about the wolves. I always knew there was something...'

A crash of thunder broke immediately above our heads. I didn't hear the end of her sentence. Jenny shuddered and the spell was broken. I rushed out into the growing darkness without bidding her farewell.

I opened my books as soon as I got back to Bemidji, but there was too much going on in my mind for effective concentration. For half an hour I tried hard to absorb the prescribed texts for the tutorial, but in the end the words just swam before my eyes. Eventually I pulled the crumpled newspaper articles from my pocket and laid them down on top of the books. For long moments I stared at them wondering what, if anything, I could do to prevent my father and his associates from bringing in the intended legislation. If the newspaper article was to be believed, their campaign was well advanced.

It might already be too late to turn back the tide of public opinion. I certainly couldn't work alone, that much was obvious and Jacob had to be my first contact. Probably he already knew about the campaign. But he didn't know my father, or what he was capable of. He would brush aside, quite savagely, anything that got in his way. A little thing like state law would be no barrier.

If Jacob couldn't, or wouldn't help, I had one trump card I could play with devastating effect: I would threaten my father with exposure over the wolf slaughter at Ambrose. By midnight, I was too tired to think clearly. I put my papers aside. Preparing for sleep I was aware of something nagging at the back of my mind. What was it? Then, drifting into sleep, I remembered and the thought brought me bolt upright.

Why hadn't Lys contacted me? She must have seen the article, could hardly be unaware of the state-wide petition, yet she hadn't phoned. I decided to phone her first thing, even before I contacted Jacob. In the event neither call was successful. Jacob was in an all-day meeting in St. Paul. I left an urgent message for him to call me. Lys' phone just rang and rang. I drove to Uni worrying about her, wondering if I needed to go back home. I didn't relish the prospect.

We collected Eighty-Seven from Sanctuary at six in the afternoon. Suzanne had been delayed with an emergency operation, a foal with a damaged leg, and when we reached Agassiz, it was already growing dark. I should have been on shift that evening, but Charlie switched me away from Sammy's night rota to the next day. To let tempers cool, he said. So I spent most of my free time studying videos on wolf behaviour in the computer room and taking occasional visits to Eighty-Seven's pen.

His leg had healed well. New hair was growing over

his wounds and in the effortless way he bounded across the uneven scrub, there was no sign of the earlier limp. I watched him for an hour or more and in all that time he was constantly active, trotting to the corners of his pen, loping back to the centre, as if searching for something - obviously ready for release. I shouldn't have been amazed at his recovery. Suzanne had cleared him for release. Yet part of me wished I'd been there at Sanctuary experiencing with him the road back to health. There was so much I still had to learn.

Agassiz Refuge measures less than forty kilometres east-west and hardly more than that in a north-south direction. It spans a maze of lakes, ponds and marshland within a sparse clothing of aspens and pines, hardly leaving room you'd have thought even for one wolf. Yet Jack's warden friend had recently sighted a group of three wolves traversing a gravel track deep in the heart of the refuge. Jack treated this with scepticism. If it were true, this was heartening news for Eighty-Seven.

Our journey into the park proved much easier than at Lost River. For one thing the ground, being low-lying, was relatively flat and hazard free, for another the track was level enough for Jack to drive the truck right up to the release site without the need to handle the crate or the resultant stumbles and disturbance we'd caused the wolves earlier.

Eighty-Seven had been given a light sedative but he was conscious and alert when we set the crate down some yards from the truck. With Jack standing beside her holding his rifle, Suzanne opened the gate to release him. But Eighty-Seven was not to be tempted out. We retreated to the truck's cab and waited for the wolf to emerge in his own good time. By signs and whispers Suzanne indicated what she thought was the cause of the trouble. After Eighty-Seven's accident he had been carried unconscious to Sanctuary. We had brought him from there in the same state; probably he regarded the crate as a refuge from danger.

It was nearly dark. Jack had reached the end of his patience. He signalled he was going to turn on the engine. If that didn't shift the wolf his next idea was to edge the vehicle towards the crate and give it a slight nudge. He did neither. Suzanne pointed into the gloom. In the shadows beyond the crate something was stirring. The figure of a wolf was approaching up the track. It was late in the season. Even without the two young wolves loping behind her, you could tell from her sagging teats that she was a female with young. If they had seen the truck they gave no indication, coming on steadily, three grey shadows in the greater gloom.

Suddenly there was a yelp from the crate. The three wolves lowered themselves ready for flight but Eighty-Seven shot out of the crate and was rapidly closing on them. I feared there would be a fight and implored Jack to fire off a warning shot. He shook his head.

Disappointed, disheartened even, I watched the lead wolf spin round. Her head went up and she appeared to scent the air then, in one bounding leap, she had flung our wolf to the ground. Eighty-Seven yelped, I thought with pain. Then all three wolves piled in for the attack. I couldn't bear to watch and looked away. Suzanne nudged my arm, 'Look'. All the wolves were now huddled together, standing bolt upright, their brushtails high and wagging feverishly. The cubs were licking Eighty-Seven's lips as if begging for food.

The wolf had nothing to give, his last meal had been in the early morning. As if the female knew this she butted between him and the cubs, tossing her head in the air and taking mock lunges at them. The cubs yelped and leapt away. With a light nip to Eighty-Seven's shoulders, she turned and trotted back down the track with her young. Eighty-Seven followed resolutely behind. Soon all four animals had disappeared into the night shadows.

Later that evening, in the darkened car park at Sanctuary I took the opportunity to check my cellphone before I went to my room. Neither Jacob nor Lys had phoned. Jacob could wait but not Lys. I had to know if she was all right. I went to my bed resolved to request a change of shift next morning.

'Wake up, wake up Dawson, Dela ...... whatever you call yourself!'

For day-time shifts, I normally got up at seven-fifteen, well after sunrise at this time of year, giving me enough time to shower and eat before starting work. I hadn't overslept. The window showed only darkness but the door into the corridor was open, the yellow utility bulbs shedding more shadows than they did light. My own room was in partial darkness. The man leaning over me appeared agitated. He shook me again. Sammy! I lashed out with my right fist catching him on the shoulder. He staggered backwards against a cupboard and yelped.

'Get out, get out of here!' I barked. Leaping from the bed, I rushed at him. But he just flung his arms wide in apparent surrender, the palms open. 'You don't understand, you're wanted.' There was real fear in his voice now.

I took no notice and pinned him violently against the wall. He yelped as his head collided with the cracked plaster but he made no move to resist. Instead, he raised his hands higher still and breathed stale breath over me. 'It's the truth, so help me!'

'If this is some mischief of yours?'

'I swear!'

'Who is it then, Charlie? Some emergency?' Still suspecting a trick, I pressed him hard against the wall. Grabbing at his shirt collar I pulled it up almost to his chin then pressed my left arm against his throat. Again he didn't resist, just tried to swallow and I felt the movement of his Adam's apple under my watchstrap. The time was three-twenty.

'Some broad at the gate,' I shivered. My grasp lessened involuntarily, but Sammy made no attempt to escape.

'You're lying aren't you, this is some dirty trick of yours?'

'It's true. Mike won't let her in of course. You know the rules, no-one in after dark. Keeps asking for you. Got something preying on her mind by the look of it.' Sammy sounded genuinely concerned.

'What's her name, what's she look like?'

Sammy looked at me kind of sorrowfully. He began to lower his arms. There was no violence in him.

'Elise, Lys - kind of small, looks a bit like you. I told Mike, didn't like to leave her alone at the gate, and came to wake you.'

My heart sank - Lys outside Sanctuary at three in the morning? I shoved him aside violently and moved towards the door. He had fallen on the bed but he called after me, 'Best put on some clothes.' His voice was gruff, without enmity.

I'd forgotten I was stark naked. In the two minutes it took me to throw on a shirt and jeans without the benefit of the overhead light, Sammy settled himself onto my bed. 'Your sister or something?' he asked quietly. 'What she want?'

'How the hell do I know?' I retorted angrily.

'Must be something bad to bring her here this time of the morning.'

'Something bad,' I agreed. I grabbed my jacket off the back of the door and left Sammy to his musings.

The security lights at Sanctuary are unlike those used in city parking lots. Instead of towering pillars shedding wasteful wigwams of light, Sanctuary's lights are set low down so as not to play across the wolf compound. Individual lights form discrete beams focused on the fence base, but they can be brought together to bear on a single target. The intensity of light can almost blind a person.

I had rushed from the building to the forecourt while pulling on my jacket. Mike was standing in the shadows at the centre of the gates where the two big leaves of metal and mesh were secured with a heavy duty lock. The gates were also chained and padlocked. Beyond Sanctuary's shadowy confines, ablaze in the fierce light, its engine still throbbing, stood one of the camouflaged Delacroix 4x4 all-terrain trucks. It had been drawn up to within a foot of the gate.

This was one of our oldest machines, the sort Gary uses in winter to transport whole moose and caribou trophies from the field. Leaning on the fence, her fingers clawing through the mesh, was Lys. She looked exhausted. I heard her pleading with Mike to let her see 'her brother Francis' and ran through the shadows calling out her name over Mike's denials. He can't have heard the news. Until yesterday no-one else at Sanctuary knew that one Francis Delacroix worked there. When the glare of the lights hit me, Lys cried out, 'Francis. Thank heavens, they're going to slaughter more wolves - just like at Ambrose.'

'Who is, Lys?' I asked, terrified at the thought.

'Leland and that man……..Talbot.' She could hardly bear to say his name. 'They were at Silver Lake today. Dad and Gary have gone with them to Devil's Lake and Mandaamin.'

'Leland and…….,' I gasped, 'the hell they are!' I swung round to Mike. As Lys was speaking I'd seen a look of concern cross his face but he stood back from the gateway, unwilling to get involved. I grabbed his shoulder. 'For Pete's sake Mike, this is my sister. Can't you let her in?'

He shook his head.

'But you heard what she said, man. There's going to be a massacre unless I can stop it,' I insisted.

'You know I can't do that Frank. But, well…. I could let you out.'

I nodded and Mike began the process of unlocking the gate.

'Devil's Lake, that's beyond Grand Forks. Jack Michelson lives there, he's got to be our first port of call,' I said. Lys looked suddenly relieved.

It was too early to phone and I could be there in under two hours in the truck. I looked round at Lys. Mike wouldn't let her in, yet I wasn't sure taking her with me was a good idea. If Charlie had been on duty I was sure he would have allowed her in, but he had gone home to Bemidji for the night. I could phone him, except that would waste precious time and time was of the essence. I had no idea what I was going to do when, or if, I got to Devil's Lake but one thing was certain, Leland and Talbot were dangerous men. I didn't want Lys with me but she'd stuck like a leech when I headed up to Ambrose. Now there was nothing for it but to head for Grand Forks and hope Jack's wife would take her in.

Lys hadn't noticed my silence, and said as if to hurry me on, 'The new estate - Mandaamin, it's not far from Grand Forks.'

'All the better. Get in the truck Lys, I need to get something.'

I rushed back to my car, pulled out the rifle and a box of ammunition and tore through the gates yelling to Mike, 'Tell Charlie where I've gone.'

I left him open-mouthed and beginning to secure the padlock. At that moment, just what he would tell Charlie, I neither knew nor cared. The truck's engine was shaking and labouring. It was close to stalling. Lys was back in the driving seat.

'Shift over, I'll drive.' Too tired to argue, she did as I ordered.

I pulled on the wheel and gingerly turned the big truck between the conifers. It cleared the nearest trunk by inches. I hadn't used that sort of vehicle for a long time, the gears were heavy, the engine sluggish to pull away. No wonder Lys looked exhausted. When we were safely running down through Bitter Springs, I turned to her and touched her shoulder. Underneath the heavy jacket she was shivering.

'You better tell me why you're driving this crate and why you didn't phone.'

'I hadn't anything to tell you before now and my new cellphone has disappeared, or perhaps I just lost it, I don't know,' Lys said, sounding dismayed. 'Anyhow, this evening, when those men left with Dad, I couldn't even make the house phone work.'

'Leland and Talbot?'

She nodded. 'And some other men. I only saw them from the upstairs window. Nasty types, I thought I recognised one or two from Ambrose.'

'Did they see you?'

'I don't think I'd be here if they had. I slipped into my room, locked the door and went out on the balcony. Dad's office is right below. You can often hear him talking but those men were speaking so quietly I couldn't hear. Part of me just wanted to curl up in my bed and hide away until they'd gone, but I knew you'd want to know they'd arrived. I slipped down the outside stairs into the dining room, careful no-one saw me. Dad's office door was slightly ajar. I crept up behind it and listened. They were in there with Pamela and Gary.'

'It was a brave thing to do, Lys.' And foolhardy too I thought, but didn't say.

'It wasn't, I was shaking like a leaf the whole time.'

'But you heard where they were going?'

'Better than that.' She pulled a folded sheet of paper from the glove compartment. Spreading it out on her lap, she said, 'it's a map of Devil's Lake, and the other lodge - Mandaamin.' It was an Indian name but I couldn't guess at its meaning. I glanced down. The cab was too dark to make out any detail on the map. I slowed for the intersection with route 71. Right headed west. Though most direct it would take me along winding country roads.

I chose left, down to Bemidji and the interstate to East Grand Forks. I took the truck swiftly round the corner and accelerated up to and just beyond the limit. There were few cars on the highway but at that time of night the truck stood out like a sore thumb. I couldn't risk being caught for speeding. When I was happy with the way it was handling I switched on the cab light. Lys' fingers lingered over the map showing two polygons joined like a figure-of-eight. There was some writing against them and a number of red crosses.

'You got hold of this without Dad knowing?'

'I got it from Dad's office after they left. Francis, I can't tell you how horrible it was listening to Dad talking with those men about killing the wolves. At Ambrose I didn't really believe Dad could be involved, though you said he was. I thought it must be some awful mistake.'

'You never said.'

'I believe it now.' She went on to recount what she'd overheard - speaking haltingly and with frequent stops to hold back the sobs which I sensed were very near the surface. I hated to ask her to speak of what she'd heard but it was necessary if I was to tell Jack everything she knew, and I couldn't put her through the ordeal twice. Apparently my father's plan was to meet up at the Devil's Lake lodge secretly and stay for several days.

Wolves would be trapped in cages, then killed indiscriminately. The bodies would be buried to avoid being discovered as had happened at Ambrose. Leland's men would stay in touch by walkie-talkie radios, amazingly Lys had memorised their callsign 'Firefly'. It was a bonus I couldn't have expected, though she didn't know what frequency they intended to use. The meeting lasted nearly two hours and Lys was lucky not to have been discovered in all that time.

When it broke up near midnight, the house had suddenly emptied. Lys watched Leland and the men, including Gary and my cousins, leave in a cavalcade of several Delacroix trucks. Dad had left with Pamela. Lys wasn't certain she was going with him to Devil's Lake. She went on hurriedly. 'I knew I had to tell you what happened, but with the phone out of action, the only way I could get in touch was to drive. Then I couldn't find my car keys, they were missing too, like the cellphone.' Lys sounded guilty, as if the loss was her own fault. I thought differently. 'Someone wanted to stop you contacting me, Lys.'

She nodded thoughtfully. Pamela seemed the obvious culprit, I doubted my father had ever considered Lys suspect, unless he'd learnt she'd been with me at Ambrose. 'Dad keeps duplicate keys for all the vehicles in the bottom drawer of his desk. The map was on top of the keys. I knew right away what it was, I'd heard that...that man distributing it at the meeting.'

The road was empty. I looked down at the map. 'Those red crosses do you know what they mean?'

'No, I didn't hear. I'm sorry Francis are they important do you think?'

We had arrived at the Bemidji junction. I slowed down for the lights and turned to Lys, 'Who knows Lys. You've done a grand job.'

'I didn't do so well with the transport.' She almost laughed. 'Once I found the map all I could think of was getting it to you. I grabbed the first key I could find.'

'Hence this cumbersome beast. How did you know

I'd be at Sanctuary?'

'Oh Francis. I didn't, I went to your digs first. That's why it took me so long to get here. I would have driven all the way to Ambrose if I had to.'

'You must be exhausted, it'll be a while before we get to Grand Forks and I need to do some thinking, why don't you try to sleep.'

'This man Jack.... who is he?'

'Head of the Minnesota Wolf Protection Department, the MWPD, he'll know what to do.'

Lys yawned, already drowsy now she had unburdened herself. Her head nodded on my shoulder. 'I wouldn't want them to arrest Dad.'

I don't think she knew what she was saying. Whatever happened at Devil's Lake my father was unlikely to get off lightly. If he did I'd make certain the media knew the real reason for his arrest - at least I hoped that's all it would come to. I hoped we would find him in time to stop the slaughter.

Lys was fast asleep when I pulled onto the forecourt of a darkened roadside café on the outskirts of East Grand Forks. It was five-fifty and a pale light was already filtering through fine high cloud. I took out my cellphone to call Jack. The ringing went on interminably. If there had been a message service I think I would have switched off and headed straight for Devil's Lake, taking the consequences later. But Jack's voice finally barked irritably down the line.

'Michelson.'

'It's.....Frank Dawson,' I said, remembering just in time to give my second persona. If Jack hadn't yet been informed of my real name he would have to be soon. 'I need to see you... urgently.'

I could hear movement. He was obviously looking at his watch, for he suddenly said down the line, 'Needs to be pretty urgent at six in the morning.'

'More than urgent - an emergency. A mass slaughter of wolves at Devil's Lake and another place called...' the map lay half crumpled under Lys' hands. She slept on undisturbed as I pulled it out from beneath her fingers, 'Mandaamin.'

'North Dakota, more than a hundred miles off. How d'you know this?' Jack became suddenly alert, his attitude hardening.

I looked down at Lys and decided now wasn't the time for explanations. 'I'll tell you when I see you.'

'That's not good enough Dawson, it'll take you more'n two hours to get here and...'

'Jack, I'm in East Grand Forks.'

He gasped. 'You've come all this way to...,'

'And I'll go on to Devil's Lake if I have to Jack, but I need your help now.'

'Where are you? I'll give you directions to the house.'

'We came off the highway two miles back and....' I described a nearby industrial complex and the darkened café, from which he was able to direct me to his house. It was only a mile away on the banks of a Red River tributary just near its confluence with the main river. I wound the growling truck down a quiet tree-lined street searching for a half-timbered building which Jack described as hidden among rank prairie grass, in front of a forest of aspens and pines. I found the place easily enough. A beam of light streamed out from the open doorway flooding the gravel track. I switched off the engine and let the truck glide to a halt yards from an open garage door. The sudden silence after the constant throbbing brought Lys sharply awake. A shadow filled the open doorway. 'Where are we?' She sounded frightened.

'Jack's place, let's get down.'

I got out of the cab and helped her down. The clouds were thickening above our heads, blotting out the early dawn and Jack shone a torch into my eyes then suddenly flicked it towards Lys. He seemed shocked. 'Who's this? You said nothing about…,'

'My sister Lys….Lys Delacroix.'

If I expected a gasp of surprise I was disappointed. Jack only nodded. Lys managed a brief smile and put out her hand. He took it cursorily and gestured towards the house. 'You'd better come in.'

Jack led us into a large pine-clad room furnished with leather couches and a scatter of tall congested bookshelves. Lys settled hesitantly at the end of a couch. She was still very tired. I turned to Jack and said, 'Before we start there's something I should tell you.'

He was wearing dark-coloured jeans and a green heavy-duty shirt with a faded leather waistcoat as if prepared for work. I wondered if this meant he'd believed me about the wolf slaughter.

'The Delacroix name, you didn't seem surprised.' As I spoke he screwed his eyes up and, looking between myself and Lys, said rather bluntly, 'If you're going to tell me your name's not Frank Dawson but Delacroix, I already know.'

'Charlie?'

'Indirectly. Jacob actually. Seems you had some trouble at Sanctuary. He thought I should know.'

'Did Jacob say it was him suggested using another

name, that I'd broken with my father?' He nodded.

'Old Louis Delacroix, up at Silver Lake. He told me something of the matter.'

'My father's at Devil's Lake right now.'

Jack had not understood the significance of what I'd said. 'Then why haven't you got him on the phone, warned him?'

I heard Lys gasp behind me. She began to get up from the couch. 'But you can't, he'll know…!' She came anxiously to my side. 'You must tell him Francis.'

Jack was a good foot taller than Lys, he looked down at her tired face and put out a hand to steady her as her shoe caught on the carpet. I spoke for her. 'My father's ordered the wolf kills, Jack. Lys lives at Silver Lake, she watched him leave late last night with some men he's hired. He's probably at Devil's Lake right now making final arrangements for the kill.'

Lys stretched her fingers out, imploring Jack's understanding, 'It's true, I swear!'

'There's no mistake, some other explanation, maybe a hunting party?' Jack questioned, directing himself to Lys. Time was of the essence.

'Lys knows what she's talking about. It's happened before Jack, up at Ambrose, he's using the same men - dangerous men. If you're not prepared to act then I'll have to stop my father myself.'

I turned towards the door. Lys' eyes flashed wildly at me. Realisation that I meant what I said, contorted Jack's features into a frown. He dropped Lys' arm and took hold of my own with a savage grip. 'Hold on there son, did you say Ambrose, up in Canada?'

'If you know about it why are we standing here talking?'

'I heard there were wolf kills up near the border. Rumours filtered down later about Ambrose - thirty or forty wolves killed wasn't it? No names were mentioned, some out-of-town landlord was blamed.'

I told him then how I'd been to Ambrose and discovered the truth about the wolf kills, describing briefly the subsequent attack on us and the arrest of Leland and Talbot. As I spoke Jack's eyes wandered from me to Lys. I watched them lingering for a moment on her face. He gave her a tender thoughtful look that any man might give a woman who had suffered some ill fate, then his gaze came back to me. I wondered if Jack's wife was asleep upstairs.

'Leland and Talbot were at Silver Lake last night with my father. Lys heard them planning the whole thing. She even found a map they are using, here.' I drew the crumpled sheet from my back pocket where I'd shoved it as we got out of the truck.

'There are some red crosses on it ...,' Lys began.

I wanted to hurry her on, offering, 'I reckon that's where they're planning to set the traps. These are vicious men Jack, we have to act quickly.'

He gave me an odd look, then took the map, spreading it out on the top of a dresser and carelessly pushing aside a huge vase of imitation flowers. His fingers traced the lines round the two inked-in polygons.

'About 20 crosses,' he mused, 'Devil's Lake, and Mandaamin, makes a pretty sizeable bit of country.'

'There's a lodge at the centre of Devil's Lake, Lys heard them arranging to rendezvous there. If you gave me some backup we could go straight there and stop this slaughter.'

'You've described these men as vicious Frank, you

can't just go walking in like that. Didn't these same men attack you before, even though they knew you were Louis Delacroix's son?'

'You can't do it alone Francis, they almost killed you,' Lys begged. She clung to my arm. I remembered being half-drowned in the lake and later the pain from fractured ribs. But nothing could stop me from facing up to Leland again.

'Couldn't you call the county sheriff, have a group of deputies and rangers stationed around the estate? Then I'll just call my father on his cellphone, threaten him with exposure to the press if he doesn't give this up.'

'You're talking about a huge spread of territory, Frank. One call from you and the whole bunch of them'll disappear. You'll just be putting off the slaughter for another day.' He was probably right.

'Then I'll go public anyhow.'

'No paper's going to publish something like this without evidence Frank. Your dad's a prominent figure well known among senators and businessmen. Along comes an estranged son with some crazy axe to grind…'

'He's not crazy, never say that!' Lys cried angrily. She stared at Jack and fidgeted with her hair, ready to challenge him again. I waved a hand to calm her.

'Bit of a sore point, Jack. Before the attack Dad deeded Ambrose to me to run as a hunting reserve. I was never going to do that. He's threatening to have me committed to get back control of the estate.'

'He'll never do it, Francis. Why, even Jacob offered to speak for you,' my sister declared.

Jack looked momentarily impressed at mention of Jacob's name. 'Nevertheless he sounds a pretty ruthless kind of guy. No, we have to think of another strategy.'

'We're wasting time, Jack. Every moment that passes another wolf may die. Surely the MWPD has the power to act?'

'Whatever jurisdiction MWPD has, it ends just three miles from here. Devil's Lake and Mandaamin are in North Dakota.'

I was furious. 'You've kept me here talking all this time and now you say you can't do anything because the reserves are a few miles outside Minnesota territory. Then I'll get back on the road right now.'

I went to push past him. I expected Lys to call me back but she clung to my arm as I headed for the door. 'I'm coming with you Francis,' she yelled, 'maybe Dad will listen to me.'

'I can't take you Lys, it's just too dangerous.'

As I turned to nudge her away, Jack Michelson came up behind me barring the doorway. He was a big man but I was prepared to shove him aside.

'Don't be a couple of bloody fools. I didn't say I couldn't help.' I hardly heard him. I tried to dodge round him but he caught me by the shoulder with his big hand. I felt my arm thrust up behind my back but the force Jack used was minimal. He just held me with my face against the wall. Lys screamed and began clawing at his back. Jack just twisted round and propelled me back into the room yelling. 'Get this hellcat off my back. I can help, I just need a little time.' He flayed behind his shoulders, got hold of Lys' hands and twisted her gently sideways. She teetered and half fell against the couch. The three of us were breathing heavily. I stared at Lys, then back at Jack Michelson. He was again blocking the doorway.

'Calm down can't you. I just said it'll take some

thinking over - that's all. Why don't you sit down.' When neither of us showed any obvious belief in his words he stood to one side and gestured towards the door. 'If you want to leave after we've talked, I won't stop you.'

Lys looked to me for a lead. I took her arm and sat down with her opposite one of the small side tables within easy reach of the open door. Jack eased himself onto the arm of a leather couch.

'Best speak your mind.'

Jack nodded but didn't shift position. 'Chain of command goes up through MWPD, they contact the Minnesota State Governor, he or she in our case, Mrs Lorna Sims contacts the Governor of North Dakota, and he contacts their wolf protection department. If he wants to.'

'And if he doesn't want to?'

'Then we have to think of a different route.'

'State governors're a tetchy bunch, liable to run amok if unduly pressed, 'I said.

'Let's cross that bridge when we come to it.' Jack insisted.

'OK so what happens next?'

'MWPD talk to our North Dakota counterparts and decide on a mutual strategy.'

'That include the sheriff's office?'

'We have powers to request their assistance, it's rarely refused.'

'Could you get enough men to put a cordon round both properties and start a search today?'

'Maybe, maybe not. It'll take some time to arrange even if we get the authority right away.'

'I warn you Jack, if it takes too long I'll get over to Devil's Lake and sort this out myself.'

Lys' fingers kneaded my arm but she didn't speak.

'Fair enough. I'll get us some coffee in a minute, but here's something I want you both to think about.' I couldn't tell if he was humouring us.

'Sure.'

At last he slipped down on the couch and was suddenly very grim. 'You say your father's at Devil's Lake?' Lys and I both nodded. 'You realise he'll probably be arrested if we organise a raid.'

Lys reached across to take my hand, saying, 'Mr Michelson, the men my father employs are evil, I learnt that at Ambrose ...,' the mere memory of the near-rape she'd suffered reddened her cheeks and brought tears glimmering to her eyes, 'but I didn't believe my father was to blame. Last night when I heard him talking and laughing with those same men, I just knew I had to stop him.'

'Those are brave words Miss Delacroix.' Lys blushed.

'Even if we stop him today Jack, he'll start up again somewhere else,' I said, my mouth very dry. 'He's got some tame senators pressing for a repeal of the wolf hunting ban. He wants to eradicate wolves from the States. There've been several meetings at Silver Lake over the last month and there's a petition…,'

Jack's forehead creased in a frown of agreement. 'I know about the petition, people sucking up to their senators for favours,' he paused, eased his big body more comfortably against the sturdy back of the couch and looked from me to Lys. What he said next caused the anger to drain away from me, and instilled a feeling of helplessness. 'The pair of you are going to have to think beyond today. From what I've learned of your father, he's bound to deny any wrongdoing. Likely he'll bring in some heavyweight politicians, those senators you mentioned, to support him. He'll claim wrongful arrest and, if I'm any judge, he'll use the whole thing to beef up his campaign. It won't take much to swing public opinion to his side.'

Lys' eyes flickered to me. She looked distraught and angry at the same time. 'Then it will all be for nothing.'

I took a more positive view. Jack wasn't saying all this to depress us, he had some plan in mind.

'What are you saying, Jack?'

'I'm saying I'll do my damnedest today to sort things at Devil's Lake and Mandaamin, organise that posse of yours, it'll be dangerous work.' I heard Lys gasp. Jack sensed her concern, 'not too dangerous if it's organised right, and I think it will be. But in the interim, we have to organise a counter attack if we want to save these wolves.'

'Muster our own forces, you mean. Run our own campaign in the media, that sort of thing?' I asked, optimism returning.

'It'll take a lot of courage, but from what I've just learnt you've both got a good portion of that,' Jack smiled and got up. Relieved of his weight, the leather slackened back into shape with a faint wheeze.

'Now I'd best make that coffee, if you two are staying that is?'

Disheartened and weary, we both nodded.

For the next half hour, while Jack phoned colleagues from a small office opening off the lounge, Lys and I drew up a list of people we felt would assist. But with the enforced delay my anxiety grew. The coffee had been drunk long since and I was becoming agitated. Jack's deep voice droned through call after call. He'd received early agreement from Lorna Sims probably because she'd no support from cattle or hunting lobbies. The governor of North Dakota had proved elusive. Later, I was surprised to hear Jack arranging with the North Dakota police department for a direct assault on Devil's Lake. When he finished, I was waiting beside his desk with the list we'd prepared. He put the phone down forcefully.

'Making progress?'

'Sure. Got four colleagues arriving here soon. Two of them know the area pretty well.'

'Minnesota people?'

'MWPD? Two are.' He gave me a self-conscious look. 'The other two are North Dakota state rangers - they'll be acting unofficial like.'

Jack took the sheet of paper from my hands. Jacob's name was prominent at the top of the list, above a set of six senators and business men across the Great Lakes states who I'd thought might be useful. At the base of the page was the St Paul News with a double question mark against it. Contact with the media would only be made when we were already at Devil's Lake and a raid imminent. I didn't trust the media with an embargoed press release. One of them would surely go for a scoop and precipitate the announcement. If my father was warned of the raid, he was sure to abort the operation - temporarily.

'And the local sheriff's office? Time's marching on.'

Instead of replying he looked down at the list. I thought he hadn't heard me. 'Pretty impressive. You phoned anyone yet?'

'I wanted you to check them over. Look Jack I know this is important, but every minute I spend here...'

He didn't allow me to finish. 'Means another wolf killed you think. Frank, I learnt something else this morning. Devil's Lake may be a private hunting lodge but this last year no-one's gone there much and it seems local fishermen have been using the place unofficially. One of them noticed some unusual activity this morning around Devil's Lake, vehicles travelling down forest tracks without any lights showing. He phoned the local police. I got through to Sheriff Dave Lawson right after the call came in. He was enraged when he learnt what your father intended. He's putting the place under surveillance right away, says he's in with us whether the governor agrees or not.'

'They should have been at the lodge hours ago Jack, supposing they're already setting out traps. If we delay any further…'

'Frank, calm down. Everything's under control. My colleagues'll be arriving in less than an hour. When they get here we'll set off. By the time we get to Devil's Lake, we'll have marshalled enough men and firepower to scare the living daylights out of anyone.'

Lys stood in the doorway wringing her hands. Her face was a pale mask as if she'd just understood what Jack planned.

'Isn't there some other way? Can't we send someone in to…. to parlay first?'

Jack stood up and went to her side. 'That may be possible Miss, I won't know until we're on site. But we could lose all opportunity of catching them if they're alerted.'

Lys gave an exaggerated sigh. Jack took her hand. 'If I can avoid confrontation Miss Delacroix, then you have my word I'll do it. In the meantime you and your brother can start phoning people on this list. There may be something we haven't thought of. You never know, it may come to a battle of wills after all.'

Lys gave him a weak smile and seemed content. I wasn't. I wanted action. Things were happening far too slowly for me. I'd just made up my mind to speak when Lys asked, 'Shall I make you some hot coffee, if your wife doesn't mind me using the kitchen?'

Previously, we'd heard footsteps moving about in an upper room. Lys hesitantly lifted Jack's cup from where it remained untouched beside the phone, an oily slick had formed on the cold liquid. Jack nodded towards the ceiling and said, without noticeable grief, 'That's my daughter Gillian. My wife died four years ago.'

The news of another female in the house heartened me. When Lys had collected our cups and disappeared into the hallway, I broached my concerns with Jack.

'Lys may want to come with us to Devil's Lake, Jack. I don't think she should. Can she stay here, would your daughter mind?'

'Yes most certainly to the first, but she'll be alone. Gillian will be going off to college pretty soon.'

'Could you ask your daughter to stay - with Lys?' I heard myself pleading. Jack looked thoughtful.

'Maybe I could, in the circumstances. Now do you want me to help you with those phone calls. It's important we get these people on our side and quickly.'

But I knew my first, most crucial call had to be to Jacob. It was half-past seven and I could see through the windows of Jack's lounge that a watery sun was poking through thin grey clouds. Jacob wasn't only up, he was in Fargo about to attend a League meeting, when I gave him the news.

Somehow my father's involvement came as little surprise to him, I even got the impression he'd been expecting a re-enactment of Ambrose. He'd get to Devil's Lake as soon as the meeting ended, Jacob told me. When I came to Jack's suggestions that the time was right for a political assault on my father's campaign he mulled over the idea for a few moments, finally coming out with some reassuring words.

'You're right. The Wolf League's been too defensive for too long, it's time we did something more positive. Yes Francis, go ahead. What approach were you considering?'

We discussed a formula for the phone calls and came up with the following wording:

An illegal slaughter of wolves is currently underway at the hunting estates of Devil's Lake and Mandaamin in North Dakota. This is being masterminded by a prominent citizen and other influential colleagues who are campaigning for complete wolf eradication. The Wolf League considers the activities of such people unconstitutional and detrimental to all wildlife. If people wanted further information, they were to contact League Offices.

Jacob agreed the use of League phone numbers. Jack and I would make the calls on behalf of the League without using our own names. Jack because he was a state employee, myself because the Delacroix name was bound to cause confusion, or worse.

'Who's on your list?' Jacob asked finally. I recounted the names we'd scribbled down. He agreed them all, even adding a couple of his own which he promised to contact direct. Jack and I started phoning. After my fifth phone call I flipped the cellphone closed, noting the battery was low. Jack emerged from his office.

'How's it going?'

'Senators Mike Hayes and Mary Jenson from Minnesota were perturbed but noncommittal. Both said they'd wait and see. Jackson Smith, a congressman from Wisconsin and Director of Smiths Incorporated' (this was an old Canadian firm, producer of high grade optical instruments and wildlife binoculars, and strong competitors with Zeiss) 'was downright outraged, says he's getting a gun and coming in with us.'

'I hope you stopped him. His word'll stand for nothing if he's seen at the raid with us.'

'Comes of having French-Canadian blood, but don't worry, he's agreed to stand back. We may have a problem with Congressman Abe Langer from Kansas City.'

'Retired cattle rancher isn't he, why d'you put him on your list?'

'Maybe it's a wild card. He's married to the daughter of a chap I met at Ely. Leroy Tucker, eighty-five years old, spoke very highly of him. He was a bit anti until I mentioned Leroy's name.' I didn't tell Jack I had volunteered the name Leroy knew me by: Frank Dawson. Probably the old boy would have completely forgotten about our conversation by now.

'I've two more for your list and two doubtfuls….,'

Jack mentioned two out-of-state congressmen who had come on board: Shauna Bates of North Dakota and Martin Emery of Iowa. Both industrial giants, they were nonetheless known for their concern for wildlife. The two doubtfuls were a disappointment. Amity Lawhead was head of the Ontario First Nation Confederation where Ambrose was sited. Gabe Tuckwell held a similar post with the Plains & Great Lakes Indian League: Devil's Lake and Mandaamin lay within his domain.

Neither body was known for its political clout, but the Indian question, even in the twenty-first century, was a fickle beast, as some politicians had learnt through ruined careers. Getting these First Nation people behind us might have deterred some of our opponents, so it was a disappointment to learn of their indecision.

'What about the wildlife organisations?' I asked. The names WWF and IFAW had cropped up in conversation.

'Bit early to call them in, maybe after the raid. Jacob can advise us better.'

I heard a footfall in the hallway. Lys came in carrying a plate loaded with sandwiches. Beside her and carrying a coffee pot and several cups was Jack's daughter Gillian. She was a fresh-faced brunette, about nineteen and looked every bit the student. Bright wispy pieces of material were threaded through her long hair which fell, otherwise unhindered, down to a bare waist. She was wearing an odd assortment of faded ill-fitting clothes, jeans, shirt and trainers with a fashionable pink half-cardigan wrapped somehow round her upper chest. But she looked a good-hearted girl and when she had laid the tray on the table near Lys's sandwiches she quickly moved across to kiss her father.

'I'll get going now.'

'Gillian,' Jack and I said together.

The girl looked bemused and gave a rippling laugh. 'I'm an old-fashioned girl, I prefer my suitors one at a time please.' For some unaccountable reason I felt my cheeks glow and redden. I let Jack talk to his daughter.

'Can you do me a favour today?'

'What's that Dad, want to borrow some cash?' Jack laughed, it was an old joke between them.

'Nothing like that. Could you…,' he looked over at Lys, appearing uncertain how to continue, 'stay here today and keep Lys company?'

Lys looked shocked, I expected an agonised complaint but it was Gillian who appeared the most surprised. There was an explosion of speech as the two woman chorused.

'Don't think I'm going to let you go without me, Francis.'

'Lys told me she was going with you.'

I was saved from answering by the crash of a knocker on the outer door.

'That'll be my lift,' Gillian spun round and headed into the hallway. Jack looked unequal to the task of stopping her. We heard a muffled gasp then a brief conversation before she returned looking slightly embarrassed, and in company with a group of people. One, a young man whom Gillian hugged and giggled with was obviously a boyfriend.

Behind them were two men and two women, all serious-looking professionals dressed in green rangers' uniforms. These then were Jack's colleagues. Each greeted him as a friend. Their ages must have ranged between mid twenties to mid thirties; why I had expected them to have the same seasoned air as Jack I don't know, but compared with his toughened exterior, they seemed very young. I quailed too at the sight of the women rangers, pondering Lys' refusal to stay behind when we left. Gillian and her boyfriend were turning to leave. I caught Lys' eye. She grinned defiantly. Raising her hand she warned: 'Not one word.'

Jack waved his daughter off, then introduced us to his colleagues. He had invited the two men because they had grown up on the Devil's Lake Indian Reservation and knew both it and Mandaamin intimately. I had already noticed a likeness in them, guessing this was due to Indian ancestry. Now Jack introduced them as Curtis and Luke Holappa, twin brothers who'd worked in the North Dakota wildlife service since leaving college. I guessed their age at about twenty-eight. Joyce Bennett and Miriam Larkin, respectively the youngest and oldest members of the group, had been employed by MWPD for some years.

Though Jack had already warned them of the dangers we might encounter, all four seemed eager to partake. None of them wore firearms and Jack didn't mention guns before herding us out towards the cars.

Lys was close by my side as if still fearful of being left behind. As we neared the outer door she suddenly cried out and ran back into the lounge. 'Wait!' she called back. I thought she'd decided not to join us after all. Instead she headed towards the coffee table. Half-empty coffee cups stood beside the mountain of untouched sandwiches. But she couldn't bear to see food go to waste. She bundled the food into two piles, wrapped them awkwardly in some serviettes, and turned back to see six curious pairs of eyes fixed on her. Slightly embarrassed but determined she handed a package each to me and Jack saying, 'No-one should go hungry, not this morning when…,' she couldn't continue and the silence spoke for itself. It might be many hours before any of us had time to eat.

We left Jack's place in three vehicles, Curtis Holappa with the two women wardens in a jeep emblazoned with the logo of his own wildlife service. Lys, Luke and Jack in an unmarked jeep to be suitably anonymous once we were in North Dakota. Jack had intended me to share their vehicle. Instead when the engines were already pumping out watery exhausts into the cold morning air, I insisted on taking the big Delacroix truck. Its bodywork was worn, but it would prove useful on uneven forest tracks, easily battering through thick scrub, a feature we might need at Devil's Lake.

Jack wasn't convinced. He insisted Luke travel with me, ostensibly to give directions, he said. But I knew Jack didn't trust me not to rush off on my own once we neared the reserves. He made Luke get out of the car and join me in the battered truck. Luke was smiling as he clambered into the agéd cab.

In just over two hours, the three vehicles were travelling along the north banks of the Sheyenne River where it borders Mandaamin Reserve. The river was running smoothly, jutting rocks showing the exceptionally low water level: portage notices across from the lightly wooded Gladstone parklands now unnecessary.

Mandaamin estate huddled behind a screen of firs and oaks of seeming equal age and height. Luke confirmed that a fire had come through the reserve fifteen years before at the end of one exceptionally dry summer. With good winter rains and scorching summers, the young trees had already grown forty feet. Wildlife had suffered in the fire, but with the breeding season over, many animals had escaped.

At the time of the fire, Luke told me, the disused

lodge was occupied only by an old caretaker and his wife. Unseasonable winds had swept north from the parched Gladstone Lakelands, leaping the shrunken Sheyenne. The flames had engulfed half the southern woods in a few minutes. Man and wife had both perished. Mandaamin lodge had been burnt completely to the ground. The only remaining structures were two small cabins which had been left to rot. Two summers back Luke had been in there following a wounded deer. The buildings were mouldering away, their footings rotted, roofs half-smashed in by pine boughs brought down in winter storms.

Jack drove slowly alongside the crowded forest, looking for tracks leading between the trees. We saw just two possible entrances where the road bordered Mandaamin. The first was a simple half moon of gravel. Beyond stood a thick belt of vegetation showing no signs of disturbance. We didn't stop. At the second, the track into the woods was clearer, demanding investigation. Jack stopped at the entrance.

I pulled the truck in behind Curtis, barely able to get the rear wheels off the tarmac. Jack was consulting Lys' map. The Holappa brothers started searching through the low brush bordering the track. I joined them silently. We all understood the need for vigilance.

The track looked unused but the vegetation gave small signs of disturbance: twisted stems and crushed herbs now recovering; a twig dangling from a stem. About twenty yards in, the vegetation grew thickly across the path. Curtis and Luke moved cautiously in that direction. The thick foliage had received a recent battering. Fresh conifer boughs littered the ground, broken bark livid yellow against the leaf litter.

Boughs higher up had sprung back into place but as the brothers pushed through they encountered another barrier. A grove of sturdy young oaks grew right across the trackway. The ground in front had been savagely churned up by tyre tracks. At about bumper height, peeled slithers of bark hung from the scarred trunks. More debris lay on the ground. All around us the trees massed tightly together. The track was assuredly blocked and there was no way through to Mandaamin. There might be no further need for silence, but none of us spoke as we returned to the vehicles.

'What d'you find lads?'

'Looks like someone tried to force a vehicle through and failed, trees all cut up but there's no way in.'

'Well I reckon we're about six miles from the boundary with Devil's Lake reserve. This is just where the first red cross is marked.'

'Maybe they'll go in somewhere else, but we haven't seen any other obvious tracks,' I cautioned, glancing at the map.

'You think the only way in is via Devil's Lake?' I pointed to a road leading out from Mandaamin lodge. At first it wound north-west almost as if trying to avoid contact, then just south of highway 2, it suddenly doubled-back and ran straight down towards Devil's Lake. The hunting lodge was sited alongside a long inlet at the eastern extremity of the lake. Every major trackway and a few of the smaller ones bore red crosses. Fewer red crosses were scattered across Mandaamin, only one near the lodge buildings.

Probably Leland or my father had used the map to choose spots near the original trackways without realising how badly overgrown they'd become. It was something which might work in our favour. Still, those signs of disturbance must mean something. I thought we should know for certain.

'This track's blocked, Jack. Perhaps I should take the truck back to that first opening.'

He looked at me steadily and I guessed what his reply would be. Luke answered for him. 'If the tracks are so overgrown Francis, you probably wouldn't get through, even with the truck.'

'You heard what the man said, best carry on to the sheriff's office,' Jack insisted.

Chapter Fourteen

We stopped for coffee at a roadside café and ate Lys' sandwiches, none of us talking much, and it was gone one-thirty when our small cavalcade entered an open lot behind the sheriff's office. The clouds had thickened to a uniform grey and a light rain began to fall, not good conditions for work in open country. As I turned off the truck's engine, the rear door of the building opened. Jacob stepped out onto the jettied broadwalk. I leapt from the truck and hurried to greet him.

'Jacob, what happened to your meeting?' He inclined his head towards the building behind him.

'Curtailed. Seemed wisest. You've stirred up a regular hornet's nest. Lawson doesn't like what's happening on his doorstep.'

'Is he proving unhelpful?' I asked, rather alarmed. Without the sheriff's help the operation was already doomed.

'Far from it, he's gone to a lot of trouble, getting help in from three counties so you'd better be mighty sure of your facts.'

'I am,' Lys had come up beside me followed by Jack and his colleagues. Jacob nodded and lead the way inside. We passed through a wide office populated by about six officers whose eyes followed us as we proceeded along the corridor and entered a room where more cops were gathered round three tables.

On one wall was a large relief map of the Devil's Lake-Mandaamin area. Now the reason for the tortuous western route from Mandaamin became obvious, a stream running east out of Alice Lake entered

Mandaamin reserve at its north-west corner. Except for a narrow strip of relatively flat land where the track spanned it, the stream plunged into a deep ravine effectively cutting off the two reserves from one another.

There was an excited murmur of voices. A tall angular man, spare of body and with thin fair hair, that occasionally swept across his forehead, came towards us with an air of authority. This then, was Sheriff Dave Lawson. He came straight across to Jack, nodded and shook hands with the four wardens, then turned somewhat more gravely to Jacob, obviously expecting him to introduce Lys and myself.

'Sheriff Lawson, this is Francis….. ' he gave me a sudden questioning look. I finished the sentence for him. 'Delacroix, Francis Delacroix, this is my sister Lys.'

The Sheriff looked baffled. 'Delacroix…. same as the guy organising this kill?'

The other officers had been talking casually among themselves. Now the room went suddenly silent. Many people shifted position or looked uncomfortable.

'Louis Delacroix's my father, and before you ask Sheriff, I split with him a month ago. I work for Bitter Springs Wolf Sanctuary now.' The Sheriff gave me a long scrutinising stare as if searching out an untruth. I met his gaze. Finally satisfied, he glanced at Jacob for confirmation and received an emphatic nod.

'You heard from the Governor yet, Dave?' Jack's question dispelled the slight tension.

'Not only heard from him, the man's coming straight here this evening with two colleagues. Jackson Smith, a congressman, and Martin Emery a big industrialist, you know anything about that Jack?'

Jack looked at me sideways and countered the

question with his own. 'What time you going to start off?'

'Governor's in a meeting in Washington. He's flying back right after, wants me to wait until he gets here this evening.'

'And you're not going to?'

'If he's already spoken to these people, news is likely to break before long. I got just three unmarked cars out checking the highways surrounding both reserves right now. Three cars to cover more than a hundred and eighty miles of road. That's hardly enough. I'm waiting on six more from Grand Forks. They can't get here until after five and I'll need to have a lot more surveillance before then. You got that map you mentioned?'

Jack handed over the now very creased map.

'D'you want to come into my office?' He appeared to direct the question only to Jack and Jacob, his intention being to exclude the rest of us. 'Your team can get themselves some refreshments.' Lys and the rangers looked disappointed.

'Curtis and Luke know the area well Sheriff, I think they should be involved,' Jack objected.

'OK. No-one else though, my office's pretty small and airless. We'll do a full briefing for everyone later.' I felt his last sentence was directed at me, but I wasn't prepared to be sidelined. As he headed for his office I put my arm out. I saw the glint of a police badge as another officer twisted around. The man eased the gun in his holster and had already taken two steps towards me as I said, 'I'd like to be involved.'

'Like I said, Mr. Delacroix, everyone will be briefed.' He glanced around at the nearest officer and shook his head. Then he glared at me as if trying to decide how to proceed. I got the feeling he still didn't trust me.

'Sheriff, there wouldn't be anything to brief people about if it wasn't for me. My whole family's involved in this, I've a right to know what you're planning.' As I spoke Lys leaned forward. 'He's right Sheriff, my uncle and both my cousins are out there at Devil's Lake too. Jack said...Jack promised there wouldn't be any violence.' Her gaze swept across to Jack Michelson who stood self-consciously in front of the Holappa brothers. For some reason he couldn't meet her gaze. The room was hot. He'd just taken off his stetson and began to fumble awkwardly with it. The sheriff saw the exchange and sighed.

'OK then, just Delacroix. The rest of you'll have to stay here.'

This time there was no arguing with him. He led the way into a room overlooked by a cluster of aspens, through which the station's parking lot was visible. Apart from the Sheriff's leather armchair and desk, the only other seats were three hard wooden chairs set round a small table. Jacob approached them and collected up his papers.

He motioned Jack into the seat. Sheriff Lawson pulled his chair across to the table and set our map alongside a larger map similar to the one in the briefing room. It seemed quite natural for the Holappa brothers to sit either side of him. I looked around for another chair. A computer console had been built into the corner of the room below the windows. Jammed beneath it was a low stool which I pulled out and positioned alongside Jacob. He remained standing.

'These red crosses..., any idea what they are?' the sheriff asked.

'That one along the Sheyenne road, south of Mandaamin. Track's marked with a cross so we took a look. It's kind of blocked off by scrub. We found signs of recent activity but there's no knowing who made them.'

'And the other crosses?'

'There was an overgrown track further east near another cross, no sign of obvious disturbance. We didn't stop.'

'No knowing what they really are then?'

'They may just be tracks, equally they could be places they're going to set traps,' Jack ventured.

'So what are we looking for then, some kind of wooden trap or just snares in the undergrowth? They must be using some kind of bait if they reckon to catch any wolves at all - any poison involved?'

'Probably too indiscriminate even for these people. They can't risk leaving the stuff around to kill anything else, someone would be sure to report sick animals.' It was Curtis Holappa speaking.

'Just some kind of crate then, baited with meat. Where'll they keep it?'

'Devil's Lake's a regular hunting lodge, it should have enough freezer space to store meat for a few days. That's how long we expect them to be there,' I offered.

'Well that's not much to go on, I was hoping for something more. I'm going to need better information before I instigate a raid and the weather's threatening to close in.'

The conversation had become depressing. I saw my opportunity to make a contribution.

'The men were going to rendezvous at Devil's Lake early this morning. If none of them knows the area they'd need daylight to deploy the traps wouldn't they? If I was Leland I'd search both reserves to make sure there weren't any campers on site before I started. Suppose they do that, and start setting the traps this evening when no-one's about. If we found out where they were working we could catch them red-handed.'

'What are you suggesting?' I'd gained the Sheriff's attention at last.

'Leland's using Delacroix trucks, four of them, just like the one I've got out there.' I gestured towards the window. 'If I took that in, no-one would think anything of it.'

The sheriff got up and peered through the window at the green truck. It seemed to tower over the nearest patrol car.

'It's too dangerous, Francis. They'll have set guards. You're sure to be recognised,' Jack argued.

'I could drive,' Luke Holappa volunteered. I ignored him for the moment.

'Jack, that works both ways. None of you knows these people, I do. How are you going to tell an innocent camper from Leland's men or even my own family? No, this is the only way you're going to find out where anybody is.'

The sheriff nodded towards the window. 'Good camouflage,' he mused.

'Sheriff, if we can isolate and target these people it'll make your job easier,' I persisted.

'Too dangerous, you'll need back up. I couldn't guarantee that until I have men stationed at all known exits and on the surrounding highways. If what you say is correct, Delacroix, I don't want them hanging around the reserves for hours getting noticed. I could time the raid to before dusk, say seven-thirty. I'll have everyone in place an hour or so before. You could go in then, check as many of these crosses as you can for traps and be sure you get out of there before seven-thirty. Any problems, you just get straight out.'

'That's hardly long enough to cover both reserves.'

'I can't let you go in until I've got all the men on station, and I can't promise that until sixty-thirty at the earliest. Those men you saw just now know the area, they've been briefed as far as is possible. The Grand Forks people are coming in cold, I've got to brief and deploy them which I can't do until they arrive. It's the best I can offer.'

Suddenly remembering my early morning conversation with Lys, I asked hopefully, 'There's one other thing, the walkie-talkies they're using. Lys says the callsign's Firefly, you got any people able to listen in to their conversations?'

'You got the frequency?' Lawson asked. I shook my head, 'Then it's pretty unlikely we'd discover it in time to be of any help.'

'That settles it, I go in - but alone.'

'I still say it's too dangerous,' Jack argued.

'I'll drive,' Luke insisted again. 'None of these men knows me and Francis can sit well back, the cab's plenty deep and dark enough. I know, I've been driving with him. As soon as he spots any trouble, we'll just drive off. Say, what if Francis wore Jack's stetson, he'd probably be unrecognisable. Look!'

Before either of us could object, Luke had flipped Jack's stetson off the table and placed it on my head. The other men laughed uncertainly.

'Joking aside Sheriff, it's a good disguise,' Jacob said.

Of the four men in the room Jacob's word carried most weight and he had also known me the longest. It was a good plan but we had to wait three long tortuous hours before Luke and I could set out for Devil's Lake.

Jack had taken his stetson back when Luke asked, 'D'you know when the North Dakota wildlife people are arriving, Dave?' He was interrupted by the ringing of the sheriff's phone. Dave Lawson spoke into the receiver 'Yep, send them in,' then nodded to Luke saying, 'Get the sergeant to find you a room.' But the phone rang again. It was a pattern which was to be repeated throughout most of the afternoon when one or other of us tried to speak to him.

As the afternoon wore on, tension steadily increased. We'd met the wildlife people in the corridor and were directed to the only free table in the briefing room. Jacob was already installed at a desk in a separate cubicle. I badly wanted to discuss the political campaign with him but he was constantly on the phone.

The six of us collected around the small table and were quickly joined by Jack's other colleagues. He briefly introduced us as Lys and Francis. Of the North Dakota wildlife people present, two senior male rangers and two vets, I only remember Mark Laidlaw's name. He was Chief Ranger for North Dakota. At first, all the talk was of deploying the two mobile veterinary vans now parked at the far end of the police lot. Mike was for keeping them on the state highways within easy reach of Devil's Lake's veterinary hospital and well outside the reserves border. Luke and Jack wanted them on standby at designated picnic lots. I was only vaguely interested; I hoped the day would end without any wolf casualties.

The conversation whittled down to veterinarian equipment. I grew bored and got up, expecting Lys to join me. She was seated right opposite, next to Jack but she didn't move or acknowledge me, so I left.

I went in search of Jacob and again found him talking animatedly down the phone. Back in the briefing room ten of the Grand Forks police had arrived. The sergeant quickly began to brief them. For a while I listened to the jargon of deployment and back-up. Several times the names Delacroix and Leland were mentioned. Talk and more talk. The waiting was getting me down. Left to myself I would have headed out directly to Devil's Lake to confront my father, but I knew he would simply laugh in my face.

At four-thirty, coffee was served in the briefing room and after long periods of study and intense discussion people began to relax. The wildlife wardens mingled with their police counterparts. Lys remained at the table deep in conversation with Jack. I sat down and was attempting to drink the hot coffee, when I heard my alias called. 'Frank Dawson wanted on the phone.'

The room hushed as I stood up. The woman vet standing nearby murmured, 'I thought his name was Francis'. The sergeant answered. 'That's right, Francis Delacroix, his father Louis's organised the wolf kill.'

I left behind gasps of surprise and irate mutterings. The phone call though, proved to be the one highlight of that long wearying afternoon: I spoke to Leroy again. Jacob was talking animatedly on a landline. He glanced up, then pulled a cellphone out from beneath a jumble of papers and handed it to me. 'Sorry Francis, chap was pretty insistent. Said he knew you, mentioned Abe Langer the congressman. I thought it might be important.' Jacob went back to his call.

'That you, Frank?' Leroy's querulous old voice asked down the line.

'Leroy, what the hell…..?'

'No swearing boy - it's not good for you, Lindy wouldn't like it either.'

'How d'you get hold of me?' But I had already guessed the answer.

'Phoned Abe about this wolf problem didn't you. Gave him your name, no nonsense.'

'Is he there?'

'One thing at a time boy, I want to hear what you got to say.'

'It's a long story Leroy....'

'I got all the time in the world, Frank. But that's not your name is it? Them people at the League office didn't know any Dawson. Mind you, wasn't really convinced at Ely.' I wondered how my behaviour could have been so transparent. Then I remembered I'd met him after my argument with Pamela and the angry split with my father. My feelings were running raw that day.

'Then how come…?' I began, but he was ahead of me again.

'Used the cellphone number, had to convince the chap to let me speak to you.'

'Well, now you've got me what can I do for you?'

'You at Devil's Lake and this other place, Manda…'

'Mandaamin, yes.'

'I'd kind of like to know who I'm speaking to boy,' he chivvied.

'Leroy, did Abe put you up to this, because if he did I'd like to speak to him. Looks like he got the wrong idea about this business.'

'Can't do that Frank. Abe's flying up to Grand Forks right this minute. Got his own private jet.'

I gasped into the phone. 'He's intending to sabotage our campaign? How could you let him, Leroy?'

'Hasn't got sabotage on his mind so far as I know, quite the opposite. Now if you just tell me your real name….,' he left the question hanging. There seemed no point in denying my inheritance, now that everyone else at Devil's Lake knew me as the son of Louis Delacroix, potential wolf killer.

'It's Delacroix, Francis Delacroix,' I said. There was a long satisfied sigh from the other end of the line.

'Son of Louis Delacroix, gunsmith and industrial magnate,' (He was repeating the headline from the Chicago newspaper article) 'that's what we figured boy.'

'So what are you and Abe going to do about it?'

'Me, I'm doing nothing at all, 'cept tell Abe who you are of course.' He paused, teasing me. I knew if I waited he was sure to divulge what Abe Langer, congressman and industrial magnate, possessed of far greater wealth than my father, actually intended.

'Got kind of fond of you up at Ely. Knew something was wrong of course, just couldn't put my finger on it. Told Abe so after you phoned. Say, you thought any more about that biology career boy?'

'Damn you Leroy, you going to tell me why Abe's heading up here?' I demanded, getting angry at the old man's prevarication.

'You ever heard of James & Langer.'

' ….that Langer,' I hissed down the phone. James & Langer was the Mid West's biggest law firm. It was known for championing lost causes against the big conglomerates. On almost every occasion they were successful. It was said their success came from simple hard work and dedication rather than the corruption afflicting many similar law firms.

'We thought the League might need some good legal support with its campaign. His brother Eric *is* James & Langer, they got the best brains and…' He would have gone on but I stopped him.

'This got something to do with your father, Leroy?' He paused before answering.

'Being pushed out of his farm like that Frank. Don't think he ever got over it, neither did I.'

'And if he'd had a firm like James & Langer behind him…..?' We neither of us needed to complete the analogy. 'But I'm fighting my own father Leroy, it's pretty serious stuff.'

'Families're complicated things Frank. All the more reason for good legal support.'

'I guess so,' I said, unconvinced.

When he spoke next, Leroy's mood had lightened. 'Got to go now, Frank…. Francis, Lindy's serving up supper. You look out for Abe. I'll tell him you're all right.'

'Nice talking to you, Leroy.'

'You get down to Chesapeake Highway, Kansas City, look out for ….'

'I know - Red River. And Leroy, I'm studying zoology at Bemidji Uni.' There was a satisfied guffaw at the end of the line, then it went dead.

I couldn't face returning to the briefing room now everyone knew of my father's part in the proposed wolf kill. I was also bored by the interminable talk and rhetoric, so I walked out onto the street and did a circuit of Devil's Lake township. It took barely twenty minutes for the obscure delights of the main street to render themselves up: a soda parlour crowded with teenage girls; older lads patrolling the streets on scooters; an ancient wooden colonial building labelled Old Glory, where old men sat on a veranda and yarned and waited for their evening meal.

One surprise at the far end of the dusty street was a riding stables where youngsters were learning the rudiments of a skill I'd practised and forgotten before my college days. I watched the antics of their small piebald ponies for a while, then let my eyes travel along a stony stream and over grassy foothills sweeping up towards the distant Coteau de Missouri where Lewis and Clark had followed the great river in their laboured search for the Pacific Ocean. How many thousands of wolves had lived here when those brave men had journeyed through that wilderness of forest and chasm, and how many had since met their deaths at human hands in these proud United States?

The thought drove me back to the parking lot. I got into the truck's cab and was checking the loading mechanism of my rifle, when Lys found me. She looked in through the open cab door. Her face was pale, her eyes weary from lack of sleep, but when she saw the rifle she started, drawing a sudden breath. Probably the ominous nature of what we planned had got through to her. I had no words of comfort to offer. 'Jacob wants to see you,' she said, turning away swiftly. Her hair swung forwards so I couldn't see her expression.

Where the afternoon had dragged abysmally, the next forty-five minutes rushed past. There was barely time to discuss with Jacob the various politicians we had contacted. Lys, Jacob and I squeezed onto an assortment of chairs round the desk he shared with a patrolman. Lys seemed lost in a world of her own. I didn't dare disturb her.

'I've also spoken to congressmen Karl Lewis and Raymond Bell, they're renowned wildlife lobbyists. Both seemed fairly positive. So for definite we've four congressmen, a couple of uncommitted senators, indecision from several more and no native American support. It's not enough…,' I could tell Jacob was despondent and quickly interrupted.

'There's Abe Langer…,' I'd left it until that moment to report my intriguing conversation with Leroy. When I finished Jacob said, 'James & Langer! They'd certainly add clout to the campaign. I doubt the League can afford their fees though, even with a public appeal for funds.'

'I could be wrong, but I understood from Leroy there wouldn't be any fee.'

Jacob mused on the information. 'You say he's on his way here?' I nodded. 'Then you'll have to sort it out with him when he arrives.'

I reminded him I would probably have left for Devil's Lake well before Abe Langer arrived.

'Sure, sure. I'll see him myself then. That brings me to the next point, it involves you both.'

I could tell Lys hadn't been listening. I nudged her arm. 'Is it time?' Her voice was low. A worried frown creased her forehead.

'Not yet, Miss Delacroix.'

'Lys!' she insisted in a whisper, but her gaze had drifted beyond the desk to an open window overlooking the parking lot. Jack and his team were gathered round the two veterinary vans. The windowless sides were emblazoned with the North Dakota Wildlife Service logo: a leaping deer. Blue emergency lights were fixed front and rear.

'You see, it's not enough to contact a few politicians, we've got to bring people over to our side, and quickly.'

As we'd sat down I'd glimpsed a phrase on the screen of Jacob's laptop and thought I knew what was coming.

'A press release?'

He nodded. 'The League governors have decided, and I'm in full agreement, that the only way we can arouse public outrage is with a press release naming names. It'll be sent to US and Canadian national papers and all the local papers, at the very moment the sheriff launches the raid.' Here he hesitated, waiting for the implications to sink in. 'I have the text prepared. You can read it if you like.' Lys glanced at him in disbelief, then she looked down into the laptop screen. She read hesitantly, and out loud, her eyes widening as the words escaped her lips.

'The Wolf League has learnt that Louis Delacroix, one time respected industrialist, hunter and upright citizen, may have turned a corner in his attitude to the country's protected wildlife....,' Tears spilled from Lys' eyelids as she read on, *'He now heads what the Wolf League considers to be an illegal campaign to eradicate the nation's wolves: a protected species which has only recently been brought back from extinction. The League condemns the action. This evening Mr Delacroix's activities at Devil's Lake, North Dakota, will reveal the depths to which he will sink in pursuing his spurious claims that wolf populations are out of control. Attended by the group of ruthless ....'*

Here my sister's voice failed her, she began sobbing quietly. Astonished at the forthright nature of the release

I continued to read for her, anxious to hear just what the League thought of my father:

'....*Attended by the group of ruthless men he has gathered about him for the purpose and continuing a process, it is rumoured he started in Ambrose hunting reserve, Ontario, where more than 40 wolves were illegally killed this summer, Mr. Delacroix may even now be engaged in activities likely to result in the illegal eradication of US wolves. Devil's Lake police department and the North Dakota Wildlife Protection team are currently investigating these allegations.*'

We sat in silence for some minutes. Jacob looking from one to other of us with a concerned expression on his face, Lys sobbing quietly, myself in a daze and trying to make sense of events. Even if no arrests resulted from this evening's raid, the press release might seriously damage my father's business interests. For one fleeting moment I felt sorry for him.

'If there's anything you want altered?' Jacob asked.

Lys didn't even know he'd spoken. I looked down at the dusty brown floor tiles, sighed and finally shook my head. Moments later Luke called me for the sheriff's final briefing. I got up from my chair, then turned back to Jacob. 'You'll keep Lys with you?' He agreed, putting a protective hand on her arm. She didn't stir.

Many of the police vehicles had already left when Luke switched on the truck's ignition. The ancient machine shuddered noisily into life. He nudged it around the remaining veterinary van which was preparing to drive down the highway west of Devil's Lake. Mike had agreed to the other van being deployed at Mandaamin's southern border. It had left minutes before.

We followed a group of police cars. Two headed due east. We followed two others on the road south. It was the route we'd followed earlier. Close behind, was the sheriff's own patrol car. Half an hour later, at precisely quarter past six we reached the woodland picnic grounds near the Sheyenne River crossing. Luke pulled the truck off the road and drew alongside the café as if looking for refreshments.

The place was closed, the sheriff had seen to that earlier. The picnic area stretched away through thick stands of pine and oak interspersed with hosts of maple trees aflame with fall colours. The woodland rose high over the river valley. Above the noise of the engine, I could hear the waters of the Sheyenne thudding over rocks beneath the road bridge. The vast grassy car park was empty except for two other cars, one blue, one dark green, parked near the entrance. They looked to be undistinguished family cars, except each housed a couple of plain-clothes detectives. Luke let in the clutch.

We passed the cars and followed a central track, marked out by white-painted stones, between shrub-lined hillocks and secluded wooded alcoves. Each was furnished with picnic tables and barbecue housings. Hoardings for vigilance against fire, and warnings of bear attacks were everywhere. Yet the place, far from the city's hubbub and the highway's noise, retained its air of isolation and wilderness.

In the summer it would be alive with youngsters and families, noisily playing out their backwoods dreams. Now at the end of a gloomy autumn day the place was uncannily quiet. In the still evening air small wisps of mist moved down from the highest treetops and the place was damp and forbidding. We had reached the farthest point of the lot, near where a small stream wound down from the forest to drop into the Sheyenne Valley. Beside a rickety wooden footbridge a trackway lead into the forest. The gate stood open, though an old sign nailed to the top spar read 'Private - No Entrance'. Neither Luke nor I spoke.

My watch showed almost six thirty. I switched on the portable radio Sheriff Lawson had given us and gave our callsign: 'Bluebird One calling Base'. Leland's callsign was Firefly. Sheriff Lawson had come up with an exotic bird name. It didn't seem particularly relevant for these northern forests but perhaps that's what he intended. His car had disappeared south along the Sheyenne road when Luke pulled into the picnic area, but I knew he meant to monitor our progress. He'd warned that his car would be waiting for us by the closed café in an hour's time. The radio sprang into life, 'Base calling Bluebird One, you are clear to proceed.' Nothing more was said.

The line buzzed expectantly and I remembered to throw the switch before saying, 'Bluebird One proceeding from rendezvous. Any further instructions?'

'Keep an eye on the time,' Dave Lawson said bluntly, 'and remember to report any incidents. Over and out.' The hissing stopped abruptly.

'Guess this is it, Francis. Best put that stetson on.'

I hadn't taken the suggestion that I wear the hat, seriously. Yet Jack had handed it to me when Luke and I left the briefing room. With a sad smile, he said, 'Look after it, and yourself.'

'No need, the forest's dark enough,' I insisted, settling back into my seat. The cab was shadowy beneath the encroaching trees and the truck was already running alongside the footbridge when Luke brought it to a shuddering halt. The forest trackway began only yards away.

'I'm not taking this crate any further unless you wear that stetson, Francis!' It was the first evidence I'd had of Luke's stubborn nature. I smiled awkwardly and played with the broad western-style hat before setting it on my head. Back at Devil's Lake the hat seemed to fit, now the brim tilted forwards so that I had to push it up to see clearly along the track. Luke laughed. He pushed awkwardly on the clutch. The vehicle lurched forwards narrowly missing the wooden posts of the footbridge but managed to collide with one of the gate's metal stanchions. There was an enormous crunch. I reached hurriedly for the door handle and yelled, 'Best if I drive.'

'Not on your life.' Luke thrust the gearstick into reverse, pulled away from the metal strut with a loud screech then changed back into first. The truck growled towards the gateway. 'You heard what the sheriff said. If you're recognised we'll have to get out of here pronto. I'm aiming to finish the survey. We'll only do that by avoiding trouble.'

I couldn't argue and surreptitiously moved my loaded rifle from the footwell onto the seat beside me, where I thought he wouldn't see it. Luke cast an anxious glance in that direction and grimaced.

'I hope you're not intending to use it.'

'Protection only, I'll keep it out of sight.'

The track wound gently uphill between thick stands of conifers interspersed with open glades of maple and oak. The canopy was often so thick overhead that little light reached us from the darkening sky. I wouldn't let Luke put on the headlights but the stetson now seemed superfluous and when I removed it Luke instantly threatened to turn back. We couldn't afford to waste time. Grudgingly, I put the hat back on and consulted the map. The first of the red crosses was approximately a mile and a half from the picnic site.

'Keep an eye on the mileage, we should be approaching the first marker soon.' Luke was concentrating on getting the heavy truck around a switch-back bend. Looking aside caused him to stall the engine and we skidded to a halt half way round the first bend. It was lucky we did. As Luke reached down for the ignition key I grabbed him by the shoulder and hissed a warning.

A huge oak tree stood alongside the outer part of the next bend. It effectively masked the view ahead but through its dense foliage I'd caught a glimpse of headlights approaching. I wound the window down and listened. The vehicle was approaching fast, driven recklessly over the irregular contours of the hill, crashing through vegetation.

The headlights bounced between the trees, then the vehicle shot out onto the track only twenty yards ahead. I feared the truck, one exactly similar to our own, would turn in our direction, but as tyres screeched and gravel scattered back along the track, the cumbersome vehicle shot forward and disappeared down the track almost as quickly as it had appeared.

I'd heard raucous laughter through the open window. Soon the sound of the racing engine faded and silence returned to the forest. Rain, which had been threatening all evening, began to fall in a fine light drizzle across the windows when Luke asked, 'Your truck?'

I nodded. It was the first evidence we'd had of Delacroix activity in the forest.

'Shall we call the sheriff?'

'Best check that track first, they'll probably have put a trap in there somewhere.' I jabbed at the first red cross on the map.

Luke manoeuvred round the bend then turned expertly into the side track where runnels formed by the careering truck were already filling with rainwater. We climbed a short rise, then the track dropped quickly downhill, which explained why we hadn't seen the other vehicle earlier. A grove of birch clustered in the shadowy base of the depression. Standing incongruously among them was an untidy wigwam of recently hacked pine branches. Spars of a wood and mesh trap about two feet high, jutted from within the branches.

Luke sneered. 'They haven't bothered much with camouflage,' he whispered.

'They probably don't expect to be discovered - or did you mean camouflage from the wolf?'

'Hardly, a wolf follows its nose to food, and its instincts. Let's take a look.'

Luke switched off the engine. As we got down from the silent cab beside the hissing of the settling engine, all we could hear was a light pattering of raindrops falling through the forest trees. Apart from the scrunching of our shoes on the forest debris there was no other noise, and the forest quickly closed around us masking all sound.

The isolation was complete, casting a malaise over me which I knew I had to shake off rapidly if we were to complete our task. Luke remained as look-out while I bent down to examine the trap. The pine boughs I left untouched so no-one would know the trap had been discovered. It had not been sprung. I checked that the wooden trigger and the wire leading to the trap door were taut before putting on a pair of gloves I'd found in the cab's door pocket. I eased myself partway inside till the glove touched the bait. It was a small cut of deer haunch carelessly thrust up against the wire at the back of the trap. I eased it away from the tripwire and pulled back out of the trap carrying the piece of meat. Luke looked at it in disgust, 'Hardly a mouthful for a self-respecting wolf.'

I shoved it into a hessian sack I found in the open back of the truck and carefully took off the gloves. 'Lets get on.'

'You're not going to chuck it away?'

'Could be poisoned.' He gave an outraged gasp then shook his head.

'Best I drive now.' I moved towards the cab door.

'No!' He thrust past me. 'You radio the sheriff.' I knew by now it was useless to argue with him. I got in and consulted the map before we moved off, following the side track towards the next red cross, then radioed the sheriff, reporting in code that we had found a trap and seen one other truck at 'Red One'. The sheriff had given each red cross a number so that he would know which location we'd arrived at. There were a further twelve crosses throughout Devil's Lake reserve and several more over at Mandaamin.

In the next forty minutes we travelled over fifteen miles and found four more traps. Luke had been right: Leland's men were little concerned with camouflage, each trap was alongside a forest track. We found them easily enough. I couldn't believe that Leland and my father had been so sure of themselves they would risk detection in this way. Well, five of the traps were unbaited now. Five hunks of meat lay festering in an open sack at the back of the truck. I hadn't thought to cover it.

We were nearing the northern border of Devil's Lake reserve when we encountered the first signs of trouble. Luke was steering the truck down a long steep hill when another truck shot out from a neighbouring track. The driver saw us instantly and let his vehicle come to rest across the track where it effectively blocked our path. Whether this was his intention or not wasn't clear. Luke gave a friendly wave, offering the man right of way but the driver, whose features were part-hidden in the deep cab, only gestured up the track behind us as if expecting us to reverse.

The man was talking into a walkie-talkie set. When Luke didn't respond, a second man got out from the passenger side of the cab and walked angrily towards our truck. He was a big, well-built man and wore a thick lumberman's jacket. It wouldn't be difficult to imagine him in that strenuous and dangerous occupation.

Worse still, I thought I recognised him as one of the men who'd been at Ambrose. I slunk back in my seat and tilted the stetson across my forehead. Thankfully the man went round to Luke's side of the truck and looked in. I kept the rifle well hidden behind my legs and at the last minute thrust the sheriff's radio between myself and Luke.

'You fools lost or something?' The man's voice was coarse with a cruel edge to it. 'Where's your damn radio?'

Luke leant forward to shield me. 'Had a bit of engine trouble. Leland sent us to a garage to get it fixed, said he didn't have a spare radio left when we got back,' Luke ad-libbed, his voice husky and less refined than normal.

The man gave a derisory belly-laugh.

'Didn't think I'd seen you blokes at the lodge.' Out of the corner of my eye, I could tell he was trying to see past Luke into the cab.

'Leland told us to double check all the traps'd been set out properly, seems he doesn't trust anyone.'

'Doesn't surprise me, don't even trust the old devil myself 'cept when he pays me.' He laughed, and then grimaced. 'Say, what's that smell?'

His head suddenly dodged to the side of the cab window and we heard him rummaging in the back of the truck. Rainclouds had begun to darken the sky. I hoped he wouldn't see the sack. When his head reappeared in the window, Luke said, quicker than I could think of an answer. 'Spare meat, 'case any of you guys forget to bait the trap, found one already.....' Luke laughed to relieve the tension, 'might've been taken by squirrels though.'

'Hope you shot'em.' Luke gave what I thought was an unconvincing laugh.

'Leland's just been on the radio, called us back in. 'If you men aren't going to camp, you'd better come back to the lodge with us.'

Camping? What did he mean, I wondered.

'We've still got a few to check,' Luke insisted. I held the map up for the man to see.

'Well you won't need to check on the traps round here. If he asks why you didn't, tell him Hollins and Jameson laid them, he won't ask any more questions. Rest of the men have already established their camps round the reserve borders, case of trouble,' the man joked as if he was actually hoping for trouble. That explained why we hadn't seen any men near the traps. Leland was covering his back. It was something the sheriff would want to know.

'Still got a few others along the Mandaamin border to do,' Luke countered. It was obviously the wrong thing to say. The man gave him a queer look. 'Boundary to Mandaamin's just a steep valley, there's no traps down there. You sure yon man can read a map properly, let me take a look.' I shoved the map towards the window and barked in what I hoped was a strong southern accent. 'He meant the track into Mandaamin. See if you can do any better,' I argued, trying to support what Luke had said.

Luke handed the map out of the window and innocently jabbed at the crosses where we'd found the traps, including the others we hadn't seen near the lodge. My watch showed the time at seven fifteen.

'Sure, no need for unpleasantness,' the man called back. 'Which way did you come from the lodge?'

'Down towards the Sheyenne, then north.' It seemed the safest thing to say. The track we'd started on led into the heart of the reserve where the lodge was sited.

'Then if you count the traps Jameson and I set you'll have checked everything this side of Mandaamin. It'll be getting dark soon, best route's back via the lodge if'n you're set on going over there this evening. Unless you want me to get Leland on the radio, see if he's got any other orders for you.'

'No!' we chorused. I let Luke continue. 'No, that'll be fine, we'll just follow you.'

'That'd be kind of difficult since you're blocking the roadway.' He stepped down at last from the fender and looked behind the truck. 'Maybe the hill's a bit steep to reverse, I'll get Jameson to pull back and you can turn round down there. We'll follow you back up there.'

To have argued further would have looked suspicious. The man trudged back down to the other truck. I let out a tentative sigh which Luke echoed. 'How're we supposed to get out of this?'

'Wasn't there an open glade back near the top of the hill? You work the clutch like you did earlier and get the truck to stall there. We'll beckon him past and say we've got more engine trouble, that we'll limp back to the lodge.' Luke looked at his watch. 'Have you seen the time?'

'Seven fifteen, I know. As soon as we're clear of them, I'll radio the sheriff with everything we've heard.'

'What if that chap insists on radioing Leland for help?'

'I hope it won't come to that,' I said, idly fingering the rifle barrel.

It wasn't until Luke had turned the truck and it was already grinding uphill that I reached towards the dashboard meaning to consult the map. It wasn't there of course, Hollins had it.

'Damn!'

'What's the matter?' Luke asked, concerned.

'Nothing.' We were nearing the top of the hill. I gestured to the right. 'Quickly, ride the clutch, that's right, now limp it into that clearing.' The truck bucked underneath us, then leapt forwards and finally staggered to a halt against the broad branches of a tall conifer, its rear end jutting out onto the track. I couldn't have managed it better myself.

I'd been watching the other truck in the rear mirror. It had been too close behind us when Luke began his manoeuvre. They had to brake sharply and the machine had stalled on the steepest part of the slope. After a couple of seconds the driver got it going again. When it laboured uphill and eventually came level with us I could see both men were boiling mad. Through Luke's open window I heard a stream of expletives.

'What the fuck d'you think you're doing?' The driver parked the truck on the crown of the hill. As Hollins got down from the cab I saw Jameson peering across at us from the open window. I recognised him as one of the men who'd dragged me from the crashed car at Ambrose.

In the lights of the JCB his face had hovered above me, screaming abuse as I lost consciousness. I felt myself stiffen. Luckily Luke didn't notice, he leaned out of the window, selected reverse gear and rode the clutch so the truck bucked and yawed, its wheels churning up the deep leaf litter which spun out in front.

'Bloody clutch has gone now,' he yelled as Hollins dodged the shower of muddy pine needles.

'Can you get it back into first gear? Leland's just radioed, wants us back at the lodge pronto.' The man had clambered up on the fender and was looking into the cab. Luke made a great play of crashing the gears and at last thudded it into first. The truck jumped forwards. Hollins lost his grip on the door, but quickly clambered back up to the door looking angrier than ever.

'Bastard!' He pulled the door partially open and looked suspiciously at Luke's feet as if he didn't trust him. Luke pressed the accelerator down hard causing the engine to scream. Hollins hadn't noticed Luke slip the gear lever into neutral. When he was satisfied with what he saw he spat towards the front of the truck. The rain caught the spittle forcing it down the window. It settled in a white spume on the black wipers.

'See if you can follow us, and not fucking well stall again,' he barked angrily.

'Hadn't we best get it back to the garage? We'll only hold you up,' I said in a slow drawl.

Hollins peered past Luke and gave me a quizzical look. Unwarily I'd let the stetson slip to the back of my head but he hadn't recognised me.

'I'll see what Leland wants to do. Hey Jameson get that radio over here.'

Jameson leapt down from his cab. He was a small man and I guessed he had taken his courage at Ambrose from the crowd around him. He leant back into the cab, pulled out the walkie-talkie radio and headed in our direction. I couldn't afford to let him get much closer, my hand stiffened round the butt of the rifle which was still hidden from Hollins by my leg. I drew the stetson down over my forehead.

'Leland'll be damned sure to want your names.'

Luke responded with equal anger. 'I thought you said he wanted you back pronto. He's not expecting us back for some time. Won't you be in trouble?'

'Trouble like that I can handle, now what's your name?' The anger wasn't far from the surface now, but he had barely spoken when Jameson came up level with the cab, brandishing the radio. He peered through the cab window. I leant back as far as I could but it was no use. Alarm instantly creased his features.

'Leave this to me,' I hissed at Luke.

'What the fuck's he doing here?' Jameson bellowed.

'You know bloody well what he's doing here, same as us. Now get on to Leland you fool.'

'No, I don't know - that's Francis Delacroix, the old man's son - the guy that got us arrested at Ambrose.'

Hollins didn't understand at first. 'You gone loco or something, what would he be doing here?'

'Gone loco have I, then ask him what his name is!' Jameson yelled. He began twiddling with the buttons on the radio. 'Leland'll want to know about this.'

I pushed Luke back into his seat and aimed the rifle through the cab window.

'Put that radio down.' Jameson's hands hesitated over the call button. I saw he had it in mind to flick the switch. 'Put it down or I shoot.' I aimed above his head and pulled the trigger so the bullet flew harmlessly over his head, then cranked the rifle for a second shot.

'He's bluffing,' Hollins called and pushed himself in between Jameson and the rifle barrel. He was braver than I'd thought.

'Bluffing am I?' Hollins was grappling with the door handle. The cab was plenty big enough for me to reach across Luke and kick the door open. Hollins was flung to the ground screaming. Blood poured from his nose as he struggled to rise. Through the window I watched Jameson racing towards his own truck. I aimed a shot above his head. The man staggered, then recovered himself. It had all happened in a split second and I was taking aim for another shot when Luke took hold of the rifle barrel and thrust it skywards.

'You'll kill him, Francis,' he barked angrily.

'If I wanted to kill him he'd be dead already!' I yelled, wrestling the rifle from him. I let off another shot. A scatter of gravel burst from the ground just in front of Jameson. He sprawled forwards in an untidy heap, but he appeared unhurt and immediately started to crawl towards the shelter of the truck.

Below me on the track, I saw Hollins' bloody hand

reach up to grab the door again. I kicked it open savagely and heard an agonised scream as it collided with his head. I tried to scramble past Luke but he grabbed me by the arm, shrieking 'Francis you've got to stop this, you'll kill someone …'

I clutched the rifle even harder and somehow the barrel swung around to point back at his chest. He must have known I meant him no harm, but he looked at me appalled.

'Don't you understand, we've got to stop him alerting Leland,' I yelled back.

I felt his grip on my arm loosen and leaped to the ground. Hollins was lying prone on the gravel, his nose bloody, a jagged tear across his forehead where the door had caught it. When he saw me he rolled forwards, grabbed at my foot and yanked hard. I fell but managed to angle my fall so that I could thrust the rifle butt down on Hollins' windpipe. I pushed down savagely till he was almost unconsciousness. I left him coughing and gagging, and struggled to my feet. I'd wasted precious seconds, Jameson had already reached the truck. He was using the front wheel to pull himself gingerly to his feet.

'Throw the radio down,' I ordered and I let off another shot. The bullet zinged harmlessly against the cab door but it scared Jameson enough to make him fall to the ground. The radio fell from his hand and tumbled into some low vegetation nearby. I strode after him, he was whimpering and trying to crawl beneath the fender. Footsteps sounded on the gravel behind me. I swung round, turning the rifle barrel towards the approaching figure. Luke stopped two yards away, his face ashen against the dark conifers. He was in shock, I had to get him thinking clearly again.

'Better get them tied up, I saw some rope in the back of the truck.' He didn't move. 'Luke, we have to get out of here.' He was looking down at Jameson, his eyes still glazed.

'Now Luke. Now! The sheriff's waiting for us.' Something stirred in Luke's eyes. He nodded and seemed to come to himself. 'Sure,' he said, weakly.

I turned towards Jameson and kicked at his leg. 'You're not hurt man, stop whimpering and get up.' He scrambled helplessly on the ground for a few seconds, then began to push himself upright. The rain was falling heavily, it streamed down his face, washing through the smeared dust and sand, leaving bare streaks on his skin. I nudged him across to our truck with the rifle barrel. Luke walked ahead of us. He was still in a daze. When I drew alongside him he was looking down at Hollins. The man was groaning and clutching awkwardly at his throat.

'Must we tie him up? He looks in a pretty bad way.'

'Don't you believe it. Now get that rope!' I didn't trust Luke to keep the rifle trained on Jameson and waited until he had pulled several lengths of rope from the rear of the truck. It was sturdy stuff, the sort we used to secure deer and moose carcasses for transportation from the forest.

I nudged Jameson to the ground and made Luke secure his arms behind his back before we tackled Hollins. Luke was right, he did look pretty done in but I didn't trust him and made Luke pull the man's arms behind his back before we secured him. It took both of us to manhandle them into the back of the truck where we laid them on blankets used to cushion the hunting trophies.

I secured the tailgate and said to Luke, 'Better get

moving. We'll take both trucks.'

Luke looked down at his watch. His sleeves and hands were streaked with blood, as were mine.

'Seven twenty-five. Hadn't we better radio the sheriff?'

'Sure, I'll tell him now. You up to driving?' I didn't give him the opportunity to say no. I dived into the cab, grasped the radio before he could object and ran across to the other truck.

'Just follow me, the map's in the other cab.'

I had gunned the engine of the second truck and looked around for our map. I didn't find it, instead there was a clipboard under the dash with another map. It was a copy of the original Leland had distributed back at Silver Lake. I identified the track we were on. We had joined it moments before encountering Jameson's truck, and I saw that it ran straight back to the track running directly from Sheyenne picnic area to the centre of the reserve.

In following it we would get back to the picnic lot all the sooner and needn't retrace our steps. The only problem was that the turning was dangerously close to Devil's Lake lodge. I pondered the problem as I watched Luke get into his truck. He still looked bewildered. When I revved the engine and took the machine forwards a look of fear crossed his face. He thought I was going to leave him behind.

Of a sudden he gunned the engine and had the truck moving sluggishly back onto the track. I pressed down hard on the accelerator and kept the revs going as the truck hurtled forwards along the bumpy track. Every so often I looked in the mirror to check that Luke was keeping close behind. He was. After a few seconds, when I was more sure of him, I flicked the radio switch and called the sheriff.

'Bluebird One calling Base,' I pressed the receiver.

'Where are you Bluebird One, time's marching on?' The sheriff sounded anxious but I wasn't going to let him ask questions.

'On our way out right now, straight through to the picnic lot.' I wanted to tell him what Hollins had said, but we had no code to cover it. In the end I just said, 'Just learnt something important, you'll need to cover all the border areas.'

I flipped the switch but there was a pause before he answered. 'Understood. But we can't hold back the deadline, Bluebird One. Do you copy?'

'We copy, there are also two people needing a bit of first aid.'

'What the hell've you been…..?' I didn't let him finish. 'Be with you soon Base, over and out.'

In less than ten minutes I reached a T-junction with a wide gravel track. Judging it to be the north-south roadway I pulled hastily onto it. If I was right Devil's Lake lodge was pretty close but there wasn't time to consult the map. The gravel spun behind the truck's wheels. I had the window open and Luke's truck was so close behind that I could hear stones pinging against the metal superstructure. It was a rough ride but I had time to think, time to decide what I would do next.

Once I'd made my decision, the hardest part would be to convince Luke to go on down to the picnic site alone. Storm clouds had made the sky a turgid grey as I neared the oak tree where we had first turned off. I had time to reverse into the side track and pull back facing into the reserve. Luke drew his truck alongside. He leant anxiously out of his window.

'I'm going back.' I called over the shuddering of the engines.

'But the raid...? I don't understand.'

'Something I have to do, and the raid will have already started. I spoke to the sheriff. Now get going.'

The rain had eased off, and a flurry of wind shook darkening leaves off the oaks. There was just enough light to make out his expression. He was trying unsuccessfully to think of a response.

'Why?' he asked at last.

'He's my father Luke, I have to give him a chance to give himself up.'

'But it'll be dangerous, I'll come with you.'

'No. This is something I have to do alone and you've got to get these men to the sheriff.'

I think he really had forgotten about Jameson and Hollins. They had received a pretty bad shaking in the rear of the truck. Jameson's head had appeared above the open sides and I could just make out Hollins lying prone on the bloody blankets, both of them were wide awake and glaring at me.

'They're OK,' I said bluntly.

He nodded, looking at them with ill-placed sympathy. Finally he turned back to me and took hold of my arm through the cab window.

'Good luck,' he said hastily, before gunning the engine. He had switched on the sidelights and for three seconds I watched them disappear through the trees. Then I turned back towards Devil's Lake lodge and whatever awaited me there.

Chapter Fifteen

Storm clouds, pushed on by a stiff westerly, were massing overhead as I drove back uphill. The rain had eased off. Though the track was barely visible in the gloom, I couldn't chance using the lights. Instead, as the engine laboured up the steep terrain, I listened to the wind buffeting the tops of the tallest trees. Conifers grew close to the track, reaching out with their dark spreading boughs. I steered cautiously round them to avoid mishap. The slope grew steadily less steep, the track widened and took a long right bend.

Suddenly there were lights ahead and the outline of a large structure which could only be Devil's Lake lodge. It rose three storeys high, the rear pressing close up against the forest. Only the front windows were lit. Several vehicles, including a couple of Delacroix trucks, were parked broadside on to the building. Another truck was parked against the side wall where the light didn't reach. I pulled in beside it, eased the door open, then shut off the engine and slipped out. Leaving the truck door ajar to avoid making more noise, I ran towards the dark shadows thrown by the lodge walls and waited, rifle in hand.

No-one challenged me. I edged to the corner and risked peering round. The lodge had a broad veranda with wooden steps leading from the forecourt. I couldn't see anyone. The wind had reached gale force, it was whistling and tearing through the nearby conifers. But above the noise and the distant crash of boughs, I heard voices. Raised voices. A door swung open, showering the steps with light. I dodged back into the shadows as footsteps sounded on the wooden steps.

A car door slammed nearby, then an engine started up and lights shone dimly down the track. Almost immediately pebbles shot out from behind the vehicle. It sped off northwards. Masked by the forest vegetation and the storm, the sound quickly died. A few seconds later, I heard a door close. I chanced another look towards the front of the building. I couldn't see anyone, but I sensed movement somewhere behind me and was aware of a faint noise, as if a piece of metal had been kicked over. I slipped back into the shadows and saw that the truck door was swaying wildly. If I didn't shut it, the thing was sure to slam and someone would come out to investigate. I took one step towards the truck.

'Hey, what do you think you're doing?' I froze.

A shadow edged out from behind the second truck. It was very dark, I didn't think the man had seen me. I dodged back against the truck's side, training my rifle in his direction. It was a mistake. A second man had appeared two yards to my right. He flashed a light into my eyes, blinding me.

'Delacroix?' Leland's voice was full of venom. 'No prizes for guessing why you're here. Get him Harry.' I heard Harry Talbot's evil laugh. I fired a shot over Leland's head, then Talbot was on me, tearing at the rifle. He landed a punch at the side of my head. I fell against the truck gashing my forehead on a projecting strut. We struggled over possession of the rifle then I twisted him round against the vehicle. His head cracked violently against the metal superstructure.

For a moment, his grasp on the barrel loosened. I had almost pulled it free when he fell sideways, yanking at the rifle. His weight carried us both to the ground, but he was still fighting. His heavy boot connected painfully with my left thigh and I risked letting go of the rifle to land a blow on his jaw. I heard a satisfying crunch. Talbot sagged beneath me. I tore the rifle away and was struggling to my feet when Leland thrust the cold barrel of a handgun into my ear.

'Drop it!'

I could do little else. I let go of the rifle and felt Talbot stir beneath me.

'Sod's damn near cracked my jaw,' he growled.

'If you can talk then it's not broken. Get him up.' Talbot got nearly to his feet then he leant forwards and aimed a sharp punch at my chest. The pain sent me reeling to the ground.

'That's not what I said,' Leland barked.

'Why not finish him?' Through a haze of pain I was aware of Talbot bending down to pick up the rifle. There was a clatter as he reloaded, then the barrel was jabbed into my neck. I let my head fall back against the earth as if indifferent to his threats. The huge bulk of the truck towered above me, I wondered if I had the strength to knock the barrel aside and roll beneath it. Once on the other side, I would have to race across the track and lose myself in the forest. I wasn't sure I could make it.

'Don't be a fool, they'll have heard the shot inside. Give me the rifle and get him up. Quickly!' Talbot pulled me roughly to my feet. The pain in my chest was so great I almost passed out. Blood from the gash on my forehead oozed slowly into my left eye, dimming my vision.

'One wrong move Delacroix, and I'll put a bullet through you.' I lifted my hand to wipe away the blood. Talbot mistook the action. He grabbed my arms, pulled them behind me and slammed my face into the truck. Blood poured even more fiercely down my face and I lost all vision in my left eye.

'I still say we should get rid of him.'

'There'll be time for that later. Just say we found a guy prowling round the place. Understand? Otherwise keep your mouth shut. Now get him up those steps.'

My legs wouldn't respond. Somehow Talbot frog-marched me around the corner of the building and up the steps. Leland was at my side the whole time, holding the rifle trained against my head. Light fell from the window across the wooden slats. I blinked through the blood and made out three figures in the room. As Leland pushed by to open the door, I heard someone ask, 'Mr. Leland, we heard a shot, is something the matter?' It was a woman's voice, one I knew well but at that moment her name wouldn't surface through my fogged mind.

'We found this prowler outside, put up a bit of a fight.' Leland entered the room ahead of us so I couldn't see passed him. When he turned aside Talbot gave me a sudden hard shove, propelling me into the room. I staggered forwards, nearly fell to my knees and swayed, barely remaining upright. I bent over and gasped for breath, trying to curb the dizziness about to overwhelm me. Blood dripped onto the polished pine floorboards. A few feet away was a soft sheepskin rug. I badly wanted to curl up on it and blank out the pain.

'Francis! Oh my God.' That voice again, followed by a shriek. Somewhere a glass crashed to the floor. I struggled to look up. The room was sparsely furnished, with a long broad table topped with the remains of a meal: dirty wine glasses, water jugs, empty plates, an ashtray. Further into the room was a lounge area.

Separated off from the dining area by a low wooden balustrade, it housed two low-backed leather couches. Three people stood self-consciously in front of them, as if interrupted in some private conversation. The look of consternation on their faces rapidly turned to horror. They were my cousins Carl and Jeff, and my ex-fiancée, Pamela.

'What happened?' Carl yelled.

'Caught him outside brandishing this rifle.'

'Francis.' Glass crunched beneath Pamela's shoes as she stumbled towards me. She took hold of my arm before I could prevent her. I managed to pull myself upright without her help. I shook off her supporting hand. She gasped at the rebuff and rubbed her hands awkwardly together. 'You need a doctor.'

'No doctor - not yet. Where's my father?'

'He's ... he's gone over to Mandaamin.'

'Mandaamin. I have to see him, it's urgent.' I tried to stand up but my legs nearly folded underneath me. I staggered towards the tabletop. Pamela leaned forward, her hand stretched out beseechingly, 'Francis, can't I do anything? At least sit down,' she begged. Her face was white with anguish. Whether this was from concern for me, or some inkling of guilt, I couldn't tell. I ignored her. Jeff was at my side guiding me towards a chair. I sank down, overcome by a painful bout of coughing. Nausea rose from my stomach. I forced it down.

'You know this man?' Leland asked, his voice all innocence. Behind me I heard Talbot spit on the floor.

'My cousin Francis, Louis' son.' Carl said.

'How were we to know, he shouldn't have come creeping round outside. Might have got himself shot.'

'He's lying. Don't …..don't listen to anything he

says…' I coughed violently and felt myself falling forwards. Jeff held me until the spasm passed, then he poured some water onto a napkin and held it against my forehead to staunch the bleeding. 'What do you mean, Francis?' he asked earnestly. I grasped the napkin and pushed myself upright. 'Leland and I have met before, he knows who I am.'

'But it's so dark out there, Francis. Mr Leland could have mistaken….,' Carl offered trying to diffuse the growing tension.

'There's no mistake. If he'd had his way at Ambrose, I'd be dead already.'

'Ambrose?' Pamela looked shocked, she started to shake and staggered backwards onto a corner of the couch. 'Were you there?'

'Didn't you know, Pamela?' I spat out the words.

'I didn't … I swear.' She clasped her hands over her face and began weeping.

'I don't understand any of this,' Carl said.

'Ambrose?' Jeff gently held my shoulder. 'The hunting reserve in Canada, Uncle Louis wanted you to run?'

'Except you chickened out and wouldn't hand it back.' Carl added mockingly. 'Wasn't there a police raid at Ambrose, some nonsense about flouting hunting laws?'

'D'you know the reason for that Carl?' I staggered to my feet, anger boiling inside me.

'Sure, everyone knows you've gone soft on wolves, haven't dared show your face at Silver Lake for weeks. Going to make a packet out of the hotel I hear.'

The pain in my chest suddenly got worse. Jeff was at my side with a glass of water. I refused it. 'Then you hear wrong Carl,' I barked, holding my ribs. 'Dad ordered Leland to exterminate wolves at Ambrose, illegally and out of season. More than forty were killed. No quota, no restrictions, just mass killing.' I hung onto the chair back, close to collapse, my vision still marred by blood.

'If that's what Mr Leland told you he must be lying. I know Louis has organised a campaign against wolves but he would never...?'

'Now listen here, I won't be called a liar!' Leland argued. I stared across at him, fighting nausea. He had restored his six-shooter to its holster, now his hand fretted over the gun. Talbot had seated himself at the table and was drinking wine, taking no part in the dispute. Probably he'd been having a cosy meal with the family, minutes before. Leland had placed the rifle on the tabletop, with the butt inches from Talbot's hand and the barrel facing towards me.

'Calm down Mr. Leland. I'm sure my cousin is mistaken....,' Carl said.

'If you don't believe me, then ask him what he's doing at Devil's Lake,' I gasped. 'Ask him what the North Dakota quota is for wolves and why he and Dad are insisting any wolf carcasses are buried instead of being handed over to the wildlife service as they should be.'

'Well there I *can* prove you wrong. Devil's Lake's overrun with wolves. Your Dad's got licences to catch and transport them out of the region.'

'And you believe that?'

'Of course. Dad just called, he wants Uncle Louis to look at a captured wolf before he takes it away for release, he's at Mandaamin lodge right now.'

'Mandaamin?' I drew a rapid breath, pain shot through my chest. 'I have to get there, I have to warn him, before…' I staggered forwards holding the tabletop.

'You're going nowhere, Delacroix.' Leland had pulled the gun from his holster. Behind me Pamela screamed. The rifle barrel was within my grasp. I pretended to slump forwards, reaching across the tabletop. Jeff leant over me, thinking I had collapsed. I pushed him out of the way just as Talbot raised a glass to his mouth. Leland shouted a warning, 'Look out!' But I'd already grasped the barrel and was swinging the butt around. I caught Talbot's glass full on, smashing it in his hand. He screamed in pain as glass fragments tore through his flesh. The remains of the shattered blood-soaked glass crashed onto the table. Out of the corner of my eye I saw Leland aim his gun at me but Talbot was in his line of fire. Jeff stood with his mouth open, staring down at Talbot's bleeding hand.

My reactions were too slow, the pain in my chest too great, to aim the rifle at Leland. He shot off a bullet, ran two paces towards the table and jabbed the gun at my head. I was dimly aware of a surprised gasp, then of something slumping to the floor. Jeff was kneeling at my feet clutching his shoulder. His face bore a surprised look. Blood pouring between his fingers stained his shirt red.

His face was ashen. He was chewing at the corners of his mouth drawing blood there too. Pamela staggered from her seat, her face pale and smudged with tears. She clutched at the balustrade but stayed there, seemingly incapable of further movement. Even Jeff's groans couldn't draw her to him.

'I should kill you right now, Delacroix. Drop the rifle.' I let it go, allowing it to clatter onto the tabletop.

'Kill him Leland, the guy's nothing but trouble.'

Talbot wailed. He was bandaging his hand with a napkin, sobbing over the bloody mess. He looked at me murderously.

'Stop it, Leland,' Carl yelled, staring down at his brother in disbelief. 'What's got into you?' His eyes flickered down to Leland's gun. It was still only a few inches from my face. I noticed with relief that he'd momentarily dropped the 'Mr'.

'He's desperate not to be found out,' I gasped. 'But it's too late Leland, the police are raiding this place even as we speak.'

I glanced at a clock over the open fireplace. It showed seven-forty. The raid should be in full swing. Where were the wailing sirens, the patrol cars? What was keeping the sheriff? Leland watched my face, sensing a lie.

'I know you're bluffing, Delacroix, but you won't save….,'

'A raid, what would the police raid this place for?' Carl shouted in outrage.

'Damn you Carl, haven't I made it clear enough. Dad, Leland - even Uncle Gary, they are all in this together. What they're doing is illegal.'

'Trapping and transporting wolves isn't illegal,' he protested.

'Killing and burying them is. You've been fooling yourself if you believe different. I came here to make Dad give himself up. Can you understand that?'

'Shut up Delacroix,' Leland ordered.

'No,' Carl yelled. 'Don't tell my cousin to shut up.'

'He's lying, can't you tell? He's trying to save himself.' Leland was breathing heavily now. He didn't seem so sure of himself.

'Who from, Leland - you? You're holding the gun. You shot my brother. You tell me who I should believe?' Carl demanded angrily. Leland swung the gun round and aimed it towards my cousin, teasing him with it. Carl's face creased in outrage. Leland laughed. 'Wolves are vermin, they *should* be wiped out. Don't try and pretend you believe what we're doing is for the good of their health.' He laughed again, creasing his eyes up in derision. Carl's own eyes widened. His lips moved but he couldn't seem to speak. Pamela had been listening to the conversation. She shuffled her feet, looking down at the floor trying to ignore everyone. Broken glass sparkled around her shoes. In the silence Carl suddenly looked across at her.

'You knew, Pamela?' She looked up then. Her gaze wandered between us as if she couldn't decide who'd spoken. She looked down at Jeff, for a moment there was pity in her eyes, then she nodded.

'Yes she knew, and if it comes to a police raid, I'll tell them you all knew,' Leland barked.

'Then you'd be a bloody liar!' Jeff had scrambled up from the floor. He grasped the tabletop, bloodying the wood with his hand and lunged unsteadily towards Leland. The man must have realised Jeff was too weak to fight. Even so, he swung the gun round aiming at Jeff as I launched myself at him. I grabbed Leland's hand and forced him to turn away from Jeff. The gun went off tearing splinters from a wooden panel behind the table.

I wrestled with him, trying to tear the gun from his grasp but he fought back viciously, forcing me down onto the table. The pain in my chest was intense, I nearly collapsed, but then I caught sight of Jeff's pale face. I let go of the gun and took a swipe at Leland's chest. He gasped and staggered back, still holding the gun. I would have lunged towards him again but Carl was there before me. He caught Leland's arm and thrust it skywards. Leland hadn't seen him coming. Carl was a strong man and he led a strenuous outdoor life. Leland was older and not as fit.

The two of them struggled. Leland's breath was roaring in his throat, I thought he was weakening steadily, but he slowly brought the gun down so it was pointing at Carl's face. Carl slashed his hand down on it. The action unsteadied Leland, he tumbled to the floor carrying Carl with him. The gun went off and Carl twisted sideways. There was a bloody gash in his upper arm.

Leland squirmed to the side then lunged forwards again but Carl didn't hesitate, he forced the man back to the ground. The gun went off again. Leland slumped onto the wooden planks. There was a gaping bloody hole in his chest and a pitiful expression on his face as if he couldn't quite believe what was happening to him. Then his eyes glazed over and his head rolled to the side. Clutching at his arm, Carl collapsed beside him.

'He's dead,' Jeff said coldly. He crawled slowly towards Carl and the two brothers helped each other stand up. Pamela was weeping quietly. Silence settled on the room. For the first time since I'd entered it, I heard the wind tugging violently at the lodge roof. Conifer boughs crashed noisily against the upper storey windows above us. Soot shot down the chimney, scattering black fragments into the empty grate. I looked at my cousins. Both had arm injuries. I didn't think their wounds were life threatening, but they'd soon need medical attention. The quickest way I could get this was by the sheriff's radio and that was in the truck.

I struggled to my feet. Talbot was at the table still clutching his hand and staring down at Leland's body. He made no comment when I lifted the rifle from the table top. I cranked the reload and handed it to Carl. He took it grudgingly. I didn't wait for a response and headed towards the door. Strangely, it was Pamela who called out. She sounded quite lost.

'Francis, where are you going?'

'To get a radio, they need a doctor.' No-one queried my decision. I guess they were all too stunned. I had a worrying few moments searching for the radio in the pitch dark of the cab then I discovered it in the footwell where it had fallen. I was back inside in under a minute to find Pamela bending over Jeff attempting to staunch the flow of blood from his shoulder. There was some colour in his face, but he still looked sick. Carl had a flesh wound. He pulled the shirt away from his upper arm, revealing a deep red scar across his biceps muscle. Blood was already congealing over the wound.

'What's that for?' he asked as I switched on the radio.

'Devil's Lake Sheriff.'

'It was true then, about the raid?'

'They should have been here ages ago, I don't understand…' I shook my head and set the radio to transmit.

'Bluebird One calling Base, Bluebird One calling Base.' I flipped to receive and heard Sheriff Lawson's anguished tones.

'Base calling Bluebird One.' Quickly flipping the switch to transmit, I yelled, 'Where the hell are you? We need help here.' I nearly forgot to set the thing to receive.

'Bluebird One we're on our way, the storm's brought trees down, tracks all blocked. What help d'you need? Over.'

'Two gunshot wounds at Devil's Lake lodge, over.' I thought I heard him curse as he came back on. 'Should be with you in ten minutes unless there are more fallen trees. Life-threatening?' he finished, briefly.

'Can't tell, just hurry.'

'We will. But Delacroix, you stay put this time, you hear.'

If he expected me to agree he was disappointed. 'Sorry, can't oblige Sheriff, just get here quick.'

I switched the radio off and turned to see three sets of eyes trained on me. Carl spoke first.

'You're going after him.'

'To Mandaamin? Yes.'

I leant down and picked up Leland's gun from beside his body. There were several bullets remaining in the chamber but I didn't like the feel of the gun. It was too closely associated with Leland himself. Carl didn't argue when I took away the rifle and gave him the six-shooter in its place. 'I'm coming with you.'

'You're in no fit state, besides you're needed here.' I nodded towards Talbot. All the fight had gone out of him. He sat in a daze where no speech could reach him.

'Gary - he knew?' Carl asked.

'I guess so...,'

'Why don't you use the walkie-talkie?' Jeff interrupted weakly. He looked up from his wound which Pamela had just finished bandaging. His lips quivered. It seemed to me he was begging me not to leave.

'Where is it?' I'd wanted to speak to my father face-to-face, but there might not be time to drive across to

Mandaamin before the sheriff arrived. Carl retrieved a walkie-talkie set from the nearest couch. He switched it on and handed it to me.

'Uncle Louis' call sign is Firefly 12, Dad's is ten.'

'Is it an open frequency?' I asked. 'What about the other men?'

'I guess they'll hear too,' he nodded.

'Can't be helped.'

It wasn't a satisfactory way to get my father and Gary to give themselves up. Others would be listening and be warned off before they could be arrested. At first no-one answered the call. We waited for a reply with the machine hissing in my hands.

Once the radio crackled into life. It wasn't my father, just a couple of Leland's men complaining they'd lost their overnight tent. They'd been heading back to Devil's Lake, but were now trapped by fallen trees. Hopefully the sheriff's men would arrest them.

I put the set down on the table beside Carl and laid the sheriff's radio beside it. 'If you need to call just press this button, give the call sign Bluebird One, then flip to receive.'

Carl seemed disturbed by the action. He eased his injured arm carefully to his side and grimaced.

'You have to go?' he questioned.

'Yes, I have to,' I paused. 'You'd better have your stories straight for the sheriff, not just about what's happened here.' Involuntarily, I looked down at Leland's body.

Jeff groaned and looked faint. 'Dad can't have known.' I couldn't look him in his eyes.

'Take care of him Carl…. Pamela.' I squeezed her shoulder, before heading towards the door.

Out in the chill night, I felt the full force of the storm. It was only just sunset but the sky was as dark as night and I could barely make out the tops of the trees. They were thrashing against each other under gusting winds that were constantly strengthening. Rain poured down thunderously. By the time I got into the cab, I was drenched and shaken.

In the distance, above the storm's tumult, I sensed rather than heard the desolate wail of sirens. I thumped the truck into gear, edged the vehicle out from the shelter of the lodge and felt the full force of the wind pressing down on the cab. It was a big truck, capable of heavy duty work in the worst terrains, yet now it yawed and trembled as I forced it uphill. There was no need for stealth. I put the main headlights full on to navigate the uneven track. It was littered with fallen boughs. Shredded oak leaves twisted around in the wind, flashing past the windscreen.

Barely five hundred yards from the lodge I braked to a halt. A huge Douglas fir, about a hundred feet tall, had crashed down from the eastern side of the track. The headlights showed a narrow gap through the broken boughs. It would be a tight squeeze. I edged forwards but one huge branch caught and held fast under the wheel-arch. I reversed and tried to push through again, the vehicle bulked but wouldn't move forwards. I pulled back a few inches then pushed on the cab door.

The wind was so strong it wouldn't budge. In desperation I pushed on the right hand door. It was partially sheltered by the fallen tree. I practically fell out and struggled through a host of mangled branches to reach the ground. The big truck shuddered as another gust hit it broadside. For a moment, I feared it would crash down on top of me.

It was a nightmare tearing the rogue branch from underneath the wheel-arch. Wind tore at my arms, branches battered and hammered against my head. Eventually I pulled it free. I fought my way back to the cab, engaged the engine and pushed a way past the tree. In the next few hundred yards I encountered further fallen trees. Most lay alongside the track and I was able to squeeze the truck through without incident.

The track turned east and now much of the fallen debris lay along the southern bank instead of sprawling across the roadway. Neighbouring aspens and sapling oaks had been brought down with the conifers, forming a weighty pile of debris. When the storm blew over the foresters would have lost a good few dollars in timber. Twenty minutes later the track wound down into a small valley. From the distance I'd travelled I guessed this to be the border between Devil's Lake and Mandaamin. Soon the truck's lights flashed across a wooden framework edging a ravine to my right, then a bridge, or what remained of it, came into view.

The barrier edging the road was intact. Spars carried power lines across, but the wooden base of the bridge had been forced sideways by a torrent of water pouring down from a jutting rock ledge. Individual boards had worked loose from their lashings. In a few moments the bridge might be impassable. I didn't have time to think, I let the heavy vehicle glide downhill under its own weight till I felt the front wheels engage with the loose planks. Part of the bridge tilted to the right. Shaking violently, it took the weight of the truck. It trembled, threatening to crash down into the blackness of the ravine, then the wheels caught and held.

In the headlights, I gazed at the gravel across the other side. Stones were being torn away by water gushing from the rock ledge. Soon the track would disintegrate. There was nothing for it but to gun the engine and, perhaps, pray. At first there was no response, all four wheels spun powerlessly as water gushed under the truck, then the vehicle shuddered and began slipping backwards. I pressed down hard on the accelerator and was rewarded by a quick jerky movement.

It was enough to get the vehicle moving. The rear wheels were rapidly clear of the bridge, the sodden gravel spinning out from beneath the tyres. Behind me I heard spars shattering, there was an almighty crack, some loose spars spun away into the ravine but I didn't wait to see what happened to the rest of the bridge. One thing was certain, no-one else could cross into Mandaamin that night.

If I'd thought the storm could get no worse, squalls of rain now showered down across the forest. Even with the headlights and wipers full on it was impossible to see more than a few yards ahead. I was negotiating a narrow bend when I saw the obstruction. Water streamed over the loosened gravel. I slammed on the brakes but the truck took ages to stop.

A venerable oak, its upper limbs bare and jagged within a lower canopy of green foliage, had been uprooted and was effectively blocking the track. Beneath it and half hidden by broken branches, the rear fender of a black saloon car jutted into the light.

It was my father's car! With my heart in my mouth I battled against the wind to open the truck door and jumped onto the gravel. The wind grasped my clothes and I had to fight hard not to be hurled across the track and down into the ravine. In the end, I bent down and crawled towards the car.

Pushing through the tossing branches, I reached up and pulled the door open. Instantly the wind whipped it out of my hands, crashing it closed. But I'd seen what I needed to. Streaming with rain, the shattered remains of the windscreen and side windows sparkled in the truck's headlights, but there was no-one in either of the front seats.

I stood up, using the door for support, and was aware of a sticky substance beneath my hands. It felt like blood. Panic gripped me. I forced myself to stagger back towards the truck, fighting the wind all the way. As soon as I got into the cab, I edged the front fender towards the car trying to clear a way through.

The great branches hurled back and forth in a torrent of wind and rain, threatening to crack open the truck's windscreen. But soon I was able to see a way between the great bole of the tree and the empty blackness where it had been torn from the soil. I gasped, realising that the tree had been pulled clean out by its roots and flung on top of the car. Where the edge of the track should have been there was a yawning gap. Only strength of will made me guide the truck's nearside wheels past the shadowy chasm and back onto firmer ground.

I let the truck glide downhill, constantly looking into the shadows beneath the flaying trees for someone slumped on the ground. The rain eased and though the track streamed with water and the surface churned into hollow ruts, I had no difficulty controlling the truck. When another ten minutes had passed, the land levelled out and the track left the ravine edge to enter a shallow cutting. Low vegetation crowded the nearer forest, then I was suddenly running through a small clearing edged with thinly ranked maple and sapling pines.

Rain smeared conifer needles on the windscreen, they collected inches deep at the bottom of the glass where the wipers couldn't shift them. Occasionally whole sheets of needles were drawn across my vision. Dimly visible through the encroaching forest the track left the clearing between two ranks of mature conifers.

I was driving towards them when something caused me to look right. Two angular block-like shadows walled off a view of the distant saplings. I saw the glint of metal and a shabby caved-in roof. I had nearly missed it! As I slammed on the brakes and revved into reverse, a figure burst out between the two wooden buildings, as I now saw them to be.

I spun the truck round and brought it as close as I could to one of the dilapidated huts that were all that remained of Mandaamin lodge. I heard Gary cry out. I forced the door open but couldn't understand a thing he said above the ferocity of the storm. Bending over in the wind he struggled towards to the side of the truck just as I jumped out. I'd left the headlights on. I caught hold of his arm and dragged him into shelter.

'Thank God you've come,' he barked in my ear. His coarse white hair was sodden with rain.

'Dad?'

'He's OK, only...,' he gestured me between the shadowy huts.

'He's only been here a few minutes,' he shouted as we approached his car. Though the car was upright it had suffered severe damage. The front fender was broken right off and the heavy oak which had smashed onto the bonnet was now pivoted unsteadily on the damaged wall of the nearest hut. Except for blown foliage and broken twigs the rear of the vehicle looked untouched. Inside it I could make out a human form. Gary saw me looking at the damage.

'Tried to get your Dad back out to Devil's Lake. His own car was shattered by some tree. He trudged down here in the pouring rain. You'd think he'd be happy to get out of here but he wouldn't go, said he wouldn't leave the wolf, even laughed when the tree came down on my car.'

'Wolf?'

'It's in a trap behind the….,'

'Is he injured…?' Rain streamed down Gary's face. He gave me a puzzled look, for a second he thought I meant the wolf.

'No.' he said rather enigmatically. 'Only … see for yourself. Best get in the front.' We forced ourselves towards the car against another squall of torrential rain then I was in the passenger seat with the rain battering so hard on the roof I couldn't hear myself think. Gary slammed the rear door and the three of us were cocooned inside the steamy interior of the car. As I turned round my father pulled himself bolt upright.

His head and clothing were sodden with rain. I was relieved his only injury appeared to be small scratch on his forehead, probably from the shattered windscreen. But there was something in his appearance, a kind of wild exhilaration, that worried me. When he spoke it was as if we had never quarrelled and we were back at Silver Lake.

'Have you seen him?' he asked, his eyes wide and excited.

'Who?' I assumed he was talking about some companion. But he hadn't heard me and went rambling on, describing the trapped wolf.

'Magnificent beast, I'll have the skin and head mounted, there won't be a hunter doesn't envy….,'

He described the wolf's features: its broad shoulders, heavily muscled body, and fine white teeth. But never a mention that it was a living creature. I had been hearing similar stories from him since childhood: the exciting chase, the prowess of the hunters, admiration for a deer's broad antlers, or the dense fur of a black bear taken in its prime. Always speaking as though, in the very act of dying, these attributes would be transferred to the hunter.

Of the creature's life essence nothing was ever said, even as it crashed down onto the forest floor with a bullet in its brain. That I'd been a party to all this, now sickened me. My father continued talking, his voice rising almost to fever pitch in his eulogy for this wolf, but while he was speaking something stirred in my memory.

'Silver grey back, the colour of birch in fall, marvellous head and neck and those silver crescents running across his shoulders, never seen anything like it.'

I was suddenly back in Pelican Lake, in a clearing where tall firs rose high into an indigo sky, snow lay thick on the ground and a family of wolves was playing about the remains of a caribou carcass. I saw again the brief flash of the yearling's flanks, the broad head, the strange, almost silver crescents on the rippling shoulders.

My father was suddenly exhausted by the effort of

describing the wolf. He fell back in his seat. He looked gaunt, his eyes sunken. In a burst of energy, quickly extinguished, he pulled himself towards my seat but I could see his hands were shaking. 'He's over there, just over…we'll go and see….,' he sank back speechless into Gary's arms and was suddenly inexplicably weeping.

'Speed? I breathed out the word almost involuntarily. Gary gave me an anxious look.

'You see what I mean, I'm sure he's concussed. We need to get him to a hospital. Louis, we're going in Francis' truck. We have to leave now.'

He shook my father gently. Louis looked at him with an old man's gaze, distant and uncomprehending, then he seemed to understand and through his tears bawled, 'No, I'm not leaving without that pelt. We'll go back to the car and get the dart gun, I'll go alone if I have …,' but he became too breathless to speak, his lips silently working over words only he could hear.

'What's he talking about?'

'He wants the pelt, won't let anyone shoot the wolf 'case they damage it. The dart carries a lethal injection, he always carries it with him…,'

I had heard of such things before, but never dreamt my father would be capable of such soulless behaviour.

'We'll leave Jenkins and Payntor here, they'll watch over the cage until we can get back,' Gary said encouraging my father towards the door.

'There are other men here?' I asked, astonished.

'Over in the hut to our left, it's barely watertight but the trap's alongside and he won't let them stir in case the wolf gets loose.'

I was horrified. If I got the men into the truck they would at least be dry. But first I would release the wolf.

It might be Speed, we were only three hundred miles from Pelican Lake and wolves could travel longer distances, but logic told me it was unlikely to be him. Either way leaving the wolf trapped for hours in a small cage, probably wet through, was unthinkable. Gary had his hand on the door handle and was urging my father to leave. The rain battered louder on the roof. I had to yell to make myself heard. 'The bridge is washed out Gary, we'll never get through to Devil's Lake that way.'

'Washed out, then how did you get here?'

'By the skin of my teeth. The planks have moved, they were cracking up with the weight of the truck, I doubt there's anything left to cross, even on foot.' Gary looked unconvinced.

'But it's still standing, isn't it worth a try?'

'Gary we have to think of some other way.' Then I had a sudden thought. 'What about your walkie-talkie, is it here in the car?'

'Jenkins has it. Your Dad left his in his car. It's only got a short range, we can call Devil's Lake, that's about all.'

'Then we'll call them. We can get an air ambulance in, but first there's something you should know.' I already had my hand on the door handle when I turned back sharply to my uncle and father. Gary looked at me expectantly, my father continued muttering to himself, occasionally clasping and unclasping his hands. 'The police and wildlife people will be there, there's been a raid.'

'Police?' Gary asked. 'Has there been an accident, is someone…?' He was thinking of his sons, then what I said got through to him.

'Carl and Jeff are all right,' I assured him, but he

wasn't listening. 'Police *and* wildlife people? You brought them here, you knew what we were doing?' I nodded.

'I couldn't figure out why you were here. I thought you'd had a reconciliation with your Dad, the way he was talking to you just now - and all the time …'

'What you're doing is against the law Gary, you know that. Dad knows.' I saw my father watching me, he seemed quite alert and I sensed he'd been listening to the conversation. He grinned, then his face became stern and he said quite like his old self, 'Gary does what I tell him. Not like my son.'

I ignored him and pushed the car door open against the wind. 'I'll get the walkie-talkie.' I didn't need to slam the door closed, the wind did it for me though its power had lessened. I had barely gained the shelter of the second hut when I heard shouts behind me. I spun round and watched my father desperately scrambling from the car. Gary was outside, attempting to restrain him. Squalls of rain thrashed down on us and for the moment I could hardly see. I tried to go back to the car but a gust of wind held me against the hut side.

'I know what you're doing,' my father bawled. 'You leave that wolf alone!' He and Gary were blown towards the hut and left gasping in its lee.

'I'm getting the walkie-talkie. Please get back to the car, Dad.'

'Jenkins? Where's the damn man?' my father yelled and began clawing his way to the front of the hut into the full force of the wind. For an old man his strength was amazing, for someone suffering from concussion it was unbelievable. I began to wonder if he had been playing to Gary all the time. I caught up with him where the door of the hut should have been. He ducked inside and I followed suit. Gary was close behind us.

The hut was no more than a shell with only two standing walls and a few uprights holding up the sagging roof. In the oblique illumination cast by the truck's headlights, I saw two men huddled around an old stove fed with struts of rotten timber cannibalised from the fallen walls The debris of decay was all around them in rotting wood and drenched leather seats coated with white mildew. The damp wood fizzed and crackled in the open grate, threatening to go out.

Gusts of wind sent sparks spilling across the floor near their feet. They seemed unconcerned. Indeed there was little chance of the sodden hut burning around them. One man had leant down to agitate the glowing spars. He looked up as our shadows came between him and the headlights. The sloping roof was low over our heads and the men's hoods, cobbled from scraps of leather, were evidence that it was barely watertight.

They looked a sorry pair, yet as soon as we entered they were both on the alert, fingering rifles slung across their legs. Each had a dark cheroot at the corner of his mouth and at first I thought this was what I could smell above the odour of decay and the evil smoke from the stove. Then I realised it was neat whisky. The knowledge made me reassess the two men.

'Get moving, you men,' my father ordered. I expected him to order them out to the truck, instead he said, 'I want the trap loaded on that truck in double-quick time.'

The men stood up immediately, shook off their temporary cowls, and moved out into the rain. One shone a flashlight at a small wood and wire structure beneath a nearby conifer. Inside something stirred, a fearful wild creature, with wide dark eyes. It had been curled up as if sleeping, its back hunched against the knotted wooden struts. The boughs of the conifers thrashed to and fro above its head and rain poured continually off the sodden fronds onto the creature. But though the fur on its head and body were sleeked down with water, where the wind tore at its pelt it was possible to see below the long guard hairs to the fine dense underfur which was still buoyant and dry.

As if aware of my gaze, the wolf stood up and turned awkwardly in the confined space of the trap. I held my breath. There on the wolf's flanks were the same silver crescents my father had described and as I'd glimpsed them on Speed's flanks. There was also a small nick in the fur at the base of his right ear from an old wound. Eight months before, Speed had been a lithe yearling. The wolf I saw now was a mature adult, his muscles solid and strong, the epitome of the vital predator.

But as the wolf raised its head and glowered from the cage, that was not a cage, into the immensity of the night, it was the eyes that told me what I needed to know. So like the eyes of Beaver and Yarka yet so different. These were wild eyes, used to hunting through the darkness for prey and enemy alike, the eyes of a creature wise to the ways of the forest, wise in the ways of one who can see the wind. I was certain now. The wolf was Speed and I had to free him from that infernal cage, whatever the cost.

It was left to Gary to yell something sensible to my father. 'What the hell you talking about Louis, the bridge is down.'

'Do as I say,' my father ordered.

'All the other tracks are blocked, Louis. You said so yourself. There is no way out,' Gary insisted.

'We'll unblock them, they won't be expecting that,' my father said in a calculating way which convinced me he had been faking the concussion. He must have realised right after his accident that the track to Devil's Lake was blocked. Knowledge that the police and wildlife people were waiting for him made him desperate to get the wolf away. With the truck he might easily force a way across country and I'd brought it to him! With a pang of guilt, I edged my way through the hut and out into the rain.

The trap was inches from my feet, I could see the latch I needed to spring to open the door. Of course, I could have let the men load the crate onto the truck. Found some way of releasing Speed later, but I couldn't risk the men overpowering me. I also had to convince Speed to escape. What if he needed encouragement like Eighty-Seven had? I hesitated too long and my father read my mind.

'Keep him away from the trap,' he yelled as I leant against the wind and grappled with the catch. My fingers slipped on the wet metal. Desperate to pull it free, I leant over the trap and heard the wolf growl. He cowered against the back of the trap then leapt forwards snarling savagely. His teeth swept harmlessly past my exposed fingers.

The man nearest me jabbed viciously at my chest with his rifle, reviving the pain of earlier injuries. I staggered back holding my ribs but found the strength to duck beneath the rifle barrel and lunge forward, more than ever determined to slip the catch.

'Get back!' he yelled.

'Get him back in here Jenkins.' My father ordered.

'Never!' I screamed through the rain. 'He's going free

d'you hear, you've done enough damage.'

'No damned wolf's going free. I'll see him dead first,' my father bellowed. He came out from the shelter of the hut into the full force of the wind. Rain streamed down his face as it did with us all but he didn't seem to notice.

'I'll not have one more of those vermin loose in this country. Payntor...' He beckoned to the second man. 'My son tries to let that wolf go, you shoot it dead, doesn't matter how many bullets you use.'

'Even if it's still in the cage?' Payntor asked, somehow perturbed by the order.

'Gary and Jenkins'll get it onto the truck.'

'No!' I yelled and heard an echo in Gary's voice.

'Let it go Louis, it'll only bring us more trouble.' Gary had come out into the rain. He looked down at the pathetic trap and shook his head.

'Let it go, let it go! Are you mad?' my father yelled into his face.

'You heard what Francis said, the police are waiting for us, you'll only make things worse.'

My father grabbed him by the arm and spat into his face. 'You're a weakling Gary, always were. I never should have trusted you with this business. Get out of my sight.'

He shoved Gary aside. My uncle fell awkwardly. He staggered against the side of the hut and tried to save himself by grasping my father's arm. He'd already turned back towards me, now he spun around again. I suppose he thought Gary was attacking him. He landed a punch on Gary's neck. My uncle fell to his knees then had to dodge another of my father's punches.

Normally I would have tried to stop the fight, instead I realised the other two men were distracted. I grappled with the catch and almost got it loose. Speed cowered in the back of the trap, disturbed by the violence. How was I to convince him that he had to rocket out of the trap, as if the devil from Devil's Lake were after him?

'No you don't,' Payntor held his rifle threateningly above my head. 'You heard what he said.' He nodded towards my father and uncle. They were writhing on the ground, clamped in a violent bearhug. Jenkins had stepped away from the trap, chewing at his cheroot. He was watching the fight with an evil grin on his face.

I shoved Payntor's rifle barrel away. I thought I had surprise on my side and indeed he reacted slowly, bringing the gun back down in an attempt to train it at my head. Behind me, Speed snarled viciously. He was twisting manically around the crate.

As Payntor's hand grappled to regain control of the trigger I swung round, forcing the gun down so his hands were pressed against the cage. The fingers of his left hand dangled through the open mesh. Payntor yelped and stiffened.

Speed performed as I'd anticipated. With a savage yelp he lunged forwards, tearing at the projecting fingers. Payntor screamed. He yanked bloody fingers back through the mesh. Shreds of skin clung to the metal. Speed continued to snarl wildly. Payntor cushioned the bloody hand against his chest. The rifle had fallen at his feet. When he saw that I was going to pick it up, he lunged towards me. 'You did that on purpose, you bastard, the bloody thing's maimed me for life!'

I was tempted to say I knew how he felt, but it was the wrong moment. Before he could land the intended punch I dodged to the side and retrieved the rifle by the barrel. In one fluid movement I swung it round and cracked it against Payntor's skull. He fell to the ground and lay still. I thought I must have killed him, but I felt no remorse.

The barrel was sticky with blood, I caught hold of it, instinctively checking the firing mechanism, then leant over the cage. With my weaker left hand I fumbled with the catch. Speed was trembling at the back of the crate. Under his baleful gaze I almost got the thing undone.

Then I remembered Jenkins. He had seen the way I'd tackled Payntor and was standing a good two feet away on the far side of the crate, his rifle barrel was trained directly at Speed's head. With all the menace I could muster, I warned, 'You shoot him and I swear you won't live to tell the tale.' The barrel of the rifle wavered but I could tell he didn't believe me.

'One wolf don't equal the price of a man's life,' he bawled.

'Try me,' I said. I brought the barrel of the rifle up with my right hand and unlatched the catch awkwardly with my maimed hand. I need only slip the door open and Speed would go free. In hindsight I hadn't pressed Jenkins hard enough, he didn't believe I would shoot and his fear of my father was greater than his fear of me. I felt myself gasping for breath. Speed's eyes were fixed on me as I yanked the door open.

The cage trembled. He prepared to lunge forwards into the bright lights of the truck. Moments later he was free of the wood-and-mesh prison and hurtling across the clearing. Too late, I grew aware of Jenkins' rifle arcing over the top of the cage. A shot shattered the darkness. Speed yelped, tumbled, recovered himself, tripped again. I glimpsed his bloody right haunch, then he'd recovered, hurling himself into the forest and was lost in the darkness.

I pumped lead in Jenkins' direction, or where the man had been before he dodged away. I got off several shots before I heard him scream. The wind took the sound up into the forest tops and a wolf howled desperately somewhere close, the sound fading in a flurry of rain. I heard another shot but I hadn't fired again. I felt a sharp pain across my forehead and a sudden heaviness. The forest floor came up to meet me. I lay in the storm's damp debris and couldn't move. My head felt as if it would burst. Stars sprang from the night sky where previously there had been only a chaos of storm clouds. Strangely the rain kept falling.

Of the next minutes, or hours, I remember little: the lights of a helicopter hovering low over the clearing sent me back again to Pelican Lake, only now incessant rain replaced the snow. Jack Michelson was leaning over me and I was trying to tell him something important, 'It was Speed, the wolf I.... I watched,' I fought for words to continue '.... Jenny will understand, she...find him Jack, he's injured, ...find him...' My voice wavered and died, light fell away into darkness. Emptiness and sorrow came in its wake.

Chapter Sixteen

My eyes flickered open, then closed against the bright lights of the hospital ward. Someone called my name or more properly my alias. 'Frank…thank goodness - you've come back to us.'

Warily, I peered through half-closed lids. Turning slightly so that I could see the woman at my bedside more clearly, I asked, 'Jenny?' The pain in my head was almost unbearable. 'What……?'

'Don't talk. The doctors said…..you shouldn't exhaust yourself. It's enough that you're back.' My hand had been lying on the coverlet. Jenny took hold of it. I watched her face flush with concern as she raised it and touched the fingers to her lips. The warmth of those kisses brought me new strength. The pain receded until it was a dull ache and I could focus on her more easily. But something she'd said disturbed me. I gazed at her and asked, 'How long?'

Her eyes creased up. I felt her scanning my face trying to decide whether to answer. Finally, she said without guile, 'Six days.' She held my hand more tightly, waiting for a reaction. My fingers tightened over hers then, slowly, I took control of myself. Though the headache was now bearable a rash of memories filled my mind: a fight at Devil's Lodge, the flight through torrential rain to Mandaamin, my father's face full of rage, two men keeping me away from an ugly crate beneath the conifer tree where an animal waited uncertainly for its fate.

I had to know what had happened during those six days. I pulled myself up from the pillow dragging a jumble of hospital leads with me. Jenny looked aghast and rushed to untangle the tube in my right arm from the oxygen tube in my nose. Grateful to find my limbs responding, I leaned awkwardly towards her and begged, 'My family, the boys....?' I laid my hand on her moving fingers and stilled them. She didn't resist. Her skin smelt of spring flowers. I kept hold of her hand and laid it beside me on the crisp hospital sheets.

'Tell me Jenny.' I coaxed. '...never mind what the doctors say.'

'Your cousins...?' she began tentatively. 'They're going to be all right. Carl's fine, he has a flesh wound and he's taken his brother home today. Jeff's going to need some physio before......'

'On his shoulder?'

Jenny nodded.

'It was a deep wound,' I agreed. 'And my father, Gary......?' Here Jenny hesitated and I felt a sudden surge of apprehension. She hurried on, 'He... they're fine. They were at the hospital the same day they brought you in. Both had a few bruises and scratches, nothing more.' So my father's concussion had been feigned.

Even as I asked the next question, Jenny's expression told me the answer, 'They're still here?'

She looked down almost involuntarily and shook her head forlornly.

'Your father learnt Abe Langer was here that day. They had a raging row right here in the hospital, it was terrible. I think your Uncle Gary might have stayed but your father insisted they leave. They haven't been here since, I don't think he's even phoned. I don't understand.' Jenny seemed genuinely dismayed at my father's behaviour.

'I do Jenny, it's nothing new. Don't concern yourself.'

'But…' she began.

'My father hasn't been arrested?' I asked tentatively.

'No, they.....there was a lot of confusion, they....'

'They...?' But Jenny wouldn't say. There was something here I didn't understand. I would ask Abe about it.

'What about Lys, my sister?'

'Oh Frank, Lys is a lovely person. She's been by your bedside from the time they brought you in.' Here Jenny breathed in quickly. I wondered how long Jenny herself had been there. 'But she's had no sleep. Jack and his daughter managed to persuade her to go home with them yesterday evening. I'll get the nurse to phone and…..,' she stood up but I kept hold of her hand.

'No,' I insisted 'Let her sleep, Lys has been through enough.'

Jenny sat back down and smiled gently, 'She cares a lot about you too.'

I nodded, then asked the question which was nagging me. 'The argument with Abe, what was it about, why was he here?' I don't know why but I looked, just then, towards the frosted glass partition separating the small ward from a short corridor. Fluted glass panels let in the noise and bustle of the hospital, but one blue-clad figure behind them seemed not to be involved in hospital routine. Jenny followed my gaze and lowered her head.

'Abe's still here,' she said softly, then offered with more enthusiasm. 'He's an amazing man Frank, you'll like him. There doesn't seem to be anyone he doesn't know or isn't willing to contact. One of his doctor colleagues let him have an office downstairs - a little bit of Congress he calls it. He's there working hard every time I pass - night or day, tapping away on the keyboard, sometimes on the phone, or both.'

She paused, preparing herself for my next question.

'You'd better tell me why he's here.' Jenny's eyes flickered back to the figure in the corridor. When she wouldn't answer, I asked. 'He's a police guard isn't he?'

Jenny bit her lip and nodded. 'Abe will explain, he can help us - if anyone can.' I didn't comment on the 'us' Jenny had invoked. I'd already decided that whatever was facing me I would face alone and not drag her or anyone else down with me. 'But you're not strong enough yet Frank, I can't let you.......,' I interrupted her.

'Every moment you're here, I'm getting stronger, Jenny.' She blushed. 'Now I'd like to see Abe. Can you get the nurses to take out these tubes, I can't see him like this....,' There were tears in Jenny's eyes as she began to stand. Before I let her go I asked almost under my breath.

'Speed?' One word, that's all it took to bring the colour back into Jenny's cheeks.

'Oh Frank, Jack found him that first day.' Tears sprang from her eyes and I feared the worst but she was suddenly laughing. She clung to my arm saying, 'He's at Sanctuary. Jack came in here that evening and told us. Lys and I were both here. The doctor's didn't think... that is they didn't know if......,'

'If I would survive...?' I asked. Jenny nodded.

'When Jack arrived with the news, you were unconscious, your pulse so low it had almost stopped, it was as if.....but the doctors told us to talk to you, so I whispered that we'd found Speed, that he was alive and at Sanctuary.'

I remembered then, I had been out in the snow-ridden prairie pacing alongside Speed, strangely matching his stride. Spectral forest trees hurtled past and a long sunset swirled above distant blue hills. Suddenly Speed turned to face me. His ears pricked to alert with his fur bristling and the muscles of his strong legs quivering. Under the broad slanting brow his eyes searched my own. Eventually I understood. The past lay between us, the future uncertain and haphazard: a tremulous vision that might never ripen to maturity. I'd felt the blood cool and thicken in my veins. With nothing to hold me back, I was slowly releasing my hold on life. Then I'd heard a voice calling from a long distance away saying that Speed was alive. That he was safe. Almost instantly I sensed the snow melting, the image of Speed dimmed and faded from the forested landscape and I began the long journey back towards life.

'I think that knowledge saved my life, Jenny,' I said.

'I know it did, my love,' Jenny said with a catch in her voice. She left to find Abe Langer.

By the time Jenny returned with Abe Langer, I'd got the duty nurse to remove the oxygen tubing from my nose and most of the medical paraphernalia surrounding the bed. She had refused to take out the saline drip, saying only the doctor could do that. Able Langer, or Abe as he wanted to be called, was a tall solid block of a man with big hands and a big character to match. The discerning gaze he gave me as he entered the hospital ward bore the same exacting study I was to see later when he studied potential adversaries. Yet, when Abe approved a man, a ready smile creased the broad lips below the russet coloured moustache he sported and you knew you had gained a friend for life.

That was how it was between Abe and myself, though I have often wondered whether his assessment of me had been formed long before, through my meeting with Leroy. With that quick assessing glance he came forward and clenched my right hand in both of his. Another man I initially thought to be a doctor followed him in.

'How are you boy ...been kind of worried about you?' He laughed and shook his head at Jenny. The pale sandy curls on his forehead tumbled forward and made him look, even in his long dress coat, like a schoolboy. It was a picture which would have disarmed many people. Before I could moisten my lips he continued, 'Better offer a seat to the young lady before we start.' He picked up and carried the single chair around to Jenny's side of the bed, almost guiding her into it before she realised. Jenny's face was a picture of amused embarrassment. I could see she hadn't wanted to sit down and leave him standing but he instantly charmed any 'women's lib' out of her. From the chair she looked up at him adoringly. I almost felt a pang of jealousy. He turned away briefly and introduced his colleague.

'This here's Jake Hemson, from my brother's office. He's going to listen in to our conversation, but don't mind him for the moment.' Jake Hemson it seemed was well trained. He stood back against the wall, immediately blending into the background. Occasionally he flicked over a page of his notebook.

'Better get straight on with the business, if you're feeling fit enough young man?'

'You'd better tell me everything before the sheriff gets here.'

'Sheriff…' He turned to look beyond the fluted glass where there were now two figures in blue uniforms. At this, one man had looked in briefly, while nodding to his colleague. 'They'll want a statement sure enough. Jake'll take care of all that when the time comes.'

'Abe, I need to know what I'm facing.'

'Then how's your memory?' Abe asked.

'Good enough.'

'Good enough to cope with a charge of manslaughter, maybe worse?'

I heard Jenny gasp, her hands tightened on my scarred left arm.

I thought of Leland lying on the floor in a pool of blood at Devil's Lake. Carl's stunned expression as the gun fell away from his hand. Other images at Mandaamin were less clear.

'Carl was struggling with him - the gun went off. Even Pamela'll testify to that.'

'You're right, but the sheriff'll still want a statement from you. But we're talking about Mandaamin. There's a dead man, Payntor, with his head smashed in and another chap, Jenkins, on life support. Your Uncle Gary says the men were threatening you but he's rather vague. Says he was quarrelling with your Dad at the time.'

I leant back against my pillow and sighed heavily. 'So that's it.'

Jenny squeezed my hand. She leant forward imploring, 'I'm sure it can all be sorted out Frank, you mustn't worry.' I looked across at her pale face, and spoke solely to Abe Langer.

'The chap who died, he tried to kill me.'

Tears sparkled in Jenny's eyes, but she didn't speak.

'Then that's what you'll tell the sheriff,' Abe insisted.

'We know quite a bit from your uncle but what about this other man Jenkins? Seems he took a bullet in the chest from a rifle, same rifle they found beside you.'

'I don't know Abe. I was trying to release Speed, the wolf, from a cage. My father had told the men to shoot Speed if I released him. I had to do it Abe, I just had to. As I tried to open the cage, Payntor put his rifle to my head. I grabbed hold of the barrel and swung the rifle round. I think the butt cracked his head open. At least, he fell to the ground. I wasn't sure he was dead. When Speed was free and running across the clearing, Jenkins shot him. I guess I went mad. I turned the rifle in his direction and kept on firing at him, until….. '

Involuntarily, I raised my hand to the bandage on my forehead. The headache had got worse, the blood pounding inside my skull. Abe looked kind of sad. I guess the full implications of what I'd said had begun to sink in.

Jenny was shaking her head saying, 'No, no.'

'You don't look too good boy, best we continue this later,' Abe said.

My eyes flew open, I grasped Jenny's hand, 'No, I'm all right,' I insisted, 'I have to know the worst. You keep mentioning my uncle, what does my father say happened?'

Abe took several seconds to answer. 'Claims he didn't see anything. Seems he and your Uncle Gary were struggling on the ground, either he didn't see anything or….'

'Or….he's scared he might implicate himself.'

'Surely he cares more about you than that,' Jenny wailed.

'You don't know my father, Jenny. It'll be attempted

murder then.'

'No, Frank no!

'There'll be mitigating circumstances....' Here Abe leaned back towards Jake who answered for him.

'Involuntary manslaughter, temporary insanity, protecting your own life, the life of an endangered species....' Jake was obviously going to continue with his list. Abe held up his hand. Undeterred, Jake gave his opinion of the likely outcome: 'Most likely suspended sentence or long-term parole ....,' before a harsh grunt from Abe finally quelled him.

'You heard the man Frank. First thing is to get you bail.'

'Am I actually under arrest then?'

'Most likely will be when the sheriff arrives, but I want you out of here.'

'Why?' I asked, surprised. Jenny had raised her head and was now staring at Abe with something like loathing.

'You can't do this, Abe,' she said, 'You can't, Frank's got enough to cope with.'

'Don't you think we should let him decide for himself?' He turned towards Jake and flicked his fingers.

'You can go now, I'll call you when the sheriff arrives.' Jake was obviously used to Abe's peremptory instructions. Unconcerned, he duly withdrew.

'What must I decide?' I asked, directing my question more towards Jenny who by now seemed overwrought and ready to do battle with Abe.

'He wants you to go to Washington with him, he's asking too much, I told him...,'

'Told him what... will someone talk to me.' I pounded on the bedclothes with my right fist and tried to get out of the bed but fell back light-headed and exhausted.

'D'you see?' Jenny shrieked offering a tumbler of water to my lips. I took two sips, then pressed forwards from the pillows. Abe was watching me silently, assessing, I guessed whether to continue. I knew from his attitude that he had something to impart, something even more serious than a charge of attempted murder.

'Your father and his powerful colleagues have contrived to convene a meeting of the Congressional Committee on Wildlife Regulations. They are putting forward a proposal to rescind all protection for wolves. They want to reclassify them under pest status regulations.'

'The hell he has!' I tried to push myself up from the bed but Jenny was at my side, gently pressing my shoulders back into the pillow. This time I hadn't the strength to resist her. I gasped and managed to continue. 'They can't think they'll be successful. International law won't allow it.'

'Most people in the States don't care about the rest of the world. Your father's people are basing their submission on evidence from cattle farmers in the Great Lakes region together with this campaign they've been running. They've got thousands of signatures.'

'But all the wildlife evidence is against them.'

'They've got public opinion behind them.'

'Even after what my father's done, hasn't that had any effect?'

Abe nodded. 'Some perhaps. Enough to raise polemics in a few national papers. But there's big money at stake, Francis, be assured of that.'

'Enough to sway the committee?'

'Unless we get more support for the League. We're

working hard on that, we've got some heavy-weight zoologists ready to testify but we need the same sort of grass-roots stuff they'll be pumping out.'

'Is that....,' I couldn't believe what I was hearing. 'Is that where I come in, you want to call me as witness?'

Abe nodded and looked across at Jenny whose anger had intensified.

'Jenny told us what you'd been through last Spring, I....,'

'But I didn't tell you so you could drag Frank all the way to Washington. He's done enough already,' she raged.

I looked from one to the other of them.

'Has he?' Abe asked at last, giving Jenny a pitying look. 'Will you deny him this opportunity to ensure the wolves' future in this country?' I couldn't look at her and sensed a new urgency in Abe's responses.

'When, when does the committee meet?' I asked.

'Next Monday, four days' time.'

'Then I'll be ready in three,' I assured Abe and saw a grateful look cross his face.

'It isn't fair to ask you Frank, it just isn't.' Tears were pouring down Jenny's face. She knew she had lost.

'Jenny, tell me about Speed.' Jenny tried to smile through her tears.

'He's all right. The bullet passed straight through the leg muscle. All Suzanne had to do was sew him up. He'll be ready for release soon. He...,' a lump came to her throat and she couldn't continue.

'Then I have to do the same.' I laughed and turned back to where Abe had been standing, only to find he'd left. Taking Jenny in my arms, I kissed her lightly on the cheek, pressing my lips over her tears. I was still holding her when Jack Michelson walked into the ward with Lys clasping his arm. Lys looked careworn and tired, but I sensed a new confidence in her as she rushed to the bedside.

'Francis, oh Francis, I've been so scared.'

She thrust her arms around me half sobbing, and laid her head on my chest, almost crushing the injured ribs. I gave her a couple of seconds before pulling her away and looking deep into her watery eyes. Jack Michelson gave me a brief nod and said, 'Glad to see you boy.'

I nodded back. Keeping my attention on Lys, I insisted, 'I'm all right Sis. I'll be out of here in a couple of days you see.'

She gazed at me disbelievingly then half turned to Jenny. 'Is that possible, has he seen the doctors?'

Jenny gave a snort of derision, 'No, but he's seen Abe Langer!'

'But....,' Lys began, looking between us. Jack came forward and took Lys lightly by the shoulders. Gently moving her aside he leant forward and shook my hand.

'It'll be Washington then?' There was genuine admiration in his voice and in the intense way he clasped both his hands round my own.

'Washington?' Lys queried unhappily. 'What are you all talking about?'

'Jenny can tell you.' I leant back against my pillows, suddenly very weary. Jenny reached across to take my sister's hand as my eyes closed. I heard Jenny's voice gently intoning against the background hubbub of the hospital.

Briefly she described my discussion with Abe and the reasons for the trip to Washington D.C. Strangely she made no mention of the charges being brought against me. Whatever she thought about him, she had enough faith in Abe to believe these would be no barrier to my making the trip. She'd hardly finished talking when I felt Lys clasp my arm once more.

'But you can't go Francis, surely you won't be strong enough in three days.'

I opened my eyes and struggled to reply.

'I have to go, Lys. Everything I've fought for, everything we've done to protect the wolves, it'll all be for nothing if this goes through. Let me do this Lys - please.' I placed my left hand over hers and watched Lys' face blanch then slowly colour again: the urge to protect her 'little brother', conflicting with the knowledge that I meant to meet this challenge. Finally she said, 'I'm going with you.'

'No!' Jack and I chorused together. 'No,' Jack insisted. 'I won't have you exposed to such a bearfight.' He appeared genuinely concerned for my sister. I wondered at their relationship and thought about Denny languishing back at Ambrose. True he was ten years her junior, but it seemed to me they'd struck up a warm friendship.

I added, 'Jack's right Lys,' I smiled at her and said, as tenderly as I could, 'remember, Dad will be there, he'll be fighting for the other side. It's bound to get nasty, and there's nothing the Press like better than a family feud. Best give them a single target and….well I want you kept out of it.'

'But I don't want to be kept out of it,' Lys challenged. She clasped her hands tightly over mine and I was reminded of the morning we'd arrived in Jack Michelson's house, how she'd fought to stay involved with the raid. This time I decided to be firmer, even if it meant hurting her.

'There's no need for you to come. You know what the press will say, Lys. Renegade daughter sabotages father's plans. Traitor, that's what they'll call you Lys - I don't want that distraction.'

Her face twisted up sorrowfully. 'But it'll be even worse for you Francis, I want to be with you.'

'I don't want you there Lys, I'll need a clear mind. If I'm worrying about you ….,' I left the sentence hanging.

Jack was gently fingering Lys' shoulders.

'You don't mean it Francis, I know you're saying it to protect me,' she sobbed.

'What if he is, it's natural isn't it?' Jack added. Lys swung round and suddenly buried her face in his broad chest. Her sobs were deep and sad.

'I'm coming to Washington as well,' he said.

This was news to me. Lys only stirred and clung to him still tighter.

As I closed my eyes and lapsed into sleep, I felt Jenny lean across the bed confiding,

'My parents'll look after Lys while you're away.'

Later, I had my first solid meal for a week and still complained of being hungry. Jenny saw this as a sign of genuine recovery and elected to return to her parents' home for the evening. I guessed she'd had little sleep in the past few days. Lys too looked tired. I'd urged her and Jack to leave earlier. So it was that I had no friends at my bedside when Sheriff Dave Lawson arrived in the early evening. Alerted to his arrival, Jake Hemson and Abe arrived in time to hear me give my version of the events at Mandaamin and Devil's Lake. When the scribe from his office had finished taking down the statement, the sheriff turned to me and said, 'I trusted you Delacroix.'

I looked down at the bed. 'My father may be a lot of things Sheriff, but I had to give him one last chance. You'd probably have done the same in my position.'

'I can't say, maybe so, but none of these deaths would have occurred if you'd obeyed my orders.'

Abe gave a castigatory snort, but I ignored him. 'Are you so sure of that?'

The Sheriff refused to answer and turned to Jake. 'On the basis of the evidence in my possession, I'm going to have to arrest your client.'

'On what charge precisely?' Jake questioned, a steely look on his face. I felt my stomach tighten as Sheriff Dawson raised himself to his full height.

'Manslaughter of Lewis Payntor and attempted murder of Allen Jenkins….for the moment.' He went through the arrest process there and then, finishing with his own demand that I shouldn't be offered bail. Jake gave him a dubious look and shook his head. I wondered if even Abe's political weight would get me bailed were Jenkins to die in the near future.

Someone convicted of murder, even in the second degree, was likely to spend thirty years in jail so it was little consolation that North Dakota no longer had the death penalty. If I felt remorse, it was solely because I'd let things go so far for the sake of one wolf. But I knew I'd been right both to release Speed and to prevent further slaughter of wild wolves.

'Next court session's this Friday morning - two days' time - think you'll be fit enough?' I nodded. This fitted in neatly with Abe's plans to travel to Washington late Saturday morning. He must have known about the court session, probably he'd even engineered my appearance.

'We'll be there,' I assured the sheriff.

Two days later, at an arraignment at Grand Forks court, I was, as Abe had predicted, placed on extended bail. Next morning I walked unaided if rather unsteadily and with a large box of painkillers in my pocket, out onto the airport tarmac on my way to Washington D.C. This was the first, and would probably be the last, time in my life I visited the capital. We were a small group, just Abe, Jack and myself, Jacob having first to attend a League meeting in Chicago. The previous evening, on my discharge from the hospital, I had persuaded Jenny to stay behind.

She had been enthusiastic in wanting to come with us, but I heard echoes in her voice of a kind of reluctance and set out to discover the reason. Eventually I coaxed the truth out of her. Her final veterinary exam, the culmination of six years' intense study and practice, was set for the following Tuesday. I couldn't let her jeopardise her career any more than I'd done already.

'Your future is more important than any trip to Washington,' I cautioned. She put her hand up to my cheek lightly touching the skin, saying, 'I'd hoped the future was something we would share.'

Abe must have convinced her the court case against me was a formality. I knew different, just as I knew there might not be any future for us. I should have told her right then but the coward in me didn't want to see her gentle face crease in a frown. So next morning, trying to look confident, I kissed her tenderly on the lips and dived into the car where Abe was waiting to take us to the airport. As we drove off, I watched Jenny turn her small jeep towards the intersection for Bigland where her parents lived. She looked to be smiling.

We arrived in Washington to the accompaniment of a heavy rainstorm. Water beat on the plane and after several minutes of jostling with strong winds we landed in the early darkness. The flight exhausted me. A fearful headache brought me close to collapse. I managed to conceal this from my companions and when we reached the hotel went straight to my room. Neither Jack nor Abe commented.

Closing the hotel door behind me, I reached for the painkillers, took three tablets, collapsed onto the bed and was instantly asleep. On Sunday morning, exaggeratedly fatigued and with an aching head, I yielded to their advice and spent all day in bed conserving my strength. Abe took Jack off to his office where the two of them made the final arrangements for Monday morning.

Sometime around midnight on Sunday I woke hungrily and ordered a ham sandwich from room-service. I hardly remembered the waiter arriving and woke in the morning to see the curled remains of the sandwich on the bedside cabinet. Abe was knocking loudly on the door.

Outside the congress building, groups of cheering Wolf League supporters greeted us with placards and banners. North Dakota was a long way from Washington D.C. I hadn't expected support to extend this far. Other protesters were equally in evidence, dour-faced anti-wolf protesters, their contrasting banners weaving and swaying in the light breeze.

The committee room could probably have held fifty people comfortably but public interest was evident in the many League supporters and the press of reporters and TV cameras at the rear, so that number was effectively doubled. As we wound our way towards the front benches, the cameras whirred rapidly. Abe was a public figure, well known in Congress and by his association with James & Langer. We followed and settled into the row behind him. The journalists took no notice of us.

Abe had given us an outline of the authorities he expected to call in support of the Wildlife Act, and of those likely to form the opposition. But there was no time to point these people out, we would learn soon enough who they were. We'd barely sat down than the hubbub in the room lessened. Directly opposite, my father was talking earnestly to a group of people huddled around him. He hadn't noticed me. Then he looked across the chamber. I saw astonishment and a kind of sorrow cross his face.

Clearly he hadn't expected me appear. He said something to an associate. The man gave me a baleful look. The room hushed as the Committee Chairman, one Adam Bains, passed between the rows of congressmen and women and took his seat on a raised bench alongside two other members: a man of rather older years than Abe and a young woman with long dark hair pulled back behind her ears.

Congressman Bains in a dark suit and with a searching gaze, was a man of middle years. According to Abe he had been a long-time financier and latterly a trustworthy politician. With a quick glance around the room he opened the session by referring to documents he'd brought in with him.

'This extraordinary session of the Committee on Wildlife Regulations has been convened to discuss a proposal that the law relating to the protection of wildlife, and specifically the Grey Wolf, is untenable. Act twenty-two, section thirty, part ninety-nine of the regulations pertains. Is everyone who needs it in possession of this document?'

There followed some self-conscious shuffling of paperwork by a few of the committee members while at the back of the room a rookie reporter from the Chicago Sprinter raised his hand tentatively.

'Yes?' Bains queried. The reporter answered that he hadn't had time to view the document. Bains displayed a wry sense of humour by responding, 'I think you can rely on your editor faxing you a copy before much longer, or perhaps sending you back to Chicago to view it.' The reporter looked dismayed. A flurry of laughter ran around the room. Bains didn't wait for it to die away.

'I should like to ask Congressman Lee Matterson to put the proposal.'

A man to the right of my father stood up and moved to a central table. He didn't take the available seat but looked around the room at the assembled host then drew his breath in very slowly. Obviously very sure of himself he began, Often laws which reach the statute book are made in haste, an over-zealous reaction to panic or to placate public concerns. Many years can pass before the fallacy of making such laws is revealed.

'Just as we are doing today, it is necessary for politicians to redress the situation. I have lodged this proposal on behalf of the people of North Dakota who elected me. They are demanding, quite legitimately in my opinion, that the depredations of this fearful animal, the Grey Wolf, cease. I call upon Maxwell Wharton, former North Dakota senator and life-long producer of quality beef cattle for our great nation, to support this motion.'

Maxwell Wharton stepped forwards from the hub of people seated around my father. He was not tall but had an imposing stature. Urbane in a dark suit which did little to conceal the solid muscle of his arms, he swept a length of greying hair from across his forehead and began to speak.

'I've been an upholder of the law in these United States all my life, please God. Glad to be so. And as a producer of prime cattle, I've been blessed with putting high quality meat on our citizens' plates for as long as I can remember.' Here he paused, obviously for effect rather than to gather his thoughts. 'When this law came in, I was told the wolf was in decline, that its restoration would bring our wild creatures, moose, caribou and deer, currently beset by disease, into a better state of health. I welcomed the law, welcomed it I say….,'

I thought ironically that he might be testifying for the Wolf League. Instead, when he resumed, there was venom in his words.

'But I was to learn better. Within just a year of the enactment of this law I started to lose cattle and latterly many sheep. Yearlings are being taken and prime steers caught and savaged without even being consumed. It's a tragedy. Along with many of the local farmers, I began to lose money: several hundred thousand dollars. Prime beef is being lost and the wolf has become a pest. This law has to be repealed.' He thumped a broad hand down on the table, making it shudder.

There was silence in the room. People appeared stunned by Wharton's vehemence. As if aware of the effect he had on them, Wharton remained silent at the witness table for several seconds. Bains asked for questions. There weren't any. He nodded to Wharton to return to his seat. The man gave a relaxed smile and was already halfway to his seat when Abe stood up.

'I would like to ask some questions of ex-senator Wharton, if the Chair permits.'

Wharton turned casually. There was nothing about the man's attitude that admitted dissent, yet when Abe asked his first question all the bluster and bonhomie evaporated and his face became a hard mask.

I had to admit Abe's tactics were superb.

'Isn't it true Mr. Wharton…,' he began, and then turned to face the three people on the bench, 'that in the last five years you have also increased the number of hunting parties on your property, that you regularly take out moose, caribou and white-tailed deer, that several times the police have encountered your hunters, perhaps unknowingly, on wildlife reserves north and west of your property? And indeed that they often, perhaps inadvertently, exceed the legal quotas for these animal kills?' There were gasps of horror from several people in the room.

'That's an outright lie Langer, I'll make you….,' Wharton shouted across the room.

Abe took no notice of the threat, continuing, 'Isn't it also true, again in the last five years, that you've severely exploited acres of forestry on the borders of your various properties? That you've sold off prime timber at high prices, at the same time laying raw marginal land down to low-grade sheep grazing? Land previously inhabited by those deer and moose and caribou, which are in such decline, and so removing both prey and habitat from the wolf. Is it any wonder predation of your cattle has increased - if this is indeed the case?'

Wharton had barely got over the shock of Abe's first accusation. His face quivered as he sought for words to justify himself. 'A man's got a right to improve his land.

American citizens are crying out for food.'

Again Abe took no notice. 'So you've made great increases to your herds and suffered a few, inconsequential, losses.'

'Not inconsiderable losses, Congressman,' Wharton blustered.

'But you've been handsomely compensated Mr. Wharton.' Abe made a point of looking down at his papers, to give Wharton more time to stew, I thought, than to verify his facts. Wharton stood looking across at him, his mouth open, a strained expression on his face.

'Isn't it true you've been in receipt of thousands of dollars in compensatory payments annually, for lost cattle and more for sheep? And money for wolf-proof fences? Money from state and national funds. Did you also know that in other states more compensation is paid out for dog kills than for any cattle killed by wolves? Doesn't it strike you as strange that Minnesota wolves should behave so differently?

Wharton's expression turned to one of defiance tinged with embarrassment. 'I don't deny I've taken compensation, any farmer worth his salt would to improve his herd for the sake of American citizens.'

Abe nodded, pleased that Wharton had begun to repeat himself. His next question was again targeted to catch Wharton off-guard

'How much are you worth Mr. Wharton?'

'That's none of your damn business, Langer!' Wharton's politician's façade of indifference was slipping. He was growing angrier by the minute.

'Come, come Mr. Wharton, your business is run as a public company isn't it, surely you have nothing to hide? I have the figures here if you would prefer......'

Wharton puffed himself up, but either couldn't or wouldn't speak.

'Then you won't mind if I read from your ten-year report 1995 to 2005 which Wharton Enterprises recently published.'

'Please yourself.'

Abe took the hint and began, 'You run several hundred thousand acres of prime land in North Dakota, more in Minnesota. Annual gross profit for 1995, ten million, net after tax and allowances eight million. In 2005, gross profit twenty-two million. Seventeen million dollars net.' He paused waiting for his audience to register these figures. 'Allowances for 1995 include new fencing and the like. Those for 2005 include land clearance to the value of a thousand dollars an acre, new barns, replacement fencing, but…..but there doesn't seem to be any mention of profit from hunting or timber.'

Wharton coughed behind his hand and explained in a low voice, 'They're run as separate businesses.'

'But of course, I'd forgotten.' Abe searched his papers, making great play of looking for something, the epitome of the bumbling showman, which he most certainly was not. I began to understand the alarm his campaigns had caused in the past.

'Mr Wharton you have heard of Yellowstone National Park perhaps?' he asked, going off on another tack, once more making Wharton uneasy.

'Of course, everyone has.'

'Then you'll know of the reintroduction of wolves into the area?'

Wharton only nodded.

'Has it been successful d'you think?'

'I….I don't know.'

'But do you think it's been *Unsuccessful?* Are the people at Yellowstone clamouring to have the Wildlife Act amended so wolves can be eradicated again, as they were in North Dakota during the last century?'

'No…., at least…,' Abe wasn't going to let him continue. 'Mr Wharton, as an ex-senator…,' Abe swallowed and appeared to look disappointed, 'when you and your colleagues put forward the proposal to repeal this law, had you researched the success or failure of the situation at Yellowstone? Are you aware of the huge increase in tourism, the boost to local business, from the presence of those very wolves?'

Wharton stared unblinkingly at Abe. Abe was breathless, but he hadn't finished with Wharton. 'Had you indeed fully researched the measures put in place by the North Dakota and Minnesota Wildlife Services and the national government? Did you realise you could improve and increase your wildlife habitats and still gain a full range of compensation payments to help you produce that prime beef of which you speak so proudly? And surely Mr. Wharton…,' Abe continued more slowly '…with all your millions, could you perhaps accept the reduction of your hunting drives to ensure the future of one of America's most prestigious native carnivores?'

Wharton stood dumbfounded in the centre of the room. Abe took no further notice of him. He gathered up his papers, directed himself to Adam Bains saying 'I have nothing more to add Mr Chairman,' and sat down.

Bains asked, 'Do you have anything more to offer Mr. Wharton?' but the man was already returning to his seat. A dazed almost forlorn look creasing his face, he hadn't the energy even to seek solace from his colleagues.

Several of them, my father included, ignored the man as he slumped down in their midst.

After the fireworks of that early session, it was a relief to settle back and listen to the next two speakers, both zoologists, both seeming experts in their own fields. Each gave powerpoint presentations to convey current knowledge of wild carnivore-livestock interactions. Much of the material and data they presented was the same, yet surprisingly they gave very divergent interpretations of the current status of the wolf in the United States.

Mrs Kathy Henderson, ex-Yale professor of Animal Welfare, spoke to my father's motion and was vociferous in her defence of domestic livestock. She was in her late fifties. Iron grey hair pulled back revealed stark features and almost black eyes, which she fixed firmly on Bains when she wasn't operating her lap-top. She stood quite upright in a long modest striped dress with a dark green Indian shawl draped fashionably over her shoulder.

True to her New England roots she spoke firmly, convinced of her own theories. Personally I doubted whether she'd ever been further west than Boston. Abe had his doubts too. When she finished, he asked, 'Mrs Henderson, have you ever been to the State of North Dakota or any Mid-West State?'

She shook her head, not at all perplexed by the question. Abe persevered, 'Have you indeed been further west than Boston?' The lady wasn't slow in following Abe's train of thought.

'I believe I visited Ohio once - as a child.' She waited until the ripple of laughter subsided. Her expression was perfectly relaxed '…. but you must know Mr. Langer that

I have spent forty years studying and lecturing in animal welfare. I have travelled to Europe and Asia, and work with experts at the highest levels of research. If you are trying to suggest my knowledge is deficient.'

Again Abe continued in conciliatory tones. 'Nothing of the sort, I assure you Mrs Henderson. I was merely trying to discern the degree of your local knowledge.'

'I...,' Mrs Henderson began, then, realising that she was being baited, merely said, 'I believe I have already answered your question Mr. Langer.'

We adjourned for lunch soon after, a brief affair, in which Jack and I ate unappetising sandwiches in a local café while Abe disappeared into his office. When the committee reconvened it was to hear the second zoologist, one Charles Peterson, ex-Harvard professor, in charge of ecological conservation and research for a Mid-West consortium. Abe believed his testimony would be crucial to our argument.

In his early fifties, Peterson still had the drive and enthusiasm of a much younger man, this couched in a lanky frame which gave him an uncoordinated air. With narrow reading glasses perched halfway down his nose, his pale blue eyes darted around the room as he spoke, entreating agreement. He had made no concessions to the committee, wearing only a thin navy-blue shirt and tight jeans, both of which had seen better days.

After forty minutes of listening to his long drawn-out phrases and often irritating pauses, there could be few in the room unaware of his own conviction, summed up by his final words and given to the accompaniment of slides portraying Mid-West lakes and forests. 'It is most unlikely that continued livestock overgrazing, excessive hunting of large ungulate game and clearance of habitat will not result in increased wolf predation, no matter what other measures are taken. Once we accept the theory of natural habitat balance, we will have begun to understand how to live alongside the Grey Wolf, in harmony.'

There was a great clamour from my father's side of the room while Peterson, more concerned with packing up his equipment and papers, at first ignored the questions thrown at him. In the end Chairman Bains restored order. 'Mr. Peterson, I am sure you will be happy to answer some questions before you leave.'

Peterson already had his laptop under his arm and turned to peer quizzically over reading glasses which he instantly removed. 'Yes, most certainly.'

Three people stood up on the opposite side of the room, my father among them. Without deferring to either colleague, he began, 'Mr Peterson, you mentioned that no-one really knows how many wolves were in the Mid-West states in the past. How can you categorically state what the balance should be in the twenty-first century?'

'I rather thought I'd answered this point. Re-assessment of historical records, carrying capacity, long-term landscape and sociological studies and of course extrapolation from similar populations in Canada, Europe and northern Russia. Yes, I thought I'd made that clear,' Peterson finished rather arrogantly, as if the question had been superfluous.

My father sat down shaking his head, obviously deciding there was little point in arguing against Peterson's extensive research, which he clearly didn't believe. It was left to a congressman to ask the question,

'Mr. Peterson, if all the measures you suggested were put in place how long do you think it would be before we reached this 'harmony' you mentioned?'

Peterson's answer was quite circumspect. 'Well the Wildlife Services are already making great strides. Habitat restoration is the most important measure of course, everything else will follow. I could say in about ten years we might reach that point, of course this would need far greater input from national and state funds, so …,'

Here Bains interrupted him. The matter of funding was a tricky topic for any politician..

'Thank you Mr. Peterson, your presentation has been most informative, but I think we have already kept you too long. You are free to go.' Totally oblivious of the veiled slight from Bains, Peterson casually bowed out of the room, his notes stuffed into his briefcase in an untidy bundle, the leads from his lap-top dangling at his side.

It was already half-past three, I was growing tired and my head had begun to thump unmercifully. I struggled with the box of painkillers in the pocket of my jeans as Abe addressed the room once more.

'I would like to call a further witness this afternoon, Mr. Chairman, someone whose experiences have spanned both the hunting and the conservation lobbies. I think he will provide members with some grass-roots evidence.'

Through a haze of pain, I saw Bains consult his watch. I fervently hoped he would delay the witness until morning, instead he nodded.

'Half an hour, forty minutes at most Mr. Langer.'

Abe nodded happily and turned towards the bench where Jack and I were seated. I expected him to beckon

Jack forward, instead I heard my name called.

'Mr Delacroix…,' a hush spread around the room. My father, looking equally surprised, stirred in his seat.

'That is, Mr. Francis Delacroix.'

To this day I don't know why Abe called me at that moment. It must have been obvious to him, as I sat half slumped in my seat, that I was dog tired. The long hours in the committee room had taken their toll on my strength. Perhaps he thought I would be more convincing in that debilitated state. In any event, I looked at him through a miasma of pain and fatigue and began to stand. I had forgotten about the box of painkillers. As soon as I stepped towards the witness table, the tablets spilled from my hands and bounced noisily onto the teak surface. Self-consciously I began gathering them into my hands. Looking up at Chairman Bains, I explained weakly, 'Painkillers.'

Earlier in the gents' room I'd first seen the jagged scar where Jenkins' bullet had creased the skin below my hairline. Sometime recently the wound had bled again and dried blood had plastered strands of hair to my forehead. I looked a sorry sight and Abe's decision to expose me so rudely seemed a sick joke. I noticed some awkward stares. People looked away in embarrassment.

Congressman Bains came briefly to my rescue.

'Take your time, Mr Delacroix… ' he coaxed, 'and your painkillers. You've recently been in hospital I understand.'

There were derisory guffaws from the opposite bench but my father raised his hand in a diffident appeal for silence. Slowly the haranguing subsided. I reached for a plastic cup, filled it from a bottle of mineral water, thrust three painkillers into my mouth and gulped them down.

Without waiting for any visible signs of relief Abe started in with his questions.

'Mr. Delacroix, you grew up in a household where hunting wild game was the norm did you not? It was accepted, almost demanded of you wouldn't you say, part of the great American dream?'

My headache was now a continuous throb. The tablets were taking longer to work each time. I could barely nod in reply. I didn't really know where Abe's questioning was leading.

'But something happened to you back last March, at Pelican Lake, Minnesota that changed all that?'

I wanted to nod but any movement of my head caused intense agony.

'Yes,' I breathed, my mouth and throat almost too dry to speak.

'I hardly like to ask in your condition, but I feel it's important that people hear your story. Can you tell us what happened to you there?'

So, haltingly, and many pauses to catch my breath, I told the story of my accident, though even now I hardly remember speaking. Abe had to coax me more than once into continuing. Slowly the headache lessened and Abe was asking, 'and this animal, Speed you called him, you didn't know he'd survived until last week?'

'Yes, that is, I didn't know.' I confirmed.

'What you saw, and what you went through, has changed your life hasn't it?' Abe cajoled. 'You now work at Bitter Springs Wolf Sanctuary.' I nodded and found breath to add, 'as part of an animal conservation degree.'

Abe now surprised me by going off on a different tack, just as he had done with Wharton's testimony.

'In addition, Francis, you've been involved in

exposing the illegal culling of wolves at Ambrose in Ontario and also took part in an official raid at Devil's Lake, North Dakota to expose a similar atrocity.'

Again I nodded, turning my face away so I wouldn't catch my father's eye.

'That's where you encountered this animal again?' Abe waited for me to nod then continued, 'The trapped wolf was about to be killed for its pelt. In attempting to release him you were yourself injured.'

'Yes,' I croaked in reply. I hung my head and shuddered, recalling the events of that night. There was a hushed silence in the chamber.

Abe addressed his concluding comments to the whole room. 'I think committee members and members of the public will agree that we have not previously been aware of the great, and unfounded, body of anxiety which the wolf engenders. We are educating our citizens about the needs of wildlife but we still have a long way to go as far as the wolf is concerned.'

His words were greeted with some nods of agreement, many from the public and reporters, but there were several growls of dissent and I wasn't given long to collect my thoughts before the questions rained down.

'Mr Delacroix, isn't it true that the number of wolves actually killed at Ambrose and other hunting estates is purely anecdotal?' One Congressman seated just behind Adam Bains asked. I couldn't see his face clearly.

'About as anecdotal as the numbers of deer killed by wolves, Congressman,' I quipped, and was rewarded by a sudden burst of laughter from the reporters. But the man had already turned away feigning disinterest.

Another Congressman, seated too near my father to

be non-partisan, asked, 'When you hunted regularly Mr Delacroix in your youth and latterly, didn't you engage in killing wolves too, because they were becoming so numerous year by year and reducing the hunt trophies?'

'It's true I killed wolves.'

'Far more than the legal quota. Like everyone else, you believed wolves were a menace to game and local livestock?'

'I believed what my father told me.' I looked around the room, seeing the grim faces and expectant frowns, and added, 'I don't believe it any more.'

The older man seated beside the Chairman now asked, 'I'm intrigued by this raid at Devil's Lake. Am I right in stating that you are on bail facing charges of manslaughter subsequent to that raid?'

He coughed as if Devil's Lake were some mythical place on the far side of the known world. His comments were followed by a sudden flurry of activity among the journalists. Cameras whizzed and flashlights dazzled. I heard gasps of exclamation from around the chamber.

'I'm on bail Sir, because the trial has yet to take place.'

'But aren't these serious charges? I'm not sure I've heard of bail being given in such cases.' He coughed again, drawing attention to his disbelief.

'I'm fully prepared to face these charges when the time comes, Congressman,' I assured him and sat back heavily on my seat, though I hadn't realised I'd been standing. The camera flashes kept coming. After a lot of ribald comments, Bains called the session to order and declared a recess until the following day.

The weakness I'd felt returned as I tried to stand. Jack and Abe came to my aid. Supporting me on both sides we merged with the jostling crowd trying to leave the committee room and had an even harder time crossing the foyer. Journalists barred our way, firing questions at me about Devil's Lake and my arrest. I didn't answer but as we ploughed towards the outer doors I heard many disturbing comments. Just one got through to me. 'You'll get five years,.... and if Jenkins dies....'

We had a subdued evening meal in the hotel restaurant. Jack and Abe discussed the day's events, balancing the evidence against the likely decision of Congress. I was too fatigued to contribute much, excusing myself early. Jack glanced at my half empty plate and offered a night-cap. I refused and found my way unsteadily to my room.

The newly-turned bed looked inviting, but there was something I had to do first. I sat down and lifted the phone. Jenny's cellphone rang for a long time before she answered. I could tell she was chewing on a mouthful of food and remembered it was only about seven p.m. in Minnesota.

After an effusive welcome and enquiries about my health, which I assured her was perfect, I gave her an optimistic rundown of the day's evidence. Jenny accepted this at face value. In return, she told me of Speed's rapid progress. Suzanne declared he would be ready for release in a couple of days. For some reason I panicked. The headache developed into a sudden sharp pain.

'Don't...,' I warned down the phone, my voice so harsh that Jenny asked, 'Frank, what's the matter - are you all right?' There was momentary panic in her voice too.

'Give me a second,' I gasped, gathering my breath,

'Jenny, promise me you won't let him go yet, not until....'

She hurried to interrupt me.

'I promise Frank, only tell me what's the matter?'

I fought for the words to express my fears. 'Jenny, I don't want Speed released in the States,' I begged.

'Of course Frank, but he has to be released soon, you know that.'

Suddenly I felt tremendously tired. I knew I wasn't expressing myself well.

'Phone Larry at Ambrose, he'll understand.'

'Ambrose? The place where....,'

'Larry's Wolf League rep in Canada, we discussed returning wolves to Ambrose.... after the massacre,' I sensed my grip on consciousness slipping, 'Jenny, it would mean so much to me if Speed could be released there, promise me you'll phone him.' But even as she gave her hesitant reply I was lying to her '.... Sorry I have to go, there's.... there's someone at the door. Speak to you soon.'

There was no-one there, of course. As the receiver dropped on the pedestal I heard Jenny's voice anxiously calling 'Frank, Frank...' then the phone clicked off and I fell half-conscious onto the bed.

It was gone eight when I woke next morning. I ordered coffee and toast from room service before searching out my colleagues. When I found Jack, he was just leaving the coffee shop. He looked me over quickly and seemed satisfied with what he saw. In the shower, I had managed to wash out the last of the caked blood from my hair, but the scar was still very obvious.

'We were kind of worried about you last night,' he

offered. He was clutching a local paper in his hand and hurried on as if vaguely embarrassed. 'I guess you'd better see this.'

He handed me the Washington Classic. On the front page, below a brief article on the Wildlife Committee session, was a colour photo of me taken the previous evening. I looked wild-eyed and deathly white. The jagged bloody scar on my forehead stood out lividly. Below the photo was a short article. 'Wolf Supporter, Francis Delacroix, testifying today to the Congress Wildlife Committee, has been accused of manslaughter in the state of North Dakota and is currently on bail awaiting trial. Another man is fighting for his life in Grand Forks General Hospital. If he dies a further charge of murder....'

I couldn't read any further, jammed the paper into the nearest waste bin and asked, 'Where's Abe?'

'Had to go out apparently. Left a message at the desk to meet him at Congress.'

'Nothing wrong I hope, other than....' Involuntarily I glanced at the scrunched-up remains of the paper.

'Not that I know of, 'cepting your dad's crew are set to speak this morning, maybe it's something to do with that.'

'I hope not.' I hadn't been looking forward to hearing my father's evidence. He was a persuasive speaker and Abe would have to keep alert to follow his reasoning. I longed for Jacob's arrival.

The crowd surrounding Congress had swelled. People spilled out on the walkway. League supporters hailed us heartily but there was an ominous presence among them. I heard shouts of 'Murderer' and 'get back to Devil's

Lake' as we pushed through the entrance. Abe's usual place was empty. A young man from his office sat there alone, thumbing nervously through some papers. He looked up expectantly as we entered but when he smiled I realised his eyes were searching behind us for his boss. He grimaced and leant back in his seat.

The man's nervousness increased as the starting time for the session approached. Amusement was mounting among my father's colleagues. Beside my father was a man of about middle years, I'd not seen before. I guessed he was an advocate of some kind. I mentioned this thought to Jack but when Henry Rawlings spoke later that morning he was to prove me wrong in a rather dramatic way.

By the time Bains entered the room, I was in despair. Had Abe's absence anything to do with Jacob's delayed arrival? Without the Wolf League's evidence we wouldn't stand a chance of success. But seconds later, Abe burst through the door. He was accompanied by a casually-dressed stranger. Leaving the man standing in front of the large wooden doors, Abe hurried towards Bains' table as the Chairman began speaking.

'I understand this morning's session will be addressed by Henry Rawlings on behalf of ……' The man I'd noticed at my father's side stood up and was picking up a set of papers quite unfazed by Abe's hurried arrival. Abe thrust a note in front of the Chairman. Bains read it, glanced at the man, then addressed himself to my father.

'Mr Delacroix…' This time there was no doubt who he was addressing. 'I am going to ask whether you would mind postponing your speaker until later this morning. Mr Langer has just informed me that our latest visitor has interrupted an international flight today, and well, perhaps he might explain himself.'

Abe had just reached his seat. His face was flushed but he was the picture of confidence as he announced, 'Mr Chairman, members, the International Union for the Conservation of Nature, the IUCN, is holding a conference later this week in Japan. This is the world's most prestigious wildlife authority. Late yesterday I learned that Kurt Meier, who you see here, a top IUCN scientist, had a three-hour stopover at Washington. I took the liberty of asking him to attend this morning and hope you will permit him to speak. His flight leaves at twelve so his time is quite limited.'

At the mention of the IUCN, groans and hurried mumblings issued from my father's ranks. Meanwhile Kurt Meier, standing upright and alert, bowed in a very European way. I saw his face and hands were bronzed. Meier was older than his clothes suggested, I put him in his late thirties. He had a wary look and seemed keenly alert to the tension in the room. Someone at the rear of my father yelled briefly.

'No precedent, send him back where he came from.' The speaker was rapidly quelled by his own team. Apparently Meier didn't understand the comment. He remained expectantly by the doors. I could see for the first time that he was clutching a laptop and a neat slim briefcase in his left hand. Henry Rawlings answered, 'Although my team had no notice of this witness, we certainly understand the reasons for this request and…,' here he gave a rather supercilious smile, 'Mr. Delacroix believes it would be churlish to turn away such a distinguished scientist. However, we reserve the right to challenge Mr Meier's evidence.'

Bains nodded his satisfaction. 'Mr. Delacroix I

certainly applaud your decision. Mr Meier, would you come forward.'

Meier had some surprises for us. Instead of mimicking the dry academics of the previous day, with their succession of sophisticated graphs, the images he showed were often disturbing, always thought-provoking. Meier had a strong German accent but his guttural phrases were often tinged with humour. His first slides were of an alpine valley under fierce blue summer skies with forested hills, gentle slopes and open fields. In the bottom of one valley sparse villages gave way to modern roadways and a central town.

'A beautiful scene, is it not?' mused Meier in his quirky accent. 'Nature and mankind in harmony you might think but this has not always been the case. Watch closely, but I must warn you many of these images are distressing. This is the same valley in photographs taken over twenty years ago.'

Meier's voice lost its humorous edge as a succession of hazy slides crossed the screen: hillsides littered with tree stumps, fields with broken fences, empty villages with crumbling houses and deserted pasture, were followed by one further, disturbing scene: a faded black and white image of an emaciated red deer lying dead from gunshot wounds. Beside the body, its head hung low, was the deer's month-old fawn, itself a scrawny creature on thin wobbly legs.

'This deer was the last to survive in the Abruzzi national forest in Italy,' Meier intoned. 'The rest had been shot by...by sportsmen I think you call them.' He smiled again and continued, 'I was to study Italy's native wolf population, initially for three months in my second summer at university. The first week I went out into the hills, but I saw no wolves. As the days passed I travelled further and further, again without success.'

Here several loud cackles were audible from my father's area. Meier looked across at them more frustrated than dismayed. 'Also I found no evidence of any deer. Forestry had removed most of the trees and just a few sheep roamed untended on the hills. You see, the shepherds had other jobs in town. But whenever they lost sheep they unerringly blamed the wolf. I have been going back to the Abruzzi for twenty years but the first wolves I saw were not rabid sheep killers, they didn't terrorise villages, nor carry off children as the local peasants would have you believe. The wolves were as close to starvation as those deer you have seen and this is where they were feeding.'

The screen showed deep snow at the edge of a lightly wooded slope, where few trees were left standing. 'This is an offal dump from the local slaughterhouse. There were no deer, so the wolves came to scavenge from this filthy fly-blown pit of rotting flesh. Starvation drove them there but it was also the place they met their end. The villagers shot them, or trapped them with wires that caused suppurating wounds. The wolves died lingering deaths. I know, I saw their mangled bodies.' Here Meier paused and shook himself, as if to dispel the harrowing memory. Nobody in the room stirred. It was as if his testimony had struck them dumb.

Meier clicked his laptop and suddenly on the screen was a playground with colourful slides, multiple swings and crowds of active laughing children. People sighed with relief and nodded to each other over the site's uncanny resemblance to the previous location.

'Yes,' said Meier, well satisfied. 'This is the same place you saw before, and this and this.' Shots of growing forests with red deer slipping between the trees, ordered farmsteads surrounded by tall fences, flashed across the screen as Meier explained. 'Now there are wolves living free in these same mountains. Wolves who have never seen an offal dump and are no danger to domestic flocks. How was this done, you ask. By intense consultation, by planning, by agreement with local people. The forests were replanted, native deer reintroduced, farmers and mountain dogs trained to protect their flocks in the old traditional ways. And because the wolves have returned a tourist industry has now grown up around them run by local people. Investment has gone to them, and because young people are finding work, they are staying in the villages rejuvenating ageing populations.'

Here Meier paused once more, gathering strength for his final assault. When he spoke again, I couldn't help wondering whether Abe had told him that Congress was considering something other than repealing the wolf protection laws. I never had the opportunity to ask.

'In Europe we have so many people, living so close together, it is often difficult to turn around a situation such as the one you have seen here. It took more than fifteen years of negotiation and of my life to reach this position. Here in the United States, with so many wilderness places, you do not have such worries. Your own Yellowstone Park: tourists now flock there and the wolf has come back from being a creature of loathing, almost to one of veneration. If this is what you will do in your North Dakota, you are doing something of which the whole world will be proud and I salute you, salute and applaud you all.'

Meier's voice had risen and a broad smile spread over his features. He raised his arms high, as if sweeping the whole room with his embrace. For perhaps three seconds there was stunned silence. Meier had already begun packing away his laptop. Then someone started clapping, weakly at first. Other hands rapidly joined in. Amidst a rash of clapping that resounded through the room, people started to rise from their seats. There were hearty cries of 'bravo' while the applause continued to mount.

Meier bowed low, a satisfied smile played over his face. In the midst of the tumult, and be assured I was there among the throng applauding wildly, I looked across at my father. He was standing among his stony-faced supporters. His face hardened into anger, then defiance, as the waves of applause washed and buffeted about the room and seemed finally to engulf him. I felt no pity for him.

The applause subsided. Meier gave one more quick bow, before he backed out of the door. Other hands took the door to let him pass. I was relieved to see they belonged to Jacob, who entered carrying a thick bundle of papers. With a brief nod at Jack and myself, he hurried to Abe's bench. He hadn't come a moment too soon. With the room barely hushed, Harry Rawlings had already taken his place at the witness table. If anything he looked more assured than before.

'I am sure we are all very grateful for Mr Meier's timely testimony….,' he began, then paused. There could be few people in the room who did not mentally add a conditional '...but', to the statement.

'Very grateful indeed. It is unfortunate though that he couldn't stay to answer some of my own questions.' There was an undercurrent of feigned dismay from my father's benches. I was dimly aware of Abe whispering to Jacob. He would have received daily reports of the proceedings from Abe. Now, I guessed, Abe was bringing him up to date on Meier's testimony.

'I should add that my own firm, the Game and Hunting Foundation, has an equally long history of research into wildlife issues, if not in Europe …,' here he paused giving us time to reflect on the relevance of Meier's evidence '…at least in these United States.' Rowdy cheers burst from my father's ranks.

I was aware of the Foundation, but they kept a low profile. I'd never seen any of their staff. Bains tapped his gavel. I noticed Jacob hurriedly writing a note for Abe. Abe read it and both men scrutinised Rawlings with steely-eyed concentration. They made a formidable combination.

'Previous witnesses have given evidence of livestock predation by wolves. I will not dwell on that here. The instances I cite are of far greater concern: the loss of human lives.' Rawlings looked sad and deferred momentarily to his notes. People shuffled awkwardly in their seats waiting for him to resume. 'Wolves are dangerous animals, make no mistake…,'

But here Abe jumped up interrupting, 'I believe Mr Meier would verify that people in Europe don't regard wolves as dangerous.'

'But Mr Meier is not here to confirm that,' Rawlings snapped. Abe thumped on the desk bristling with anger. Jacob laid a restraining hand on his arm.

'I have in my hand a list of verified instances where

those same wolves which Mr. Langer is trying to protect, have attacked and killed American citizens.' Rawlings voice had risen a little above his usual well-modulated tones. Jacob tapped his files. The League had investigated every reported wolf attack for the last ten years. The sum of their research must lie there. He was content, at first, to let Abe speak for him.

'1991 - Bismarck city, North Dakota, lone hunter, Zack James, killed by wolves one evening in his own cabin.' A wave of horror swept around the room.

I saw Jacob write just one word for Abe.

'Unverified, Mr Chairman.' Abe countered.

'I assure you Mr. Langer...,'

But Abe looked fierce. He glanced over the sheet of paper Jacob had handed him.

'Doctors later confirmed that James, who was 73, died of heart failure. His body was mauled after death by brown bears.'

Rawlings nodded but appeared unruffled.

'Then I will proceed with other undeniable evidence. 1998 Sioux City, a young girl was savaged and killed by a wolf while trying to protect her own pet dog, which also perished.'

Jacob was at Abe's elbow, ready with his evidence.

'Again not verified, Mr. Rawlings. At least four townsfolk shot the 'wolf', and subsequent DNA studies proved this animal was a dog-wolf hybrid. The unpredictability of such crosses, divorced from the stability of a pack, is a known fact.'

But Rawlings was not to be quelled, though I detected a hint of unease in his voice. He eyed Jacob, with suspicion, but said, 'It seems you have access to recent information on these cases, Mr Langer, which has not shown up in my research. Let me continue then, with some cases you can hardly dispute. 2003, Mille Lac, a cyclist attacked by a rabid wolf. But for the intervention of a hunter who shot the wolf, the cyclist would have been killed. As it was, the man was left permanently disabled.'

Murmurs of 'shame' issued from the opposite benches. But Jacob was so keyed up he by-passed Abe, interjecting, 'Tragic, but not so….,' he paused and addressed himself to Bains'. '…I should explain Mr. Chairman, my name is Jacob Leason, and I speak for the Wolf League. As Mr Rawlings has said *our* evidence is often more complete than his own. We make in-depth studies of every case, interviewing witnesses again and again to come at the truth.'

Bains nodded, 'I am aware of your organisation Mr. Leason. You are free to proceed but be aware that members are equally free to re-evaluate all the evidence they hear.'

Jacob nodded. 'Several years ago an orphan wolf cub was adopted by a family in Mille Lac. But pure-bred wolves, or even wolf-dog crosses, make unstable pets, they grow aggressive and demanding. A wolf taken into a family home is not a pet, it is a time bomb. By the age of ten months this Mille Lac wolf weighed sixty pounds and was so considered unruly by the man's family, that they gave him an ultimatum - the wolf had to go.'

'But this man - let's call him Mr. Smith - was too tender-hearted to turn the wolf over to a zoo to spend its days behind bars. Instead he drove a hundred miles north to the Chippewa National Forest and left the animal there to fend for itself. Four weeks later the wolf had found its way back to Mille Lac. Mr. Smith is also a cyclist. The confused and hungry wolf may simply have rushed the unfortunate cyclist thinking the man was his former owner. We can never know the truth of that encounter. Mr Smith had recognised the carcass as his pet wolf, but he was too scared to speak, fearing he'd be blamed for the attack. Long after the furore died down, he confessed his ownership to the League. I have his written affidavit here in my hand.' He waved a single sheet of paper.

Rawlings' appeared only marginally diminished. He shuffled his notes then looked at Bains. 'Mr. Leason is very exacting in his research Mr Chairman, but I have here some further cases the committee might be interested in. May we continue?'

Bains nodded giving a wry smile. Perhaps, like many of us, he gained a perverse pleasure from the men's sparring. Even so, it was disheartening to think the committee's decision might depend solely on strength of personality. Bains let them continue their cat-and-mouse game for a further fifteen minutes with Rawlings quoting cases: 'date, state and events,' and Jacob retaliating with the fruits of his own research.

Jacob faltered just once. Two weeks since, Rawlings intoned, a twelve-year-old boy, recently trained in rifle use, had gone out alone to hunt his first deer. He startled a wolf that had recently killed. We were told the animal had lunged towards the boy, who shot wildly at it. The boy survived, the wolf did not. The room remained hushed.

People waited expectantly for Jacob's usual forceful response. Instead he lowered his head. Raising it again he looked around the room as if gazing at every person in turn. Finally his expression hardened.

'I regret Mr. Chairman, that this event is so recent the League hasn't had time to complete any research but, I submit, none of us can be certain that this wolf meant to attack the boy. It may simply have been trying to escape.'

Cries of 'shame' and 'liar' rose from my father's cohort. Jacob raised his hands in a gesture of frustration. 'Naturally I am glad the boy wasn't injured.' Pausing once more he continued, 'What I find hard to accept, is that our society allows a twelve-year-old child to handle a lethal weapon, much less fire it.'

There were some angry murmurs of agreement from among the women in the room. But these were also accompanied by angry shouts of 'renegade' and 'traitor'. Rawlings returned to his seat, a triumphant smile playing on his lips. There were no further witnesses, and Bains brought the proceedings to a close.

We waited three long days for the Committee's decision. I spent most of the time at the League's H.Q., learning how they accumulated the material that Jacob had presented. Jack's extended leave from the Wildlife Unit ended with the committee hearing. He took the first available plane back to Grand Forks.

Abe disappeared into his office for hours at a time though I saw him each evening. I kept in touch by phone alternately with Jenny and Larry. Ambrose, it seemed, would be ready any day to receive Speed and two further wolves, both females, from Sanctuary. I couldn't believe the despatch with which Larry had acted. When I congratulated him he told me that further surprises awaited me at Ambrose.

The terms of my bail prevented me from leaving the country, even to travel to Canada. Larry must know there was no possibility I would be there for the release. Sorrowfully, I'd told him to go ahead without me. I even had to repeat this when he called on the third day after the hearing. 'That's where you're wrong,' he shouted down the line.

I was at League H.Q. having coffee with two members of the team when he phoned. I turned away to insist, 'I can't come, Larry, that's final. Don't make it any more difficult than it is.' I stood up and walked across to the window. The restaurant was on the tenth floor, yielding a perfect view across Washington. A radiant October sun shone from an eggshell blue sky. The Potomac River glinted silver through coloured chestnuts and I was reminded of the richly toned aspens lining the drive down to Ambrose.

'I just can't be there,' I insisted, hoping he would finally understand. What he said next shook me to the core. 'Presidential parole! Just for the day.' I couldn't believe what I was hearing. 'You get that committee sorted out soon and Chrispin Mores, Canada's deputy Prime Minister, has promised to be here to keep an eye on you.'

'Larry if this is some awful joke…,'

'Nothing of the sort I assure you. Just give me a bell when you're free to come. That girl of yours - Jenny isn't it - is just waiting for the signal to load your wolves onto her truck. Bye now.'

I was left reeling. Somehow I managed to push open a door and found myself on an open terrace. I stood there, bathed by the warm October sun, wondering whether I had the courage to visit Ambrose again, only to have it instantly snatched away from me.

Three hours later, after a hurried phone call from Abe, I was in a taxi speeding towards Congress. Abe had heard rumours the Committee's decision was about to be published. The crowd of League supporters had dwindled to thirty or so die-hards and only one anti-wolf banner was in evidence, carried by some young men in hunting gear.

The tension of the last days lay heavily on people's shoulders. Banners drooped, many of the placards had been folded up and stood askew against the classical pillars of the façade. Beside them sat three journalists, a man and a woman were playing cards; another man, a smoker, was blowing smoke rings above his head. They were obviously bored. The sun went in and a chill breeze nagged at our clothes. The waiting seemed interminable, though it probably lasted no more than thirty minutes.

Abe came out onto the top step of the stairwell. Jacob stood in the shadows, behind him. Through the double door behind them came a courier. The thin sheet of paper he carried was caught by the breeze which threatened to snap it away from his fingertips. After a brief struggle he pressed the sheet up against a noticeboard and secured it with clips. Jacob remained beside a pillar, while Abe gestured me forward.

His face was a bland mask. I feared the worst and let several people run up the steps ahead of me. A brief ominous silence ensued while the first few supporters read the notice, then suddenly they were cheering wildly. Whoops of joy followed, buffeting against the solid marble pillars. The rest of us jostled into position where we could read the notice. Under the full committee title 'Congressional Committee on Wildlife Regulations Act Twenty-Two, Section Thirty, Part Ninety-nine', it read:

'In view of the great public interest in the proposal recently made to repeal the wolf protection laws, the Committee has taken this unprecedented decision to make formal preliminary declaration of intent.

There followed four, short, damning sentences:

'The Committee is NOT minded, now or in the foreseeable future, to advise the repeal of the Wolf Protection Act.'
'The Committee is recommending to Congress and the Nation that further support be made available for wildlife teams engaged in restoration of wolf habitat'
'The Committee is recommending to Congress that extra funds be made available for the education of all its citizens in the wildlife code.'
'The Committee is recommending to Congress a stringent revision of hunting licences in the United States.'

Two women standing beside me took me by the arms and we swung round in a circle to shrieks of joy. Others joined in and we were a milling mass of people amid squabbling journalists and some newly-arrived photographers. Every so often I caught sight of Abe. He was standing on the top of the stairwell, smiling heartily, his broad figure even more puffed-up than usual. Jacob was down in the throng talking to reporters.

Next morning we set off for Thunder Bay in Abe's small plane. It was full to bursting. A capable pilot, Abe was in the co-pilot's seat. Two of his congressional assistants, myself, Jacob and four of the Wolf League's top officials, were crammed into the narrow shell of the aircraft along with two stewards. They kept us supplied with champagne, which Abe had thoughtfully installed before we left Washington.

If Abe was used to the public tide of support which had broken out across Washington's media the previous evening, League members were not, so the bubbly liquid flowed liberally and our conversations were equally bubbly and effusive. We had just left Chicago air space and I was holding out an empty glass, clumsily trying to catch the flow of champagne from a bottle, when the news came through. Abe opened the flight door and beckoned me forwards.

He had to shout to make himself heard over the din we were making. He had a pair of earphones around his neck and he looked grim.

'Francis!' I didn't want to acknowledge the warning look in his eyes. I got up unsteadily from my seat and had to push past a new-found colleague. Rob Philips, PR Executive for the League, hadn't heard Abe calling and stood up in the gangway vigorously shaking my hand. The collar of his suit was twisted all anyhow, his face flushed and brow sweaty. The champagne spoke through him as he said 'Great guy, great guy'.

Abe called again. I encouraged Rob back into his seat and continued on towards the cockpit. Abe signed me forward and closed the door behind him. Though he was breathing heavily he was silent for several seconds while I looked out through the cockpit window down onto a land of shining lakes and dense forest.

'Bad news Francis …' Abe's gaze followed my own, his eyes settling on the green land passing below us. 'Sheriff Lawson's on the radio, wanting to speak to you.'

Without warning my legs buckled beneath me. I felt myself sinking into the co-pilot's chair. With a long drawn-out sigh, Abe slipped the earphones off his neck and onto mine. He gestured to a switch on the control panel.

'He wanted us to land back in the USofA right now. I told him we had Presidential clearance for this trip. There was nothing doing. Just flip that switch when you're ready.'

'Why would he want….?' I began. Abe looked up.

'Best you speak to him yourself.' Abe opened the cockpit door. A clamour of inane comments issued from the cabin, then the door had closed behind him and I was left staring at the pilot, Carl Rice. He ignored me and looked studiously ahead at a fine haze of cloud we were approaching, as if it were some artistic masterpiece. I flipped the switch and gave my name. 'Francis Delacroix, what can I do for you Sheriff?'

I expected crackling, some interference at least, that would distance me from the man. Instead Sheriff Lawson's voice came over the airwaves loud and strong.

'Delacroix I want you back in Grand Forks. Jenkins is dead. As of now your bail's cancelled d'you understand?'

I suddenly felt sick. 'I understand,' I responded almost involuntarily. Lawson couldn't have heard me.

'I wanted your flight diverted, but your influential friends stalled on me. Be assured I'll be waiting for you at Grand Portage international crossing.'

His voice was rough and rasping. I sensed he was after blood. He clearly saw my behaviour at Devil's Lake as a betrayal of trust. I had caused the deaths of three men but Lawson's people would hold him responsible. I'd made a bad enemy of him. Now he was seeking revenge for loss of face.

'I'll be there,' I croaked.

'I'm upping the charge to murder,' Lawson barked down the radio.

'I said, I'll be there,' I hissed through clenched teeth and threw the headphones down angrily. They bounced on the floor at my feet. As I left the cockpit, I heard Rice flip the radio off.

I'd been away nearly three weeks. Ambrose could hardly have changed in that time. With its solid brick walls stained a more intense crimson by the westering sun, the sturdy portico looked solid and enduring. Now, just as it had done on my first visit, the place looked neglected, the bare courtyard and sightless windows offering no welcome.

And if today I saw in its solid walls a kind of vicarious refuge, I would not be admitting to the anguish and heartbreak the place had caused me. Ambrose Estate had been a millstone around my neck but, if we were successful today, I would carry away memories that would have to last me a lifetime, however long that was. The recollections, I knew, would always be bitter-sweet.

Abe edged the first of our three cars onto the empty courtyard. There was no-one about, but I signalled for him to stop. I stepped out of the car to breathe the sweet air of freedom. I would not think beyond today. All the bright aspen leaves had fallen, they littered the grass beneath the trees and without their finery the pale bare stems looked forlorn. I bent low to pick up a red-gold leaf, keepsake of a turbulent autumn, and heard my name called from somewhere near the house.

Rick raced down the steps and hurried towards me. In his smart blue suit he looked every inch the confident businessman. Gone was the gauche young man I'd met barely a month before. A secretary hurried after him with a mobile phone offering a call from the Audubon Society. He asked her to put them on hold. He grasped my right hand so tightly, I could hardly wrench it free.

'Good to see you Rick.' We clasped arms but he held on to me as I tried to draw away, desperately patting my shoulders. I couldn't get him to stop. When at length I managed to pull away, he wouldn't look at me.

'You look great. Business good?' I nodded to the waiting secretary.

'Oh Francis...' Rick blustered, forgetting his hesitancy. 'You can't imagine, conferences with the Audubon people, and IFAW. Of course it's partly Larry's doing, he's so many contacts... '

'The conference people are doing their bit are they?' I thought of the interim contract we'd agreed.

'We've all the equipment we need, more if we want it. I can't think why they......,'

'No need to be modest Rick, you're a damn fine businessman, you sure sold Ambrose to me.'

'The truth is Ambrose sold itself Mr. Del... Francis...,'

Two cars carrying the rest of our party were just entering the courtyard. I drew Rick back towards the house so we shouldn't be overheard. 'Rick, I wanted to talk to you about Ambrose.'

A shadow crossed Rick's face.

'We have to ensure its future, I've been uneasy.'

'Francis, I know I pushed you into....,'

'Rick you don't understand...,' I paused to catch my breath. Rick looked more anxious than ever. 'That's why I've decided to make the hotel business over to you.'

'No! No....I can't take it,' Rick stammered. 'Not like

this.'

'If you refuse Rick, then you're not the businessman I thought you were.'

'Think of me how you like, I just can't do it. Francis, you gave me my first break when no-one else would. I can't take Ambrose from you.'

'Rick, I'm unlikely to have any need for it, now, or in the near future.'

'Everyone needs money, Francis... no matter what...,' he stumbled over his words, 'I'm not saying we'll make millions, but it wouldn't feel right. Suppose...,' he gulped and the sparkle came back to his eyes. 'Suppose you made over a controlling interest to me, say 51 percent. I could run the firm and know I wasn't letting you down. I'd feel happy about that.'

I put out my hand to my new partner, agreeing. 'You drive a hard bargain Rick. 51 per cent it is.' Suddenly Rick was all smiles. He patted me on the shoulder, rather harder than before.

'Hadn't you better join Larry?'

'Is he here, I didn't see any cars?'

In truth I'd been disappointed by the absence of media interest in the wolf release, even doubting Larry's claim about the attendance of Canada's deputy prime minister. Probably there had been too little time for any publicity. Rick only laughed and clamped his hand over his mouth.

'I wasn't supposed to say. They…..that is he's round the back with some girl and a truck full of your four-legged friends.' The subdued laughter managed to trickle out from his half-closed lips.

'Damn you Rick!' I laughed. I returned to the cars and directed Abe around the back of the building. We had just passed the lake when a loud roar went up from a marquee half-hidden behind the beech hedge. Rick hadn't been honest with me!

People came running out waving flags and shouting wild greetings and I caught sight of two video screens beyond the marquee. A host of journalists and cameramen, kept in check by the wooden barrier, jostled for a view of the approaching cars. Abe stopped the car. Hundreds of people surrounded the vehicle. Many were complete strangers. Others I recognised as parents and children I'd seen on the Wolf Fun Day; in the distance our volunteer guards: Hamilton and Merrick, their heads turning, constantly scrutinising the crowd; Lionel and Denzil half lost in the milling throng and at the forefront Avril and Larry. Above the marquee's entrance a brightly coloured banner flapped in the light breeze.

When it settled for a moment I read the words, written in red against a brilliant blue background, 'Ambrose Welcomes Back its Wolves.' Beaming madly, Larry opened the car door and shook my hand even before I could get out. I was overwhelmed by the sudden expression of support, but there was one face missing.

'Where's Jenny?'

He shook his head and yelled above the crowd.

'She's here.' And then, when I wouldn't move from the car added, 'Wouldn't leave the wolves. There's too much noise and disturbance. She's taken them down to the release site by Pearl Lake. Good lass that. Now come and meet the deputy Prime Minister.'

'You were telling the truth then.'

'Did you think I wasn't?'

'So much has happened …..I don't know what to think.'

'He's in here.' He guided me into the marquee. 'Better have a word with the press afterwards....,'

'No Larry I can't, not now, not......' I insisted, backing away from him. Larry scrutinised my face.

'Bad news?'

I nodded.

'I'll try to keep them off your back then.'

'You're not taking them to the release site are you?' I asked, worried the presence of such a host, journalists included, would jeopardise the planned release. Speed needed peace, I knew that. But now, more than ever, we had an obligation to publicise his release. What happened today would act as a signal that wolves deserved a place in our hearts, as well as in the world we shared.

'Not likely, too much disturbance as Jenny says. That's what the video screens are for. The pictures are going straight onto the website so the press and anyone else can use them.'

The meeting with Chrispin Mores was mercifully brief. He broke off a conversation about the price of land with some local politicians and took my hand, a little warily I thought. 'I understand you achieved remarkable success in the US Congress, Mr. Delacroix.'

'The success belongs to Abe Langer and the Wolf League, Mr Prime Minister, my part in it....,'

I turned towards Abe who was standing right behind me taking in the general adulation. He ignored my entreaty and said, without any hint of irony, 'It's your day Francis, enjoy it.'

Then he leant his ear to some journalist, and beside me I heard Mores saying, 'You needn't be modest Mr. Delacroix, I know what you've done already and what you're doing at Ambrose today has struck a blow for our native wildlife. You have great courage …,' here he paused, 'I only hope your current …. difficulties will be quickly resolved and you come back to us absolved of guilt.'

'I'll try to live up to your faith in me Mr. Mores.' With a slight sigh he turned back to his fellow-politicians.

I grabbed Larry's arm. 'Get me out of here,' I begged.

We left the noisy crowd behind us. Just Larry and myself in a jeep heading through the approaching twilight down the dusty track towards Pearl Lake. The rest of our party, Jacob, Abe and their colleagues were left to mingle with the assembled diplomats and journalists who were already broadcasting their interviews. Speeches would follow and they would all watch the release of Speed and his fellow wolves on video.

As we neared the small hollow in which the lake lay, my memories of the yurt depicting native Americans long since gone from the landscape were replaced by a camouflaged truck standing isolated amidst the dry pasture. To either side of it, two video cameras had been set up which were to send back pictures to Ambrose lakeside. Larry switched off the jeep's engine and let it glide to a halt beside the truck. True professional that she was, Jenny eased herself out from the cab and tiptoed across to where we sat.

'Good to see you Francis,' she whispered. Through the open cab window she clasped my hand warmly. 'I'm sorry to have to hurry you but the wolves should be released right away. They've been in the crates far too long, I was almost ready…,'

'To let them go without waiting for us. No need to

apologise, Jenny. Let's get going.'

She nodded back to the truck. The off-side door opened and Charlie's big form rolled out. With nods and smiles he gestured me round to the back of the truck where the three crates stood, each covered in a grey blanket. With Larry's help, we hauled the crates down to the ground still with their coverings intact and positioned them side by side in the deepest shade of the nearby conifers.

'Better turn on the cameras,' Larry whispered.

Jenny ran lightly between the two apparatus. When she was satisfied the pictures were clear and properly focused she drew back alongside me and squeezed my hand. Remote control swung the cameras in our direction. I heard the mechanism whirr, then all my attention was on the grey blankets. With a hesitant smile Jenny pointed to the nearest crate, 'He's in there. Do you want to .....'

But there was no further need for words. I leant forwards as I'd seen Suzanne do, pulled up the end of the blanket and resisted the urge to peer inside before pulling up the doorway. The catch came away easily, unlike the luckless crate at Mandaamin. I waited breathlessly beside it.

I thought I was ready for the release this time, yet as Speed shot from the crate, the broad silver crescents blooming against the dusky night, the flashing muscles speeding him through the prairie grass, the same lump came to my throat and the same tears to my eyes as when we'd released those first two wolves, weeks before. Larry gave me a moment, then managed to catch my eye. I nodded. Charlie and Jenny leant over the remaining crates and unfastened the catches. Just as Speed had done, the two young females streaked through the grass and were quickly engulfed by the shadows of approaching night.

I shook hands wordlessly with Larry. Wolves had come back to Ambrose, now it was my turn to leave. Somehow I got him to agree to return to Ambrose in the truck with Charlie. Jenny and I were to follow in the jeep. We sat in the vehicle watching the rugged truck disappearing into the approaching gloom before I turned towards her. She put out her arms expecting me to embrace her. I had to disappoint her.

I looked down, took both her hands in mine and told her of my one-sided conversation with Sheriff Lawson, and about the helicopter Abe had arranged to take me back to Grand Portage, in case Lawson got tired of waiting and sent the Mounties after me.

'But it won't make any difference will it, Mr... Abe..., they were so certain...' She pleaded, grasping my arms.

'Jenny. It was a charge of manslaughter before, now it's murder.'

'But they can't find you guilty, they can't,' she said, half sobbing.

'Lawson obviously thinks they can, and Jenny....,' I looked over the top of her head at the encroaching night. 'I can't be sure I didn't intend to kill Jenkins. Everything happened so fast. The fight with Payntor. The storm at its height, rain pouring down. We'd been arguing viciously and when Jenkins shot Speed, I just went mad.'

'Then tell the sheriff. And if it comes to a trial tell them again. You're innocent Francis, I know you are.'

'Jenny, Jenny we have to face facts. I killed a man, pumped shot after shot at him, couldn't help myself.'

Inexplicably I saw a flicker of hope rise in Jenny's

eyes.

'But he was killed by a single bullet Francis, doesn't that mean something to you?'

'It means I'm guilty Jenny, guilty as hell.'

'No Francis, it doesn't….,' she was laughing into my face shouting, 'didn't you say you're an excellent shot? All your life you've handled guns. Well if you tried to murder someone, you'd have killed him with just one bullet wouldn't you. It's terrible that a man died Francis, but that doesn't mean you were trying to kill him. That's what murder implies doesn't it - intent to kill?'

'You're grasping at straws my girl.'

'Am I …. ' she gulped '…. your girl?' Tears glistened in her eyes. I drew her towards me and hugged her tightly, trying to think beyond myself. She had taken her final veterinary exams four days before, amid the trauma of my arrest and the Congress hearing. The exam had gone well, she'd told me on the phone. I hoped it had. Success shone out from everything she did and her association with me could only tarnish her career. How could I let her suffer the horrors of a trial, and whatever followed?

'Jenny I can't put you through all this. Perhaps it's best if I leave now.'

She raised her head and searched the evening sky through the jeep's window. Stars had begun to sparkle above the eastern horizon. A blemished ruddy glow showed in the western sky. The lights of a plane blinked far above us and the only sound was the whispering of meadow grasses.

'The helicopter?' she asked innocently.

'No - just disappear.'

She looked at me aghast. 'Go on the run?'

'It would be better for everyone.'

'Everyone who supports you - Jacob, Abe, everyone at Sanctuary?'

'Everyone I've let down.'

'You've let no-one down Francis, everyone respects what you've done.'

'That's not how they'll feel if I'm convicted. Best to bow out now.'

'So you're just going to abandon Speed. How many more wolves are there like him Francis, how many?' She thrust open the jeep door and pointed into the wilderness of shadow beyond the prairie. 'This campaign's only just beginning, Francis.'

'Other more qualified people can take up the reins,' I insisted, but cool night air swept across my face as she twisted in her seat and leapt out of the vehicle. Calling back through the doorway, her voice echoing and lowered by sadness she said, 'You're a fool if you think that Francis. You think you've failed us don't you? Then ask yourself why you had such success at Congress, why the deputy Prime Minister and so many journalists were here today. They were here because you cared about Speed, cared so much you were willing to risk your own life. Politicians, journalists come and go Francis, but you stood out against your own father. You told your own story and it's gone to people's hearts. You can't give up now.'

I got out rapidly and moved awkwardly to her side. Her cheeks were wet with tears as she looked up at the darkening heavens. I took her by the shoulders and pressed my lips against her forehead. I felt her stiffen and draw back.

'What kind of life would you have - have you thought

of that?'

'I'll get by,' I insisted through dry lips. I felt my stomach tense, and thought of the empty days without her. Incredibly, she laughed. A low-pitched sound that made me uneasy.

'Oh yes, mister backwoodsman. Living by your wits, always moving on, always ......,' she paused as I nodded. 'Francis, there's something more isn't there?'

Slowly I let go of her arms. I expected her to cling to me. Instead she just watched as I walked two paces away.

'Jenny....Jenny I do love you please believe that, but I can't ask you to wait for me. I don't want you wasting your life.'

'Isn't that my decision Francis? I love you for what you are and for what you're doing.'

'But, if I go to jail...' I began but Jenny came forwards and placed her lips gently on my own. They were cool from the night air and her cheeks were wet from tears that continued to fall. She drew back briefly saying, 'Let the future take care of itself,' before she kissed me again. I felt her strength run through me and held her like that for many minutes.

Much later we returned to the jeep and headed back to Ambrose and its empty marquee. Together with Abe, we watched the lights of a helicopter draw near and saw it land beside the lake. I mounted the running board with him. We left the door partially open and turned back to bid Jenny farewell. Her cheeks were now quite dry. She stretched out her hand to me.

'Remember Speed!' she cried above the roar of the engine. 'He's *free* Francis and so will you be - I know it.'

The helicopter jerked upwards a few feet. I looked down at Jenny and naively asked 'When?' but my voice was lost in the thundering engine. Jenny stood beside the lake, her hair blown anyhow by the downdraught. A buxom girl, she looked suddenly lost and fragile. For one fleeting moment I fought the urge to leap down beside her, then the machine lurched sideways. Abe grasped my arm as the helicopter lifted away from the ground. He shook his head and frowned. He'd seen the expression of despair on my face. For a long time we stood together by the open door watching Jenny's small figure disappear into the night shadows. The lights of Ambrose dissolved and were gone.

SPEED

He ran through the night and through the dawn,
until light entered the sky.
Until his stomach no longer felt hunger,
nor his heart fear.
Running beside him, eyes intent, his mother and his
father. And far behind, unable to match his stride,
the two young ones.
All five together pacing through the snowfield and
the forest, until exhaustion overtook him and
he dropped and slept and woke - alone.

****